To Chris

Best wishes

Thank you

[illegible]

VICKSBURG

Thomas R. Stubbs

authorHOUSE®

AuthorHouse™
1663 Liberty Drive
Bloomington, IN 47403
www.authorhouse.com
Phone: 1-800-839-8640

Published by AuthorHouse 1/27/2012

ISBN: 978-1-4685-4440-4 (sc)
ISBN: 978-1-4685-4439-8 (hc)
ISBN: 978-1-4685-4438-1 (e)

Library of Congress Control Number: 2012901085

CHAPTER ONE

It was now somewhere around the middle of April. We had been told last night that in the morning we would be marching off to Vicksburg, but morning came and nothing seemed to happen. It did seem obvious that something was up. On talking to some of the other troops of the 31 Mo. regiment that had been at Milliken's Bend for awhile, they related that General McClernand and his corps and part of General McPherson's troops had already left camp and marched down across the peninsula a few weeks ago. Just where they were headed, none of the troops that I had talked to seemed to know. These troops had been in the garrison at Milliken's Bend for several months and had welcomed our arrival yesterday by celebrating over a few jugs of corn liquor.

They had related last evening all of the abortive attempts they had made so far in attempting to take Vicksburg. The first attempt had been by General Sherman who had tried attacking at Chickasaw Bayou up a steep bluff north of town, in face of impossible odds. There they had attempted to land troops on a narrow triangle of damp ground, bounded on the west and east by a bayou, or flooded swamp, in places over head high and at other places up over the knees. On the western side, it had been bounded by deep sloughs and swampy ground so that the only practical way of marching was down a patch of ground that pointed directly at the bluffs. The bluffs had been extremely steep, so that it was impossible to walk or climb the bluffs and the troops had been reduced to crawling on hands and knees and trying to pull themselves forward with brush and clumps of grass in order to climb the bluffs to get at the troops. This had been a disastrous attempt and as I recall one of the troops had said that

Sherman had complained that it would cost them 5,000 casualties to take Vicksburg and they may as well lose them here. Such a cavalier statement hadn't set well with the troops. The attempt had been disastrous, as they knew it would from the start.

Then the other troops had related similar escapades that the military commanders had engaged in, such as digging a canal across the peninsula. De Soto's point, as the peninsula was called, was nothing but mud and swamp and the attempt resulted in failure when heavy rains washed out the dams and flooded the works that the troops had spent months on. Then there was the attempt to blow the Mississippi levees upstream thereby flooding the farmland east of the river and making a giant lake that would allow the Union troops to travel by steamboat south to get in position for an attack on Vicksburg from above. An attempt was also made to dig a canal through the swamps west of the Mississippi to reach Lake Providence from which, it was thought, the army could travel by steamer to reach to reach the Mississippi River and assault Vicksburg from below. Whether we would be off on another expedition to dig passages through the swamps or whether they would come up with some idea for another boat trip on the rivers, no one seemed to know.

That morning we didn't receive any orders and we were uncertain as to what the actual intentions were. Sometime after noon, we received orders to march down to the landing to help in loading Admiral Porter's ships. When we got to the landing, there was an incredible bustle with troops and sailors at work on the steamers and gunboats. The boats had been strangely modified. On the port side of the ships some large bales of cotton had been latched that had been soaked with water. Some ships had strange structures put together out of planks and wood that changed the outlines of the ships in an attempt to disguise the structures on board. We received orders to help with loading and formed lines to pass boxes and crates of ammunition, food and clothing down from the banks and up onto the ships where the sailors took it and stowed it below decks or inside the superstructures on the steamers.

Some of the troops seemed to feel that this indicated that the steamers would be attempting to run the river past the Vicksburg batteries on the bluffs. Barges were similarly protected with bales of water soaked cotton and loaded with supplies to be pulled behind the steamers. We worked feverishly throughout the day, loading the barges and steamers and, after it became dark, the troops were marched back to the barracks.

We had a late meal that evening and gathered around on the levees facing the river to watch for the anticipated passage down the river. We seemed to wait in quiet anticipation for hours. Just when the steamers actually moved away from the wharf, I don't know because they left so quietly that it was impossible to detect the true time of their departure. Not owning a watch, I think it was probably well up towards midnight before we heard cannon fire from across the river. I feared the attempt to run the bluffs without being seen, hadn't gone so well.

Still, it was so dark, I was sure that the confederates on the other side of the river wouldn't be able to hit anything from the heights of the bluff. But, shortly after that, flames sprang up in the east and quickly became almost like a blazing sunup. The whole eastern shoreline seemed to be bathed in bright light. Then flames appeared to spring up from the western bank and also from what we assumed was the center of the river. I was amazed to think that the Confederate fire could have been so accurate. Silence settled over the troops as we watched from the levee. We were quite fearful that all of the steamers and barges had been hit and set on fire and now were burning in midstream or running to ground on the western shore causing this illusion of an early sunrise.

We felt sorry for the sailors on board the steamers and the barges as we were sure that the entire expedition had been shot out of the water or set on fire. There wasn't anything that we could do, however, and being quite late we were finally ordered back to the barracks for the evening. It was a dejected and disheartened army that finally hit the bunks and went to bed for the evening. We believed that another attempt on Vicksburg had ended disastrously like all the previous ones over the last several months.

Getting to sleep that evening was difficult. As I lay there, attempting to drift off, I thought about all that had transpired to me over the last year and a half. It was hard to believe that so much had happened in that time. It was in October of '61 that I had lost my family in the massacre at Osceola. After that, I joined the Union Army and had gone through training and been deployed just in time for the Battle of Shiloh. We had been on our way to Corinth when we had been attacked at Shiloh by a rebel army that we had no idea was in the vicinity. After the battle, we had spent several weeks reorganizing and had spent another month marching the 30 miles to Corinth which had been our original objective. There, we spent the next six months battling mosquitoes, chiggers and bad water. It seemed like once we had got to Corinth, no one knew what to do next. Eventually the rebels had found us in Corinth and decided that they really didn't want us there and had tried to force us out. We had endured the two day battle at Corinth and soundly defeated the rebels but neglected to make any meaningful pursuit.

Disappointed and dejected, we had spent another few weeks in Corinth before being marched back up the way we came and had, in the end, disembarked from Shiloh Landing and gone back to St. Louis to refit and recruit to replace the troops that had been lost from the 21st Mo. Regiment. We had then been transferred from the 21st Missouri to the 31st Missouri Regiment and had trained the new recruits before being embarked to come here to Milliken's Bend in preparation for the assault on Vicksburg. But it looked like the assault on Vicksburg wasn't going so well. I lay restlessly wondering how long we would be stuck in Milliken's Bend before the brass decided what to do next.

It seemed I had no sooner fallen asleep, than I was awakened by the bugle and roused out of bed. After dressing, we assembled in the muddy parade ground for roll call and breakfast. I was surprised by the exuberant nature of the troops as they gathered on the parade ground. I thought that the fleet that had attempted to run the bluffs on the river had been utterly destroyed, but surprisingly, except for the loss of one steamer and a couple of barges, it had been entirely successful. How they could have received word of the success of the expedition so quickly surprised me. But the troops seemed to feel that this boded good for the army and that we would be soon on our way marching with all the rest of the troops across the peninsula to wherever they had gone south along the Mississippi.

After breakfast, we returned to the barracks and I went through my gear again. I removed the two Remington revolvers that had once belonged to my father and older brother. The revolvers, along with the Henry repeating rifle that I had given to Sergeant Shawnasee, were all that I had salvaged from the smoldering ruins of our homestead on the banks of the Osage River. I considered loading the Remington's but decided not to. It wasn't a good idea to leave the guns loaded for an extended period of time because the powder could become damp or the beeswax blocking the cylinders could become dislodged if left unattended. Just because we anticipated marching out directly didn't mean that we would actually be seeing any combat, so I decided not to load my weapons.

Nothing much seemed to happen for the rest of the day and we merely wandered around through the camp at Milliken's Bend, talking and speculating on what would happen next. Nothing much did that day, nor did anything much seem to happen for the next several days. It was nearly two weeks later before we received any meaningful news. Then we were instructed to pack our gear and be ready to move out in the morning. Once again, I considered loading the Remington's but decided not to. The anticipation of action was almost overpowering but, until we had more conclusive evidence that it was imminent, there was no sense getting further prepared.

The following morning after the bugles roused us up for roll call and breakfast, we returned to the barracks and loaded up our gear and marched off down to the landing. At last, it seemed that something was really going to happen. A number of steamers had been assembled and we were marched down to the water and up the gangplanks. We assembled on deck or in the salons and, after our regiment and several others were on board the steamers, set off down the Mississippi. I was rather apprehensive that they would be attempting to run the river with steamers loaded with troops in broad daylight. Maybe they had only lost one steamer and a couple of barges in their run down the river at midnight, but this was another story entirely.

Yet, down the river we went but, before we came to the big bend, the steamers turned off to the east and went up what the troops told me was the Yazoo. We went for a few miles up the Yazoo and then the steamers slowed, pulled into the banks and disembarked the troops. Some of the troops that had been there before were shocked and apprehensive. They thought that we were going to attempt to storm the Chickasaw bluffs as they had back in December just around Christmas.

I have to admit I was dreading this. I can't say that I've ever been scared before and I had been in the battles of Shiloh and Corinth, but then I hadn't had time to think about it. At Shiloh, we had marched off not knowing that there were any Confederates in the vicinity and, when we ran head on into the entire Confederate Army, the action had been so intense, confused and, to me, disorganized, that I hadn't had time to think of being afraid. It had simply been load and shoot as fast as you could, retreat, form up, shoot some more and then run like hell. The same had been true at Corinth. We had had no idea that the Confederates were there in force when we had marched out of town. Once again, we had run into a major Confederate force and had to conduct a fighting retreat. This time, it looked like the Confederates knew we were coming and were prepared for us and I was afraid we were about to repeat the disastrous attempt to take the bluffs. Indeed, the troops that had been there the previous December apprehensively pointed out that this was the same identical ground, the same broad triangle of dry land between the bayous and the sloughs that they had marched across so senselessly six months ago.

But, we went marching across the broad base of the triangle and up the river and into the woods on the other side where the generals ordered us back on the steamers that had proceeded upriver after having disembarked us. We sailed back down the river to the west where we disembarked and then marched across again. We did this for the entire morning and most of the afternoon, disembarking and marching across the field, and then re-embarking to the east above the opened triangle of dry ground, and then sailing back down to the west and disembarking again.

By now, most of the troops that had been here previously seemed to feel relieved and actually quite jubilant and we began marching with pride and nonchalance. It seemed that the troops realized that we were only putting on a demonstration for the Confederates on the bluff. Just what the purpose of that was, we were uncertain, but it certainly boded well for us.

That evening, we steamed back down the Yazoo, then up the river to Milliken's Bend and returned to the barracks. We had done a lot of marching, shouting, cheering and bluffing, it appeared. But, now we were back in Milliken's Bend and uncertain as to what the next move would be. It wasn't long in coming.

The next day, after the buglers blew and we had assembled in the parade ground and had breakfast, we were ordered to the barracks to retrieve our gear and be ready to march. It looked likely that we were on our way to join up with McClernand, McPherson and Grant someplace south along the river, but we were disappointed. General Steele and General Tuttle, who were part of Sherman's 15th Corps, left that day on the march to join up with Grant and the rest of the troops, but General Blair's Division of which we were apart were left behind in Milliken's Bend.

We remained there in Milliken's Bend, feeling rather lonesome. The fort had held, I don't know, somewhere between 20,000 and 30,000 troops at one time, and now we were down to a few thousand. We stayed there for several more days until relieved by troops who had come down from Memphis and then we followed the rest of the 15th Corp on the march down through Louisiana. We marched along fairly dry ground at first but soon found ourselves marching though the swamps. Tall oak and cypress trees crowded the levee on both sides and in places the limbs entwined over our heads. Mosquitoes and biting flies swarmed around our heads and as we marched we flailed the vermin off ourselves and the man in front using pine limbs we had torn from trees we passed. As we marched I looked from side to side, studying the country we were passing through. It was springtime in the south and it was enchanting. The smell of honeysuckle permeated the air. Spanish moss and other vines draped the trees; and everywhere I looked it seemed there were trees or shrubs in bloom. If it weren't for the biting insects it would be a nice place to live

We were marching along the levee with an open area of lily pad covered swamp on our left side. There were a number of long legged blue heron and other large birds feeding in the grass 20 or 30 yards away. I was admiring their brilliant plumage and gracefulness as they moved slowly picking their way, when suddenly the water exploded in a shower of mud and vegetation. There was a thunder of beating wings as the birds took off, and as I stared a large ugly creature thrashed the surface of the swamp with a heron in its mouth. It looked like an eight or nine foot long lizard and was covered with horny, thick, leathery looking hide. It whipped its large head from side to side, then tossed it back and swallowed the bird whole. As it opened its mouth once more, as if to belch, I was stunned at the sight of its enormous teeth. I had been skeptical of the tales the troops had told about alligators. But, in truth, I found them even more fearsome looking than I had imagined. It took two days before we were able to wind our way through the bayous but finally we struck the Mississippi at a place called Perkin's Plantation. We had marched somewhere around 50 to 60 miles.

The weather had become miserably hot and dry. It reminded me of Corinth, Mississippi. It's hard to believe that the winters could be so wet and nasty with rain nearly every day and the summers could be so dry and blistering. Once again, we had been troubled, not so much by mosquitoes as by swarming clouds of buffalo gnats. These things seemed to fly straight in your face and bite as they went by. I swear the nasty vermin didn't even take the time to land before they bit.

The following day we were allowed to walk around the landing. There were a number of houses and assorted buildings that had all been burned to the ground. The rumor was that this had been a plantation belonging to Judge Perkins who was the brother-in-law of Jefferson Davis himself. Some of the troops insisted that the old judge had burned his own plantation rather than let the Union troop quarter in the buildings. I don't know if that was true or not. I suspect that it may have been burnt in retaliation of the fact that he was related to Jefferson Davis, even if only by marriage.

In the morning we continued our march down the west bank of the Mississippi and finally arrived at Hard Times, which was the name given by Grant to their camp on the west bank across from Grand Gulf. The camp was enormous but not nearly as well constructed as the camp at Milliken's Bend. It was obvious that Gen Grant didn't plan on wasting time here. The following morning, we boarded up on the Forest Queen, a medium sized steamer that transported us across the Mississippi to Grand Gulf. The rumor was that Grand Gulf had been Grant's original choice for landing on the east side of the Mississippi but, due to the rebel fortifications that had been erected, he had been forced to go even farther south to land on the eastern shore and had then moved inland and north to cut the rebel line of communication and supply inland. This had resulted in the evacuation of Grand Gulf by the Confederates.

Standing on the shores and looking up at the fortifications that the Confederates had erected on the hills above Grand Gulf, I felt that this had been a very intelligent decision on General Grant's part. Maybe these generals weren't all as stupid as I had been thinking.

The rebels had fortified a steep hill, which appeared about as formidable as Chickasaw Bayou, with rifle pits and entrenchments, line upon line all the way to the top of the hill. All along the top of the hill, they had had at one time numerous cannons and large siege guns to defend the river landing. It was quite unnerving to contemplate.

We spent the rest of the day helping unload steamers that crossed the

Mississippi back and forth between Grand Gulf and Hard Times, bringing over all the supplies, ammunition, food and clothing that was necessary to maintain the army.

That evening around the campfires, we were brought up-to-date on the gossip by troops that had been there for several days. Apparently Grant had landed at a place further south on the eastern side of the Mississippi and had moved inland. There had been several sharp battles between the troops at a place called Fort Gibson and a place called Fourteen Mile Creek. At Fourteen Mile Creek, General McPherson ran head-on into a Confederate force commanded by a General Gregg. This had resulted in a severe fight in the tangled woods lining the banks of Fourteen Mile Creek. The rumor was that the fighting had been severe and intense, that the troops had been intermingled in the woods and were so close that troops were actually burned by muzzle flashes as the lines exchanged fire from only a few feet apart. But everyone seemed exuberant and excited. It seems that the Union forces had been successful in all of their engagements. They had managed to break through the enemy lines and Grand Gulf had been evacuated and our troops were continuing to move eastward.

The following day we broke camp and the rumor was that we were to be on our way marching to a placed called Hankinson's Ferry. I assumed that this was someplace on the road to Vicksburg, but getting there looked like it wouldn't be easy. The road was narrow and crooked. The last couple of days had been extremely cold but, once again it had gotten to be quite hot and dry. The road was extremely dusty and water was scarce. The countryside was surprising to me. It seemed like the dry, crooked, dusty road wound along the top of ridges in a very irregular fashion. Looking off to either side of the road, it seemed like the land stood on edge. There were extremely steep hills bordered by hollows chocked with thick brush. It looked like the land had been plowed by a drunken giant. The tops of ridges seemed to run in all different directions. Some ridges were broad and had been cleared and cultivated. The tops of other ridges were narrow and covered with tall timber and thick brush which made it impossible to tell which direction we were actually marching for most of the time. The road was so narrow that frequently wagons, and at one time even an ambulance, had gotten off the edge of the road and overturned, rolling down the bluff to come to rest in the scum covered water and mud of the bayou.

We were able to march, I think, only 15 or 18 miles and were so tired and thirsty that that evening when we were allowed to stop, we simply dropped down in an old cornfield and slept in the dirt. As we had laid there trying to sleep, the men became quite talkative. It had been several days since we had had much to discuss and the troops were all quite anxious as to where we were headed. One of the younger of the troops, Johnny Applebaum, who really wasn't much older than I, probably somewhere around 18 or 19, was quite talkative. Johnny was one of my favorite soldiers. Possibly because he wasn't much older than I and possibly because of his thick German accent and his good sense of humor, I took quite readily to him.

"Sir," he said. He always called me 'Sir' which I found humorous since he was really a few years older than I. "Sir, do you have any idea where we are headed?" Affecting my best Irish accent in imitation of the Sergeant, I replied "Well son, beings how Colonel Fletcher doesn't take me into his considerations much, I really don't know any more than you." To which Christian Nichols, another of the German immigrant volunteers, replied "And I bet General Sherman doesn't take Colonel Fletcher much into his discussions either." Which prompted me to reply "And sometimes I wonder whether General Grant tells General Sherman anything." Feeling rather devilish I went on to say "And you know what the big meetings the officers have in the evening is all about, don't you? They all get together and ask each other 'Just where in the hell are we now?' This prompted somebody in the squad to join in with "Yea, I can see them all sitting around smoking their cigars and saying 'Well, does anybody have any idea just where in the hell we are?' And then the other general says "Well, I saw a sign laying on the ground back a ways that said Fourteen Mile Creek but, beings how it was laying on the ground, I couldn't tell which direction it was pointing." Then someone else butted in, "Well every little hollow we pass has a creek in it and so Fourteen Mile Creek is probably the fourteenth one east of the Mississippi.

Hans Verner replied in his best imitation of an officer "But where are we in relation to Vicksburg?" To which I replied "Well, we must still be south of it because I think we would have surely seen it if we had marched north of it." This sparked great peals of laughter from the whole squad who replied "Really, I'm not sure anybody would have noticed it." Of course, this was all just good natured jesting. At one time when we had been stuck in Corinth for six months, suffering from the mosquitoes, chiggers and heat and diarrhea that was rampant in the place, my impression of officers had not been so high.

It had only been when I had related to these same soldiers while we were training and recruiting at Benton Barracks how Colonel Moore had conducted the troops at Shiloh, fighting a retreat for two miles from our initial conflict with the Confederate army in the cotton field south of Shiloh all the way back to camp, that I realized just how important the training and discipline was that enabled us to deploy from column into line, fire several volleys, reform and then retreat again. It was one thing to good naturedly joke about the officers in command of the troops but I knew that we all had a deep and profound respect for them. We ridiculed and made fun of Sherman in his attempts to take Chickasaw Bayou. And we made fun of Grant and his numerous escapades; with his digging canals and steaming up and down bayous and rivers trying to get to Vicksburg but inwardly we did possess a deep admiration for them, especially for Sherman who was the general of our corps.

The 31st Missouri was a regiment in the 15th Corps under Sherman. That irascible old bastard had been thoroughly ridiculed by the press in his younger days and there was even a rumor that they had labeled him as being totally insane. Thus, Sherman had very little use for the newspapers and the reporters that traveled with the army.

We had been teasing each other about whether Grant or Sherman might have missed Vicksburg when we were marching which prompted one of the troopers, Frank Martin, to bring up the story that he had heard about how when we were in Milliken's Bend, and General Sherman had been with Grant on the Mississippi at Hard Times, General Sherman had rejoiced at the loss of one of our steamers. Admiral Porter had successfully made the trip around the peninsula below the bluffs of Vicksburg. A few days later the navy ran the gauntlet again. This time the only loss was the steamer that held five or six reporters. Frank joyfully related how he had heard that when Sherman received the news of the loss of the steamer with the reporters, he was quite gleeful and shouted that we would be receiving news from hell shortly now. This brought a great roar of laughter from all the men. Having relieved their fears and frustrations with pleasant criticisms of the officers in command, we gradually settled down and fell off to sleep.

Over the next couple of days, we managed to march only three or four miles. The weather had continued to be unbearably hot, dry and dusty but then we had a couple of days of fairly hard but intermittent rains. We had been ordered to move from our position and into Raymond. We marched down out of the high bluffs and ridges west of the town and along wet, muddy roads which slowed the speed of the march considerably. It seemed that Raymond was on the other side in a lowland area and the hills all seemed to drain into this narrow ground which held the water until the land was nearly saturated.

We marched across the lowlands and into the town of Raymond while the 17th Corps under McPherson was still departing out the other side of town. We joked and speculated how the southerners must all be thinking that they may as well go ahead and surrender, what with all of these Union troops marching through their little town.

Raymond wasn't much of a town. Someone said that before the war there were about 800 inhabitants. Apparently General McPherson had had a rather sharp little fight there just yesterday and, as we marched, we passed the Raymond Courthouse that was filled with rebel wounded and passed by an old hotel that was packed with rebel prisoners that were taken the day before. We camped for that night just east of Raymond, some troops even having the benefit of sheltering in some homes along the eastern side of the town. It rained hard again all night.

The following day we were up early but it was continuing to rain hard. Most of the corps never got out of the immediate vicinity of Raymond. Some time in midmorning it seemed that the rain was slacking off some and the corps began marching out towards the east. As we were marching, we heard a brief flurry of gunshots and what sounded like a quick cannonade. Word spread back down the ranks that the Confederates had attempted to hold the Union advance along a small creek to the east. Some people reported that this was called Lynch Creek. The engagement hadn't lasted long before the Confederates fled and we continued marching across the creek and towards Jackson, Mississippi. I was rather astounded at this point to find out that we were headed for Jackson, Mississippi which some reported was 40 to 50 miles east of Vicksburg. But at least we seemed to be making good time in that direction, for whatever reason.

When we went into camp that night, the men were quite exuberant as they felt that we were at least halfway to Jackson. Then the talk gradually turned again to the officers commanding the regiment. Johnny Applebaum had a story about how Colonel Seay of the 32nd Missouri Regiment had been placed under arrest and had been threatened with court martial. The 32nd Missouri was in our brigade and was considered to be a sister regiment, having recruited men in and around the St. Louis area also. It seemed that Colonel Seay a couple of mornings ago had taken a shot at a red squirrel in a tree. I guess the Colonel considered squirrel stew to be a change in diet from the usual hard tack and pork. He missed the squirrel but managed to arouse the animosity of one of the superior officers who had had him placed under arrest. This didn't sit too well with the rest of the men in the squad who felt that it was rather an exaggerated reaction for someone who just had a taste for squirrel stew. Johnny Applebaum said "Too bad you hadn't been there. You could have shot the head off that squirrel and still spared the cheek. I laughed and said "damn right, the cheek is the best part of the squirrel," which caused a round of laughter from the rest of the boys in the squad.

Morning came and we were bugled into wakefulness early and soon back on the march to Jackson, Mississippi. It seemed that Sherman and his 15th Corps were approaching from the southwest while McPherson and the 17th Corps were approaching from the west. Some time shortly before noon when we were barely two miles from Jackson, fighting broke out to our north. There was a sound of artillery firing and several sharp volleys of musketry, but then things quieted down again. I don't believe the engagement could have lasted more than 10 or 15 minutes.

We continued on the march and followed some railroad tracts into Jackson itself. The town was surprisingly quiet at the time. It seems that the rebels had made their withdrawal shortly before we actually arrived upon the scene. Most of the noise and bustle that could be heard were from the cheers and the exultations of the troops that had reached the town, the capital of the state of Mississippi, taken it and accomplished all of this with little, as far as we were concerned, fighting or loss of life.

Orders were soon received that we should destroy as much property of the Confederate army and military as we could and to destroy as much of the railroad as feasible. Just how we were supposed to determine what was the property of the Confederate army and government was never really explained. Any buildings that were close to the railroad were set on fire. Several were found to have cotton and other military stores but a few, I suspect, were burnt out of sheer jubilation. One building that was presently up in flames could possibly have been considered to be housing the Confederate supply of liquor since a lot of the troops fleeing the immediate vicinity were carrying jugs and boxes of whiskey or other types of liquor. I suspected that it had probably been somebody's bar at one time and actually had nothing to do with the military but I guess certainly liquor could be considered to be a type of supply.

We began pulling up the rail tracks from the bed and tossing them off to the side of the roadbed and suddenly someone came up with the idea of burning the ties also. Mounds of kindling were gathered and piled up and set on fire and the ties were laid crisscrossed on the top of the fires until they were burning fiercely. This gave off a thick cloud of black smoke that had a horrible stench. I was told this was due to the creosote that they soaked the ties in to prevent them from rotting in the moisture. Whatever it was, it certainly stank and caused the eyes to water.

We took the rails themselves and laid them on the stacks of burning railroad ties and heated them up until they were flaring red hot in the middle at which point parties of men would approach the fire from each side, lift the rails and carry them away from the fire. We then forced them against telegraph poles, wrapping them around the pole in a knot so they would be unusable. We did this with several rails until the stack got to be four or five feet high and then found that carrying the rails to the next telegraph pole was rather cumbersome and unnecessary. We cut off all the telegraph poles close to the fires, about five feet up, and then we could wrap the ties around them in a pretzel fashion and then lift them up over the tops of the telegraph poles and throw them along the side of the railroad. This seemed to be great fun and the troops enjoyed themselves immensely. We worked until late in the evening and then stacked the fires up so they would burn through the night and turned in.

The following morning we were up early to resume our work of destroying the Confederate railroad. Generals McPherson and McClernand were dispatched west, in the direction of Vicksburg again, but General Sherman's troops were given orders to continue the destruction of Jackson. We went further into the town, destroying any buildings that looked like they might be housing supplies or even having housed troops for the Confederate army. We continued the work of pulling up the rails, stacking the ties, setting the fires and burning and otherwise destroying the tracks.

While we were engaged in the destruction of Jackson, I began reminiscing about Osceola. I had the feeling that we were doing to Jackson, what Jim Lane had done to Osceola. This got me to thinking about my family and the tragedy that had befallen them that had resulted in the death of my parents and my older brother, William.

As we worked, tearing up track and burning ties and bending rails, the creosote smoke burnt my eyes and stung them so much that I'm sure that the men in my squad couldn't know that the tears running down my cheeks were more for my family and my own personal loss than due to the smoke from the creosote soaked railroad ties. There were several railroad bridges across different rivers in and around Jackson and we felt it was necessary to destroy these also. We salvaged barrels of tar and coated the trestles and the tracks with the tar, setting it aflame. This worked remarkably efficiently and shortly every bridge near the town had been burnt and fallen into the rivers. We continued to work about the destruction for the next two days and then received orders to march off to the west towards Vicksburg.

As we were beginning the march to Vicksburg, rumors suddenly spread that the other army corps were in a major battle somewhere outside of Vicksburg. We quickened our march in an attempt to get up in time to participate in the battle but, as the troops presently engaged in combat had marched out two days previously there wasn't much chance. Nevertheless we marched hard but, when it became late in the evening, we went into camp never having heard the sounds of any fighting in the distance.

We had just crossed a small bridge, which we had burnt quite quickly and laid down for the night in the cornfield just on the other side. Shortly after we had laid down to rest, having eaten what supplies we had on-hand, Colonel Simpson passed through the camp and announced that General McClernand had fought a tremendous battle another's day march to the west at Champion Hill and had been overwhelmingly successful in his endeavors. The story was that the Confederate General Pemberton who had been in Vicksburg had moved east, apparently attempting to join up with the Confederate forces in Jackson and had run head-on into the Union forces advancing from Jackson. Pemberton had been severely defeated and had lost several thousand troops killed and wounded, and several thousands captured. The story was that Pemberton was now in full retreat back to Vicksburg. We cheered lustily at this good news. It seemed to me that we had been marching all through the southern territory without much resistance. Certainly Vicksburg would be ours soon.

The following morning we were up early and marching rapidly. Sometime shortly after noon, we passed a hill off to the south which was pointed out and we were told that that was Champion Hill where Pemberton had confronted General McClernand the day before. We marched on past and came to a river which I was told was the Big Black River. There were some Confederate troops still on the eastern side of the river but they retreated quite quickly as soon as we showed up in force. We didn't even have time to get the regiment into line to confront them before they were gone. We came to a halt on the east side of the Big Black and waited while troops threw up a pontoon bridge across the river. This took four or five hours and it wasn't until late at night, probably 9 or 10 o'clock, before we got across the river to the western shore and went to camp for the night there.

We spent a rather restless night. I doubted that we were in much danger but our regiment was one of several that had crossed the river while the majority of the division was on the other side. Thankfully the night passed peacefully, although slowly, and in the morning we were up early to move out. The rest of the division was still crossing the river on the pontoon bridge when we ran into some rebels who had decided to contest our advance. They had some artillery in the distance which they brought to use. We spread out in line and advanced rapidly. There were rebels visible in the distance and, as we advanced, we were continually taking shots at them. At times a battery of flying artillery would charge up, unlimber and fire at us and in response our artillery would gallop forward, unlimber and fire back. We continued this long range skirmishing throughout the day, continually moving forward at a fairly rapid rate. I shot so often that once again my arm and shoulder was so sore that I could hardly stand to fire that damn heavy musket.

We were marching, skirmishing and in continual action it seemed for most of the day but nobody seemed upset. The boys in the squad all seemed exceptionally cheerful as we were making such rapid progress and, despite the heat and the lack of water, it was an exhilarating sight to see the Confederates fleeing so rapidly at our approach. We continued the rapid advance throughout the day and towards evening we were rewarded by seeing the high bluffs and the town of Vicksburg in the distance. I don't think I will ever forget my first view of the city on the bluffs. The land in all directions seemed to be bare of trees and vegetation for several miles around the periphery of the city. The rebels had done a marvelous job of clearing any thing that might offer protection or concealment. We moved off to the right, as ordered, and circled north of Vicksburg. As darkness approached, we found ourselves on the edges of some high bluffs looking down towards the river in the distance. Off to the southwest we heard heavy firing. It seemed that the leading troops were involved in a vigorous skirmish. It lasted possibly an hour but must not have amounted to much since we weren't ordered up. All along the top of the bluffs ran a line of abandoned fortifications. We were ordered to halt here for the night.

As we went into camp on the high bluffs looking down over the river to the north of Vicksburg, we intermingled with troops of some of the other regiments. One of the sergeants of the 32nd Missouri Regiment suddenly exclaimed "By damn, boys, you know where we're at, don't you?" Of course, I really didn't know but, as he began pointing out things in the distance from the bluff that we were on, it became quite clear. He said "Yonder is the Yazoo, and just down below is the Chickasaw Bayou. See there, you can make out the rifle pits and the abatis that the Confederates had built. That's where we were back in December when Sherman ordered us to attack these same bluffs that we're on now." Then he exclaimed "By damn, it took us six months and we took the long way around but here we are on the top." This brought a loud cheer from all the troops within hearing as it suddenly became quite clear to me that this is exactly where we had been when Sherman had made his feint a few weeks ago.

We had been out there near the river at the base of the triangle looking at these self-same bluffs. From the top of the bluffs where we were now, I could look down and see where the troops had fought in the bayou and the swamps at the base of the bluff. It was amazing to me to think that anyone could have seriously considered attacking here. Or that they could have even climbed these bluffs. It was amazing that the Confederates who had fled when the troops had taken the rifle pits at the foot had even been able to climb these bluffs while being under fire. I couldn't believe that officers could even contemplate ordering troops to attack here. I listened and looked where a veteran of the battle pointed. There was where Col DeCourcy led his troops over the causeway. There was where Gen Blair pushed his stumbling troops through the swamps. And there, to the left was the Indian mound and the location where the artillery had worked such dreadful effect on Gen Thayer's brigade. But now here we were on the top of the bluffs looking down over the Yazoo River in the distance and the Chickasaw Bayou and directly to our south was Vicksburg. We had made it.

CHAPTER TWO

That evening we did our best to relax in the remains of the Confederate fortifications looking down over the Chickasaw Bayou that General Sherman had attempted to conquer last Christmastime. I lay back, gently resting on my elbows and my knapsack, with the members of my squad surrounding a small bonfire. Off somewhere to the north, fiddles were playing and further to the east there was the lonesome warbling tones of a harmonica that seemed to be playing a rather mournful song. We were still jubilant and cheerful. Although it was against regulations to have liquor in camp, I ignored the bottle that the boys were passing around. I had felt that they had earned a few sips for relaxation.

I wished we could have been more joyous in our celebrations, but possibly we were still somewhat subdued in spirits. Not more than a mile away to the south, on sheer, steep bluffs, stood the Confederate fortifications of Vicksburg. We were jubilant, but I was sure the rebels were resigned to defeat and excessive celebrations in the face of their remorse just didn't seem appropriate. About that time, we were startled by a dense Irish brogue. "There you be, boys," announced the Sergeants' arrival. It seems that he could conjure up this dense Irish brogue at will and at other times he was completely capable of speaking perfect English. In fact, I believe that he spoke English better than I did.

I was delighted to see the Sergeant. It had been four or five weeks since we had have any conversation. I had spoken to him a half dozen times during the last few weeks, but only in passing. I know that I had truly missed our near nightly conversations at Benton's Barracks but I felt that it was inappropriate to bother him on campaign. I'm certain he had much too much to worry about without having to wet nurse me. Also, I felt that since I had a position of authority and a lot of men to look after myself that I couldn't appear to be reliant on anyone else. Therefore, whenever we met for conversations, it had been brief and to the point. However, he was here now and I couldn't help springing up and shaking his hand rather vigorously. "Sarge," I said, "It's good to see you." He said "I just had to come by to see if there was anything you boys might be needing." He made this inquiry while scanning my squad of men from left to right. Johnny Applebaum spoke up immediately and said "Hard tack, Sarge, hard tack." Hans Verner replied "Yeah, Sarge, hard tack. We have been eating way too much green corn and green sweat potatoes and pork. It doesn't set easy on the stomach." That was true. All that rich food and fatty pork seemed to go right straight through.

"Anything else, boys?" the Sarge asked. Then he said, "Hey there, Mr. Cantrell, haven't you spared a sip for the Sarge" as Robert tried to slide the half empty Whiskey bottle into his blouse. "Why sure Sarge. But only a sip. There is barely enough for the boys as it is." The Sergeant took a small sip and passed the bottle back to Bob Cantrell and then announced that he must be off to check on the rest of the squads.

Before he left, he took me aside to tell me in private to make sure and keep the boys under control. Then he said under his breath that in the morning we would be launching an all-out assault on the Confederate works on the bluffs ahead. This shook me to my heels. I had thought that once we had surrounded Vicksburg, had it isolated and fully encompassed, that the battle was over. We controlled the Mississippi to the west and had 30,000 men surrounding the city from north to south. We had troops stationed over the river also and the rebels were completely cut off and isolated. It was only a matter of time before they were forced to surrender. I thought that our job was done and could see no sense in attempting to storm the fortifications on top of the bluffs.

I spent a restless and near sleepless night in anticipation of the fight I believed was coming in the morning. I hadn't seen the confederate fortifications myself, but feared they might be as formidable as the works we had investigated the night before. Morning came and we formed up to move out. The troops under Col Wood moved off to the southwest following the road that wound along the top of the bluffs by the earthworks. They had been down this road last night and had encountered a line of rebel rifle pits along a ridge top and had skirmished unsuccessfully for upwards of an hour before dusk came. Now they were back at it and this time they were taking artillery. Well at least they knew what to expect.

We moved off to the east; parallel to the road we had traveled yesterday, then formed line and turned south. I led my squad well forward and began moving in skirmish formation though the dense trees. At first we followed along the top of a ridge but soon dropped down its near vertical edge and were forced to cross a shallow slough of standing water. It was only several inches deep but was covered with a thick, oily scum of greenish slime. The mud clung to our boots and we sank up over our ankles with every step. It was nearly impossible to pull my feet out without losing my boots. I wondered how deep it would get then I shivered as I wondered if alligators lived here. It was impossible to see more than a few feet due to the thick growth of bamboo, so I called out to the squad to stay close and not get separated. Thankfully we soon crossed it but had to struggle and crawl up another steep ridge. With all the mud on our boots it was impossible to stand up and climb. We had no sooner reached the top then we could see the main line of troops through the woods even with us. We had been a hundred yards ahead when we started but obviously they had been moving on a ridge parallel to our position and had been on dry ground all the way. We had climbed a spur that connected to the ridge they were on. I looked back and forth but couldn't see the sun through the trees so had no idea what direction I was headed. Damn it anyhow! I decided to keep going the same way. At least we were back in line, so to speak.

It was only a few yards and we came to the edge of the spur and had to descend again. We had only taken a few steps before, one after another, our feet flew out from under us and we slid down the bluff on our backsides. I splashed into the stinking, scum covered water and struggled to get up. The water was only a few inches deep, but the mud was several inches deep and I could only regain my feet by turning on my side, then my knees and pushing myself up with my rifle butt. Double damn it! I took a moment to take stock of the situation I called out to each of the men in the squad and was relieved to know I hadn't lost any. We were supposed to be skirmishing, searching out the confederates and doing so as stealthily as possible. At least it was unlikely there would be any rebels dumb enough to be down here in this mud.

We crossed another couple of ridges and waded across another couple of sloughs, then came to some level, dry ground that looked as if it had once been cultivated. Thirty or forty yards away was a tangled abatis of felled trees lying on a steep slope with their sharpened limbs pointing in our direction. Looks like we've found the rebs, I thought, and motioned the men back into the brush. I felt lucky none of us had been shot. Then I moved forwards keeping low and concealed. Carefully I scanned the slope, then the top of the ridge across from us. I could make out a line of rifle pits or some type of earthworks but they seemed to be empty. Just then firing broke out to our left. It rose rapidly in volume, as if a whole brigade was involved, then just as rapidly ceased. Still everything seemed quiet here. I moved back into the bamboo and told the boys what I had found. "I want you to stay here. Stay concealed but cover me. I'm going to check it out. If there's anyone up there, shoot him before he shoots me." Then I moved to the edge of the bamboo, waited for the boys to get ready, took a deep breath, and took off at a run. I ran doubled over at the waist and jigging from side to side. It seemed it took forever to reach the shelter of the abatis. The downed trees with their interlocking branches made an excellent barricade, but an equally adequate shelter. Just as long as there wasn't any artillery I thought! I wiggled my way through the limbs until I found a sheltered spot where I could observe the ridge above. I didn't see or hear anything.

Finally I motioned the rest of the squad over. I wished I had told them to come one at a time, but as soon as I waved they all came with a rush. I raised my rifle carefully scanning the ridge and ready to fire at any movement. One by one the men reached the downed trees and moved forwards to where we could communicate. "Appears the rebs have pulled back" I said. "I want half of you to stay here and give us cover, the rest spread out and let's climb this ridge. Keep your guns up and ready." Then we started out. We were five yards apart and climbed or crawled our way up. I was constantly expecting, any moment, to get shot. But, thank God, the rebels truly were gone. On the top of the ridge were a long line of rifle pits but, as far as I could see, there were no emplacements for artillery. This ridge was only a hundred yards in length then fell off steeply on each end. I suppose that was way it had been abandoned. As I looked union troops came out on the ridges both east and west of us. Finally the rest of our regiment caught up with us. As they were struggling through the abatis I took the time to survey our surroundings. South of our position was a deep and wide valley. It appeared as if it had once been cleared but now was grown up in brush and weeds. Scattered throughout the bayou were numerous, dense tangles of felled trees. The confederates had been busy as beavers; they had cleared all the trees from this point to their defensive works on the other side of the bayou. And they were there now, in force. I could see confederate troops thickly lining the fortifications across from us. It looked as if they had dug entrenchments across the entire top of the ridge that seemed to be unbroken as it ran from west to east. I could see five hundred yards in each direction and everywhere I looked were earthworks crowned with upright log palisades or horizontal logs with head logs to provide a firing slot. Worse than that, I could see several artillery emplacements

Suddenly I felt a whiff of air blow by my left cheek then heard the report of a rifle. I immediately dove into a rifle pit to my right. Damn, I thought, the rebs had shot at us. We were at least eight hundred yards away and I had felt perfectly safe. Worse the bastard had nearly killed me. I was just starting to rise up to peek over the lip of the pit when I was crushed to the dirt as Johnny dove in on top me. "What the hell" he said. They're shooting at us". "I know" I replied. "And someone is damn good at it". Soldiers from the rest of the regiment were just then starting to move on the top of the ridge and we called out for them to take cover or be shot. They immediately began scrambling into the rifle pits as several shots went whistling by

Suddenly I heard my name being called. I recognized Sergeant Shawnasee's voice and called back "Over here Sarge". I shifted to the back of the rifle pit and searched for the Sergeant among the troops along the edge of the ridge. It wasn't hard to spot the Sergeant as he stood nearly six foot four inches, although now he was on hand and knee trying to make the last few feet to the top of the slope. "Stay there" I called, "I'll come to you". I scrambled on my knees quickly back over the rim and dropped on the ground next to the Sarge. "What's going on up there" he said. A brisk rifle fire had broken out as our troops replied to the rebel snipers. It sounded like a real fight. "Ah, the boys are just wasting lead" I said. "The rebels are eight hundred yards away, but they have some mighty fine sharpshooters who won't hesitate to take a shot if they see a big enough target". "You better stay here for now, there's no cover, all the rifle pits are full and you're definitely too big a target" I joked. Then I added "Besides they have artillery that is positioned to sweep the ridge if we tempt them too much". "Come with me" he said.

I followed the Sarge as he slid back down the ridge and wound his way back through the abatis. We approached a group of officers who were clustered standing safely on the edge of the bayou. I recognized Col Fletcher who commanded the 31 Mo regiment and Col Seay of the 32. Sergeant Shawnasee led me up to them and introduced me. My first thought on being introduced to the officers in command was what a miserable impression I must be making, standing there covered head to toe in mud. Even Col Manter was there. "Well, Corporal Everett, report please" he said. I went on to describe what I had seen, even going so far as to draw out in the earth the locations of the artillery emplacements. Then felt so bold as to add my opinion that without earthworks we would be too exposed to attempt occupy the top of the ridge. Col Manter smiled, then ordered shovels and picks to be brought forward. It seemed they already had a good idea of the terrain and of our position and had come prepared. Then he suggested Col Fletcher accompany me back to my rifle pit and inspect the situation himself. I supposed there was no sense in too many officers exposing themselves recklessly.

I turned and led the way back to where we had exited the abatis without another word. Then we picked our way through the tangled, sharpened branches and crawled back up the bluff. As we crept to the edge of the rim I called out to Johnny to confirm our location. He instantly replied and I called back "Do you still have room for one more". "Sure, plenty of room in the inn" he said. I would have liked to have seen his expression as Col Fletcher scrambled forward and joined him in our hole. In a few minutes Col Fletcher was back and thanked me for my report. "Very observant" he said. He made his way back down the ridge and through the abatis, at one point being forced to crawl on his hands and knees. I watched till he disappeared from view. Turning to the Sarge I said "Next time give me some warning if I'm going to meet the brass. I must look disgusting". The Sarge just laughed and said "Son they cared more for what you had to say then how you looked". We lay back against the slope, bracing ourselves with our feet. "What now Sarge" I said. It was, maybe, around ten o'clock. The Sarge had said last night that we were to launch an assault on the confederates this morning. But surely we couldn't attack across eight hundred yards of open bayou and up a hundred or more feet of near vertical bluffs. "Now we wait for the shovels to come up then dig in". Hopefully we'll have better opportunities elsewhere down the line" he said. I could only shake my head in agreement.

We lay on the slope and soaked up the warm southern sunshine. I took several large swallows from my canteen, but felt no need to converse further. It felt good just to be near the Sergeant. About a half hour later soldiers arrived bringing up shovels and picks. I took one of each, finding it difficult to carry them and my rifle also. I turned to the Sarge and said "Take care now sir, we need you". "You too son, you too" he replied. With only a seconds hesitation I scrambled to the top of the ridge and made a crouching run for my hole. I dove headlong in the pit landing on Johnny. "Damn it, be careful" he called. "You nearly stabbed me with that pick". "That's no way to talk to someone bringing you presents. Now get to work" I said. "How am I supposed to use this lying on my back" Johnny said. "Find a way or stand up and get shot" I joked.

I lay on my stomach and grabbed the handle of the shovel just above the blade and began scraping and scooping at the ground. The earth was unlike anything I had seen before. It was grayish in color and of a strange clay-like texture. But it was easy to dig and didn't seem to have any rocks. I shoveled it up and threw it on the south side of the pit. Johnny lay on his back stabbing away at the clay to his left side, and attempting to widen our hole. After a while we traded implements and I began picking at the earth on my right side while Johnny scooped dirt and piled it out at his head. Gradually we widened and deepened the hole and soon had room for other soldiers to join us. I transferred the head logs to the confederate side of the pit and peeked through the slot beneath the log, feeling greatly relieved. I studied the rebel works, keeping my head back from the aperture beneath the log. I knew they were watching us, as I was watching them

Our hole was deep enough now to stand and Johnny had given our shovel and pick to the other troops. While they worked Johnny joined me as we spied on the rebs. "What are you thinking" asked Johnny? "I was just thinking about how close I came to being dead" I said. I haven't noted any wind, but that's still a damn long shot. I've never attempted any near that far. Dad always said there was no sense wasting powder and lead at anything over a hundred yards, although we sometimes practiced at two hundred yards against a backstop where we could dig out the balls. Dad was always that cheap". "I'm thinking this would be a good place to sight in this rifle". "Sight it in" quizzed Johnny? "Yeah, sight it in" I said.

It was around noon. The rifle pits had been widened and now formed a long line of entrenchments on the top of the ridge. Sergeant Shawnasee joined us in the trench. "Looks like we're still planning to assault later" he said. "When the firing starts we are to join in. Keep the rebs occupied, so they won't try to shift their troops". Thank God I thought with relief. Attacking here was pointless. I almost smiled thinking I would be given a chance to sight in my rifle after all. Then the Sarge was off, passing down the line to spread the word, and giving me some time to think things over.

I realized that simply firing away at this distance was pointless. I was too unfamiliar with the rifles trajectory. I needed a definite target and someone to watch for me since I wouldn't be able to see through the black powder smoke once I pulled the trigger. I carefully studied the confederate lines. Just to the right of our position their line bent ever so slightly back. There was a horizontal barricade consisting of one large tree on top of the earthworks and a head log on it. The stump of the base log stuck out from the line and was probably a foot in diameter. It made an excellent, stationary target. I pointed it out to Johnny and explained what I had in mind. Now all we could do was wait.

Around two o'clock artillery opened a heavy firing to the east. It was soon followed by the rattling crack of small arms fire. I guessed it was nearly a mile away. I could almost imagine I heard cheering as the troops rushed to victory or death. I nudged Johnny and asked "Are you ready". Johnny took two steps to his right and nodded. I took careful aim, using the log to support the rifle, and having raised the rear sight to maximum elevation. Gently I squeezed the trigger and was surprised when it discharged. Instantly my vision was blocked by the muzzle blast and the thick gray, stinking smoke. All up and down the line our regiment let loose. As I reloaded Johnny simply shook his head. "I couldn't tell" he said. Well, I hadn't expected it to be easy! I fired three or four more shots at the stump before Johnny suddenly exclaimed "There, a foot low and a foot to the left. I'm sure. I fired once more to be sure myself, and Johnny said "No doubt. I could see it knock dirt". Then I fired three more shots, having made my correction in aim, and was pleased to hear Johnny cheer each time he saw wood fly from the stump. Then I fired three shots at the stump, using the different markings on the rear sight, as Johnny noted the effect. "Your turn" I said and traded places with Johnny.

I watched carefully as Johnny took aim and fired. Since I had a good idea where to look, it wasn't hard to spot his shots. Johnny seemed to have trouble keeping a steady aim, so I watched and coached him as he emptied his ammunition box. By the time he was empty he had developed a real knack for it. We had been so intent on our business that I had failed to notice that the rest of the regiment had already ceased firing. Only then did I realize that a lull had settled over the whole battlefield. At least an hour had passed as Johnny and I carefully sighted in our rifles. Surely the fight wasn't over. As if my thoughts had inspired the Gods of War all hell broke loose again to the east. And this possibly prompted an outbreak of heavy fighting to the west where Gen Wood's troops were. Artillery sounded in the west then, once again, small arms joined in. The fighting seemed intense but finally dwindled away and ceased. Once again the battlefield was quite. Throughout the rest of the afternoon there were occasional outbursts of explosions and what sounded like sudden volleys of rifle fire, but the fight seemed to have stalled. Darkness gathered and as the sun went down in the west, I could only wonder what we had accomplished

We settled down in our hole and dug out some hardtack. I realized then that we hadn't eaten since breakfast. My mouth was so dry I couldn't chew the stuff and had to take a swallow of water with each bite. Sergeant Shawnasee passed down the trench and sat down across from us. Honestly I don't know how he had the energy to still be moving about. "Well, Sarge, what's the word" I mumbled with my mouth full of mushy hardtack. "Can't say for sure, my boy, but we didn't make any headway today. We'll have to try something else. I expect we are in for a long siege. Have to starve them out I suppose" he said. Then he passed us a flask of whiskey. I took a sip and passed it to Johnny. We only took a tiny sip. I knew the Sarge liked to share it with the other sergeants and corporals, it made us all feel closer. "There are barrels of fresh water at the abatis below he said. Better gather up your canteens and get some for you squad". Then he moved on, checking on the rest of the regiment.

I passed down the trench speaking to each of the boys in turn and collecting their canteens. They hadn't been injured, only a little worse for wear. But most were out of water. I was exhausted but needed to learn to be more thoughtful. That was what made the Sarge so special, and so well liked. I shambled down the bluff, made my way through the abatis, and found the barrels of fresh water. As I waited in line I listened to the talk. The rumor was that Gen Sherman's assault hadn't gone well. Gen Blair's

Second Division had made the attack. Gen Kirby Smith's Second Brigade had attacked along the Graveyard road. To their right Gen Giles Smith had attacked across a bayou filled with felled trees and sinkholes.

The troops had managed to get to the confederate fortifications, called the Stockade Redan, but had been pinned down by the murderous confederate fire. The rumor was that Gen Sherman had lost nearly a thousand men and had nothing to show for it. I merely listened to the talk and when my turn came I filled the canteens and made my way back. It was all I could do to crawl back up the ridge with nine canteens stuffed in my haversack and clutched in my hands. Finally I reached the trenches and passed them out before slumping to the ground next to Johnny. I took one long drink then lay back to sleep. I couldn't begin to worry about tomorrow.

The next two days passed without event. Hot meals were prepared back down in the shelter of the bayou and we were allowed to go down by regiments to be served. Otherwise we spent time improving our trenches. We dug trenches running perpendicular to our lines back over the lip of the bluff and cut steps to aid in climbing back up. Now we were safe from confederate sniping as we moved back and forth to our positions. We cut and carried limbs from the abatis to lay parallel with the earthworks and placed spacers for the head logs. We were instructed to set logs perpendicular under the head logs and across the trench to the other side so that if the head log was dislodged it wouldn't fall back in the trench on top of us. An emplacement was prepared on the east end of the bluff and after dark one night a battery of artillery was manhandled into position. We were here to stay, but what of the confederates? I found out later that night.

Sergeant Shawnasee came by just after dark with the news. The squad gathered together as he filled us in. "Boys" he said "Gen Grants whole command has come up. We've dug entrenchments completely around the confederate works. All the available artillery has been positioned and in the morning Gen Grant has decided to try again. Attacks have been ordered all up and down the line". Before I could ask, he went on. "All we can do here is to fire away again, keep their heads down. No way we can cross that bayou. It's too far and the bluff's too steep. But we can keep them distracted, unable to shift troops. Get some rest and be careful tomorrow". Then he was off to spread the good news.

Shortly after sun up artillery thundered up and down the lines to the south and east. Even Admiral Porter's gunboats joined in the fun, lobby shells over the city. We expected to add our fire to the battle but instead received orders to abandon our entrenchments and march to the rear. As we filed down the bluff and across the bayou I watched as a skeleton crew of men spread out to occupy our positions. We marched across the low ground headed slightly to the northeast and found a gently sloping ridge to climb. We were soon on dry ground on a ridgeline that I thought was the same that others in our brigade had traveled two days before. It had been our bad luck to have to march on the southwest slope of this ridge through sloughs and up the steep sides of spurs that projected from the main ridge. I had no idea where we were headed. Around mid morning the artillery slackened and rumbled to a close. All up and down our lines to the south and east small arms fire flared up. It sounded as if Gen Sherman was having another go at the Stockade Redan. And this time he had support. The entire army must be on the assault. I listened intently, as we marched, for any indication that the fight was advancing, but it's hard to judge progress by noise alone. We must not have succeeded because the sounds of combat in front of Gen Sherman's position dwindled off after an hour or so. Fairly heavy firing continued off to the south however. Maybe we were having better luck there.

We marched for several hours. I lost track of time and location. I was more interested in listening to the battle that continued to rage off to the south. It waxed and waned throughout the day but never entirely ceased for any appreciable length of time. I wondered again where we were headed. At times we halted for long periods. I began to think we were lost. I remembered how, at Shiloh, one of the generals got lost with his whole division and missed the fight entirely. Or so the story had spread. About mid afternoon the sounds of heavy firing commenced again from where I thought Gen Sherman's forces were. And further south it intensified. Then finally we spied union troops ahead in a bayou. We marched off a ridge and found ourselves reunited with Gen Thayer and the Third Brigade of the First Division Fifteenth Army Corp. As we came to a halt to await developments I took the time to have another drink and dug out some hardtack. I realized that the battle in front of Gen Sherman's location had faded and nearly ceased. Then, surprisingly all hell broke loose again. Gen Sherman had a bee in his bonnet, no doubt. I watched as a group of officers conferred ahead. Finally they broke up and Gen Woods troops marched forward to the southwest and approached a ridge behind which Gen Thayer's troops waited for the order to advance. It wasn't long in coming. Up over the ridge went Gen Thayer's brigade, followed by Gen Woods who had his men attack in columns by regiment. Immediately confederate artillery swept the top of the ridge, I watched it plowing the ground, knocking men left and right. Then they were over the ridge and soon rebel rifles rattled out their volleys to join in the bedlam that was combat. Now I could only listen as our troops endured the hail of lead projectiles I knew were bringing many a noble life to its end. I began to fidget; my mouth was so dry I couldn't swallow. I looked at Johnny and he replied with a nervous smile. But time passed and we remained where we were. The fighting lasted about an hour then the sky began to darken, the firing ceased and after it was dark the troops began to filter back. Another day at Vicksburg came to an end.

CHAPTER THREE

Two days after Gen Grant's second assault on Vicksburg found us back in camp on the bluffs over Chickasaw Bayou. Some of the regiments in Col Manter's brigade had been assigned to man our previous lines along, what I learned, was called Mint Spring's Ridge. Others worked on building a road for easy access from the main camp here on the bluffs to Mint Spring Ridge. And still others were detailed to march to the rear. My squad had been allowed to pack up our gear and join several other squads from the regiment as we marched to the rear where we were given a two day rest and allowed to thoroughly wash our uniforms and bathe. Then we were put to work on extending a supply road from the top of the bluffs down to the west to get supplies up from the landing at the Yazoo River.

Troops had already cut a road through the top of the bluffs and down the gentlest edge of the slope towards the river. We joined work parties from below as they cut logs and laid them across the northern edge of the bayou and then placed dirt, grass, brush, and other branches across to bridge the mud of the swamps. We continued working in this fashion for the next couple of days. At last, we were relieved and ordered back to camp. We got to camp that evening in time for a good meal and managed to clean our uniforms again and ready our equipment. It paid to take good care of all your gear. I particularly liked to keep my rifle and revolvers clean and oiled. I was leaning back against my knapsack and haversack, putting a sharp edge on the Damascus bladed knife that had belonged to my grandfather, when Tom Sinclair came over. "Have you seen Frank Martin recently? I haven't seen him since supper" he said. "No", I replied. But in all honesty I hadn't been paying any attention. "Why do you ask?" "He doesn't appear to be anywhere's in camp and it's getting close to taps" Tom said. "If he's gone, he'll be in trouble" he added. More likely, I thought, you're afraid WE would be in trouble. Over the last five or six weeks I had gotten to know the men in my squad much better. Campaigning was much different than being quartered in a barracks with someone. It really showed people for what they were.

Take Tom Sinclair, for instance, Tom was a quiet, no nonsense type of fellow. He seldom joked, but was always ready with a quick smile or a kind word for the troops. He was in his mid twenties and had worked on his parents homestead somewhere around Caledonia, Mo. Tom had a sweetheart, back home, and had been planning on marriage as soon as he saved enough money to get his own place. I thought that showed just how dependable and solid Tom was; homestead first, then wife and family. To most of the troops he was almost like a father, even though he was only six or seven years older than most.

Then there was my favorite soldier amongst the squad, Johnny Applebaum, Johnny was one of the four Germans in the squad. They all came from St. Louis and had been acquaintances. Johnny was the youngest, only a few years older than I, and was everybody's friend. He was always ready with a joke and loved to play tricks on people. He especially liked to harass Otto Kerner.

Otto was older than the other three German's, being in his early twenties. I would have thought he was much older. He never smiled and seemed perpetually gloomy; or angry, it was hard to tell. Most of the others in the squad left him alone. But not Johnny, Johnny went out of his way to tease and joke with Otto. I think Johnny found him to be a challenge. Surprisingly Otto always responded to Johnny's jibes in a friendly, although gruff, fashion. I believe I even saw him smile, once or twice.

I suppose I was allowing myself to be willfully distracted because I didn't know what to do about Frank Martin. Tom cleared his throat and I looked up and said "I'll go look for him. You stay here". Then I slipped my knife in my boot and got up. I wandered through the camp, but Frank was not to be seen. The bugle blew announcing the fact that we should turn in. I went back to our tent and when I ducked in Tom looked at me as if to say "Well". I merely shook my head. I thought I should inform the Sergeant but couldn't do it. I didn't want to get Frank in trouble. I decided to wait till morning; there really wasn't anything anyone could do tonight. I spent a restless night waiting and hoping Frank would turn up. Shortly before sunup I finally fell asleep only to be awakened by Frank as he came stumbling in and actually fell over me. "Where the hell have you been" I cursed. "I've been to see the whores" he laughed. "What" I almost hissed. "The ladies, the ladies" he said. "There's tentfulls of them down at the Yazoo. I found them when we were working on the road". How the bastard could have made it back across the swamp and up the bluff in his drunken condition, I couldn't even imagine. It was amazing he hadn't drowned in the swamp. Or been eaten by alligators, which would have served him just fine. And what of the sentries? It was a wonder he wasn't shot. "Damn you, I snarled. Go to bed and shut up".

I should have known right away where Frank was. It was all he talked about. Whiskey and women! The son of a bitch, truthfully, had been born in a brothel. He talked constantly of his life working on the rivers. It seems he had been up the Ohio, down the Mississippi, up the Missouri, and God only knew where else. And everywhere he went he spent every dime he made on whiskey and women. I found him repulsive, but also fascinating. His talk about women was starting to interest me. I was just over fourteen and had had little contact with the opposite sex. And Frank liked to go into amazing detail about his escapades. I wondered how much of it was true. In truth I thought women would have found Frank disgusting. He was the shortest man in the squad, if not the army, and he was flabby. He was starting to go bald, even though he was less than thirty, and he had bad teeth. Worst was his face. He had close set eyes and his lower lip was turned out so the flesh showed. It looked like he was always getting ready to spit. Well, I guess, it just went to show that anything could be bought if you had the money. As I rolled over to get what sleep I could Frank was already snoring.

CHAPTER FOUR

The following morning, we were roused by the bugle, had breakfast and then received orders to begin siege warfare in earnest. We were issued pickaxes, shovels and spades, and then we were ordered to begin digging trenches towards the Confederates on the bluffs north of Vicksburg. We marched southwards along the ridge to where Col Woods was entrenching. Then turned eastwards and marched along his trenches to the end, descended to the north slope and continued to the east. After a ways we were ordered to dig perpendicular to the bluff so we could stay safe from confederate snipers. Once we had dug across the ridge we heaved large bundles of bamboo cane on the southern slope, for protection, and then started digging again towards the east. For some reason the brass wanted a continuous trench all along the ridge. I guess they wanted to ring the confederates in. I couldn't see how we were in any danger here. We were four and five hundred yards away, on the top of a nearly hundred foot bluff with near vertical sides. The confederates couldn't hope to break out here. Maybe they just wanted to keep us busy.

We went along digging earth, shoveling it and throwing it on the side of the trench nearest the Confederate emplacements. We dug the trench about 10 feet wide and about 4 to 5 feet deep, piling the dirt up on the southern side and making a mound nearly 10 to 12 feet wide at the base. We worked in shifts throughout the day, being encouraged to work for about two hours before being relieved and allowed back to rest in the trenches. We were given a couple of hours of rest to refresh ourselves, had lunch and then went back to work.

Over the next week, work progressed fairly rapidly. I was still impressed with the nature of the clay like soil. It cut easily and held its shape. Even when it rained! The water seemed to run off and it wasn't necessary to shore it up. But, as we neared the southern bluff, we were forced to take more precautions. We would dig the trenches safely during daylight, but wait until after dark to do work on the parapets that we were erecting. We would try to pack the earth and smooth the tops. Then we would bring in logs and lumber to form breastworks on top of the parapet. We would place several logs side-by-side lengthwise following the trenches, and then place sandbags filled with earth on top of these and further logs on top of the sandbags. This made room for sharpshooters to stand on the embankment looking between the logs at the Confederate works and snipe at them with relative safety.

Finally we were rotated back to the main camp over Chickasaw Bayou. We marched into camp, found our tents and dropped to rest. Everyone but Frank, he had a fidgety, suspicious manner about him. I watched him as he moved about the tent then said "Frank, if you sneak off again I'll have you shot for desertion". Rather I could, or not, I didn't know. But he didn't either! He said "I ain't deserting" in an indignant manner. "Well" I replied "You'll just have to wait till we get leave to visit the ladies". I could tell he didn't like me reading his mind. Then I tried to relax and began studying the rest of the squad.

I had two other Germans from St. Louis in the squad, Christian Nichols and Hans Verner. They were both nineteen and looked enough alike to be twins. In fact, they were first cousins. Their fathers had married sisters. They both had light brown, somewhat reddish, hair. They stood about five foot eight, slightly taller than Johnny or Otto. Usually you could find them together. They were both even tempered and mild mannered. I considered them dependable, if not forceful. Finally there were Robert Cantrell and Michael Francis. Both were just over twenty. Robert came from Hannibal and had worked on the steamship landing loading freight. He had once traveled the river but had married and settled down. I couldn't imagine how he could leave his wife to enlist. He sent everything he was paid home. He was sturdy, exceptionally strong, but somewhat introverted. Michael was friendly and seemed to look up to Johnny. He liked to joke but somehow lacked Johnny's charm. If he messed with Otto he would usually provoke him. I often thought they came near to blows, but Michael always realized his peril and apologized just in time. I truly liked all the men, except Frank.

We rested through the rest of the day, sitting around the tent. Then were treated to a hot meal and returned to the tent. I made sure to keep an eye on Frank. Surprisingly Tom did also. It seemed he felt as responsible for him as I did. I thought it was going to be impossible for Frank to elude us both. Somehow we got involved in talking about the war. We all knew how it had started and why, or so we thought. What I didn't know was why the rest of them had enlisted. I was here because I had decided I had to help free the slaves. My own grandfather had come here from York, England. He had arrived as an indentured servant for a southern plantation owner around Rome, Georgia. He had saved his money and on his release had moved along the Tennessee River to Memphis. Eventually making his way to Natchez, Mississippi he had worked overseeing slaves on a cotton plantation. When he left he bought two slaves to take with him as he settled west of Osceola, Mo. Grandfather had often bragged that he could only afford such a fine slave as Abraham because he ran off to be free so much that it was too expensive to hire trackers to bring him back. Grandfather had become friends with Abraham and had bought Sara to be his wife promising both their freedom after seven years if they would work as his indentured servants. Grandfather had always bragged that he "never" owned slaves, only "indentured servants". Abraham and Sara had stayed on to live at our homestead and I had grown up with their grandson being the same age and best of friends. Everything changed when Kansas jayhawkers had burned our home and killed my parents and older brother. They had killed Abraham's son Isaac also leaving my best friend Abel without a father. I had been filled with hate and burned for revenge, but didn't know who to blame. For a while I came to blame my grandfather, thinking we had been punished for his sins. Then had decided our tragedy had merely been due to the war, the main cause of which was slavery. I had developed a strong antipathy towards anyone who tried to justify slavery and especially to anyone who would fight to defend it. At times I thought I had become slightly unhinged. But anyone involved in this war must be unhinged I thought.

I was curious to know why the other men had volunteered. When I inquired everyone was silent at first. Then Johnny, looking strangely sheepish, said "I think it was mainly because of our fathers. I know that was true for me. Our parents came here looking for freedom, they thought

America was a special place, and now they encouraged us to fight to protect it. They can't bear to see it torn apart". "Freedom from what" I said, not sure what he meant. "Freedom from the lords and the church" surprisingly it was Otto who spoke. Then he had gone on to explain how two hundred years ago Germany had been devastated by thirty years of non stop war. In parts of the country over half the population had died. His family had lived in Stuttgart and he implied that the vast majority of the people in that region had died, either in fighting or from starvation. And the lords had been fighting because of religion! It had been a war between Catholic and Protestant kingdoms! I couldn't believe it, Christian fighting Christian, because of church doctrine.

Then Otto went on to describe how Germany had been a collection of dozens of small kingdoms that constantly were fighting each other. Even though they all spoke the same language! They would even ally themselves with foreigners to fight each other. "I don't want to see that happen here" he said. I had never heard Otto talk that much. Tom Sinclair spoke up. "Can you imagine what it would be like if we were separated" he said. "America has a chance for true greatness that can never be realized if we allow the South to secede". I knew Tom was a deep thinker, but was surprised by his perspective. Who would be thinking about future greatness? Bob Cantrell merely said "It was going to happen sooner or later. Might as well get it over and the sooner, the better". Surprisingly no one mentioned slavery.

After several days spent relaxing in camp we were surprised to be allowed our own chance at sharpshooting at the enemy. Sergeant Shawnasee passed by and mentioned that Col Fletcher had agreed to allow my squad to practice long range rifle fire. The Sarge had made the suggestion himself, speculating that at least a couple of the squads should be proficient at it and could thereby serve as more efficient skirmishers when leading the rest of the regiment as we moved into combat. I couldn't help but wonder if he had mentioned that it was originally my idea? Col Fletcher had agreed and had done one better. The Sarge had proudly announced that he had arranged for us to spend a couple of days under the tutelage of sharpshooters from the Twelfth Mo. We rapidly gathered our gear and hustled off, following the road to the southwest along the bluffs then moving east through the trenches we had helped dig on the top of Mint Springs Ridge. Finally we arrived at the sharpshooter's location on a southern projection, or curve, of the ridge. We were now roughly five hundred yards from the confederate lines on Fort Hill Ridge and within rage of some confederate artillery.

I introduced myself to the officer in charge, a young lieutenant who didn't seem pleased to see us. He was abrupt to the point of rudeness and acted like we were wasting his time. I felt like mentioning that we were all in this together, and helping to improve my squad's efficiency could only benefit us all, and then thought better of it. He might consider that type of comment to be insubordinate. He did seem like the touchy type after all. But leave it to Johnny; he leaned over to Otto and whispered, loud enough to be clearly heard, "We should get out of here, the corporal can shoot better than any of them anyhow". "Yah, Dat he can' said Otto, for some reason putting on a dense German accent. The lieutenant chose to ignore them; calling out to a sergeant he said "Let's see what they can do". The sergeant was beaming as he led us over to the parapet. He seemed like a pleasant fellow and tried to be most helpful as he said "There's a slight westerly breeze. We're five hundred yards; at this range your shot will drift about five inches to the left". I studied the ridge across from us, then announced "See that log on the slope below the artillery; I'll aim for its center". The log in question was about five feet long and ten to twelve inches in diameter and was lying vertical on the slope having been dislodged from the artillery emplacement. I raised the ladder sight and chose the third setting on the rung. Then I rested the end of the barrel on the parapet log, gently grasped the barrel and sighted in. I took a deep breathe, letting half slowly out as I gently squeezed the trigger. The kick of the gun surprised me; my squeeze had been so soft. And instantly Johnny cheered as splinters flew from the center of the log. The sergeant cheered also, and then said "By damn you don't need no practice". The lieutenant merely snorted and walked away.

The sergeant then asked for the next man. Johnny happily volunteered and stepped forwards. This time the sergeant was even more helpful and seemed downright enthusiastic. He took his time coaching Johnny in holding the rifle, controlling his breath, gently squeezing the trigger, and judging windage and elevation. The rest of the squad listened intently, awaiting their turn. Johnny calmly set his sights and prepared to fire. His first shot was only a few inches to the left. The sergeant exclaimed "You caught a quick breeze, just bad luck". Try again". Johnny fired several more shots, the last few being dead on. The sergeant encouraged him by saying "My own men can do no better". I believe he meant it. Otto stepped forwards next. Despite all Johnny's teasing they had formed some type of close bond. He was determined not to be out done. He listened patiently and intently as the sergeant again went through his precise instructions. Then he took his place at the parapet. His first shot shaved wood from the right side of the log. The sergeant positively howled in surprise "You boys can all shoot". Hot damn"! By now the sergeant was absolutely enjoying his assignment. To some people shooting is pure pleasure, and seeing it done well is a joy. Otto fired a half dozen shots and the sergeant continued to be impressed. I had halfway expected Johnny to do well since I had coached him so much that one day, but I was surprised by Otto. When he was done I shook his hand and slapped him on the back calling him "Hawkeye". I'm not sure he knew what I meant but he grinned widely anyhow. I don't think I had seen him grin before.

One by one the rest of the squad stepped forwards and took their turns. I suppose they fired twenty rounds apiece before the sergeant signed off on them. At last it was Frank's turn. He seemed apprehensive. His shot's seemed to kick dirt from all over. He was often close but never successful. No matter how much the sergeant tried he couldn't help "pulling" the trigger and jerking his shots. I wanted to try to coach him, but felt he resented me. He didn't seem to understand, why I couldn't just look the other way when he went to see the ladies. I had tried to explain that I was responsible for maintaining discipline, men couldn't just wonder off when they felt an urge. But he remained petulant and sullen. The hell with him I decided. The sergeant persevered. He had Frank fire all forty cartridges, and then borrowed more. Finally he gave up. I had been watching closely and began to wonder if Frank wasn't just being obstinate and deliberately jerking his shots. I wouldn't have put it past him.

The sergeant proudly congratulated us calling us "As fine a bunch of sharpshooters as he had ever met". And I thought he meant it, with the exception of one. He then offered to let us spend the rest of the day practicing or actually sniping. I hadn't seen any rebels, with all that shooting they were keeping their heads down, but decided to try anyhow. The sergeant excused himself and wondered off, while we lined the parapet. We spent the rest of the day sniping away at the confederate walls themselves; they must have found it annoying. But we weren't doing any damage. I began to feel we were wasting a lot of ammunition. But, as the artillery kept up a nearly continuous bombardment of the town and the naval vessels in the river kept up a continuous fire, I couldn't see that we were wasting any more lead than they were. Besides, it probably did serve to force the Confederate artillery men on the bluffs to keep their heads down and, anyway, it had been a long time since the boys in the squad had had any practice.

We stood on the sloping sides of the parapet, peering between the head logs and waited for an opportunity. I passed through man to man explaining the concept of windage and elevation, and then we would stand there patiently, waiting for an opportunity to practice. The thought occurred to me that, whenever Confederate cannon replied to our bombardment, that the Confederate artillery men would move in to swab out the barrels and reload the cannon so, whenever we noticed a blast from the Confederate lines, we would aim at the spot that the fire had come from and then deliver a volley towards it. I wasn't sure if we were having any effect but possibly we might get lucky. This only happened rarely.

Dusk approached and we headed back to camp. The boys were still excited by the day's adventure and quite pleased with themselves. When the Sergeant came by they boastfully related their tales. Johnny gloated when he described how my first shot had been perfect and how the lieutenant had been miffed. The sergeant just smiled and said "Well done, boys, well done". Then he informed us that tomorrow we were to help widen the road down the bluff to the Yazoo and help corduroy the road though the swamp. Gen Sherman wanted it wider and another bridge built across the water at the foot of the bluff. In the morning we set off for road detail. It was the first week in June and it was hot and humid. The work was brutal. We cut logs, carried limbs and brush and shoveled tons of dirt. Time seemed to move slowly. For a couple of days, we were given a respite from digging and working in the swamps. The only thing exciting was the occasional alligators. But as far as I know they never hurt anyone, being intimidated by all the noise and all the men. Although some troops were designated to stand guard with rifles I don't think any alligators were actually shot. Tom and I kept a cross watch on Frank, and he knew it. To be so close to his desire was almost too much for him. He remained quiet and morose. Finally we were allowed to wash our clothes and bathe in the river at the foot of the bluff. The guards seemed to take delight in periodically calling out "Look out alligator". The first time caused a scramble of naked men, but after a while they lost interest. I only hoped they continued to remain vigilant. We were marched back to camp at the old Confederate fortifications and allowed to rest and relax. During this whole time, it seemed that our artillery fire and fire from the gunboats on the river never ceased, especially at night. I suspect that maybe Grant had come to the conclusion that if we kept the Confederates up all night and deprived them of sleep; they would soon tire of resisting.

But, we were soon back up in the trenches and there wasn't much to do. We were about where we had been originally on the nineteenth of May at the time of the first assault. We were too far away to move forwards, the terrain did not allow it. However the rest of the army was kept busy digging and fortifying and moving ever slower forward. They spent a couple of weeks in digging the diagonal zigzag trenches towards the Confederates and had covered nearly half the distance to the foot of the bluffs on which the confederates were entrenched. I heard that they were digging nine approaches to the rebel lines. As they neared the Confederate entrenchments, they began digging the trenches slightly deeper and slightly wider. I had been contemplating what we would do when we got closer to the Confederates on the bluffs. The closer we got to the bluffs, the more the height of the Confederate fortifications would allow them to shoot down into the trenches.

The trenches were widened and deepened and, on the side of the trench furthest from the Confederate lines, the depth was increased a couple of feet deep for three or four feet wide. This left an elevated step three feet wide or so on the side nearest the Confederates. Since the trenches were deeper and the mounds of dirt on the Confederate side of the trenches higher, lumber was brought in to reinforce the inner walls to keep it from collapsing back into the trenches. This resulted in the deepest part of the trenches being probably 15 feet lower than the height of the head logs on the exposed side. To provide more protection to the troops in front of the trench digging the excavation forward, large sacks full of sticks and brush were constructed which could be rolled forward, offering them more protection as they performed the initial work.

As the weeks passed, it seemed like the Confederate response to our bombardments gradually slackened and nearly ceased and, in addition, it seemed like our bombardments slowed. There would be several hours throughout the day, especially, when the only sound that could be heard were the curses of the troops as they dug and the clanks of shovels and pickaxes, but I don't think that a night went by without the splendid fireworks of the bombardment of the town.

As we continued to approach the Confederate city on the bluffs, we were given more and more time at sharpshooting, and now since we were within a half mile of the Confederate works, we practiced the profession in earnest. Before, it had just been a distraction to force the Confederates to keep their heads down, but at this distance, a truly good marksman could spot individual Confederate soldiers and fire with lethal effect. Of course, the same was true for them.

I would peer between the head logs while ordering my squad to keep their heads down and pick out a target. I would call the location and describe the objective, call out the windage and the elevation and then, on command, the squad would put their rifles between the head logs, take quick aim and fire a volley. I felt that was much safer and more effective than having the troops individually scanning between the head logs looking for individual targets. I think we must have actually been effective because it seemed to draw the Confederates' ire. The number of shots that we received in return increased exponentially. But, as we only showed ourselves for a couple of seconds, their sniping had no effect. Then, suddenly, we received what seemed almost like a volley of shots in our direction. I ducked my head down cursing at the Confederates and looked back down the line to see if any of the boys had been injured. I quickly ceased cursing at the Confederates and directed my insults elsewhere.

There was Johnny Applebaum with his cap held erect on two ramrods, marching down behind the parapet, occasionally rising the hat up above the head logs high enough that he was attempting to mimic a soldier walking with a jaunty stride. The Confederate shots were kicking up woodchips and dust all around his hat. "God damn it, Johnny," I said, "What do you think you're doing?" He said "I bet Hans that those rebs couldn't get more than three shots through my hat." "Cut that out," I said, "you're going to get yourself killed for no reason." But, the boys just laughed, thinking it great fun.

We continued our intermittent sharpshooting while the rest of the army proceeded with trench digging and the weeks seemed to pass. Now, it seemed seldom that the Confederates bothered to reply with artillery to any of our provocations. Our entrenchments were within a couple of hundred yards of the Confederates on the bluffs, so I had been told, when suddenly one day the earth seemed to lift under my feet and bounce me in the air. The ground trembled and dirt fell back into the trenches. We were covered with loose dirt and dust from the trenches and then seemed to be struck by a brief strong wind which ruffled our clothes and actually lifted the kepi on my head. This was soon followed by an ear shattering explosion. I looked up facing the south in the direction that it seemed that the blast had come from. As I watched, I saw some heavy material lifting into the air, followed by some light dust and quickly followed by a thicker, blacker cloud and watched as it mushroomed up into the air. It seemed like it must have gone nearly a mile in the air and then seemed to fall back to the earth.

As the dust and debris settled back below view of the bluffs on the hill, a terrific cannonade erupted in its vicinity. This seemed to last for 10 or 15 minutes and was quickly followed by intense volleys of musketry and I imagined that I could hear cheering and exaltations from that direction. My initial thought was that a Confederate ammunition magazine had accidentally blown up. I couldn't have imagined what else would have caused such a catastrophe.

We stood there watching towards the south and gradually the sounds of musketry faltered and died out and all became quiet after a couple of hours. It was several minutes yet before we resumed work on the trenches. Even where we were at the head of the ridge, rumors seemed to spread quickly that the Union forces further south had set off a mine under the Confederate lines. About that time, the firing intensified again and there was a short intense round of artillery firing. This seemed to slacken and then was followed by occasional volleys of musketry and dull explosions. It lasted for several hours, and then gradually faltered.

We were soon relieved and allowed back into the camp for a few days of rest. All of the talk in the camp was about the Union attempt at mining the Confederate fortifications. Apparently, General Hickenlooper had dug a long tunnel under the Confederate fort and hauled in a ton or more of black powder and detonated it. I wondered if this was the same Hickenlooper from Shiloh, but no one seemed to know. When they set off all that black powder, it had resulted in the tremendous explosion and mushroom cloud that we had noticed.

After the debris had settled, the Union had opened up a fierce artillery barrage and, when that had ceased, rushed a couple of regiments or more into the enormous crater that had been blown in the Confederate lines.

However, the Confederates had rushed troops up from the other side and the fighting had faded out.

All this occurred on June twenty fifth. The explosion had created a tremendous crater in the confederate line but achieved nothing else, unless it was to give us something to talk about for a few days. Just when the talk started to die out we detonated another mine. I think it was even bigger, but the results were no more successful. However it did provide an even better story. The story was going around that one black man who had been on top of the Confederate fort had been blown a hundred feet or more through the air and into the Union lines. They said when they had helped extricate him from the dust and debris that had showered down around him, they asked him how far he had been blown in the air, and he replied that he didn't know but he thought about three miles. That had caused peals of laughter throughout the camp but it seemed remarkable enough to me that he could have been blown at least a couple of hundred feet through the air and survived.

After a few days of rest in camp, we went back to resume our watch on the trenches. I was wondering what we were going to do when we got still closer to the confederate lines, when a turmoil spread down the row. Soldiers were throwing their hats in the air in jubilation and firing their muskets off into the blue. I thought they had gone nuts but the rumor spread that Vicksburg had capitulated. It must be true, I thought, or else someone had a very poor sense of humor. We quickened our pace back into camp and soon it was apparent that the rumors were true. Vicksburg belonged to the Union. And today was the Fourth of July.

CHAPTER FIVE

The Confederates had surrendered. Vicksburg was ours. The news spread through the camp like a grassfire on a high wind. The news seemed to spread from one man to the next. I stood there in stunned disbelief. "Who told you that?" I asked Otto Kerner. "I think it was Bob Cantrell who said it." But no one seemed to know where the rumor had originated. I assumed it must be true because shortly after that, volleys of musketry sounded. A thick cloud of black rancid smoke drifted through the camp as the soldiers celebrated by firing their muskets off into the air. We couldn't resist joining in the jubilation and let loose a volley ourselves. But it seemed just moments later that officers were passing through the camp, chiding us for our stupidity. They were keen to join in our celebrations but only wished to direct our energies in a little safer fashion. As one officer told me, "Anything you shoot off straight in the air, will go up about a mile, drift a little bit on the wind and then come back to earth. You could be killing soldiers in your own camp with your stupidity."

Well, of course, he was right. I opened my mouth with the thought of asking him if it was okay if we simply bit the bullets off and spat them on the ground then fired off the black powder but, from one look at his expression, I decided it would be best if I just kept my mouth shut. It wasn't long after that that the first of the bottles and jugs began to be passed around from hand-to-hand. Drinking in camp was officially forbidden but it seemed there were always plenty of jugs available on the slightest excuse for a celebration. It's amazing how bottles could be passed through a group with so little notice taken.

But we had an abundant excuse for a celebration on this occasion and any hint of discretion was entirely abandoned. Jugs were raised in the air to loud cheers of jubilation and the tin cups clanged and were tipped in abandon. From somewhere in the camp the joyous notes of a fiddle broke out and were soon joined by the sound of drums and bugles blending into the revelries. I couldn't even identify all of the musical instruments that seemed to join in with the celebrations. It seemed that the general consensus was that, if you couldn't play a musical instrument, you could at least sing or dance. It seemed the whole army was infected with the desire to make noise and join in the celebrations.

It wasn't long until we noticed a curious aroma on the wind. We lifted our heads and sniffed the air. There was always an odor of wood smoke around a camp but this smoky odor had a strange and tantalizing difference. Small groups began to break off from the celebrations and move towards the northwest and, sure enough, just beyond the limits of the camp, giant open pits had been prepared over which beef carcasses were slowly turning and roasting. The cook fires had been roped off and guards were present, I suppose to keep the troops from trying to enjoy the meal before it was actually prepared.

We stood around as close to the ropes as we could and watched as the cooks turned the meat on huge spits propped on posts driven deep in the ground on each side of the charcoal pits. It was then that, for the first time that someone mentioned that it looked like we were going to be having a fine Fourth of July celebration. It's easy to lose track of time with the monotonous day-to-day duties of a prolonged siege and somehow I hadn't even realized that it was indeed the Fourth of July. I didn't know if it was some type of an accident, or if may be the rebs had some strange cause for holding out till the Fourth of July to finally surrender. I had a strange thought as to what kind of celebrations they would be holding in the town of Vicksburg itself for this fine Fourth of July day. What could they possibly have to celebrate and was it possible that they had anything in the way of supplies to celebrate with.

I suppose I wasn't the only one to have this thought because Johnny Applebaum spoke up and said, "Maybe we should go up and invite the rebs to come down to our celebrations." I was glad I hadn't made that suggestion as I watched as Johnny was rather roughly shoved from one of the boys to the next. Someone even made a suggestion that we should roast

Johnny on a spit, to which a couple got his feet and a couple got his arms and they began hoisting him, trying to lift him over the rope barriers. It was all in good natured fun but some of the guards around the barricade probably didn't realize that as they were rather rough in shoving us back to our side of the line.

Then another rumor seemed to sweep through the crowds as we gathered, watching them barbeque the beef and, almost as one, the troops turned their backs on the pits and began moving in the opposite direction. I had no idea why we were moving off but it seemed like there was a general consensus that something was worth seeing to the east of the camp. We arrived on the eastern edge of our camp near the road that went through between the Union camps and on up and entered into Vicksburg itself. There, lining the center of the road, were several wagons pulled by teams of mules and horses. The wagons were surrounded by troops. And then the rumors seemed to pass back through the troops nearest the wagons that we should all get our tins or some other type of container. The wagons were loaded with kegs of beer. They were forming the troops up in line to get a cupful.

The squad turned its back as one man and moved back through the camp to our tents. We wrestled through our gear to get our tin cups and head back to the wagons before they were all out of beer. As we formed up again around the wagons, we were roughly gathered in a line. Johnny managed to make his way to the front of our squad and it was only as he neared the head of the line that we noticed that he was carrying a coffeepot. "Being a little bit optimistic, aren't you, Johnny?" the boys said. He simply laughed and said, "Well, I couldn't find my cup, and I was afraid you boys would get all the beer before I could get there." Then, he laughed as he stretched his coffeepot forward and the sergeant manning the keg, laughingly filled it completely full. Then he said, "Now, you can share that with the rest of the squad later."

We stretched our tins out as we passed through the line, one after the other, to get our ration of beer. I think the keg must have been practically empty because my tin was at least half foam. I opened my mouth to object but we were quickly ushered through the line and out the other side. We were not allowed to congregate here but were directed further away from camp. It seemed the officers wanted to make sure that everybody got at least a little portion of beer. I wasn't sure that they had enough kegs that they could distribute some to every man in the whole corps. I doubted they had that much beer in the whole Union army! I wondered if the generals had been planning on having a Fourth of July celebration in the first place and possibly this Confederate surrender was just convenient.

We wandered back through camp, got some hardtack to munch on along with our beer, downed a few more bottles and jugs of liquor and continued the celebrations. We formed up to make several passes back through line towards the wagons with the kegs of beer and it seemed that they never ran out. The wagons could be seen coming up the hills from the direction of the Yazoo River and I thought the supply of beer would be never ending. We wandered off to the west of camp where the beefs were being roasted and later that afternoon, approaching on early evening, we were in time to see them start shaving off generous portions of beef. We had been anticipating this moment throughout the day and had been carrying our tin plates and eating utensils. We passed through the lines and were given generous portions of beef and beans and fresh baked bread and butter.

Towards the evening, a few fireworks were shot off but nothing to compare to the usual nightly bombardment of Vicksburg. In that regard, the celebrations were rather lacking. We had a glorious feast that evening but, sometime after dark, the beer finally ran out, although the bottles and jugs of liquor never ceased to flow.

The bugles blew to order us to bed but they couldn't order us to sleep and couldn't quiet the celebrations. We talked while we sipped liquor until late at night and enjoyed the sense of calm and peace that seemed to settle over the whole camp. It was as if the whole war was over and we hadn't a care in the world. I didn't know if there was a hostile rebel within fifty miles and couldn't have cared less. Vicksburg was ours!

It seemed I hadn't even fallen totally asleep before we were rudely awakened during the middle of the night. We were first aroused by bugling and then rough shaking as our officers passed through the camp. We were ordered to pack up our gear and be ready to move on the moment. I had gotten in the habit of always making sure there were several pots of coffee boiled up before we went to bed. I saw to it that each man in the squad filled his canteens with coffee or fresh water. We loaded up our gear and were ready to move shortly, but it seemed like it was another hour or so before we received any orders to form up and march out.

There was a rumor that General Johnson, whom we had last heard of when we chased him out of Jackson, was on his way to attack us here in Vicksburg. We marched out in the dark. It was much too dark to tell just which road we were traveling on. We passed through the rest of the Union camps, judging as best as I could from the North Star in a roughly easterly direction and then, once beyond the camps, turned south and marched more southeast. We came to what seemed to be a fairly well defined road and, again, turned to where we were marching more or less straight east.

The sergeant passed as we were stumbling along the road in the gloom of the early morning. "Where are we headed Sarge?" I called. "Looks like it's a race to the Big Black. Johnston's reported to be on his way and we plan to stop him at the river" he replied in a joyful Irish twang. "Looks like it will be a fine morning for another glorious whooping" he said as he marched past encouraging the troops to move faster. After all of the celebrations of the night before, I thought that we would march only a short distance and then be allowed to take a brief respite, but the order never came to drop out to rest. Gen. Sherman must be taking this new threat very seriously I thought. As it was still too dark to see what was happening, I managed to relieve myself as we marched along in line. I was beginning to wish I hadn't drunk so much beer last night. I managed to sneak a few sips of diluted coffee from my canteen as we marched and I'm sure that most of the rest of the men in the squad did likewise.

We marched for several hours until a faint pink glow began to brighten the horizon in the east. Sometime after the sun itself was up above the trees and the low bluffs in the distance, we were allowed to fall out and rest for a few minutes. We took advantage of this brief rest by breaking out some hardtack and washing it down with water. It wasn't long until we were ordered back in line.

We were marching along rapidly. I had the nagging worry that all this hurrying and bustle portended dire events. How General Johnson and his Confederate forces could have gotten so close, I couldn't quite understand, but from the general sense of anxiety moving through the troops, I expected to come upon him any instant. I was listening carefully for any sound of action in the distance and even began to sniff the air cautiously as I attempted to pick up any scent of Confederate troops in the vicinity. I almost felt like laughing at my anxiety.

The day brightened and became miserable and unbearably hot. It was well along in the morning, probably nearing 10 o'clock as near as I could tell from the angle of the sun before we were allowed to break out again. We snacked briefly on hardtack and washed it down with the water. I was attempting to conserve as much of the water as I could but, because I was so excessively dry from the night before, I think I was below half a canteen already and the day was just getting started. I tried to conserve the water as much as I could throughout the day but, by mid afternoon, it was gone. Some of the troops began breaking out of line to fill their canteen from puddles or any other type of depression in the ground that held the slightest trace of moisture. I couldn't bring myself to do that. I wondered if they were ever going to allow us to rest.

The sun had moved well past the south and was starting to color the western sky before we were allowed to break line and go into camp. I believe we must have marched fifteen to twenty miles that day. I was able to pick up a faint smell of water in the distance and, as it began to darken, it seemed that the air took on a slight dampness. As we made camp, some of us were allowed to spread out and search for water.

Johnny and I gathered up the canteens from two of the squads and made off to the north, only a few men being allowed to go in search of water. We took a couple of empty haversacks to carry the canteens and departed. It seemed to me that the ground sloped more in that direction. I knew that we had come across the Big Black River on our way to Vicksburg from Jackson. I thought that it was still a few miles, at least, to the east. Judging from the lay of the land, I felt there was quite likely a small creek or stream of water that flowed from the north towards the Big Black within a few hundred yards of where we were camping and, indeed, we found a shallow creek containing maybe eight to ten inches of water.

Johnny and I filled our canteens and each drank down a canteen full before we filled the rest of the canteens. Then, before heading back to camp, I downed another half of a canteen and refilled mine. We made our way back to camp, each of us carrying ten or twelve canteens. The slope hadn't seemed so steep coming down, but carrying all those canteens of water sure made the climb back up difficult. We dropped as soon as we reached camp and slept a rather exhausted night through.

We were awakened well before sunup again, but no orders came and we merely sat around in the camp for several hours. The sun came up and still we received no orders so we breakfasted on hardtack and water. Soon, coffee was boiling and all was quiet. We drank several pots of coffee and then went back towards the stream to fill our canteens. Along the way, we noticed thick brambles and clumps of blackberry bushes, especially as we neared the lower slopes around the creek. We refilled the canteens and set them aside while we filled our kepis with the sweet fruit. Johnnie and I ate our fill, laughing at each other as the berries stained our hands and mouth black with juice. At last, our kepis filled with blackberries, we gathered the canteens and headed back to camp.

We spent most of the day in camp here and, towards afternoon, marched a couple of miles down to the Big Black River and crossed on the bridge that had been erected there. We marched only a couple of miles and then went into camp again. Things seemed much more relaxed and almost carefree this day. I began to think and wonder about the reasons for the forced march that we had endured yesterday and if there had ever been any dire threat from General Johnson.

But, we were up the next morning and marched out again rapidly. It seemed there was a sense of determination and almost anxiety again. We marched hard, being allowed but little time for a break. The canteens that we had filled as we crossed the river were soon empty and the troops began to suffer greatly from lack of water. Throughout the day, we passed numerous troops that had staggered to the side of the line of march and collapsed. They were being given as much medical attention as possible but what they really needed was water. Troops were drinking water out of any little depression in the ground that they could find. There simply wasn't enough to be had. It's amazing how you can be within a few miles of a river but still be dying from thirst. It also amazed me how unbearably hot and dry it could get within a few days' time.

We marched again until well after dark. I had managed to conserve my water as long as I could but my canteen was long since empty. I was thinking of finding one of the officers to be allowed to go out and search for water since we had not received any permission to do this. I was beginning to think that we couldn't go much longer without some respite, when the Heavens seemed to hear our prayers and opened up a merciful deluge of rain. I tipped my kepis upside down to catch as much rain as I could and then used the brim to try to pour this into my canteen. It rained hard for a couple of hours and I succeeded in filling my canteen to the brim and, even had quenched my thirst from the kepis itself. The sweatband was stained with dirt and with salt from weeks and weeks of sweat that had soaked into it, but it was water.

The following day, we were up early but it was probably midmorning before we marched off. As we marched towards the east, we heard the sound of skirmishing in the distance. Then, there was a brief round of cannon fire and what sounded like several volleys of musketry. Isolated shots rang out for the next half hour as we moved off towards the east. We hadn't seen any Confederate forces ourselves but certainly they must be in the immediate vicinity. I think we had marched eight to ten miles that day before going into camp.

After breakfast in the dark the next day we moved out and seemed to head more in a northeasterly direction and, as we marched, we noticed off to the south a small town. There was some skirmishing still going on in the immediate vicinity. As we passed to the north, we noted one vigorous volley and exchange of musketry to the south, but then we were beyond the town and began circling down from the north. We struck a broad, well defined road that we were told went directly through to Jackson. We marched for a couple of miles further along the road and then went into camp on both sides. In the distance, we could make out clusters of houses and other buildings. We must be on the outskirts of Jackson, I thought.

As we settled into camp, we could tell from the dust and vague movements of groups and small bodies of troops that the Confederates were still in the town. We made camp and threw up some fortifications along the southern and eastern edges and barricaded and reinforced the entrenchments as best as we could. Then, we settled down for the night, wondering what the morning would bring.

CHAPTER SIX

We had approached Jackson, Mississippi from the northwest, following the road from Clinton, Mississippi. We had come into the vicinity of Jackson and had camped for the night three to four miles out. The following day, we moved further to the south as other troops were brought up and went into position north of us. It looked like we would be in for another siege. It was still pitch black when we were roused up that morning to begin the assault of Jackson. We moved out to the south and spread out in line.

The 31st Regiment began moving forward in the blackness towards the lines that we had seen in the distance that seemed to be occupied by the Confederates. My squad of men was advancing slightly in front of the rest of the regiment. We moved forward through the darkness, bent nearly double at the waist, watching for any movement or any sign that the Confederates were in front. Musket fire broke off to the left of us which caused us to bend even closer to the ground as we moved forward. The firing became rather furious for a while and was so intense that we could make out the flashes and the light from the musket fire to our north. Artillery fire from the Southern positions soon followed which prompted our artillery to respond. I had no idea what they were actually firing at as I don't think any troops could clearly be seen. I suppose they were simply firing where the musket flashes were more intense.

One of the boys off to my right spoke up. His voice was a coarse whisper from the darkness. I could tell from the German accent that it was one of the men from St. Louis. "I don't like this at all," he said. "I can't see a thing." I whispered back, "Shut up, you fool, you'll get yourself shot."

We moved forward in the darkness for several hundred yards, it was hard to tell how far. We had been sent out as skirmishers and I knew the rest of the regiment were following behind but, how far back they were, was impossible to tell. I whispered out, "Hold up, boys. Let's wait until we can tell just where we are." We dropped to our knees, looking forward toward the Confederate positions and I was listening intently for any sound of movement to indicate that the enemies were in the vicinity. It seemed that we had waited for several minutes before I could hear movement to indicate that the troops were catching up and coming up from behind. Then, we began moving out, searching for the Confederates to our front.

Fighting broke out to the south this time. It quickly escalated until it was nearly continuous. We halted as if by mutual consent and watched the musket flashes in the distance. I had an unnerving impression that, since we had had firing both to the left and right, we must be closer to the Confederate fortifications than I had suspected. We had had orders to advance towards the Confederates to drive in the pickets and skirmishers and I felt that we had gone far enough. We dropped to our knees and watched carefully towards the east for any sign of Confederate activity. Behind us, I could hear the sounds of spades and pickaxes being put to good use. It was still much too dark to see and I nervously shifted position, going from one knee to the next. It seemed I could imagine the sounds of movement to my immediate front and I peered carefully and cautiously in that direction, but I was unable to make out anything definite.

I wondered if a lot of the firing we had noticed to the left and right of our position were simply troops firing at imaginary rebels and shadows. I wasn't about to fire at anything I couldn't positively identify and I whispered and told the men to make sure of any targets before firing. I knew that the first musket shot would prompt a volley from my men also which might result in any rebs returning fire. Then again, I was a little nervous that in the dark we might have wandered off to the left or right and might actually have other Union skirmishes behind us that would prompt us to be shooting each other.

I ordered the boys to lie down in the dust and be alert. It seemed that the passage of time was interminable. Minutes seemed like hours. Then, gradually I seemed to notice a slight light in the east. Slowly it became brighter until the trees and the outline of Jackson in the distance was revealed by a light outlining the tops of the structures. We had left camp during the night with a full canteen but the temperature seemed to be every bit as hot as during the day, or possibly it was just fear that parched my throat and mouth. I had felt the constant need to sip water throughout the night and knew that I would regret this tomorrow.

The sun had come up enough that I was beginning to feel extremely exposed, so I whispered softly to the men in the squad, "I think it's time to get out of here," I said and, with that, we turned and crawled back towards our troops. We moved back fifty yards or so and then came up to our knees and stood up, still crouching at the waist and staying low to the ground. We moved back another hundred yards or so and came into the rifle pits that our fellow soldiers had dug during the night. It was with intense relief that we dropped down in the pits and were greeted by our comrades in the company. "Damn," I said to the soldier whose pit I had slipped into. "I thought you boys could have dug these things deeper while we were out there." He just laughed. "I wish you had my blisters," he said.

I rolled over and looked back toward the Confederate lines from the direction we had come, and then looked back to try to determine where we had camped the evening before. We had managed to extend our lines probably seven or eight hundred yards during the night. As I looked to north and south, we had a new continuous line of rifle pits and shallow entrenchments made. I could only hope that these would suffice to protect us from Confederate fire in the morning. It still looked like we were three miles from the Confederate entrenchments and Jackson was even further beyond that in the distance. I was afraid that at any moment we would receive orders to rise up out of the rifle pits and charge toward the Confederate emplacements, but thankfully the orders never came.

Nevertheless, I was feeling extremely exposed where we were. Our entrenchments it seemed were barely enough to provide meager shelter from any Confederates sniping or artillery fire. I wondered what it was that was keeping General Johnson from attacking our positions as it looked to me that we were extremely exposed, but throughout the day things remained quiet in our immediate vicinity. Keeping my head low, I slithered from one pit to the next to check on my boys. Johnny had taken shelter in the trench nearest to me. The first thing he said was, "Have you got any water, Sir?" I told him, "I still have about a half a canteen." "Can I have a drink, Sir?" he said. "What happened to yours?" I asked. "Well, I drank it all during the night, Sir." "Sure," I said, "Have a swallow." I knew how he was feeling. I had been so dry and parched from nerves and the heat of the night that I drank about half of mine and thought I was doing badly.

I moved from man to man in my squad, crawling and ducking from one rifle pit to the next. It seemed we were all in the same situation. Most of the boys had saved some of their water but others had consumed every last drop of theirs. This looked like it could be a real serious problem. We had extended the lines seven or eight hundred yards during the night but it seemed that no one had thought to provide sufficient water. I asked any soldier that I could find as I moved up and down the line for extra water if they could spare it, but no one had a drop to spare. It seems that digging trenches was every bit as tiring and as dirty a job as the one we had spent in the middle of no-man's-land cowering from Confederate detection.

The troops were still digging and scratching at the ground and shoving the dirt to the east in front of us and between the Confederates. The trenches were becoming more adequate and I was certainly feeling safer from Confederate fire, but the lack of water was becoming nearly unbearable. I moved back and forth between the members of my squad, gathering up all their canteens and told them to stay put until I got back. And then, bending over at the waist and taking advantage of what cover I could find, I made my way back across the ground that we had advanced over during the night to our original positions. I had to move well back beyond our original line looking for water which couldn't be found. Finally I decided to head to the north, back to the Clinton Road, in hopes that supplies of water had been brought up. I managed to locate a wagon with several barrels of water and filled each of the canteens, and then I made my way back to the squad. As I distributed the canteens, I told each of the boys to be careful with it. "I don't know where they're getting the water but there doesn't seem to be much of it, so take it easy," I told Otto Kerner as he tipped his canteen up and seemed to drain half of it in one gulp.

We spent the day sheltering in the entrenchments as best as we could and baking in the hot July sun. The soldier whose rifle pit I was sharing at the moment inquired as to where I had gotten the water. I told him that on the Clinton Road, back in the main lines, there were some wagons with barrels of water. He gathered up the canteens from the rest of the men in his squad and went off in search of moisture. When he returned, he had a canteen for each of his men but relayed the bad news that he wasn't sure there would be anymore that day. "Yea," he said, "They're having to send them back several miles to that small stream we passed a night or two ago for the water. They're bringing it up as fast as they can." Then, he said that somebody from Company G had told him that some of these farmhouses had cisterns that had water in them and some of the troops had gone there in search of water.

I looked around in all directions to see if I could see a farmhouse or structure that might indicate there had been a building that might have a cistern. The only structure that I could spy was several hundred yards ahead and to the left of our position. I couldn't tell if it was a house or a barn from this distance as it was obscured behind a small stand of trees, but it was far enough ahead that I didn't feel the inclination to go and investigate. Besides, we had a full canteen for now.

The day passed slowly. Possibly it was passing even more slowly than the night had, but it eventually became dusk and then moved on into pitch darkness. We stayed in the entrenchments where we had spent the day while the squad that had dug the entrenchments the night before moved off in the darkness towards Jackson. We waited another hour or more after they left and then moved out cautiously behind them. We moved forward for several hours, slowly and carefully. Once again, as it had the night before, firing broke out up and down the line at intervals. It seemed like there would be one shot, followed by a quick volley, and then volley after volley would follow. I wondered, as I had on the night before, just what they were shooting at. We moved on carefully for another hour or so and then I felt that we had gone far enough and we broke out the shovels and pickaxes and began digging rifle pits and entrenchments. We dug steadily throughout the night and long before dawn we had used up all of our water, but yet we had to keep digging. We needed to have these entrenchments as deep as we could before it became light and I didn't want to have the soldier from the other squad chide me on how we hadn't managed to dig pits as deep as theirs.

Eventually it began to lighten in the east towards Jackson and soon after the other squad had made its' way back into the entrenchments with us. The first thing the corporal of the other squad asked was if we had any water left. I said, "Well, I don't but maybe some of the other boys do." I moved off down to the line but, on inquiry, the men in my squad were as dry as I was. It seemed digging made you even thirstier than worrying.

I looked around for the cluster of trees to see if I could identify the building that I had noticed yesterday. The sun was coming up but it was still dim. Looking at the sky, it seemed that we might be in for a cloudy day, possibly it would even rain. I could only hope so. I gathered up the canteens again and moved off towards the north and then back towards the west in the direction of the buildings I had noticed the day before. It turned out indeed to be a small farm. There was an abandoned farmhouse that was still standing and on the one corner was a cistern. Someone else had already discovered it and it appeared to be dry. I was just cursing my luck when two other soldiers showed up in search of water. "You're too late, boys," I said, "It looks like it's all gone." "I know," they said, "We have been here before, but hopefully we can find some still." They were each carrying a pickax and a spade and they had a short section of rope. "We figured there might be some water if we just dug it out deeper," they said, and I could only applaud their good thinking.

I knocked a hole in the wall of the farmhouse and secured one end of the rope to the frame. I then helped lower them into the cistern. I stood guard around the top of the cistern while they began excavating in the bottom for moisture. It didn't take long until they had a pit three feet square and three feet deep dug out that began to fill with moisture. It was muddy and dirty, but it was water. They filled their supply of canteens and passed them up to me and I lowered mine down to them. We soon had as many canteens as we could carry and I helped pull them up out of the cistern. We left the rope where it was, but they took the pickaxes and spades with them.

Ducking and weaving, I made my way back to the squad and passed out the twenty canteens that I managed to take with me. Each of the boys in my squad had a canteen as well as the squad that we were working with. I told them where the cistern was and that there was a rope there, unless someone had taken it, and that, if we needed more water, we could go back there with pickaxes and spades and see if we could get anymore. "With luck," I said, "The hole that we dug will fill up while we're here." "If it does," said Christian, "Someone else would get it before we get back." "Probably," was all that I could think to say. Then, I began scanning towards the east for any other structures that might indicate recent habitation and the possibility of water.

What water we managed to get in the canteen was soon gone. We had been thirsty during the night and it remained dry all throughout the day. The corporal of the other squad had gone back to the main entrenchments looking for water. He was gone most of the day but towards evening returned. It seemed that General Sherman was bringing up barrels of water as fast as the wagons could roll but that the lines along the road to get the water were so long that it took the better part of the day to get their canteens filled. They shared their water with us but, by the time it became dark enough for us to move forward to skirmish with the rebs, we had already finished all of it. It seemed that day-by-day we were getting by with less water. We hadn't even started the night yet and our canteens were dry.

"Tom, Tom Sinclair," I called out. "Here," he said. "Come here, Tom." Tom moved towards me in the near dark. When he got close enough to talk to in a whisper, I told him, "Tom, I want you to take charge of the squad tonight. You know what to do, skirmish forward for another six or seven hundred yards, keep an eye on the rebs and then hold up there while the boys in I Squad dig the rifle pits and entrenchments. Otto, come with me." Otto Kerner seemed to me to be one of the more steady and reliable men in the squad. "Otto," I said, "We're going to move forward and see if we can find a cistern at that farmhouse. You get a pick and shovel and a length of rope, and let's move out."

I dumped my haversack out on the ground and Tom filled his sack with my possessions, then I filled my sack with canteens. Otto filled his with the canteens from the men in the other squad and then took the haversack from the other corporal and filled it also. Otto was soon back with the pickax and shovel that one of the soldiers had only too gladly loaned him, but he had been unable to find a segment of rope. We had orders to move out in skirmish formation and I couldn't delay any longer, so I ordered the boys forward. I knew that Tom would see to it that they followed instructions. The boys were well enough disciplined that I could probably have counted on them, but it's always best to have someone who is known to be in control.

Otto and I moved forward, crouching low to the ground and trying to be quiet. We moved in the direction of the farmhouse, listening carefully for any sound of rebel skirmishes or even Union troops. I knew that this was dangerous. My own squad was behind me and there were other skirmishes to the left and right. We were in the middle of no-man's-land between the two armies. If any firing broke out, we could be shot from either side. That's why I had wanted Otto to come with me. I knew that he appreciated just how dangerous the situation we were in was.

Johnny Applebaum was a good soldier, steady and brave, but I could just imagine Johnny, if startled by a noise to either side, suddenly whispering loudly, "What was that?" or "Who's there?" We had to be careful, quiet and, above all, cautious. Moving through the darkness was rather terrifying. I knew I had a good sense of direction and I had taken careful notice of just where the farmhouse had been, but moving in the dark, trying to be, above all, quiet, it was hard to tell how far one actually had traveled. When the moon came up, I knew we would have enough light to be able to make our way to the farmstead, but I had hoped to get there while it was still dark. I was beginning to think that I must have passed north or south of the farm when suddenly I could make it out near at hand. It's a good thing that we had been so careful.

A cracking noise to my left made me realize that we were not alone. "Who's there?" I whispered loudly as Otto and I dropped to the ground. A voice to my left replied angrily, "Who do you think?" It certainly didn't sound like a Mississippi accent to me, so I whispered back, "Corporal Everett, 31st Missouri." "Corporal Lynch," he said, "13th Illinois." We moved cautiously through the dark until we came in contact with them. He was there with another man, like I, all of us in search of water. They had gotten there before us. "Have you found anything?" I said. "No," he said. We have been through the house looking for a pump and knocked over a chair, but we haven't found anything. "Well, the cistern that we found water in last night," I said, "was outside the house. It had a wooden door over it like a root cellar and some pipes going from the gutter on the roof leading to it."

We moved off in a small group, circling the house, and on the opposite side, sure enough, located a cistern. We pried the wooden cover off with the shovel and peered down into the darkness. It was still too early for the moon to be up and we really couldn't see anything. We fastened our belts together and secured the canteen to one end and lowered it down into the darkness. I dangled the canteen back and forth as far as I could reach, but never noticed any splash to indicate water. Then, Otto had the idea of securing our linked belts to the sling of his rifle and, holding the rifle by the barrel, lowered it as far down into the cistern as he could. I was thrilled with emotion as I heard the sound of the canteen splash on the top of the water. It must have taken us a couple of hours to fill the forty or fifty canteens that we had amongst the group.

Long before we had finished filling the canteens and loading up our haversacks, other stragglers of Union soldiers joined us. Corporal Lynch and the private with him were standing guard at each corner of the building while Otto and I filled the canteens. Periodically they would call out as more thirsty soldiers gathered around the farmstead. To their pleas for water, Corporal Lynch would explain in his rather coarse and vulgar manner, "You just have to get the hell at the end of the line."

We finished loading up the haversacks with the canteens and handed them to Corporal Lynch and his private, whereupon he insisted on going through each haversack to make sure they had the right number of canteens and that each was indeed filled before he would relinquish his position at the head of the line. Then, he and the private moved off around the northwest corner of the farmstead while Otto and I moved around towards the southeast corner and back towards the direction that our squads had last been in.

The moon was well up by now but, still we moved cautiously, staying low to the ground. I was trying to estimate from where I thought the position of the farmstead had been to where I thought that our troops would now be and it was with relief that I could make out the shapes of soldiers kneeling and shifting position on the ground immediately to my left. I could tell by the outline of their bodies that they were facing, leaning towards us. I thought that we had managed to move through the dark and get this close and hadn't been noticed. I almost felt irate that we hadn't been challenged before now.

I called out in a loud whisper, "Corporal Everett, 31st Missouri," and was relieved to hear Tom Sinclair call back, "I know who in the hell it is. If I hadn't recognized you, I'd have shot you." I had known I could count on Tom. I distributed the other canteens to the boys and sent Otto back with his load to the squad that was digging entrenchments. Otto and I had each drank as much water as we could tank up on while we had been at the cistern and it's a good thing that we weren't thirsty because, in no time the boys had downed at least half of their water, only pausing when I reminded them not to drink more than half of it because it would be a long night and day tomorrow and I doubted, by the number of men who were forming line around the cistern, whether there would be any water there if we went back.

We spent another hot and dry night and, as the sun started coming up in the east, we made our way back to the rifle pits and entrenchments. We were moving up slowly, but by now we had cut the distance to Jackson nearly in half.

CHAPTER SEVEN

We were relieved the next morning and allowed to wander back to the rear while other troops were rotated forward to take our positions and continue the work of digging our lines towards the Confederate fortifications. We moved cautiously across the open ground that we had covered during the two preceding days. When well to the rear, we found the wagons with the water barrels. For whatever reason, they hadn't brought them up any closer.

As we formed into line to get water, I thought about asking a captain who seemed to be supervising things, why the water wasn't brought any closer to the front so we didn't have to walk so far to get it. We had been without water for several hours now and were thoroughly parched. But, then I decided that the captain probably wouldn't wish to be questioned by a mere corporal, especially one who was barely 14. Besides, I liked to try to deduce their reasoning on my own. Then, the thought struck me. Several wagons loaded with barrels of water and a large number of troops clustered around waiting in line to get it, might create too tempting a target for the Confederate artillery, if it was much closer. And, satisfied that I had come to the proper conclusion, I smiled inwardly to myself.

Minutes seemed to be hours as we stood around, thoroughly parched, and waited our turn in line. When it seemed to be my turn, I unthinkingly asked the Sarge if he might pour a small amount in my canteen so I could rinse the mud out. And then, wisely, decided to ignore his suggestion as to where I might go. As I took my canteen back, I decided not to mention the fact that he had only filled it about three-fourths full. We went through the line and then stood around in a group as we sipped on the water. I took a single mouthful and rinsed my mouth and enjoyed letting it trickle slowly down my throat before taking another small sip.

I finished about half my canteen, and was thinking about going back and getting in line when the captain seemed to read my mind and suggested we should move on. We wandered further down the road and at about fifty yards came to a cook tent that had been set up and joined the line there. We were all anticipating having our first hot meal in the last two days. We went through the line and the cook loaded our plates with the usual beef and beans, a white starchy grain and cornbread. I wasn't sure what this new food was but, if they were going to put it on my plate, I was going to eat it.

We wandered a short distance from the cook tent and took our seats cross-legged on the ground in a group. I didn't hesitate to start woofing down everything on my plate, but Otto Kerner spoke up as he flipped the white grains with his fork and said, "Was ist das?" Otto was one of our German boys from St. Louis and, whenever he was excited, inevitably reverted back to his native German. Often he did it on occasions such as this, merely to be funny. "Das ist rice, you dumb German," Johnny Applebaum said. "Haven't you ever had rice before?" I had never had rice before either but wasn't inclined to mention this fact. I suppose it was something that was grown in the south and that the foragers that we sent out must have found a considerable supply of it somewhere.

We had been living off the land; so to speak, for the last several weeks. We had relied almost exclusively on the foodstuffs that the Confederates had stored when we first arrived in Mississippi. The supply lines had been fairly well established by this point, but still foragers were being sent out to return with any type of supplies they could find to subsidize our food supplies.

I ate the rice and, although I found it to be rather bland and tasteless, it was truly filling. Then, I rinsed it down with half of what was left of the water. We sat around joking and relaxing and basking in the Mississippi sunshine. I felt full, warm and contented. Now that we weren't being forced to dig trenches, the sun didn't seem near as bad. We relaxed for another half hour before deciding that we should be making our way back to the line.

As we passed the water wagons, I thought about joining the line again to see if I could get another full canteen before going back to the front but, as I glanced at the captain, I could tell that he had his eye on me. I wasn't sure how he knew that we had already been through the water line once that day, but it seemed like he did. Hesitating for only a moment, we continued our way back towards the front and moved back into the first trenches that we dug and took our place there. I decided we would probably be given a couple of days' rest in the furthest trenches before being moved up towards the front again.

Most of the boys in the squad lay down along the edges of the trench and were soon asleep. I found it hard to sleep in the middle of the day, especially with troops passing up and down the trenches, stepping on your feet and jostling you, so I crawled to the top of the trench and peeked over the embankment. For whatever reason, General Sherman had elected to start the usual zigzag diagonal approach towards the Confederate fortifications.

I supposed that now that we were this close to the Confederate line that he felt this was the safest way to continue. Off towards the extreme south and east of where I thought our lines would be, a furious battle broke out. The sound of cannon fire was intense as the thunder of the guns rolled across the fields towards us. Volleys of musketry fire arose and a veritable cloud of black powder smoke darkened the horizon in that direction. This continued fierce and unabated for thirty minutes and then gradually tapered off and, within an hours' time, everything was totally quiet in that direction. I wondered what had transpired. If General Sherman had ordered an attack, I would have thought that it would have been all along our entire lines. But, during the height of the action, I watched as our troops in front continued digging.

By late afternoon, it was apparent that the troops were digging a parallel trench to the Confederate fortifications. I suspected that they decided to go no farther that day. By the time it was getting to be dark, I estimated they had dug the parallel trench a hundred and fifty yards or more from the end of the diagonal. It looked like we were going to be satisfied with merely advancing our lines a quarter of a mile or so that day. I finished off the rest of the water in my canteen and lay down at the foot of the trench and went to sleep.

The following morning, we went back to the water wagons, refilled our canteens and had a hot breakfast. Then, we went to the supply train and received rations for the next couple of days. Finally we wandered back to our places in the trenches. I looked out over the fields and saw that during the night the troops had extended the parallel trenches for probably half a mile in each direction and were now commencing to dig diagonal again towards the Confederate lines. We were ordered to collect our gear; it was our turn to be back in line.

We spent the next couple of days digging diagonal and parallel lines until late one afternoon when we realized that there didn't seem to be any activity in the Confederate entrenchments. We ceased digging and, as I peered carefully over the top of the embankments, I noticed several groups of skirmishers approaching the Confederate works all up and down our line. They would move forward cautiously and frequently drop and take cover in the open. Meeting no resistance, they disappeared up over the top of the Confederate works and into their lines. I watched with bated breath, anticipating Confederate resistance in a sudden volley of musket fire and artillery, but all was quiet. I watched as, all up and down the Confederate lines, signals were given that all was clear and the order came for us to advance up and into the Confederate works.

We marched out in line, anticipating any moment that we would be met with gunfire and were most relieved to find the fortifications truly empty. A joyous celebration broke out all up and down the lines as troops cheered and threw their hats in the air. We possessed the Confederate lines but it was obvious there were still Confederates moving through the town of Jackson itself.

We weren't given much time to continue with the celebrations before the officers had us busy reforming the Confederate works. We began digging embankments facing the town of Jackson to protect our troops in case of a sudden sortie by the Confederates. How many troops General Johnson had in town was impossible to determine. You could see troops moving along the streets from building to building but their numbers were impossible to count. By dusk, we felt we had achieved a considerable strengthening of the walls toward the Confederate town and laid down to rest.

Since I finished off my canteen of water during the day, I was quite thankful when, after dark, water was brought up to the troops in the front. Just before we laid down to sleep that night, word went through that the 31st Missouri would be moving out in the morning to try to circle around the town of Jackson. By the light of the campfires, I carefully loaded the Remington's and placed one in my belt and one in the pocket in my blouse. My rifle was loaded and ready.

As I lay down to sleep, I didn't seem the least apprehensive and was soon peacefully slumbering, but it seemed no sooner was I asleep, than we were being roused up to move out. We moved through the Confederate fortifications and proceeded towards the east. We came to the Pearl River, which was east of the town of Jackson, and waded through it just at dawn as the first rays of the sun topped the trees in the east.

We were moving along the road in column towards a town called Brandon that was somewhere ten or fifteen miles east of Jackson. We marched about, maybe, an hour and had covered four or five miles, I suppose, when firing broke out at the head of the column. Troops were moved into line north and south of the road and we advanced forward cautiously. My squad took its place at the front of the line and moved out in skirmish formation. This had gotten to be our customary position in our company since Sergeant Shawnasee had decided that my squad was probably the best marksmen under his command.

I had worked diligently with the boys and felt that they were as good as could be found in the whole regiment. When we had been in the siege lines outside of Vicksburg, we had worked on our marksmanship. Often we had been allowed relief from digging trenches and had been allowed to snipe at the Confederate sharpshooters in their trenches outside of Vicksburg, and I had instructed the boys as we had practiced our marksmanship. I would pick out specific targets, call out the range and the windage and advised the boys on where to hold their aim and watched to see the results of their fire.

I felt confident that at least half the squad was capable of firing with deadly effect at long range. Most were capable of making even a snap shot at a Confederate at a hundred yards or less. All of them were deadly at two hundred yards if given enough time to take careful aim and fire. Tom Sinclair and Otto Kerner, I felt would be deadly accurate even with a hurried shot up to three hundred yards. And, as the sergeant had often watched our careful practice, I knew that he felt that we were as sufficient as any in his whole company.

So, we moved forward a couple of hundred yards from the rest of the line as we advanced cautiously towards the east. We moved from tree to tree until we spied in the distance Confederate cavalry skirmishing with the head of our column which had deployed in line. We were well south of this skirmishing and continued moving forward, hoping to flank the Confederates along their position on the road. We got into a fairly brisk skirmish with Confederate infantry who were moving forward directly opposite of us. They had skirmishes out also.

I had spied them first and had the squad kneel carefully, taking as much cover as they could behind the trees and I carefully picked out the Confederate that I felt was in command as they moved towards us. I don't think they had any idea that we were there as they carefully felt their way forward. The squad held their fire as they knew from previous experience that I would be the first one to shoot. As the man that I had selected stepped around a tree and moved forward, I fired. This prompted a quick volley from the rest of the men in the squad. I glanced quickly down the line to note the effect of our volley. I felt thoroughly confident that four or five had fallen but, due to the muzzle blast and the dense black sulfurous smoke from the powder that still lingered in front of our positions, it was hard to tell, and besides the usual reaction of a soldier at the sound of a gunshot is to drop to the ground for cover.

As I quickly reloaded, I scanned left and right down the line. About two hundred yards to my left, I noticed other Confederate skirmishes moving through the woods. I had finished reloading as the one closest to my position dropped down to one knee behind a tree. He was kneeling on his right knee with his left foot up, leaning forward around the right side of the tree and starting to take aim. Although I couldn't see from where I was, I knew that Union skirmishers must be moving through the woods to my left and were just now coming into range of this ambush. I didn't wish to lean to the right around the tree to take aim since I felt this would expose me too much to any Confederates directly in front who might be looking for anyone foolish enough to do that.

I switched my rifle to my left shoulder and leaned around to the left of the tree, taking aim with my left eye. I sighted quickly and, as the most exposed portion of the Confederate soldier's body were his buttocks, that's where I shot him. The flash of the musket cap and the blast from the muzzle obscured my vision but I felt certain that I had seen him fall. I had been in two major battles and several skirmishes. I had seen both Union and Confederate dead and wounded, but thankfully I had never seen anyone that I could say that I had definitely shot. The thought gave me some comfort. It made it seem like it was all almost a game.

I scanned carefully across in front of our own position. I scanned quickly up and down the line where the Confederate skirmishes had been. The best way to locate your enemy was watching for any movement and I knew that my peripheral vision was best for picking out movement. If you focused on one spot, for some reason it was actually harder to notice motion. I couldn't pick out anything and began looking directly, trying to pick out any shapes of soldiers lying motionless on the ground, whether dead or wounded, or attempting to hide. I knew there were soldiers there but couldn't locate their positions. Then, glancing quickly up and down the line, I picked up some movement, both to my right and left. It became obvious that the movement was further back in the woods than where the troops had been that we had fired upon and soon it became evident that Confederate infantry, in force, were moving up. This wasn't looking so good for us.

I glanced back behind and failed to note any of our Union troops coming up in line. I thought we were two hundred yards or so in advance of our lines when we had spied the Confederate skirmishers. I was thinking our boys must be unnecessarily cautious as they moved forward since there was still no sign of them. I picked out another party to fire at, even though I didn't feel like I had a good shot, and blasted away. This prompted the rest of the men in the squad to fire. I felt this would slow the Confederates up for a few minutes and motioned to the boys that we should move back.

We faded away carefully through the trees back towards our own troops. Luckily we had moved towards the rear no more than fifteen or twenty yards before I could make out the boys in blue coming forward. I spied Sergeant Shawnasee down the lines and waved rather energetically to get his attention and indicated to him that the Confederate infantry was there in force. The company came to an abrupt halt.

While I moved forward to converse with the sergeant, he indicated to an officer further down the line who signaled and it seemed that the whole regiment paused. When I got up to the sergeant, I reported that we had had a run-in with the Confederate skirmishers in our front and that there was a line of infantry moving towards us. I knew that other skirmishes up and down the line were reporting the same information.

We had been sent on this march with three regiments. Under the best of conditions, that would have meant roughly three thousand men but, with the action that we had been through during the last month, we probably were not numbering more than two thousand. Just how many troops we were actually presently facing was impossible to say.

I had the impression that there must have been at least a regiment of Confederates advancing towards us and our original encounter had been with cavalry. General Johnson still had troops in Jackson and, although they seemed to be evacuating, I had an uncanny feeling that there might be considerably more Confederates either north or south of where we were.

I think the officers in charge made an excellent decision as we failed to advance any further east and, after having maintained the line for upwards of a half hour or more and not having encountered any Confederates advancing towards us, they elected to move back. We faded away towards the west, still in line, and after having moved at least a mile, formed back up into column and marched westward into our fortifications around Jackson. It had been an interesting day.

That night, I slept fitfully. For some reason, I was haunted by visions of Confederate dead and wounded. I imagined myself moving forward from our skirmish line and into the positions of the Confederates when we first fired on them. I pictured the man that I had first fired on, lying on his back with his fist clenched, and his back arched as his glassy eyes stared towards the sky. I think that his mouth opened with a slight trickle of blood at the corners of the lips and then was shaken by the moans and screams of the wounded Confederate just behind me. I turned and found a young Confederate, not much older than myself, lying on the ground, being shot through both hips. He was unable to stand, walk or crawl due to his injuries. As I looked at his wounds, I knew that my bullet had shattered both hips and burst his bladder and bowel. I knew that he must die but why couldn't he die quietly.

I woke up in a cold sweat and was unable to get back to sleep for the rest of the night. I had never been troubled before by such thoughts and couldn't imagine why I was having them now. Gradually, the sun came up. I moved to the top of our earthworks and glanced towards Jackson. Up and down the lines, groups of skirmishers had begun moving forward into the town itself. I could see as they motioned and waved back towards our line and was cognizant of the fact that larger groups of infantry moved forward, gradually and carefully, into the outskirts of Jackson. I listened for firing and watched for any type of activity, but all seemed quiet. Up and down the line, troops began moving out from our position, carefully, and then more confidently. It seemed that the Confederates were gone. Jackson was in our hands.

CHAPTER EIGHT

We moved into Jackson cautiously at first. I couldn't believe that General Johnson had surrendered the town without more of a fight than what he had offered. We went from house to house, searching carefully and apprehensively for Confederate troops. It soon became apparent that there weren't any. Reports came back from cavalry that were scouting to the north and east. It seemed that everything was quiet.

We spent the next hour moving through town. We had destroyed a good portion of the town, mainly along the railroads and the downtown central area when we had been here two months ago. The word came down that we were now to destroy what was left of the town. I watched as troops went from house to house, taking delicious delight in setting them afire. Their homes were ransacked for whatever was felt to be of any value. Orders came down from above forbidding this, but no one paid much attention as troops stuffed their knapsacks with their little treasures. Fine furniture were piled in the street and set on fire. The troops seemed to take special delight in destroying anything that they thought may have been especially prized by the southerners. No one could object to the troops stuffing their knapsacks with food supplies or even items of clothing.

Soon, flames were leaping from the roofs of homes throughout the town. I watched, not feeling an urge to join in this wanton destruction. Tearing up railroad ties, heating and bending rails and burning cotton in warehouses was one thing but this was another. I heard soldiers say that if the army in Virginia would do as much as we did that the rebels would soon lose heart and this war would be over. I wondered as much to myself, practically thinking that this may well have the opposite effect. I thought it was just possible that it would encourage them to fight that much harder. I wondered that, if the Confederates knew what was happening, if it wouldn't make them fight with that much more zeal to protect their families and homes.

As I wandered through the town, keeping my squad with me and watching the work of destruction, we bumped into Sergeant Shawnasee. He, like I, was merely watching the work of destruction that the soldiers engaged in. We had time for a brief conversation that I had sorely been missing over the last several weeks. "It looks like the boys are doing a fine job, Sarge," I said. To which he merely replied, "That it does, son that it does." "Sarge," I said, "Why do you think we're doing this?" To which he replied, "That's war, boy. It's a cruel business." Then he said, "You know, after we pulled out back in May, the rebels have done a fine job of coming back, repairing their railroad tracks and building the town back up. When we move out this time, we want to make sure there's nothing left worth coming back to. It's the only way," he said.

The approach of darkness brought an end to the destruction. We were ordered back out of town, into the fields between the old Confederate fortifications and the town, where we had now established our camp. I don't know whether it was because the officers felt they couldn't keep a close enough eye on us to prevent looting after it was dark, or whether they feared an attack by the Confederates while we were disorganized, but the town was abandoned to burn and smolder. When we returned to our camps, we were treated to a hot meal and plenty of water.

The boys and I were up early the next day. It seemed that the officers were in a hurry to get us back to the work of destruction. But, instead, we received orders to gather three days' rations and be ready to march out. General Steele led the division, this time, in person. We marched through Jackson to the Pearl River where I made sure to take the time to fill my canteen. Then, we headed back out on the Brandon Road where we had been a couple of days previously. Glancing around at the numbers of soldiers it was apparent that we had the whole division and not just three regiments. I felt that we would be ready for anything that the Confederates threw up against us.

We marched rather proudly in column. We had cavalry out front and skirmishers on each side and, of course, the head of the column would have skirmishers out beyond them also. We had some delay getting over the bridge at the Pearl River and it was later than what was intended before we got well on the march. It was another of those hot, unbearably dry, Mississippi summer days. The sun seemed to soak all of the moisture out of your body.

We soon came to the spot where we had skirmished with the rebels a day or two before. Still, we had seen no sign of them. A halt was called and we were allowed to drop out along the road and rest for a few minutes. I sipped carefully from my canteen, wetting my mouth and swishing it before slowly swallowing. I drank about a fourth of the canteen, hoping to ensure that I had plenty of water to last throughout the day. There was no telling what we would be finding ahead.

We reformed in column and marched out to the east. Then, restlessness seemed to pass through the column. Whispered messages were passed through the ranks. The rumor was that the Confederates had elected to contest our advance. We had marched another four or five miles from where we had called the halt at the scene of our previous skirmish. The column was formed into line on both sides of the road. We marched to the right along the southern side of the road and formed up in line on the edge of a large cornfield. We moved through the stalks of the corn that were over our head.

We had had no sight of the enemy ourselves, but the fear was that they were not far from us. The ears of corn were full and robust. Some of the troops broke off ears and tried to stuff them in their knapsacks as we moved forward. The corn leaves caught on our clothes as we passed through it. I kept my rifle up, using the stock to brush aside the corn as it scratched my face and skin. Then, suddenly, we were through the corn to the other side.

On this side of the field, the corn had been harvested and intentionally knocked down by the rebels. Just beyond the edge of the cornfield was open pasture and on the other side the Confederates had formed line. It appeared as if they had dug some shallow entrenchments, piling the dirt up to face us and lining the top of the mounds with split rail fencepost. The work was hastily and poorly constructed. In places, their defense was nothing more than the old split rail fence itself. Unfortunately, looking left and right down the line, I could see where they had at least three batteries of cannon in position. I was heartedly thankful that we had come out of the corn about halfway between two different batteries and had none directly opposite ours. We were far enough south of the road that it was only possible to make it out faintly in the distance.

Sending out skirmishers was unnecessary. The rebels were there immediately in our front at eight hundred yards and seemed determined to make a stand. Orders were given for us to advance forward. My squad was on the front of the line. I had a disturbing memory of Shiloh. This is how the rebels had come at us. They had marched out of the woods across the open field and straight into our guns. At Shiloh, I watched as the rebels had marched in step, rifles up and head high, out of the woods and into the field, and began moving across it. There, we had waited impatiently for them to get within two hundred yards before firing our deadly volleys.

There, I had admired their courage and discipline. I had wondered how any man could have the nerve to march directly into the muzzles of loaded guns. And, now, here I was doing it. Seven hundred yards. Six hundred yards. Five hundred yards. Four hundred yards. And, then our artillery opened up behind us. They were firing over our heads and over the cornfield behind us. I wasn't sure how they could see their targets, but their fire was having affect.

Explosions erupted in the Confederate lines, some short of their lines, some past their weak defenses, but a lot of our fire was spot on. As I watched, portions of split rail fence flew in the air. Then, the Confederate artillery opened up. Thank God there was none directly in front. Orders were given to fix bayonet. We marched forward and then were ordered to stop and proceeded to fire a volley. Our lines were engulfed in black smoke and flames, and out of the smoke we charged.

It's not easy to run in those clumsy boots the army provides, and the ground was rough and partially broken. But, on we went, screaming at the top of our lungs. As we neared the Confederate lines, our order was becoming more and more chaotic. When we were about a hundred yards out, the Confederates rose and delivered a volley into our lines. A number of soldiers on each side of me stumbled and went to the ground. I couldn't turn to see who they were. What I had thought was an opened field, was actually a field that had been previously planted and harvested and plowed.

There were clods of dirt and old stalks of corn that were in an advanced state of decomposition, but which served admirably to catch at your boots as we stumbled along.

More and more soldiers went down, but at last I had come to the split rail fence. Directly opposite of me on the other side of the fence was a Confederate soldier, hurriedly trying to reload his rifle. He was standing a few steps back from the fence itself and just starting to remove the ramrod. He was almost beyond reach, but I held the stock of my rifle in my left hand and the butt grasped in my right and thrust it at him. I let go of the stalk with my left hand and, holding the butt of the rifle, I thrust it at him at arms' length, almost like throwing a spear. I think he was surprised and terrified at the same time. He threw his left arm up in front of his chest and the bayonet pierced it from side-to-side. He dropped his rifle and turned to run. He straddled my rifle and went stumbling off with it trailing between his legs. He carried it off with him for five to six yards, before it pulled loose and fell to the ground.

My first thought was that I needed to get my rifle back and I kicked the fence rails down and stumbled across them in search of it when suddenly I remembered the Remington in my belt. I jerked the revolver up and fired left and right. Our Union troops had succeeded in dislodging the rail fence and were coming through unimpeded. Men to my left and right were thrusting with bayonets or clubbing with rifle butts at the Confederates who stood their ground. I switched the Remington from the right hand to the left hand and continued firing and pulled the other Remington from the inside of my blouse with my right hand. It seemed that the rebel forces had lost all interest in this fight and were fleeing rapidly towards the east. I emptied both revolvers quickly as I moved forward to get my rifle. Then, all up and down the line cheering broke out. The rebel force was in full retreat.

We formed up there on the other side of the rail fence where the Confederates had been and caught our breaths. Everywhere up and down the line men were shouting, "They're getting away! They're getting away!" And, others said "Let them go." I seemed to be shaking from head to toe. It had been an unnerving march through the cornfield and a terrifying charge across an open field. I was winded and struggling to catch my breath. My mouth was so dry, I could hardly swallow and, I was so relieved to still be alive that I couldn't quit shaking. I fumbled at my canteen and took a slow swallow. I watched as the rebels disappeared in the distance. I thought I had made good time across the field, but they were making even better time in the distance.

While I stood there treasuring the moisture as I swallowed it from my canteen, I recognized Johnny Applebaum's voice as he called out, "Corporate Everett! Corporal Everett! Where are you?" I turned, searching for the origin of the voice. I had a horrible fear that Johnny was in need of my assistance. But then I spied him still on the western side of the split rail fence. He saw me about the same time I saw him and motioned frantically. I rushed to his assistance. As I stumbled across the split rail fence, I was looking at Johnny trying to discern where he must be injured but as I neared, he said "It's Michael. Michael Francis."

I went rushing back across the clodded field, following Johnny's lead. A hundred yards from the rail fence was a line of Union soldiers on the ground. Johnny led me to one that was lying facedown and motionless. There was a pool of blood around his head, soaking into the dry dust of this Mississippi field.

I rolled him gently on his back and noticed that his face was covered in blood and mud. There was blood in his eyes and it still trickled down from his forehead, but I thought it was a good thing that his eyes were closed and not staring up at me with that empty, vacant, glassy stare. I poured what was left of the water in my canteen over his face and washed the blood and mud off. He didn't seem to be responding. I took Johnny's canteen and some cloth that he gave me from his knapsack and washed the blood out of Michael's hair. I found the wound just at his hairline on the right side of his forehead. I poured what was left of Johny's water in the wound and brushed at it with the cloth. This made it bleed even more but then, thankfully, when I felt in the wound itself, I couldn't feel any broken, sharp edges of bone. I took the cloth and held it tight against his head to staunch the bleeding. Then, I carefully looked for any other wounds and was relieved to find that there wasn't anything obvious. Michael was still breathing, although it seemed faint.

I had Johnny sit by his side and placed Michael's head in his lap and had him hold pressure. I unbuttoned his blouse and felt for a heartbeat in his chest and it seemed strong and steady. I felt relieved, thinking that he had merely been knocked senseless by the shot which seemed to have just creased along the top of his forehead and through his hairline, raising a furrow from front to back.

Then, I went in search of the rest of the boys in the squad. I moved to the left and then back to the right down the line of soldiers that lay in the dirt. The next soldier I came to had a wound in his leg. It was about mid thigh, but thankfully on the outside of the leg. I knew that the major blood vessels ran down the inside of the leg. The wound went from front to back and, on the back of the leg, was a hole in his pants as big as an egg. I took some clothes from his pack and pressed against his wounds, front and back, and cinched it up tight with his belt. Then, I placed his knapsack under his back and shoulders to raise his head up as I thought this might help him breathe. I didn't know what else to do.

I found another soldier with a gunshot wound high in his right chest. He was struggling to breathe. I sat him up against his knapsack and removed his blouse. The shot had gone straight through. I wrapped his blouse over the wounds and used the sleeves to cinch it in place. I didn't know what else to do. Up and down the line, other soldiers moved, attempting to render assistance. Soon, there were soldiers with stretchers moving back and forth picking up the wounded. I went back to check on Michael who had come around and was sitting up, leaning against Johny. He still seemed to be stunned but was talking, although not making much sense.

One by one, the other boys in the squad showed up. I was quite relieved to see that they were all capable of walking on their own. Otto, of course, was in high spirits, talking excitedly in German. I had no idea what he was saying. Sometimes I would actually understand what he meant. There was a considerable similarity between English and German, at least in some cases. This time, Otto was so excited and talking so fast that I couldn't make anything out.

I asked Johnny what he was saying and Johnny just simply laughed and said, "Well, that stupid German seems surprised that some rebel actually tried to kill him." I watched and listened as Otto mimed to Christian and Hans how the Confederate soldier had thrust at him with his bayonet and how Otto had been lucky to deflect the blade. However, he was pointing out a slice through his sleeve on the right biceps where the blade had cut as it had been lifted up by his rifle and thrust to the side.

I went to look and, sure enough, he had a cut from front to back on the outside of his right arm that, although not deep, had bled profusely it seemed, at least for a while, but which had now ceased bleeding. All-in-all, I was greatly relieved and actually broke out laughing as I slapped him on his left shoulder and said, "You're going to be alright. Now, start speaking English again, damn it!" The whole squad broke up into laughter as they shoved Otto back and forth between them, and Otto laughed and said, "Ya, I think I speak English now."

I was even more relieved when I turned and saw that Johnny and Tom Sinclair were helping Michael to his feet. He stumbled forward a few paces between their arms until he was able to regain his balance and support himself. It looked like we made it. I spied Sergeant Shawnasee moving up and down the line and waved and whistled him over. I told him about the one seriously wounded soldier with the chest injury and asked if we couldn't see that he got carried to the road for assistance as soon as possible. The sergeant walked with me to where he was still lying, struggling to breathe, resting against his knapsack. Sarge said, "Yes, son, it looks like he needs help quickly." So, I ordered Johnny, Michael and Otto to assist in carrying him to the rear.

Johny and Otto grasped their wrists as they passed their arms underneath the wounded soldier and lifted him in the air. Michael seemed steady enough to support his head as they carried him carefully away toward the road, in search of an ambulance to take him back to Jackson. Then, we formed up the rest of the squad and rejoined the column as it marched off to Brandon.

By dark, we were moving into the town. Our cavalry and skirmishers had reported that the town was empty. As it was dark, we simply moved into the town and then went into camp. Just before we entered town, the heavens opened and poured down a torrential downpour. Most of the troops had used up their water and took delight in the heavy rain. We were thoroughly soaked, but delightfully refreshed.

General Steele ordered a very strong sentry to be posted and sent pickets out in all directions a mile or more from town. Then, we broke into our rations and, after having eaten and refilled our canteens from the wells and cisterns in the town; we set up our tents in the street and bedded down for the night. General Steele had forbidden us to seek shelter in the homes in the town itself, I think wishing to keep us together as much as possible.

I lay in my two-man tent and tried to rest, but it was impossible. There was a tremendous bustle in the town. Sometime after dark, a large number of prisoners were marched in and quartered in a warehouse along the railroad. A strong guard was placed around them. Cavalry made its way up and down the streets, the beat of the horses hoofs jolted the ground and aroused us any time we felt that we might be close to falling asleep.

As soon as the sun was up the next day, we began our work of destruction. We concentrated on the railroad at first. The whole regiment would line up on each side of the tracks, grab the rails between them and pull them up with the ties. Sections of rails a hundred feet long would be lifted in this fashion. We would throw it to each side of the rail bed and then grab the ties and pile them up in the center. When the railroad ties were burning fiercely, the rails were knocked apart and placed on top of the fire. After the rails were sufficiently heated, we would bend them around nearby trees or telephone poles.

We worked unceasingly through the day on our job of destruction. About noon, we were given a break to eat. We went off to the edge of town where we found that large beds of burnt coals had been prepared. Green corn still in the husks had been thrown on the coals and, as the husks gradually dried, shriveled and burnt off the corn was cooked on the cob. I found it to be quite delicious, being steamed in the green husks of the ears.

While we sat on the edge of town snacking, the prisoners who had been picked up the day previous marched by towards the road back to Jackson. Johny, Otto and Michael turned up while we were relaxing around the beds of coal. They had made it back to Brandon during the night but hadn't been able to find us in the dark, that day they had joined in, burning and destroying the town. Obviously they hadn't been able to locate us because we had been concentrating on destroying the railroad itself. Then, Johnnie said, "But we knew where we would find you at lunchtime." To which I replied, "Yea, and the only reason we came here was because I knew that's where you would be."

After lunch, we resumed our work of destruction and, by the time we left Brandon the next day, there was nothing standing in the town. We marched the twelve to fifteen miles back to Jackson in high spirits, singing and stomping our feet in anticipation. The boys were looking forward to getting their hands on what was left of Jackson.

For the next two days, I wandered through the streets of Jackson and watched as the town was ravished. I could walk from south to north and east to west through the town and, everywhere I looked, were smoldering ruins and ashes. There was a rumor going through the soldiers that General Sherman had officially changed the name of Jackson, Mississippi to Chimneyville. Whenever this gossip was repeated, the boys would breakout in loud laughs and cheers for Chimneyville. Well, I thought as the sergeant had said, "That's war."

CHAPTER NINE

When we marched out of Jackson, after having completed our work of utter destruction, practically the only thing left to be seen were scattered piles of ash and debris and an occasional tree that had somehow escaped the destruction. That, and the stone and mud brick fireplaces that showed how well we had completed our work.

We marched all day and towards evening, went into camp just on the outskirts of Clinton. Clinton I don't think had ever been much of a town, but it surprised me that there was more left of Clinton than there was of Jackson.

The following day, we marched rather leisurely along, heading back for Vicksburg. Perhaps we marched too leisurely because late afternoon found us still several miles from the Big Black River that we would have to cross. Crossing rivers was always somewhat of a challenge, even at the best times. It was possible that some of the troops were even then congregating along the banks, waiting their turns to go across the bridges that were nowhere near adequate, at least not for a large body of troops at the same time.

Thus, events found us making camp just north of Champion Hill. It was on this very ground that a few months ago the Union forces had fought a severe and bloody battle with the Confederates. As the troops went into camp, I used what little considerations were given my rank as corporal and was given permission to visit the site of the battle.

I wandered out from camp and immediately headed for the tallest height in the near distance. We had passed near Champion Hill earlier on our march to Vicksburg, but hadn't had the time or the opportunity to see the site for ourselves. Now, as I wandered up the reddish, steep sloping hill, I was amazed that two months' time could do so much to obscure the scene of the battle. There were occasional places still exposed where the ground had been disrupted by shells, but the grass had covered most of the scenes of action on the slopes of the hill. The most telling evidence of the ferocity of the fight were the blasted trees along the slopes and especially near the top where the fighting had been most severe, that and the mounds of dirt that indicated where the troops had been buried. It appeared to me that the troops had been buried in long trenches probably as close to where they had fallen as possible.

As I wandered over the site of the battle, past the mounds that now entombed the bones of the soldiers, a kind of melancholy seemed to settle over me. What was so special about this place that all of these soldiers had to meet here to die? Had the Champions, when they had first founded their farm here, who could say when, had any inkling that in the future such a ferocious battle would take place on their property?

The railroad from Vicksburg to Jackson ran not far from here and the road passed relatively close, but neither went directly to this farmstead. I couldn't see what was so special about this ground that it was worth fighting over. It made me think that this battle, or possibly the whole war, was simply an accident that should have been avoided.

I began to think that I shouldn't be here. I wished I was back home on the farm with my parents, but then I remembered that my parents were dead and the farm had been burnt and I really had no home. I had come to the conclusion that this was all because of slavery in the country and had enlisted with the intention of seeing the war through until slavery was abolished. Abolished? It's funny how I had picked that word up. Two years ago, it wasn't in my vocabulary. Now, it was a word and a phrase that was repeated on a daily basis.

I wandered back into camp and ate a rather melancholy meal with the men in the squad. Even Johnny, who was usually so talkative and humorous, seemed to have been affected by the gloom of the place. I wondered if, due to the recent fight, that possibly the souls of the departed were lingering around the field. It was an uncanny feeling.

We had passed close to Champion's Hill on our way to Jackson, but had passed through in the daylight while at the beginning of the march to the east and I hadn't noticed any of the glum that seemed to be lingering around here then. I decided it must be the dark that was making me feel so uneasy.

The following day, we marched on to the Big Black River and gathered on the eastern shore as troops passed over the rickety bridges. It took most of the morning for the 15th Corps to cross over to the west and we marched a few miles and then went into camp again. We didn't feel that we had much to fear of the Confederates at the time and merely went to camp just south of the railroad bridge.

We were up at first light and marched a few miles further south along the Big Black to a place called Hankinson's Ferry and, there, proceeded to dig and strengthen some old fortifications so that after a weeks' time of digging and repairing the trenches, we had a very secure and well defended camp. It reminded me considerably of Milliken's Bend. I think it may have been near the 1st of August when we finished our preparations. I thought we would be going into camp here probably for the winter.

We spent the next several days digging and building up fortifications. The line that had been selected seemed to follow the course of the Big Black River. We piled up dirt ten feet high and ten feet wide. At points, we piled mounds in front of the main earthworks themselves. Here, we positioned cannons. I had never seen cannons this large before. They were simply monstrous. I think they had probably come from Vicksburg itself. I knew they had huge cannons there but, until you saw it up close, it was impossible to appreciate the size.

The biggest pieces were placed facing straight out across the river towards the east and south as if we should be afraid of Confederates approaching from that direction. Smaller pieces of cannons were placed to enfilade down along our own lines in case the Confederates were brave enough to swim across the river and assail our earthworks. I found that hard to believe, but then surely we ourselves had done even more stupid things than that.

We erected tents all throughout the fortifications and, after a few more days, plank lumber was brought into camp. This wasn't green wood. It had obviously been seasoned and some had even been painted once upon a time. Where the scavengers had managed to find this, I couldn't imagine.

I thought we had burnt anything within fifty miles, but it was obvious at some point in time this lumber had been part of some Confederate homestead, maybe some southerner's house or barn. I wondered if some of it could be coming from Vicksburg itself.

We used this to set up plank houses in camp and to form the roofs of dugouts along the earthworks. We would dig shallow caves into the front of our embankments, then brace the walls and roof with lumber and cover this with a mound of dirt. We dug countless pit latrines throughout the camp. We were well supplied from steamers along the river, but still on a daily basis foragers returned, bringing in fresh food, greens and meat that they had confiscated from the southerners. I thought that we had forged for anything that could have been eaten over the last three months, but surprisingly they still they managed to keep us well supplied.

After a week or so, word went out that we were to be given furloughs to go home for a spell. Most of the troops that were allowed home were troops that had been wounded or who had taken sick during the last campaign. Fortunately none of the men in my squad had been severely wounded or had been extremely ill. Only a percentage of the troops were being allowed to go, so, after discussing with the squad, we decided that Michael Francis and Bob Cantrell should be allowed furlough. Michael had come near to being killed in the fight outside Brandon and Bob was then suffering from dysentery and fevers for the last several days and we felt that the rest would do him good. Besides Bob was the only married man in the squad and had two small children who, we decided, would like to see their father.

Bob and Michael proceeded on down to the Mississippi to board steamers back to St. Louis. The rest of us settled in to make ourselves at home until the officers decided where to send us next. We moved into one of the dugouts that we had constructed and shared it with another squad from the 31st Missouri. The dugout had been built large enough to accommodate two full squads, that meant at least twenty men, but due to the fact that the wounded and sick were cared for elsewhere and the other squad had had two men killed in their recent campaign, there was plenty of room in the dugout. We were not accustomed to this degree of luxurious privacy.

One evening after supper, the sergeant made an appearance. He had been bunking in one of the plank houses with other sergeants and even some of the junior lieutenants. I wasn't surprised to hear rumors throughout the regiment that, due to his solid dependable character and considerable good sense, he was being considered as officer material. He came to the dugout and passed around, talking to all of the soldiers and spending more time with the corporals of the other squads. He inquired about their health, their families and their concerns.

Earlier that morning, we had received a large shipment of mail. We hadn't had any mail; at least I hadn't had any mail, since we had left Benton barracks. But, possibly, due to the fact that the campaign seemed to be halted, at least for the moment, the mail had finally caught up with us. I had read the letter from home as soon as I had gotten it that morning, and was sitting with the men in my squad on one side of the dugout re-reading it by the light of the lantern when the sergeant made his way around the dugout and came to our group.

He talked to each of the men in turn, inquiring about their needs and concerns, and at last spoke to me. "And, how have you been doing, son?" he said. And then, without pause, he said, "I see you have a letter from home. What have your folks got to say?"

There had been several pages to the letter. The first page was from my uncle and he replied to the letter that I had last written and mailed to them from Benton barracks. He wrote briefly about what was happening and their trading post at Osage City, informed me that my sisters and younger brother were well and how enjoyable they were to have around the house. Then, there was a page from my Aunt Susan, and a page from each of my two sisters, Mary and Elizabeth. There was even a short note from my younger brother, Jesse. It seemed so strange that he could actually write. After all, he wasn't more than seven, no, I think he was probably eight now. Anyhow, it surprised me that he could write.

Rather than trying to relate everything that had been written in the letter, I looked up at the sergeant. I knew he had no family left, at least in the United States. He still had brothers and sisters in Ireland but I doubted that they ever kept in contact. I looked up at him and said, "Would you like to read it, Sergeant?" And, I was rather surprised as he stretched out his hand and took the letter and settled down on the floor, leaning back against the wall of the dugout and, by the light of the lantern, read the letter through slowly from front to back.

When he finished, he handed the letter back to me and commented, "You know, son, it sounds like they really love you and miss you." Then he said, "Don't you ever miss home?" As I took the letter and folded it and put it back in my blouse pocket, I commented, "You know, Sergeant, the thing I miss most about home were the evenings that we sat around by the fireplace and just talked and told stories." I suppose I was in an excessively talkative mood at the moment.

I told him, "You know, one of the things that I especially miss was listening to my grandfather talk. He had a way of telling a story that kept you motionless and completely enthralled. I had absolutely loved to hear stories about when he was young, growing up in York, England. He would tell stories about how his father had been a fishing boat captain. His father actually had two boats that he owned and several men that worked for him, and our grandfather especially liked fishing and took great pride and pleasure out of going with his dad out on their trips. He would often tell us stories about how he marveled at his father's ability to find the fishing banks where the schools of fish gathered. He also remarked on how uncanny his father's ability was to sail out on the seas out of sight of land and then make his way back to the coast and back home, when all that he himself could see was water and sky in all directions."

The sergeant leaned back against the plank wall placing his folded arms behind his head, "Yea," he said, "It does sound wonderful. Why ever did he leave?" I hadn't meant to get caught up in a long family history, but now I was forced to relate how my grandfather's father had been lost at sea with one of his boats and all of the hands on it. My grandfather's older brother had captained the second boat and had made it back to York, just barely. Grandfather had been on the boat that was commanded by his older brother and he said that, when they had left, his father had sailed north in search of the schools of fish while they had headed south. It seems they had been fishing later than usual and the fall weather was turning cool and brisk. The storm had blown up quickly out of the northwest and, seeing it coming, his older brother had turned and sailed as fast as they could to the southwest and made it into the coast well south of York, and then worked their way up to the north along the coast when the weather had abated.

I then went on to explain as briefly as I could how my grandfather's mother had remarried a man who ran a carpentry business in York. It seems that he and my great-grandfather had been good friends since he was the one who built great-grandfather's boats and kept them in repair. Grandfather had been eight or nine years old at the time and had gone to work, learning the carpentry trade, making barrels, wagons, wagon wheels and repairing fishing boats. Apparently his mother refused to allow him to join with his older brother in the fishing business and, not seeing much future in York in the furniture and carpentry business, grandfather had taken advantage of an opportunity to move to the new world as an indentured servant for a Georgia plantation owner.

I tried to keep the stories short and brief as I didn't feel real comfortable talking about my family. I thought about asking the sergeant about his family, but then remembered that his wife and children had all died in the cholera epidemic that had swept through Canton, Missouri just before the war and how his two sons that had survived, had both been killed fighting for the Union army in small insignificant battles up around Kansas City and someplace else in northern Missouri. He had told me previously how he had left Ireland, seeing no future there due to the strict British rule and I was at a loss as to what to say to him, so I went on talking about my family anyhow.

I told him how my father especially liked to tell stories about ancient Greece and the mythological heroes. Father had had a book that he had acquired as a youngster from my grandfather's trading post at Osage City. It was full of stories about ancient Greek philosophers and heroes. I told the sergeant, "You know, the thing that I remember most about that book is the fact that it was falling apart. Father had it for maybe thirty years and the backing was cracking and split, pages had fallen out and were put back in and, when you tried to read it, they would often fall out all over the floor. How father kept them in the proper order was always amazing to me. He tried to keep it up on the mantle above the fireplace and we had strict orders that we were never to touch it, or the bible that mother always liked to read from," I said.

I went on to tell him, "I think my favorite stories were the stories about the kings of Israel. I especially liked the story of King David and how he slew Goliath with a sling shot." And, then I laughed and said, "I couldn't imagine a boy killing a giant with a slingshot." "Oh, why not?" he said. "Well," I laughed and said, "It's only a slingshot." At which the sergeant laughed and said, "You know, a slingshot can be a mighty dangerous weapon." I rather skeptically said, "You're joshing me, Sarge." "No, no, I'm not," he said. "You know, the Roman legions had companies of slingers with them. They used it as a type of short range artillery, you might say. A good slinger can throw a stone nearly as far as a man can shot an arrow. And, they can do it with deadly accuracy," he said. "And, the thing is, when an archer runs out of arrows, a slinger can usually find rocks readily at foot." And I thought he was going to say 'readily at hand' and laughed at his joke. Readily at foot, indeed.

Then the sergeant went on to say that, as a boy, he had always carried a sling in his pocket. "You know, the British forbade us to have any kind of weapons. You couldn't be seen carrying a knife or a bow and arrow or even a club. But, it was hard to tell if someone had a sling in his pocket. I often used a sling just for fun, or for practice. You know, young boys have a need to find weapons of some sort to play and practice with. So, slinging rocks at things just came natural. Still, you had to be careful that you weren't caught at it. So, whenever I could, I practiced slinging stones at anything I felt I could hit. With enough practice, you can get to be uncannily accurate. I often used to kill rabbits, ducks and geese for the family. Of course, if we were caught killing animals on the Lord's lands, I would have been in big trouble. The British Lords laid claim to anything found upon their land, even if there was a goose merely flying by."

Still feeling somewhat skeptical, I said, "Yea, but there's a lot of difference between a rabbit or a duck and a man." Then the sergeant said, "You know, I used to think that when I was a youngster too, but then one day I took a piece of one inch oak plank that was lying around the barn and propped it against the stone fence out in the field. I decided to use it as a target, thinking that I wouldn't have to keep looking for rocks if I just kept slinging at this one board against the stone fence. My first shot split that old oak plank plumb in half. It just cracked it wide apart. I never did that again because I thought the British Lord would soon get suspicious if all of his planks started disappearing. But, you know, a good sized rock would split a man's head open like a melon. I'm sure it would break ribs even if it didn't penetrate."

Well, I knew the sergeant liked to tell stories, but one thing that I was certain of was that he wouldn't lie about such a thing. And, so, we spent the time talking till late in the evening and I listed to more of the sergeant's tales about Ireland. I felt much better now listening to him talk than talking about my own family. The time passed quite rapidly as

I sat listening to the sergeant. I became aware that most all of the other men in the squad were listening to the sergeant's stories and were just as comfortable sitting there listening as I was. It reminded me of life at the homestead before the war as we all sat around listening to the sergeant talk.

He finished his present tale about a lost sheep roundup and remarked that it was getting quite late and he needed to get back to the cabin before taps. He excused himself and said he would be back in a day or two. I knew that he liked to mingle through the squads in the company and keep himself well informed and up on the soldiers' concern. It made for good morale and helped discipline. I couldn't help but hope that it wouldn't be long until he stopped back for another visit.

CHAPTER TEN

The sun came up the next day as hot and dry as usual. It was a good thing that the fortifications were built on the banks of the Big Black River, I thought, since it hadn't rained for several weeks. There was plenty of water in the river so the camp didn't lack as far as that was concerned. But I couldn't help wondering if, with as many troops as were camped up and down the river; it might be possible to drink the whole thing dry. Looking at the river, it did seem to be lower than it had been when we first moved in here two weeks ago. I couldn't believe it had been that long.

That morning after breakfast, the squad was given leave for three days. We were free to do whatever we wanted. On sudden inspiration, I suggested that we go to Vicksburg. After all, when we left St. Louis, we were told that we were headed to Vicksburg. We had been sent to Milliken's Bend and then down to Hard Times. We had been across the Mississippi River to Grand Gulf, marched to Jackson, Mississippi and back to Vicksburg, then back to Jackson and back to our present location. During all that marching, we had only managed to catch an occasional glimpse of Vicksburg itself. The closest we had actually been to Vicksburg was when we were in the fortifications along the northwest line overlooking the Chickasaw Bayou. The Confederates had been right there on the bluff in front of us, but their lines were a distance from Vicksburg itself, maybe a half a mile or so. We had only ever seen glimpses of the tallest buildings of Vicksburg a time or two and only from a great distance. I said, "You know, boys, it's about time we got to visit Vicksburg." And, so, we took off.

We passed through our troops along the road and went into the town from the southeast corner. We passed through one Union entrenchment after another and worked our way up the bluff moving beyond one ring of devastation after another. Just when we actually entered the city of Vicksburg, I couldn't say. The homes and buildings on the edge of the city had all been destroyed in the fighting, or else cleared to provide better fields of fire. I was surprised to see that the structures near the center of the city had been largely spared. I had not expected to find the remains of a town. I had thought that there might be an occasional home or public building still standing but was astonished to see that most had survived. I had thought we might see nothing but destruction where, like Jackson, there were only some faint indications of where the streets had run. When we were done with Jackson all that was left was collapsed or burnt buildings with the chimneys pointing skyward. There had been nothing that resembled a town.

But in Vicksburg most of the city had survived although it had been shockingly altered. What we found before us resembled nothing that I could think of except a giant anthill. There were trenches, holes and pits dug all throughout the top of the bluffs where the town stood. Even though it hadn't rained for a couple of weeks, some of the holes in the ground were big enough that they still held a few inches of water. There was nothing but plowed and disturbed earth in all directions. I don't think there could have been more than two or three trees still standing within my vision, and the ones that I could see didn't have more than a couple of limbs apiece. There were no shrubs or bushes and surprisingly, I couldn't even see any grass. It looked like nothing but dry, plowed and overturned clods of earth.

As we walked along the top of the bluff, we noticed numerous holes dug in the sides of the bluff. We passed one that had the frame from a house with a door positioned in the opening. Feeling rather curious, I walked over, knocked on the door and, getting no reply, opened it and we walked inside. Inside was a room no more than eight by eight feet in size. Planking had been used to form a ceiling and walls. There were a couple of beams resting on planking that looked as if they were intended to hold the whole roof up. It appeared to be a rather flimsy and unsteady construction. I suggested to the boys that we get out of there rather quickly for fear that it might cave in. How it had ever withstood all the bombardments the Union troops had thrown at it, was a mystery.

We passed numerous other excavations on the hill where Vicksburg stood that were nothing more than dirt tunnels dug without any support. Of course, these rooms were quite small, usually not big enough to hold more than a couple of people at a time.

Then, as we proceeded north along the line, we came to one excavation in the hillside that had a large carved and decorated door on a frame built into the hillside. Once again, I went up and knocked on the door before opening it. There had been no response to my knocking, so we didn't hesitate to move into the room and wander about. It was a large room; about ten by twenty feet, and the roof, walls and floor were reinforced with planking and solid beams. There was even a potbellied stove with the tin chimney extending out through a hole in the roof. There was a table and chairs and a couple of soft chairs.

There were two doors in the opposite wall from where we came in that opened into two smaller rooms about ten by ten feet, one of which held a four-poster bed. I supposed it had been the last refuge of one of the wealthier denizens of Vicksburg. How it had managed to remain intact surprised me. There was even some fine china in a cupboard along the southern wall of the bunker.

As we left and shut the door behind us, I realized that we were nearly as far north in the town as you could go before entering the Confederate lines of fortifications. As I turned and looked back towards the south, I observed some soldiers boxing up furniture and possessions and carrying them off to the south.

The thought went through my mind that the china, cupboards, four-poster bed and soft chairs would probably soon be boxed up and carted off to the landing to be shipped home for some Union officers' prize. I could picture the Union officers hauling off pianos much like Jim Lane had done at Osceola, but then I thought that they may as well take it. I doubted if any of the southerners would be coming back to this town anytime soon, as it had seemed to be largely deserted. When the heavy fall rains came, I didn't think that any of these underground structures would stand the weight. I could picture the mud sliding and, in the spring when the grass came back, as I knew it would, there would probably be no sign of these excavations.

Johnny suggested that we proceed to the northern limits of the Confederate fortifications because he wished to see where our camp was from the Confederate viewpoint. This seemed to lift the spirits of the boys. I think they were feeling somewhat melancholy, as I was, after having wandered through the ruins of the Confederate city.

We hustled off to the north and soon were at the limits of the Confederate walls. We had no trouble looking down from above and picking out where we had camped about eight or ten weeks ago. I still had trouble remembering dates. It didn't seem that there was much difference between one day and the next and, despite my best efforts, it was hard to tell just what the date actually was. I think we were probably into the second week of August.

We looked down on our camp above the Chickasaw Bayou and picked out the ditch that we had so eagerly sought to reach without being killed. Looking at the ground below us from above, it was obvious to me that if we had persisted in trying to cross the remaining ground and assaulting the bluffs, none of us would ever have survived.

We moved east along the top of the Confederate fortifications until we came to the Stockade Redan. I had learned that that was the name of the Confederate fortifications at the point of the bluff before it turned back to the south. From here we could look down the Graveyard Road and get a good view of where the main assault of the 15th Corp had been in our first attack on Vicksburg. We could pick out the graveyard road as it wound between an opening in the bluffs across from us and approached these bluffs that were so heavily fortified by the Confederates. We looked down into the ditch where our attack had ended so disastrously. It was appalling to think that a few days later we would attempt the impossible again.

The rumor had gone out after the battles that we had lost nearly a thousand men total in the two attempts made to attack these fortifications. My only wonder is that we hadn't lost more. It seems our attacks further west and north were an attempt merely to keep the Confederates from rushing more troops to defend this location. I actually thought that whatever number of men that they had had here would have been enough without reinforcing it anyhow. I wondered if both Grant and Sherman had known that their attacks would end in failure, but had felt obligated to at least make the attempt for political reasons. Or possibly just to satisfy those damn reporters that Sherman hated so much.

We wandered further south along the Confederate works and came to the first of the great mines that the Union had set off under the Confederate lines, and then we continued moving to the south and west until we returned to the spot where we had first entered Vicksburg. This had taken most of the morning and a good portion of the afternoon and, as we still had time left before dark, we wandered down to the landing. Here, tents were set up to serve beer, whiskey, meals and whatever other luxuries a soldier found himself in need of.

The landing had been considerably repaired and extended far beyond what I think its capacity had been before the war. Even now, there must have been a dozen steamers and gunboats tied up along the wharfs. A small town of tents and ramshackle buildings had sprung up along the waters edge. I felt confident that at high water most all of this would be washed away, probably in the first of the spring rains, I thought. But, for now, the structures held a multitude of people.

By unanimous consent, we made our way to an establishment that looked like it was more prosperous than the rest and was offering hot meals. This establishment was run by some Confederate ladies and several black women that I supposed had been former slaves, possibly even of theirs. We sat down and ordered a hearty meal. I started off with a rather spicy soup that had crawdads and fish and an assortment of vegetables. I'm not sure what all was in it, but it was delicious. We sipped on warm and, I imagined rather muddy tasting beer and waited for our steaks to cook. I ate roasted potatoes and a steak that was certainly well done along with some spicy, vinegar flavored greens. The greens reminded me of spinach. Then, we topped it off with apple pie and more beer.

We wandered through the rest of the tents along the river landing. I was looking for black powder and percussion caps for the Remington's, needle, thread, beeswax and anything else that I thought would be useful. We wandered from tent to tent for nearly an hour until I sensed the boys were getting restless with my endeavors. Frank was the first to disappear. I was surprised he had accompanied us as long as he had. Gradually, one by one, we separated. Finally only Johnny and Hans remained with me while I searched for supplies. I had told them that they might well find something to buy that would end up saving their lives. The rest of the men in the squad had already taken off in search of whiskey and women. Anywhere an army went, both could be found in ready abundance.

It was starting to become dark. We had been given a three days' pass and didn't have to be back in camp so we weren't inclined to make the long walk back. We made our way to a tent that was doing a lively business. The front flaps were wide open and there were trestle tables along each side with kegs and bottles on them. The back flap was open and led out into a small clear space that was circled by wagons full of liquor with guards keeping a careful watch on the contents of the wagons.

Bartenders behind the trestle table were dispensing liquor as fast as the soldiers could extend their tin cups for more. The tent wasn't big enough for many people to occupy at once, so there was a steady line passing through along the sides and along in front of the tables and back out the other side where the soldiers gathered in the streets to drink, tell stories and return to form back in line.

We came upon Otto and Christian and they joined us for a few drinks until we had built up our courage and then Johnny, Hans and I followed them down to an establishment that they had found earlier in the day. It seems it was here that they last seen Frank Martin. This establishment had been set up in one of the few buildings along the waterfront that had escaped the bombardments. It looked like it had once been a warehouse.

Where we entered was a large opened area with a trestle table bar along one wall. Ladies of various colors and different stages of dress and undress moved around the open floor. There were stairways at each end that led upstairs to what may have been offices at one time. The rooms now conducted business of a different nature, I'm sure. The main floor was divided off in some locations by plank rooms, but in most cases privacy was afforded merely by blankets suspended from ropes, screening off areas of the building.

Most of the working women were blacks of different shades and different ages. There were extremely young girls and fairly old women. One thing I was sure of is that they took to their new emancipated condition with enthusiasm. I had never seen women so wild and excited to be free. I chose one young girl, not much older than myself, I don't think, with brassy red hair. We went off to her screened in cubicle in the corner of the room and I paid her several times the customary rate. I told her I wasn't planning on leaving till sunup. I thought that she looked most flattered, but possibly she was merely relieved. Maybe she was thinking she wouldn't have to work as hard.

We undressed and snuggled up in the blankets and cushions on the floor and she was soon hard at work. I had never been with a woman before and the circumstances were somehow embarrassing for me. I found it hard to make conversation and she seemed to have no inclination for small talk either. But I was not just a man, I was a soldier and life was short. Besides this was extremely exciting so I made sure that she earned her money throughout the night. I only let her take a few short naps until early morning. Then we slept soundly for several hours and it was considerably after sunup before I woke up. Before I left, I put her back to work one last time and then dressed.

I left the establishment being unable to find any of the other boys in the squad and wandered up along the riverbank and through the buildings. I found my way back to the tent where we had eaten the night before and, sure enough, they were serving breakfast. I had breakfast and lots of coffee as I was feeling rather sleepy from the night before. I thought I had actually slept well, but for some reason I was rather exhausted, it seemed.

I wandered through the shops along the landing and filled my knapsack with supplies and assorted trivial knickknacks that I had taken a fancy to. I found a cheap little brass box with a sliding lid that I thought the brassy red haired girl would like. It wasn't much, but she had seemed rather sentimental to me. Rooms in the boarding houses were practically as expensive as a night with the ladies, so I had already decided to return. I thought it was as good a way as any to work my way into her good graces.

Right on the banks of the river, another business had been set up where they were cleaning uniforms. I stripped down and gave them my clothes to have them washed and cleaned and went for a swim in the river. I swam for an hour or two, being careful to keep my eye on my knapsack on the banks of the river while they cleaned, dried and tidied up my uniform. I wandered back through the small town that had been set up beneath the bluffs and then up to the city on the hill. I passed the courthouse and came to an excavation just to the south. I nearly passed by but had a sudden impulse to enter so turned, crossed the street and walked in. I was surprised and mortified to find that this one was occupied

"Excuse me, Sir" I stammered. "I didn't expect anyone was still living here" I attempted to explain. Glancing around the room I noted that he seemed to be alone. He was sitting on a straight chair next to a cot, but on closer look I realized the cot was occupied by what I took to be a child. Slowly he looked up and seemed to notice me for the first time. 'Hello" he said, in a voice lacking the deep Southern draw, "How can I help you". Feeling guilty and certain that he believed I was there to rob him I hastened to explain "I was just passing by and I don't know why but I felt the need to come in". "Perhaps it is the will of Jehovah" he said, with his gaze fixed on my face. "Why are you still here" I said "all of the other caves seem to be empty". "It's much cooler here than in the house" he replied "I thought it would be better for him" as he nodded in the direction of the cot. I looked again at the child on the cot and realized that the face was that of a young man with the scruffy beard of youth. I took a step or two forward to obtain a better view before I realized the truth. It was when I noticed the thin bloody drainage seeping through the blankets and recognized the foul aroma of corruption that I understood that the youth had no legs. I backed up a step and timidly suggested "I should be going".

"No, don't go. I haven't had any visitors for weeks. That is, except for Dr. Stone, he stops in daily to check on us and bring what food he can spare" the man said. "Don't you have family here" I inquired. "Just my son" he said, almost in a whisper as he motioned at the cot. "I insisted my wife and daughters leave months ago. I sent them back home to New York so they would be safe. I wish we had gone with them". "Why didn't you go too?" I asked. "I had a business to run, a home to look after, and a naive conviction that no one would bother a New York Jew and his son living in the South" he said. "I shouldn't have been so stupid". "What kind of business did you have" I said, hoping to change the

"I worked for a group of investors that speculated in cotton. I arranged for the purchase, storage, and transportation of cotton for the company and managed a mercantile store of my own" he explained somewhat proudly. "We lived here for the last eleven years and they were good years" he nearly choked. "But it was obvious that this war was inevitable. I did my best to try to convince these folks that the North would never allow them to secede, but they wouldn't believe me. Now just look at us" he said. I glanced from him to his son and pictured in my minds eye the devastation of Jackson and Vicksburg. Yes, I thought, just look at you.

"God damn Yankees" he suddenly exclaimed. "Why couldn't they leave us alone"? I almost saw fit to remind him that I was a Yankee, even if I was from Missouri, but thought better of it. Instead I began to suggest that if the South hadn't insisted on maintaining slavery there would have been no reason for the war. He looked at me with an expression of awe, or maybe exasperation at my innocence. Then calmly, almost patiently, he said "You realize the war isn't just about slavery, don't you"? I was shocked by that. "Of course it's about slavery, what else?" I queried.

He calmly answered "Certainly the issue of slavery was the predominant catalyst for the conflict but there were others. For instance, in Dec. 1814 a delegation of politicians from states in the northeast met in Hartford, Conn. to discuss seceding from the union because they were opposed to the war with Britain. They were advocating secession because it was in their economic interests to do so. Why did they think they could secede then, but the South can't now? And you know, I'm sure, that secession was threatened again in 1852 and 1856 because of taxes imposed by northern states on the sale of southern cotton to foreign nations" he said, then took a deep breath and calmed himself. "No, this war has been coming for some time. I just wish I could have kept my family out of it".

I remembered how often I had heard my father say the same thing. "Why didn't you?" I asked humbly but sincerely. "Oh, I tried' he said. "But when Grant landed his troops at Grand Gulf and invaded Mississippi my son was determined to fight to protect our land from the northern invaders. No one I knew in Vicksburg was in favor of secession. In fact, the majority of the population voted against it, and we never owned slaves! He wasn't fighting for slavery; he was fighting for our home". And with those words he lowered his head and began to weep. I quietly backed out of the room and shut the door. As I wondered, rather aimlessly, I contemplated what he had said. If northern states had first proposed secession, maybe we didn't have the right to force them to remain in the union. And how could one part of the country impose taxes that specifically affected only other states. It was all so confusing. But then I decided that none of this mattered. I was fighting to abolish slavery, and that was all that counted.

I managed to locate most of the rest of the boys from the squad as I wondered through Vicksburg. We went off for a few drinks and another hearty meal and then made our way back to the ladies.

I found the little brassy redheaded girl and gave her my gift which brought tears to her eyes. I paid her for another nights' work, but we spent the next couple of hours sipping drinks along the bar and dancing to the music. It seems she didn't much care for the foot stomping dancing that I was used to, but preferred the slower music where she could glide light-footed and gracefully over the floor, that is as light-footed and as graceful as you could be with me clutching to her who had never experienced this type of dancing. But, after 15 or 20 minutes, I seemed to get the feel for it and greatly enjoyed having her hanging off one arm as we strolled around the dance floor, or clutching her around the waist with my right arm as we held hands with the left and circled around the other clumsy dancers who seemed to be doing their best to imitate us.

It was well after dark before we retired, that meant that it must have been 10 or 11 at night which, although quite early hours for that type of establishment, was later than I had planned. It seemed that the attention, the dancing and the talking had increased our anticipation and she went to work with what I felt was true enthusiasm. I had the impression that she had once been accustomed to much better times, even a life of luxury and privilege. It was well after sunup before we roused and she rather leisurely and gratefully went back to work on me.

When we were both up and dressed I took her out to breakfast at the little tent that I had first found on Friday afternoon. After breakfast, we made our way back to her working establishment. It was Sunday morning and the girls were already back at work there. When I turned to leave, she asked me if she would be seeing me again. I told her yes, as soon as I got leave I would be back, and I meant it. She smiled graciously and beautifully. I know she believed me.

I left and wandered through the landing, managing to find about half the boys in the squad and, after lunch, we headed back towards our camp. We had never managed to find Frank Martin again after we broke up on Friday night. Johnny Applebaum suggested that he had probably gotten drunk, fallen into the Mississippi and drowned. I hadn't really thought about this. Frank was notorious for the amount that he liked to drink, always seeming to have a bottle and be half tipsy at the best of times. Now, I felt responsible and negligent. I was worried that when we got back to camp, I might be in trouble if one of the boys had indeed drowned while in a drunken stupor. Then, I worried that possibly he had slipped onboard one of the steamships and had run off.

I was almost relieved to find when we got back to camp that he was already there. Johnny looked at him and said, "Frank, where the hell you been?" He said, "Well, I have been right here since Saturday morning." I said, "Saturday! Why on earth were you back here Saturday morning?" He said, "The first place I went when we got to the landing was in search of a woman. I had my share of women and too much whiskey. Saturday morning, I awoke, and found myself in a ditch just beyond the southern end of the landing. My knapsack was missing, my money was all gone and it's all your fault." "My fault!" I said, "How in the hell is that my fault? I hadn't even noticed when you left." He said, "That's why it's your fault, corporal. You know I can't control myself. You knew the first place I would go was for the women and then the whiskey and you should have kept a better eye on me." I laughed and said, "Now, Frank, there are way too many damn women down there and way too much whiskey. I wasn't about to go sticking my head behind every curtain in that camp looking for you. If you want me to nursemaid you, you're going to have to stick with me. I had my share of women and whiskey and still came back with most of my money." Then Frank said, "Well, maybe you should teach me a thing or too. I have never been able to manage that." With that, he broke out into a wide grin, and slapped me on the shoulder and I knew that he had been teasing all along. Maybe he wasn't as bad as I thought?

The following day we were back to work strengthening the fortifications for whatever reason, I could not determine. I felt the fortifications were strong enough and I didn't think there was a rebel left in the state. But, like usual, when the officers didn't know what else to do, they found places for us to dig. Then, we were back to the usual marching and drilling. A couple of weeks later, Michael Francis and Bob Cantrell returned, and it seemed that they brought the rains with them. I wasn't used to Mississippi weather. Back home in Missouri along the banks of the Osage, it was usually late September, even October, before we got much in the way of rains. But, this was Mississippi and it did seem to rain a whole lot more here, at least throughout the spring months. I supposed it might be true of the fall also.

It rained fairly hard for several days and the dugout held up pretty well, but there is only so much rain that loose dirt and dust can absorb before it starts leaking through. I knew that when the earth above had had a chance to settle, that it would become more watertight, but it didn't take long before the rain was soaking its way through the loose dirt and dripping through the planks above and running through the planks along the walls of the dugout. But that was okay because we stretched ropes across from wall to wall and suspended our rubberized ponchos over these and made our beds beneath these flimsy covers.

It was now late August. I was wondering if it was going to continue to rain like this for the rest of the fall. I was beginning to wish that we could be moving on someplace other than here, but the rains only lasted for a few more days and then the weather turned hot and dry again. The sergeant made two more visits over the next couple of weeks. I found myself talking more and more about my family. The sergeant seemed to be especially interested in stories about my grandfather, how he had worked as an indentured servant in Georgia, saved up some money, headed west, volunteered to serve with Andy Jackson in the Creek Indian wars in Alabama and how he had served also with Andy Jackson when they marched down the Mississippi to New Orleans. He especially liked the stories about how my grandfather had been there when they utterly destroyed the British troops under General Pakenham at the battle just south of New Orleans. The sergeant had a strange fondness for the British as soldiers, but an intense hatred of the British as a people. It was kind of hard to reconcile his feelings towards them.

We had had three day passes on two other occasions and I had spent my time, as much as possible, with the little brassy redheaded girl. It seems she had developed a true fondness for me and I actually began picturing spending the rest of my life with her after this war was over, but I never said any such thing to her. I knew that was impossible, so there was no sense to speak of it. She never mentioned it either; although I'm sure it crossed her mind. We were both making the best of a bad situation. I wondered if a few years ago she would even have considered talking to me. From things that she had said and the way she carried herself, I'm sure that she must once have been part of the southern nobility. I had never asked her name, but had taken to calling her Brassy. It sounded better than just calling her Red. I think she actually liked the name.

Now that the weather had dried off, I was beginning to think that I wouldn't mind just staying here in Vicksburg and making a visit in to see

Brassy every couple of weeks, but good things can never last. Towards the end of September, we were ordered to make ready, and pack all of our gear together because in the morning we would be marching off. The sergeant had come by to give us this information and even he didn't know for sure where we were going.

In the morning, we loaded up and marched out of Camp Sherman and headed west instead of east as I supposed we would be going. We marched back to the landing at Vicksburg and I kept my eyes peeled for any sight of Brassy. I supposed that she might even be watching for me as it was obvious that major troop movements were at hand, but I never spied her distinctive colored red hair in the crowds.

CHAPTER ELEVEN

It seemed that we milled around on the road next to the landing for hours as steamers loaded troops and supplies then backed away from the landing to be replaced by others. Finally we made our way to the front of the line and marched up the gangplank. I was still looking for that girl, but I never did make her out. I don't know why it seemed so important to me. As we passed around the bend and out of sight of the landing, I thought to myself that she was probably hard at work anyhow. While we were passing the fortifications at Milliken's Bend, word spread that we were on our way to Memphis. Well, that was a reasonable guess! Beyond that, no one knew. .

I spent my time circling the deck and watching as the river rolled by. A couple of hours after passing Milliken's Bend, we steamed our way past a point where Grant's army had blown holes in the levy in their abortive attempt to circle around and come down the rivers from the north above Vicksburg. The weather was hot and dry again. The trees were thickly leaved out and still green but there were occasional yellow and brown leaved walnuts visible. Walnuts were always the first to turn color in the fall. There were high stands of grass and brush along the riverbanks making the details of the landscape rather hard to distinguish. But I couldn't recognize any steep loess bluffs like at Vicksburg. I did so enjoy watching the country pass by! Once again I imagined myself piloting a riverboat after the war. Maybe I could travel the river and visit Brassy regularly? I actually considered what would happen to her after the war, surely there would be no need to continue in her present employment.

I soon became bored with watching the riverbanks and trying to pick out details and with dreams of a life with that red haired rebel girl. This war was never going to end. Those damn rebels were too proud, too stupid, or maybe just too determined to surrender! I made my way into the salon and sat down amidst the rest of the men in the squad, leaned back and napped throughout the day. I think that we had exhausted most of our conversation over the last several weeks of rest in Camp Sherman. We were on our way to Memphis, but what we would do after that seemed to weigh heavy on our minds. No one seemed to be very talkative.

The trip seemed to take forever. The steamboat had to make frequent stops along the shore to stock up on wood for the furnaces. With all the troops and supplies on board, and fighting against the current, the steamer used a lot of wood causing the trip to take forever. Dusk turned to dark and we stretched out where we were to make ourselves comfortable throughout the night.

Just as the sun was starting to come up in the east and the light was showing above the bluffs, the boat turned sideways into the current and edged into the eastern bluffs. When we sat up to look around, we could see in the dim that we were moving into a landing at the base of a moderately high bluff that was crowned with the outline of numerous buildings. We had made it to Memphis.

The gangplank was lowered and we lined up to disembark. We jostled our way into line and made our way down the plank, then formed ranks along the landing. When everyone was accounted for we marched off in formation up the bluffs and through the town, that was still pretty much quietly sleeping, and into camp on the eastern side. Roll call was taken again and then we were marched off to our designated area within the camp and dismissed.

We had been assigned a large barracks building that held most of the members of our company. Our squad moved to the opposite wall from where we entered and dropped our gear on the beds we chose and sat down to make ourselves comfortable. Johnny Applebaum spoke up and commented, "I can't believe how prosperous Memphis looks." "Of course, it's prosperous, you dumb German," Otto Kerner said. "With all these troops stationed here and all of the supplies coming and going, everyone in this town is a millionaire, unless you're in the service," he said. I sat there laughing as I listened to them banter back and forth. I don't know why it was that the German soldiers in my squad always called themselves dumb Germans. I expect they had heard that from other people all their lives.

Anyhow, Johnny said, "Well, what I meant was, I thought when we got to Memphis we would find it about like Jackson, nothing but a pile of rubble and mud." Then he looked at me and asked, "Corporal Everett, why do you suppose Memphis hasn't been destroyed?" I hadn't really thought about it. Of course, Johnny was right. There was no sign of destruction or devastation, the buildings seemed to all be intact and I wondered how the Union forces could have taken this town so easily. I just looked at him and said, "How the hell should I know? I just got here myself." Then Johnny called out, "Sergeant Shawnasee, sir!" As I looked around, I spied the sergeant making his way through the barracks, conversing with other squads in the company. The sergeant made his way over to our group and Johnny didn't hesitate to ask him, "Sarge, why do you think Memphis is still standing?" To which the sergeant just smiled and laughed and said, "Well, because the rebels did the smart thing and decided to surrender it without a fight." Then he laughed again and said, "Of course, if they all had good sense, they would just quit now." We all laughed, thinking that was pretty unlikely. But Johnny seemed exceptionally persistent in his desire to get an answer to this question. "No, really, Sarge," he said, "It didn't look like there had been any fighting at all here."

Then, seeing as how Johnny wasn't to be put off, the sergeant became thoughtful and after a few seconds, replied in a serious tone of voice, "Well, maybe after Grant had taken Ft. Henry and Ft. Donaldson and gone down the Tennessee River to Shiloh that essentially split the state in half. And when we finally took Corinth and kept control of the railroad there, well, maybe the rebels decided that any armies in Memphis would be in danger of being surrounded and lost." Then he said, "You know, there was a tremendous battle out on the river between the Union fleet and the Confederate fleet here at Memphis. Several Confederate steamers and other vessels were sunk in the Mississippi not far from the landing. What, with our side controlling the river and having major forces to the east, Memphis just wasn't worth fighting for," he said.

Well, I thought this made perfectly good sense until I took a moment to think about it. Then I said, "Well, you know, Sarge, after we had taken Corinth and then bypassed Vicksburg and crossed over at Grand Gulf and destroyed the railroads at Jackson, why didn't the Confederates just evacuate Vicksburg? I couldn't see any difference." The sergeant thought about this for a moment, got a serious expression on his face and then said, "How the hell should I know?"

One after another, the boys in the squad all broke down in laughter. I think the sergeant had been listening to our entire conversation because his last reply had been a near perfect imitation of my own voice. Vicksburg, which at one time had been a larger, more prosperous city, or at least I had been told that, than Memphis had been reduced to a pile of mud and mostly deserted buildings on a hillside. But Memphis stood there looking majestic and untouched. There was nothing about war that seemed to make any sense.

Our company remained in the barracks for the next several days. Trains came and went. Different regiments of the army marched down to the tracks, loaded up in freight cars, or aboard platform cars, while some even had the luxury of being in regular passenger's coaches as they departed towards the east. It seems our destination was Corinth, Mississippi again. Finally it was our turn. Well, at least we were past the worst of the summer heat and, with all the time we had been in control of Corinth, maybe they had managed to drill enough wells that we would have a plentiful supply of water. I didn't think it could be any worse than what it was when we were there before.

We marched down to the tracks and boarded into a freight car. It seems they packed us in there even tighter than I thought was possible, then they shut the doors, leaving them open about a foot on each side. Otto spoke up and said, "Why did they have to shut the doors? Why couldn't they leave them open so we could get some air?" And Johnny responded quickly, "Well, you dumb German, if they didn't shut them, the way we're packed in here so tight, some people would be falling out."

The engine whistled a couple of times, the cars rattled and jolted

and away we went. I was preparing to settle in for a long trip to Corinth, but it seems that we had barely gotten started when the train began to slow and then came to a stop with a jolt and whistle. We could hear people moving outside and then the doors opened and we were ordered out. I don't think we had even gone 8 or 10 miles. We gathered around along the tracks on the one side of the train and wondered what was happening as the officers came along the line and told us to shuck our packs and drop our rifles here. Then, we were marched east along the tracks towards the head of the train and came to the platform car loaded down with steel rails and railroad ties. We marched up along the side of the platform car and, as soldiers handed ties down to us, we took them on our shoulders and formed into line, then marched off past the head of the train. Sure enough, just beyond the front of the train was a section where it appeared that the rails and ties for at least a mile had been pulled up, burnt and destroyed.

Troops with picks, hammers and shovels were even then beginning to smooth the ground and position the ties. The rebels may have abandoned Memphis, but they hadn't given up on tearing up the tracks. We worked for several hours to repair the section of tracks that had been torn up. We managed to use up all the ties and rails on two platform cars. Then we marched back to pick up our packs and our rifles and some were loaded back into the freight cars. Thankfully now we had a lot more room since we had two empty platform cars that we could occupy. We marched back off towards the head of the train and the squad took its position on the platform car. At last we were off again towards Corinth.

It turned into a bright, hot, sunny late summer's day and I was quite happy that we had been fortunate enough to have an open platform car to ride on. It was a little bit windy, but that made things just all the better, I thought. We sat there towards the center of the platform car, leaning back to back for support, and watched the countryside go by. We talked and joked as we rattled along, but still managed to keep a careful eye out for any sign of Confederate activity. You couldn't see much of the tracks ahead from back here but, whenever we came to a long curve, I looked ahead to see if I could tell if the tracks were still in position.

We approached numerous small rivers or creeks running through rather steep ravines and, as we rattled over the rickety trestle bridges, I kept a close watch out since there was a fear in my heart that some rebels might be ready to detonate a charge to destroy the bridge beneath the wheels of the train. Rumors had been circulating that that had indeed happened more than once. In late afternoon, we pulled up, took on water and wood and were allowed to leave the train to stretch our legs and relieve ourselves. We had munched on rations and water throughout the day and took the time to refill our canteens, then we loaded up and took off again.

As it became dark, I began to regret the decision that we made earlier to ride on the platform car. I wasn't sure just how much further it was to Corinth or what time we would be getting in there. The idea of sleeping on an open platform car as it rolled along the tracks in the dark was not very reassuring. I don't think it was much after midnight, if even that, when we came into Corinth, slowed, rattled and jerked to a stop and disembarked. We formed up, marched off and were shown where to bed down in a row of tents not far from the tracks. We were back in Corinth. Of course, it was much too dark to see, but I scanned in all directions anyhow. I had the feeling that nothing had changed.

We were shown to our tents and we made ourselves comfortable, or at least as comfortable as nine men in a tent can be. I was sure it was well past midnight and expected in another four or five hours we would be bugled awake. We made our beds quickly and lay down to sleep. I had no sooner lain down, than I had fallen asleep, but it was a rather fitful, restless sleep. I awakened well before the bugle, coming out of a fearful deep sleep. I had been dreaming that I had been killed in battle and been sentenced to hell and that's why I was back here in Corinth. I rolled over, and tried to go back to sleep. It couldn't be as bad as I remembered.

We had endured an entire summer here a year ago. Every day seemed to have been the same. We suffered from thirst due to the lack of water in the area. The water we had was nasty, foul and disgusting to taste. Half the troops were sick with dysentery, cramps and diarrhea and it seemed like the other half of the troops were sick with fevers that I think were due to the clouds of mosquitoes that seemed to infest the area during all times, except for the very heat of the day. During the heat of the day, the biting flies were at their worst, that and the chiggers that were invisible as they crawled up your legs, under your stockings and bit. In fact, I thought I could feel chiggers biting away at my ankles already. Surely we wouldn't be here too long this time.

We had arrived in Corinth somewhere around the first of October. We spent the next several days which passed slowly in marching and drilling around camp. Trains came and went on a daily basis and gradually the number of troops assembled in Corinth increased to the point where the camps were crowded and bustling with activity. Then one morning we formed up and marched out toward Iuka Springs, Mississippi.

Parties of troops had been working on the railroad throughout the last week and had repaired it as far as Iuka Springs. We marched throughout the day and came into camp about halfway to Iuka. The weather was still warm, but nowhere near as hot as it could get in Mississippi in the middle of the summer. The nights were actually quite pleasant.

We went into camp that night and merely placed our groundsheets along the side of the road and slept on our haversacks. At that time of the year, for whatever reason, the mosquitoes and chiggers were not very abundant. All in all, it was a pleasant night.

The following morning we were up early and continued our march to Iuka and I found it to be a delightful little town. The battle that had been fought here the previous year had been outside of town somewhere to the south and west. I was told that we had marched right past the battlefield, but was surprised to see that there really wasn't any trace of it after only a year's time. We were lucky enough to be granted a rather extended stay in Iuka.

Rumors seemed to circulate throughout the company that Sherman had been ordered to repair the railroad all the way from Corinth to Chattanooga. That was the name that had come up several times in the last week. The rumor was spreading throughout the troops that a tremendous battle had been fought there a month or so ago and that the Union army had been disastrously defeated. They had fallen back from Chickamauga and were now being besieged in Chattanooga which was a town on the south bank of the Tennessee River. The story circulating at the time was that Grant had been dispatched to Chattanooga to try to salvage the situation and that Sherman was attempting to rebuild the railroad to bring in enough supplies for Grant to break the siege.

I wondered myself why it was necessary to rebuild the railroad all the way to Chattanooga. It was on the banks of the Tennessee River and I didn't understand why it couldn't be supplied by steamboat. But none of the boys in the company knew. Certainly we were not privy to the intelligence and information that the officers had, however it seemed that they had no desire to keep us informed either. We didn't know if there were troops out ahead of us working daily on the railroad or not, but I reasoned to myself that there wasn't enough room at the head of the tracks for all of us to be up there working, so they were just rotating us through, maybe a regiment at a time.

For now we were in Iuka Springs and were allowed time to truly enjoy the situation. Iuka was a fine little town. It had a number of mineral springs, both hot and cold. Before the war, it seems that wealthy planters and business men and farmers had come from miles around to take the mineral baths and relax. There were a number of fine hotels, restaurants and gift shops. The houses all seemed to be well cared for, most of them having white picket fences around the small yards which were planted with vines and shrubbery and neatly cared for. Even though it was late in the year, somewhere around the middle of October, there were a number of plants that I didn't know the name of that were still in bloom. It seemed like the war was a thousand miles away.

We had just received a couple of months' back pay and the men in the squad were all eager to spend it as rapidly as possible. Ordinarily that would have meant a few nights of riotous debauchery and drunkenness. It may have been due to the charming, rather sophisticated environment of the town itself, or due to the fact that shortly after our arrival a series of prayer and revival meetings broke out in the town. I don't know whether this was arranged by the officers of the 15th Corp to keep us in line, or whether it was a sudden inspiration on the part of the local politicians and business leaders. Whoever was responsible, they succeeded admirably. I had thought that with this many troops in town, it wouldn't take long for the troops to wantonly destroy it with their drunken celebrations. The town seemed peaceful and the air of Christian rejoicing seemed to keep the troops in line.

I had my uniform cleaned and pressed, went to the mineral hot springs myself, enjoyed some delicious food in a nice restaurant and only got marginally drunk on a couple of occasions. I think Frank Martin was the only man in the squad who was drunk on a daily basis. When he wasn't drunk, he was always bragging about his adventures with the loose women of the town. If there were bordellos of loose women in this town, you could count on Frank to know where they were.

By the time we were ordered to march out and move forward, Frank was already trying to borrow money from the other boys in the squad. I couldn't imagine how he could have spent two months' pay so quickly. I was almost reluctant to move on when the orders finally came.

We marched out one lovely morning, just as it was starting to get light. The sun was coming up in the east and the whole eastern horizon had a light purple glow that quickly changed to pink and then orange and yellow. The land was heavily wooded but relatively flat. It was easy marching and, as the weather was cool, was almost enjoyable. We were relaxed and almost nonchalant. We knew there were a considerable number of troops further ahead along the railroad and were not expecting any surprises from the Confederates. We marched a fair distance and went into camp unusually early that afternoon. As we were making camp, we heard gunfire in the distance. There was only a brief flurry of gunshots and then it was all quiet again.

Over the next few days we advanced rather leisurely towards the east. We heard skirmishing in the distance on nearly a daily basis now, but it still seemed as if the war was a long way off. Gradually the terrain changed. We had been marching on fairly flat level ground, but then the ground seemed to drop off steeply and quickly in all directions. We topped out on a rise and looked out over a deep wide valley. It seemed like the ground gave way in a series of broad steppes.

In the distance below in the valley, a stream could be seen as it cascaded down from higher ground in the south and broadened as it moved to the north. The ground seemed much more hilly and uneven in the north as we watched the stream broaden as it disappeared into the distance. We were moving along a road at that time. The railroad was off to the south and could not be seen from where we were. From where we stood looking down over the valley, everything seemed quiet and peaceful. Below us there was a large pine forest which, as we looked down towards the valley beneath, gave way to brown leaved oak trees then yellow leaved chestnut trees and finally greenish sycamore trees along the banks of the stream. There was only an occasional cleared space that indicated human habitation and the farmer with a small homestead.

We moved down the road towards the southeast to the bottom of the valley that was several hundred yards wide at this point. Here, most of the land had been cleared and the pastures were still green and thick. We moved across the bottom of the valley, crossed the stream and, moving still to the southeast, wound our way up the eastern escarpment. Just exactly when we moved into Alabama, I really couldn't say. There was nothing to mark the border.

We marched a fair distance this day. I actually hated to leave the beauty of the valley behind. As we marched further east, the ground seemed to become flat and slightly more open. We were back amongst mainly scattered pine trees. As the sun started to settle in the west and the sky to darken, gunfire and even artillery sounded towards the east. We had traveled probably 14 to 15 miles this day, the most we had marched at one time for at least a week. We were in Alabama. I was uncertain how far we still were from Chattanooga, but it seemed that the Confederates had decided to oppose our further movements. As we went into camp that night, we were unsure what the following day would bring.

CHAPTER TWELVE

We had a restless night. As we lay on the ground with our blankets and ponchos covering us, we found it hard to sleep. I lay there with Johnny Applebaum on one side and Frank Martin on the other. Johnny, as usual, was quite wound up and talkative. "What do you think of that?" he said. "They finally realized what they have in General Sherman. They have given him command of his own army. We're now part of the army of the Tennessee. General Sherman is now in command of the 15th, 16th and 17th Army Corp, and General Grant has been named commander of the army of the west. He won't have to worry about General Halleck always trying to demote him or court martial him."

"Yea," I said. "Now that Grant's in command, I expect we'll be seeing some real fighting soon instead of just building and protecting this railroad. I'm getting tired of this. It seems we no sooner get the tracks repaired, and then the Confederates tear them up again". "Haven't you boys been listening?" said Frank Martin. Frank being several years our senior always tended to call us boys, even though technically I was his superior beings how I was a corporal and he was still a private. "We're on our way to Chattanooga," he said. "Well, I had known we were headed towards Chattanooga, but I thought we were principally involved in trying to get the railroad established to link up with Chattanooga."

Frank then went on to say that he heard that we were marching directly to Chattanooga and railroad be damned. I thought for a few moments then, without speaking, that if that were the case, we would surely be involved in fighting soon enough. Then Johnny said, "What do you think we're going to do once we get to Chattanooga?" We all knew that the Union had a strong force in Chattanooga and were presently being besieged in the town by the Confederates. The stories made it sound like Vicksburg in reverse.

"Well, the first thing I'm going to do when we get there is go pay a visit to the ladies," said Frank Martin. I laughed and said, "That's all you ever think about, isn't it?" Frank said, "Damn right, what else is there?" I laughed and said, "Well there's always whiskey. Isn't that what you always talk about, whiskey and women?" Frank just laughed and said, "You're right, but you don't understand. The women in Chattanooga are the best along the rivers."

It seems that Frank had worked for several years on the river. He had been down the Mississippi to New Orleans and back several times and had been back and forth on the Tennessee. "Yea," he said, "The ladies of New Orleans don't even compare to the ones in Chattanooga. They have some fine establishments just right along the banks of the Tennessee. From what I have heard, the troops had been making good use of them, too. I heard that half the troops in Chattanooga are suffering from the pox. It seems General Rosecrans passed an order and placed the establishments off limits to the troops. I think they just want to keep them for the officers." "What are you talking about?" I said. "What's this pox?" Then he went on to explain that there were a number of diseases that could be caught from working women."

I began to feel distinctly uneasy. I hadn't been aware of this when we had visited the ladies in Vicksburg. I was distinctly worried and asked him, "How do you know if you've got this pox?" He just laughed and said, "Believe me, if you've got it, you'll know it." I asked him, "Well, have you ever had it?" He just laughed and said, "Hell no, my dad taught him to take better care of my equipment than that." Now, my curiosity was definitely aroused. I said, "What do you mean, take care of your equipment?"

Frank went on to explain, "Well, before you go visit the ladies, you should drink at least a couple of pints of beer. Make sure your bladder is nearly bursting before you entertain the ladies. That way, as soon as you're done, you can urinate and wash your plumbing out. Then, always have a bottle of whiskey and wash the outside off. That way, you won't catch anything. I have been doing that all of my life and I have never come down with anything. What, didn't your father ever teach you anything?"

I almost felt like laughing. The thought of having any such discussions at home was quite hilarious. I'm not sure my father even knew anything about such ladies as Frank Martin preferred to visit, although thinking about it, I wondered about my grandfather. He had been up and down the rivers on keelboats to Natchez and New Orleans. He had also served with Andy Jackson in the Creek Indian wars and at the Battle of New Orleans. I almost laughed to think of my grandfather in some New Orleans bordello. I could remember my grandfather talking about how he knew Andy Jackson personally and I briefly imagined him and General Jackson making the rounds of the establishments down along the Mississippi. I thought it was quite funny.

Then I asked Frank, "Well, if the establishments in Chattanooga are off limits, how are you ever going to get in?" He just laughed and said, "I would like to see them try to keep me out." It's all Frank ever thought about and all he ever talked about, whiskey and women. Well, it was better than thinking about bullets and bombs, I thought.

As I fell asleep, I was thinking with pride that we were now part of the army of the Tennessee with General Sherman as the commanding officer. I seemed rather proud of the fact that we were in the 15th Corp, 1st Division, 1st Brigade, and our old commanding general was now in charge of the whole army of the western theater. It was something to be proud of.

It seems like we had no sooner fallen asleep, than we were being roused up. I didn't think it could be much beyond midnight. We rolled our blankets and groundsheets and poncho up and packed our bags. It was late October and the weather was fairly cool, especially in the middle of the night. I put on my greatcoat and placed my revolver in my belt and slipped the other in the pocket of the greatcoat.

It took a couple of hours to get the army ready to move, but it was still pitch black when we moved out. We had the cavalry screen in front and it wasn't long before they had discovered the rebel pickets. There were intermittent volleys of musket fire and on occasion even artillery joined in. Our brigade was in the lead as the 1st Division made its way towards Tuscumbia, Alabama.

We marched in column. The cavalry was in front and the sounds of near constant skirmishing kept us on our toes. Further out ahead of the column, regiments had been ordered into line both north and south of the road. They sent skirmishers out and we moved carefully forward. We seemed to make good time for several hours and I expect we covered five to six miles before the column ground to a halt. It seemed that the rebels had decided to make a stand up ahead. The regiments at the head of the column turned off to the left and formed into line facing east. We marched off the road to the right and formed into line.

As we moved away from the road along the railroad, we came into a stand of trees. The pine trees were rather sparse and widely separate and my squad moved forward as a skirmish line. Suddenly artillery sounded from both sides. The firing was hot and furious for a while. It was soon followed by volley after volley of musketry. We were moving through the woods carefully. We resorted to our usual skirmishing formation. Johnny and I worked as a team, as did all the rest of the men in the squad. I would keep him covered as he moved forward behind a tree, and then he would cover me as I moved forward in turn keeping a careful eye out for any sign of rebel forces directly in front.

As we moved forward, the pine trees thinned. Looking off to the north, we could see the Confederate positions. They had artillery positioned on the edges of a small cemetery. There were Confederate infantry in the protection of the cemetery itself, hiding behind tombstones and using the split rail fence around the cemetery as cover. Our infantry was advancing along the road directly on them. We took position on the edge of the woods and opened fire on the Confederates from our positions.

I estimate that we were probably still 300 yards from the Confederate artillery as they straddled the main road. It was long-range shooting, but it was worth it, even if it only distracted them for a few minutes as they attempted to reload their cannon. We fired volley after volley at them. I'm sure I saw more than one gunner go down. The rest of the regiment in line began making their way forward around us. It was too much for the Confederates as they promptly began bringing up their horse teams to hook the cannon up to withdraw. As the cannon rattled off down the road, the Confederate infantry began a fairly abrupt withdrawal also.

We let out a loud cheer, seeing them withdraw and we stood in line watching them go. They moved quickly across some low ground, and across a small creek, but I was rather dismayed as it seemed that the teams of artillery moved left and right of the road and reestablished another position on higher ground not much more than a mile from where they had been. Their infantry continued down the road and spread to left and right in the fields along the road on the high ground and in the low ground between the two ridge lines. We had been on a slight elevation to the west and now they were facing us on a slight elevation to the east with low swampy ground intervening.

We were on the edge of the woods and there were a few scattered thickets of wood and brush in the valley between us. The Confederates had no sooner taken up their position, and then they began firing artillery across at us again. I was grateful that we were further south along the line because it seemed that they concentrated their fire on the troops to the immediate right and left of the road as we began advancing again.

We moved out in skirmish formation once more. There weren't many trees to take advantage of as we moved forward. As we moved, we tried to stay to the low ground. The fields were fairly empty, but there were low places that appeared to have been drainage ditches dug to allow excess water to funnel off into the creek that ran north and south across the middle of the valley. Bending over at the waist with my hands barely above the ground, we moved forward, pausing occasionally to take shots whenever we saw Confederate skirmishes at our front. We made our way down the drainage ditch to the creek which had two to three feet of water in it and splashed across to the eastern bank and crawled to the top, careful to keep our heads down. Probably a hundred yards further across the valley was a line of Confederates sheltering in a shallow ditch facing us. We let loose a volley and then slid back down the banks of the creek as we reloaded. The creek soon filled up with our infantry as we continued to skirmish with the Confederate line.

Most of the brigade was now in position to the left and right of our squad and, as they began to slither to the top of the banks, I noticed that the Confederate line began to withdraw en masse. There were five pieces of Confederate artillery on the high ground opposite us. They had been posted firing mainly down the road at our troops and had been keeping up a brisk fire. As the Confederate line from the bottom of the valley began moving towards them, they limbered up once again and retreated back down the road.

Once the artillery had left the top of the hill, our lines moved forward fairly rapidly and the Confederate infantry at our front seemed to melt away. We moved forward briskly now. My squad moved out in skirmish formation. Once again, we began entering woods at the bottom of the ridge on which the Confederates had been. I was feeling much more comfortable now. Slipping from tree to tree, we moved forward. I was beginning to think that there were no Confederates in our immediate front. I thought maybe they had had enough and had decided to retreat all the way back to Tuscumbia.

We moved forward for another two to three miles without even seeing any Confederate skirmishers. We crossed the ridge on which they had taken momentary pause and through a moderately thick stand of fir along the top of the ridge and moved through this from tree to tree. As we came to the opposite side of the ridge, the trees began to thin and, as we looked down the ridge, we saw another fairly open valley and there upon a hill which seemed to project forward of the ridgeline on the opposite site of the valley, the Confederate artillery had once again formed up. The artillery was north of the road as it passed through a gap in the ridgeline. I suppose they were still a mile or so distant, but they were quite clearly visible. As I looked along the ridge to the east on the opposite side of the valley, you could see Confederate infantry moving south, facing across towards us.

My squad and I stood there watching them as the Union line came up behind us. We stood there watching the Confederates form line and make their dispositions as the rest of the brigade and the entire division came up behind us. It looked like they were planning to make a stiff resistance at this point and we merely watched and waited as our own forces came up around us.

The Confederates were occupying some high ground across the valley, positioned to our northwest. Directly to the east of us was a small hill that seemed to extend towards the northwest and approached closer to the Confederate positions on the main ridge. There was what appeared to be a valley centered between this small hill and the hill on which the Confederate troops were taking up their position. Directly east of us, the open meadow extended further to the south.

While I stood there watching the Confederates across to the northwest, orders were received for us to cross the open valley directly to our east, and to take up position on that hill on the other side of the valley. The two regiments that were further south of us began crossing the valley and I watched, expecting them to come under fire from the artillery in the Confederate positions. They made it halfway across the valley without receiving any hostile fire. It was only as they approached the southern flank of the hill to the east that the Confederates' artillery opened up. There were only a couple of volleys of long-range artillery fire until the troops were passing into the safety of the hill that was partially obscuring them from the Confederate direct line of sight. By that time, we had been ordered across.

We started rather hesitantly at first, and then, when we neared the vicinity where the Confederates had opened fire on the first two regiments, we quickened our pace and covered it nearly at a run. As we were moving into the safely of the trees on the lower edges of the north slope, a faint ringing of bugles in the distance sounded. This was then followed by rousing cheers of Confederate voices and a thunder of hoofs as what I estimated to be an entire regiment of Confederate cavalry charged out of the safety of the woods on the hillside to the northwest and across the narrow valley towards the southern part of the hill that we were just now beginning to ascend.

The first two regiments that had partially descended the smaller hill that we were presently climbing opened up with volley after volley of musketry fire at the Confederates as they stormed across the narrow valley between them. Our artillery from behind to the west opened fire at long-range at them. It was a glorious spectacle to behold. The Confederate cavalry, in line at the start, had seemed extremely organized. They came out in column, and then spread left and right across the field and proceeded at a walk, and then a trot, and then a gallop. By the time they were halfway across the narrow valley; their lines had been devastated by volley after volley of musketry and artillery shot. Still, they came on.

There was one group towards the center that seemed to gradually break away from the rest of the Confederate line. We must have been a thousand yards from them at that point. It was much too far to attempt a shot. I simply watched as an officer in a splendid uniform with a big feather plum in his hat seemed to emerge from the Confederate lines. I watched in amazement, expecting him to pull up and turn around, as he was creating some space between the rest of his troops, but still he came on. Then suddenly his horse faltered, stumbled, and went down pitching him headlong over his neck. He landed hard, but rose and came up on his feet seeming to shake himself to regain his senses. Just as he started to straighten up to stand erect, he suddenly shuddered, spun and crumpled to the ground.

As I watched, suspensefully, a few troopers came up on each side and dismounted and, between them, managed to hoist him up on the back of one of the horses and then, with him lying across the saddle, they turned and headed back towards the Confederate hill with two troopers running on each side of the horse, holding onto the saddle and steadying him in position. All firing seemed to cease, both from the Union and Confederate forces as they made their way across the valley and rounded the eastern end of the hill where the Confederates were positioned.

I could only admire their courage, but was rather skeptical of their thinking. They had launched this spectacular charge with probably no more than two hundred and fifty men. While on our side on the hill below me, there must have been at least several hundred Union infantry. Our troops were on the edge of the woods on the upper and lower slopes of the hill. They had protection from the trees and were able to stand on the ground and fire volley after volley at the Confederates who were attempting to cross, probably seven to eight hundred yards of open ground. Who knows what they could have been thinking.

The rest of my regiment came up around me and we made our way to the top of the hill to join the first two regiments who were by then starting to dig in and fortify their positions. They were further to the east on the top of the hill and even extended somewhat to the south where the hill turned sharply before opening into a shallow valley with the headwaters of a creek. As our regiment dug in and fortified their position on the northwestern slopes, I made my way across the top of the small hill and could see how this hill overlooked the shallow creek at the southern edge of the hill where it turned sharply to the west.

The rest of our brigade lingered behind in the valley and took refuge in a ravine that ran to the south and which was below in the field which we had crossed. As I wandered around through the woods on the top of the small hill where we were then making our fortifications, it was possible to see in the distance two or three miles away a small town that I knew to be Tuscumbia, Alabama. Immediately east of our hill was a creek. Immediately north was a much larger hill that was heavily wooded with the eastern side of the hill opening down on the creek that seemed to be much wider there.

I knew that in the distance to the north lay the Tennessee River. The rest of our division was scattered out in a rather circular fashion, going back to the hill to the west where we had descended and then across the valley where the railroad tracks and the road ran and extended further to the north into the hills on that side of the railroad. I made my way back to where our fortifications were being erected and located my squad. It was late in the afternoon and I felt it was unlikely that we would attempt any further advancement that afternoon. We continued to scratch out a trench along the slope of the hill and dragged down logs to form a small barricade in front, and then we settled down for the night.

It was a rather uneasy night. The Confederate artillery continued firing, it seemed to me randomly, in all directions, but thankfully most of the fire was directed to our west to where the bulk of the division was then sheltering along the railroad and along the wooded hillside that we had abandoned early that afternoon. Only an occasional barrage came directly south at our fortifications. I was thinking that in the morning we would have a major battle trying to force the Confederates off their wooded hillside.

Morning came and at first light, I was watching nervously off to the north, expecting that at any time orders would be given for us to advance across the opening to attack the Confederate positions. But thankfully that order never came. Suddenly off to the west a tremendous artillery barrage sounded. I could tell by the deep throated booming rumble of the guns and the great clouds of black powder smoke that darkened our line, that during the night we had brought up some mighty big guns. I watched the Confederate positions on the hill to the north as they went up in smoke, dirt and debris. The Confederates answered with a barrage of their own, but it merely served to plow dirt in the valley between us. I knew from prior experience that the most common cannon in the Confederate artillery were twelve pound Napoleons. They were smooth bore cannons. They were lacking in range. I speculated that we must be firing twenty pound rifled parrot guns at the Confederate positions and the best they could do was to fire back with their twelve pound Napoleons. It was obvious that we had the range on them and their position was untenable.

It didn't take them long to realize it either. Soon we could see what was left of the Confederate artillery moving across the road to the east and headed towards Tuscumbia. Our artillery left off firing at them and shortly after the Confederates had disappeared from sight, we were given the order to advance. The regiments that had been posted to our right on the hill, I found out last night were the 3rd and 27th Missouri Regiments.

We moved down the hill to the north and west, still in line, and moved towards the road. As we advanced, I carefully watched for where I had seen the Confederate cavalry officer go down the evening before. I had it in mind to see if his cavalry saber was lying on the ground next to where he had gone down. I thought that it would make an excellent souvenir for Sergeant Shawnasee. I spied the horse from a hundred yards away and carefully angled my approach so that we would walk by it. I didn't want to attract any attention to myself. The ground where the horse had gone down was fairly flat and the grass had been grazed over and was fairly short. I was rather disappointed in that I had passed by the horse and hadn't noticed any shiny metal to indicate where his saber may have fallen. Just as I passed by the head of the horse, right by its left ear as it lay on the ground, I spied the handle of a small revolver. I picked it up quickly and stuffed it in my belt. Then, on impulse, I reached down and grabbed a leather saddlebag that was positioned just in front of the saddle on the withers of the horse. Only one side of the bag was showing, the other was still under the horse, but I tugged it free and threw it over my shoulder as I went by. Not that I was planning on stealing any money or valuables that might be in it, I was only optimistic that the pouch might contain ammunition for the revolver as well as percussion caps and a cleaning kit. It never hurt to have an extra gun or two.

We made our way to the road that ran along the railroad tracks, formed up into column and continued our march towards Tuscumbia. We marched into town without opposition. I expected the rebel forces that we skirmished with for the preceding two days would have barricaded the streets and made a fight of it to protect the town, but it seemed that they had spent the night destroying the railroad in town, while the town itself was undamaged. It was a fine village that reminded me a lot of Iuka

Springs, but there must not have been any hot springs in the vicinity because it was lacking in fancy hotels and spas. I had just enough time to take a quick look at the town as we marched quickly through to the eastern periphery before we were ordered to start fortifying our positions where we were. General Sherman wasn't taking any chances on a night attack, we would have to wait till tomorrow to explore.

CHAPTER THIRTEEN

Tuscumbia was a well kept and rather prosperous appearing little hamlet that looked like it might escape the true ravages of war. After having dug trenches and thrown up some fortifications, we were allowed time for rest while still keeping a watchful eye for any Confederates lingering in the vicinity. Then we settled down as we waited for the night.

Later that evening, we were allowed to go regiment by regiment to the town where the cooks had prepared hot meals for the troops. We went through the line and got our tin plates filled with potatoes, beef and beans and bread. We found places to sit on the boardwalks surrounding the streets and ate a hot meal. It was surprising that, with all the troops in the vicinity and the occupants of the town which must have numbered at least a thousand, how quiet the place could be.

The curtains were drawn in all the stores and homes, but I could still feel an uncanny sensation as I imagined we were constantly being spied upon by the inhabitants. We were given just enough time to finish our meal, wash our utensils off in the barrels of water set along the street and then were directed back to our place in the fortifications. At that time of year it was surprisingly dark, I think, probably by no more than 5 o'clock. I rolled up on my groundsheet under my blankets and was soon asleep for the night.

I had anticipated that in the morning we would be off following after the Confederates that we had been battling for the last two days. They had last been seen retreating towards the east and I knew from rumors that

Chattanooga lay to the east along the Tennessee River. For the last week, we had been marching on the south side of the Tennessee River and on occasion had been able to catch glimpses of the river in the distance when we had been passing along the top of a ridge and been able to look to the north down a ravine or valley into the distance. So, I was rather surprised that, after we were bugled into awareness, we didn't pack up and move off at once.

We lingered in Tuscumbia and had another hot meal. No one seemed to be in a hurry. After breakfast, I returned to our position along the eastern limits of Tuscumbia and sat down to relax; leaning back against the shelter I had thrown up around my rifle pit. The rest of the squad gathered around, sat down to relax and awaited orders.

I hadn't had a chance to inspect my booty from the fallen Confederate cavalry officer as of yet. I found the revolver to be most interesting. Most of the officers and a good percentage of the sergeants even, carried revolvers of some sort. Most preferred a Colt or a Remington; however, I knew there were a multitude of revolvers that were all very similar in function. The one that I had retrieved from the battlefield looked like a small Colt and, indeed, when I pulled it from my belt for further examination, distinctly etched into the top of the barrel were the words 'Address: Colonel Sam Colt, New York, US America.' I turned the revolver from side-to-side and back and forth, inspecting it. I clicked the hammer back and forth carefully and, as I rotated the cylinder, I noted that there were still two balls left unfired. I let the hammer down carefully so as not to discharge the weapon on a loaded cylinder.

I found the gun fascinating, mainly because of its small size. The barrel was much shorter than any I had seen before. I think it was probably less than half the length of the usual barrel. The cylinder had shallow grooves cut in the side that went over half the distance of the length of the cylinder. It looked a lot like the Colt Navy revolvers that I had seen officers carrying except for its size.

I passed it around amongst the men in the squad who were all fascinated by it. I made sure to point out to them that it was still loaded and they should take care in handling it. As they passed it back and forth, inspecting it, Christian happened to mention that it only had five cylinders. I hadn't noticed that myself when I had rotated it through, but indeed that was true.

After the gun had made its way around amongst the boys and had come back to me, I inspected it further and decided that I should probably clean the weapon as it had obviously been fired at least three times in the last engagement. It had a screw and wedge on the left side of the revolver and I knew that it could be broken apart by removing these; however, I didn't have a screwdriver to fit. On sudden inspiration, I remembered the small set of saddlebags that I had retrieved. It seemed logical to me that the Confederate officer would have kept his powder and balls in the saddlebags; maybe he had a cleaning kit also.

I pulled the saddlebags out from under my blankets where I had been leaning back against them and opened them up to inspect the contents. The saddlebags, at first glance, appeared to be symmetrical; however, I found that that wasn't the case as I opened them up. As I lifted the flap over the first saddlebag, I found that it was divided into two compartments. Each compartment was lined with red velvet material. In the upper compartment was an identical revolver to the one that was presently lying in my lap. Even the walnut grips appeared to have been made from the same piece of wood as they each had a similar dark, almost black reddish hued tint. I thought the revolvers may have been purchased as a complete set. I lifted the tray that had contained the revolver from the saddlebag thereby exposing the second compartment.

In the second compartment was a small brass flask of gunpowder. This compartment was divided in half with the flask of gunpowder being in one chamber and the second compartment containing the lead balls and percussion caps. The lead balls were in a small velvet drawstring pouch, the percussion caps being in a small tin. This compartment had a rectangular sleeve that had tabs in front and back that could be grasped to lift it out of its place in the saddlebag. Beneath it was another compartment. In it was a tin of circular wads that were impregnated with wax that I knew were used to seal the chambers to prevent cross firing. There was another small drawstring velvet bag to hold more bullets also.

I placed the container with the wads and the bullets back in position in the bottom of the compartment, then slipped the tray with the pouch of bullets and percussion caps back on top and replaced the tray that had held the revolver. Finally I tied down the flap on the saddlebag.

The saddlebag on the opposite side was different. When I lifted the flap up on it, I found that it likewise had two compartments, but these were one on top of the other with the front of the saddlebag being divided horizontally in half. Each compartment was able to be accessed by flipping the front of the saddlebag down and then a tray could be pulled forward, exposing the contents.

In the bottom compartment was a complete line of cleaning and lubricating solutions in stoppered glass bottles. The upper compartment contained the tools for the care of the revolvers. There were powder measures, cappers, screwdrivers and tiny ramrods. There were also brass bristle bore cleaners and a small hammer with a hard rubber tip.

I slid the trays that held the cleaning instruments and the cleaning and lubricating solutions out to inspect them further and, as I did so, I found folded behind them a quantity of bills in both Confederate and Union currency. I immediately passed this over to my right to Johnny Applebaum and told him to distribute it amongst the men. Confiscating a Confederate's weapons for my own use was one thing, but taking the money felt too much like stealing. Besides, all the boys had noticed me when I found it. The only one who made any comment on the money was Frank Martin. He said, "You know what this means, don't you, Boy? I'm going to buy you a night on the town with the ladies in Chattanooga. In fact," he said, "I think I have got enough money here to buy you two women." I had never bothered to count the money, but at first glance it appeared that he was probably right, but then I wondered if they would take Confederate money now that the Union controlled the town. Well, who knew? Maybe the Confederate troops soon would be taking it back.

We still hadn't received any word as to when we would be packing up and leaving, so I decided I had time to at least give the guns a quick cleaning. I removed the screw and manipulated the wedge out and the gun broke in half for easy cleaning. I pulled the cylinder off and carefully washed the three cylinders out so that I didn't get any water in the two that were still unfired. Then, I cleaned them out with the cleaning solution, let it evaporate and dry, and then swabbed the barrels out again and carefully reassembled the revolver and reloaded the one cylinder, leaving one empty under the hammer. This was the first time I had taken apart and cleaned and reloaded a Colt revolver.

I could see why my father had preferred the Remington because, in an emergency, the cylinders could be interchanged with just a flick of a lever. Taking out a screw and a wedge and then reassembling was rather tricky, especially if you were in a hurry and it did require having the proper screwdriver and hammers for reassembly. But I was quite proud to have this matched set of Colts. I couldn't wait to get a chance to fire them.

I just finished reassembling the Colt and was still listening to Frank Martin describing the Chattanooga brothels to the rest of the boys when Sergeant Shawnasee passed by. He took one look at the new weapons I had acquired and said, "What do you have there, Son?" I held it out for his quick inspection and was delighted by the keen interest he took. It's hard to believe that men can find a weapon of destruction to be a thing of beauty, but indeed he and I both agreed that these were just that, things of beauty.

I offered to give him one, but was quite relieved when he turned it down. He patted the butt of my father's Henry as it hung down suspended from his left shoulder by its sling. He laughed and said, "I think the seventeen shots in this should be enough." Then, I decided to change the subject. I said, "Sergeant, Sir? When will we be moving out?" He just laughed and replied, "I'm not sure we're going to be going anywhere today." Then he said, "Even as we sit here talking, some of the troops have gone out to the east tearing up all the track as far as they can and we're tearing up the track to the west behind us." Now, I was really confused. I said, "I thought that we were supposed to repair the track all the way from Corinth to Chattanooga. We have been building bridges, laying rail and erecting fortifications to defend the rail all the time we've been moving on from Memphis. Now, we're going to go back and tear it up?"

The sergeant just laughed and said that, from his information, the decision had been made to run the rail straight north from some rail station to the west and to connect to a rail on the other side of the Tennessee River. We were now to destroy the entire railroad south of the Tennessee River so that the Confederates couldn't use it. It seemed that headquarters had discovered a real urgency for us to get to Chattanooga. He said, "You had better rest up boys, because in the morning we're in for a hard march."

I took the time to clean my boots, then oil them and wax them down good and clean my uniform. I always took care to make sure that my uniform was kept patched and repaired and my equipment oiled and waxed. I think that I was the only man in my squad who paid any attention to anything other than his weapon. Most of the men had already disposed of their spare uniforms, preferring not to carry any extra weight. They seldom brushed or made any attempt to clean or repair the clothes they wore and certainly never bothered to wax their boots. I think they anticipated that, with winter soon approaching, they would be issued new uniforms and new boots. Indeed, despite all the meticulous care I had bestowed on my own uniform and boots, they were becoming rather shabby appearing and I wasn't sure they would offer much protection from cold, wet and damp come winter anyhow. But, nevertheless, I had time on-hand, so I decided to spend it in this rather forlorn endeavor to maintain my appearance.

It was quite an uneventful and pleasant day. Apparently the Confederates had moved clear out of the area because I didn't hear even a stray shot to indicate any hostilities. Looking around in all directions, the only obvious sign that there was a war going on were the big clouds of black smoke that were seen in the distance east and west of town. I knew that indicated that ties were being burnt and that rails were being bent, but if you hadn't known better, you might have supposed that it was merely a farmer clearing fields and burning brush. The day did pass too quickly. We had another hot meal prepared that evening and hit the blankets just after dark.

The following day, we were up early and were amongst the last of the troops to leave to Tuscumbia, Alabama. We were marching west along the road, following the rail tracks that apparently the rest of our division had spent the previous day destroying. It seems that their curiosity had gotten the better of them because the Confederate cavalry were again following us fairly closely.

Throughout the day they would make sudden charges on us from wooded positions where they had remained undetected until we were quite close. They would charge forward, fire off a volley, and then disappear just as quickly. We took to carrying our rifles carefully, ready to bring them to shoulder at the first sound of any ruckus. We marched fairly leisurely. I suppose we were marching only as fast as the troops up ahead could tear up the ties and bend the rails.

At night, we camped along the road. We kept our weapons to hand. The second night of our march back towards Iuka, we were attacked in the dead of night by a strong Confederate cavalry force. We could see flashes of gunfire in the night and could hear horses and men rushing through the darkness. I hesitated to fire in return because it was too dark to see more than a few yards and I feared firing into our own troops. I don't think that others were as careful as I was because several sharp volleys blasted out from our positions up and down the road. Possibly the Confederates were a lot closer to them there than they were to us, or maybe they were just shooting each other.

Despite all the turmoil, confusion and firing, it was surprising to learn the next day that only a single man had been killed and a few others wounded. I thought the Confederates may have just decided not to let us get any rest that night. A day or so later we turned north and moved down the hills and into a short valley that led to the Tennessee River. We moved down to the river and, even though it was becoming dusk and soon would be pitch black in the bottoms along the river, we began crossing.

It took most of the night to get the whole division across the river with the wagons and artillery batteries going first. We were amongst the last to cross the Tennessee. We spent what was left of the night on the northern banks of the Tennessee and were up early the next day which soon turned blistering hot and extremely dry. I had hoped that the Confederates would have stayed on the south side of the river, but it seemed they were determined to follow us as they constantly made rushes upon our columns as we marched along and at one point even managed to set fire to some of the wagons following us.

The next day was surprisingly cold. It's hard to believe how the weather can change so much overnight. It blew up quite a storm and rained all day and, with the high winds and the cold, it was quite miserable. The roads turned to a quagmire of mud that was up over the tops of our boots as we slogged along through the wind and rain. We made camp that night and spent a miserable time in the rain and mud sleeping along the road.

We were up early in the dark and marching again, it seemed, before we had even gotten a chance to fall asleep. I suppose that it was just as well to be marching in the mud and rain as trying to sleep in it. The rain seemed to dissipate about sunup, but it left the valley shrouded in a thick heavy fog that took nearly until noon before it could burn off.

In the middle of the afternoon we passed through the small town of Florence, Alabama. It was nearly directly across the Tennessee River from Tuscumbia, Alabama. As we recognized the place where we had spent two days peacefully just a week or so ago, I couldn't help but remark out loud to the boys that I couldn't understand what the hell the generals were thinking. We could have crossed the river here and only had to march a mile instead of the probably fifty miles we had marched the last few days. I suppose they merely wanted to wear out our boots.

I think some officer must have overhead my comments because, shortly after passing through Florence, we turned north and spent the rest of the day marching in that direction. Soldiers like to talk and the rumor had been that we were heading to Huntsville, Alabama which was further east, but now we were marching north. Well, the good thing was that it had quit raining and was actually fairly warm. It wasn't hot, but it was much nicer than it had been the last day.

It was rather sunny and only a few scattered fluffy clouds were seen passing gracefully overhead. We continued marching north for the next four days, and then the lovely sunny weather took a sharp turn for the cold. We woke up one morning to find the ground covered with a thick frost and, upon arising and kicking off the blankets and packing up our gear, I noticed that the ground had frozen fairly solid during the night.

We passed through the small town of Pulaski which sat in a basin in the hills. The hills were exceedingly steep and I was amazed to see that nearly all of them had been plowed and cultivated. How anyone could actually manage to farm these hillsides was quite beyond me.

The next several days consisted of nothing but brutally cold frosty weather and long marches. At least the marching kept us warm, it was only at night that we suffered from the cold. We had spent the last several days marching pretty much east from Pulaski to wooded and hilly, gently rolling countryside. We marched to Fayetteville and across a beautiful deep blue mountain stream. The bridge was made out of solid limestone and was a truly beautiful structure. The stone had been cut and fitted together and had a high arching span across the deep blue water as it ran over the rocky bottom. It was so clear that you could see the rocks on the bottom, even though it must have been ten feet deep.

In the distance we could see higher mountains that, the rumor spreading down the line was, were the Cumberland Mountains. I recalled my grandfather talking of passing through the Cumberland Mountains on his way from Georgia to Memphis. I knew he had followed the Tennessee River west even as I was now following it east. For whatever reason, we turned south and were marching steadily in that direction. I decided not to make any comments on the wisdom of the high command. It's probably a good thing I didn't because a couple of days later we came into a small hamlet at the foot of the Cumberland Mountains that, the rumor was, was Maysville. Someone said it was only ten miles or so west to Huntsville where we had been headed in the first place over a week ago. I hated to think that we had marched a hundred miles or more and were back to within ten miles of where we had been in the first place.

The mountains off to our north and east were quite impressive. They seemed to arise directly from the valleys and ascend at a seventy or eighty degree slope. The tops were covered with oak, beech, chestnuts and cedar trees. It was a truly beautiful view off to the north and east, but I wondered how people here could make a living at farming. The soil was deep red clay that didn't appear to me to be worth cultivating.

We passed a very narrow, but exceedingly deep, stream that ran through the mountains. The engineers were hard at work in rebuilding the railroad bridge here. We managed to get across on a rather flimsy plank bridge. As we marched across, the whole thing seemed to shake and tremble beneath our feet. As we were still bringing up the rear of the division, I felt fairly confident that it would stand our weight, and I laughingly made some comment to that effect to Johnny who was marching immediately next to me. His only reply was, "I hope the bastards haven't worn it out though."

We turned to the north again. To the east, the Tennessee River could be seen down in the gorge as it wound its way through the mountains. We continued marching along the railroad where it seemed that at times the tracks were laid on the very edge of precipices that dropped dangerously down to the river below. We passed through a small town of only a hundred or so inhabitants. I believe it was called Stevenson.

A couple of days later, we arrived in Bridgeport. This was a small town on the west bank of the Tennessee River and the railroad crossed here heading towards Chattanooga. Frank Martin was ecstatic. He said, "Chattanooga isn't more than forty miles, Sweeties I'm on my way". Johnny spouted off, "Why don't you keep marching, Frank? You'd be able to be there by nightfall". Frank fired right back, "And why don't you come with me, Boy? We could march all night and by morning we would be there to spend the whole day with the ladies". Then he proceeded to tell us, in detail, what all he was going to do as soon as he got to Chattanooga. "I'm going to hire myself three ladies to escort me and I'm going to prance all about town with them, General Hooker be damned" he said. Then he went on to explain how he had heard that Gen Hooker, an officer from the Army of the Potomac, had been transferred out west. According to Frank Gen Hooker had a reputation back East of walking the streets and attending military balls and events accompanied by a bevy of prostitutes. He was so notorious that people had started referring to his whores as "Hookers Ladies".

We had been paid about two weeks ago and he had a couple of month's worth of money in his pocket and he sounded like he was ready to spend it all in one wild day of drinking and whoring. Well, I thought, he had never married and had nothing better to do with his money. At least he didn't gamble. What he spent his money on was always a sure thing.

We had gotten into Bridgeport just at dusk, so we settled down for the night. I was totally exhausted and munched a few pieces of hardtack, washing it down with water, while listening to Frank complaining about Gen Hooker hogging all the loose women and the officers putting the brothels off limits. As I drifted off to sleep the last thing I remember hearing was Johnny laughing as he told Frank "I'm sure nothing can stop you".

CHAPTER FOURTEEN

The next day we were up early, crossing the bridge to the eastern shore of the Tennessee. Frank could hardly contain himself. The weather, which had been fairly nice, brutally cold but dry, took a turn for the worst and throughout the day it started to rain, heavy at first, but then it turned into a torrential downpour. We slogged on through the mud following the south shore of the Tennessee at this point. We only made it about six miles before we stopped for the night; just near the mouth of a great cave that we were told was called the Nickajack.

Frank was entirely beside himself since we had only managed to make it a mere six miles, but it had taken a considerable time to get the troops across the bridge and bring across the artillery and the wagons. The Nickajack was a huge cave. I spent time with my brothers and sisters exploring some caves near where we had lived along the banks of the Osage River west of Osceola, but I had never seen a cave like this. The mouth of the cave must have been a couple of hundred feet wide and the roof of the cave must have been a hundred and fifty feet high or so. It went back at least a hundred yards before it seemed to narrow down fairly rapidly. A good number of troops had spread their bedrolls on the floor of the cave and were settling down to sleep. I was awed by the size of the mouth of the cave and wondered how far back into the mountains it went.

I questioned one of the soldiers who had taken up his position just beneath the edge of the overhang. He said that no one really knew, but he had heard it went for twenty miles or so. Then he said that they had guards posted further back in the cave to keep soldiers from setting out to explore it. It seemed that four or five days before that a lieutenant and four soldiers had gone spelunking and had never returned and couldn't be found. I don't know whether that was true or whether it was just a rumor being spread to keep people from wandering off on their own. As I looked further into the gloom at the back of the cave, I could see that there were indeed men standing who seemed to be patrolling. I suspected there might be some truth in the rumor.

As we settled down for the night, Frank was again all talk of his escapades with the ladies of the Chattanooga brothels. The man was actually becoming somewhat tiresome with his single-minded determination.

We were roused early the next morning while it was still pitch black. We lined up in column and, as we began to march out, we passed by the commissary wagons and were issued four days' ration and another sixty rounds of ammunition. This boded ominously for us as it indicated that we were marching into battle shortly. Frank Martin was especially perturbed because he thought we would be marching into Chattanooga and he would have some time with the ladies before seeing any action.

It seemed that it had been raining nearly daily for the last week, but this morning it commenced a downpour such as I had never seen before. We left the Nickajack, marching on a muddy, rocky, uneven road that seemed to cling to the very side of the mountains. The cliffs on our left dropped at a seventy to eighty degree angle down to the Tennessee River below. It was thickly covered with trees and brush. In places, it was a perpendicular wall of rock. The road we were on had been cut directly out of the base of the mountain. Not far above us was another cut where the railroad ran. Beyond that was a sheer precipice of three hundred feet or more.

Marching in the deluge with perfect torrents of runoff racing down the side of the mountain, washing out the road beneath our feet, and then spraying over the sides to fall away into the Tennessee River, which was rising even as we watched, was somewhat terrifying. Occasionally bright flashes of lightening would illuminate the darkness and the thunder seemed to reverberate, bouncing off the mountain and echoing down the valley. Stumbling through the mud and shallow rivers of overflowing runoff, made me fear that at any time I might lose my balance and be washed over the edge.

Then, we rounded a bend in the mountainside and the road took a turn to the south. Now we had sheer mountain cliffs on each side. We were marching through a narrow ravine through which a rushing stream ran. The road ran back and forth through the creek as we moved south and then southeast. The sun came up and was somewhat more reassuring in that we could see where we were placing our feet. Crossing back and forth through the creek was a treacherous undertaking. It was lined with small boulders and pebbles and, with the heavy runoff from the mountains on both sides; the footing was precarious at best.

Thankfully the water was never more than waist deep. I wondered if it kept raining this hard, if in a few hours the stream would even be fordable. We had passed through a small hamlet in an area where the ravine had broadened as we neared the top of the mountain. We marched across another stone bridge and shortly thereafter made camp for the night.

It was a miserable night, what with the rain and the wind whistling across the top of the mountain, the thunder and the lightening booming all around us and trying our best to rest in the mud. I couldn't imagine anything more miserable. I was almost thankful that in the middle of the night we were up and marching again.

We were moving down the eastern slope of the mountain into the valley beyond. Even though we were heading downhill, the wagons continued to get stalled in the mud and we frequently had to halt the whole column as we strained, pushed and pulled to move them forward.

Through the night we thought we could occasionally make out campfires in the valley below and on a mountain two or three miles in the distance. They would be visible for a short period of time before being obscured again by the clouds that seemed to hang around the sides of the mountain. Just as the sun started to come up in the east, we reached the gentle slopes at the bottom of the mountain and shortly thereafter were on relatively flat ground on the west side of the stream that came down from the south and emptied into the Tennessee which was visible in the distance to the north a half a mile or more.

We marched up and were allowed to fallout and make camp next to another division of the Union troops that were encamped along the stream. We were directed off the road further away from the stream and, as we arrived at our designated campsite, simply dropped where we were. The rubberized ponchos that we wore had served only slightly to keep the rain off. I was drenched from head to toe, but was too tired to care. We simply dropped, squatting cross-legged in the mud. I wondered how we had even survived the march.

It seemed that we were all too tired to even talk and sat huddled in a group, leaning forward, heads together, trying to protect ourselves from the wind and the rain, but it seemed to whip and whirl and hit us from all directions. No one seemed inclined to want to lie down to try to sleep.

A couple of hours later, the rain seemed to slacken and became a light drizzle and then ceased. By midmorning, the fog in the valley was starting to burn off and the sun was warming us up. I felt inclined to rummage through my haversack to break out some hardtack for breakfast. No one was inclined to try to light a fire; I doubt that there was any wood that was dry enough to get one started anyhow. I simply placed the hardtack in my mouth and let it gradually moisten until it became soft enough to bite off a chunk. What, with all the rain, I didn't even feel inclined to drink anything to wash it down. I was waterlogged already.

As the sun gradually warmed us up, sometime around noon, we felt inclined to get up and stretch our legs out. Sitting cross-legged in the mud tended to stiffen the joints. We got up as a group and wandered off towards the other division that was encamped just south of us. I think we were all rather curious to get to know who these boys might be. Personally, the smell of coffee was a strong attraction. I needed something to warm me up and wash down what was left of the hardtack.

As we moved up to the campfire, hoping to warm ourselves and beg some coffee from these new soldiers, Johnny, who was always ready for a joke and a good laugh, suddenly called out, "Well, howdy, generals." To which they all laughed. Then one of them said, "What makes you think we're all generals?" And Johnny replied, "Well, you all have stars on your caps. Doesn't that make you all generals?" Before anyone had a chance to reply to that, Otto spoke up and said, "No, you dumb German. They can't all be generals." "I know that, you dumb German," Johnny said. Then everyone broke out in laughter.

One of the men spoke up and said that that was their corps badge. I hadn't even noticed the stars on their caps, but as I looked around, I saw that indeed everyone had a star on their cap and even their wagons and tents had stars. Still laughing at Johnny's joke one of the sergeants asked us what our corps badge was. For some reason, Tom Sinclair, who usually didn't join in jesting much, slapped his cartridge box and, in his best Scottish accent said, "Forty rounds in the cartridge box and forty rounds in the pocket." The whole group broke out in laughter.

Coffee was passed around and we stood around in the mud, stomping our feet, and drinking coffee as fast as they could boil up a pot for us. We washed more hardtack down with the hot coffee and had a pleasant short little visit. It wasn't long until some officers came, directed us back to our own camp and brought our pleasant little meeting to an end. I guess they couldn't have the troops all wandering off, intermingling with each other; it would be too much of a hassle to get them straightened out later.

We moved back to our designated spot and, as the sun was coming out and the mud was at least warming up somewhat, we elected to put together our tents and try to get a little rest. It didn't look like we would be seeing any action today. We managed to get a few hours of sleep and then woke up to the smell of hot food. It seems we had finally gotten all of our wagons and gear up and cook fires had been built and we were to be treated to a hot meal of some bacon, beans and cornbread. It wasn't long after finishing supper that we went back to our tents and went to sleep.

The morning was cold, damp and foggy. There was a light drizzle which occasionally turned to a brisk downpour, it would soon dissipate and never lasted long. We were up while it was still dark and stumbling around in the camp. Daylight seemed to take forever to come, possibly because we were in a valley between two high mountains and possibly because of the dense fog that blocked out any rays of light. Breakfast had been prepared, but no one seemed to have much of an appetite because we had been told that on this morning we should be attacking Lookout Mountain. The mere thought was daunting and discouraging.

We had been told to strip for combat and leave our knapsacks and any excess belongings behind. I took one Remington and the two extra cylinders from the compartment in my knapsack. I placed the Remington in the belt of my trousers and the two cylinders in the pocket I had sewn on the inside of my blouse up over the right breast area. I took one of the Colt pocket police pistols and placed it in the pocket over my left breast area. I put some hardtack in my trouser pocket and made sure my canteen was full. I had forty rounds in my cartridge box and another sixty placed in my pockets. I took one blanket, wrapped it up in my greatcoat and tied it with twine, rolled that up in my groundsheet and secured it and then rolled the whole affair up in my poncho and tied it up tight. Then, I slung the whole contraption over my shoulder and dropped my knapsack in the wagon that had been assigned to the regiment. At last, we formed up in column and were ready to go.

The wait seemed unbearable. We knew there were Confederates on the other side of the creek and all along the side of the mountain beyond that. The thought of even attempting to scale the mountain in the fog, rain, damp and drizzle, seemed forbidding. We had all seen how steep it was and knew from past experience how hard it was to maintain footing on damp grass and muddy earth. The thought of rebels firing at you pointblank from fortified hidden positions on the side of the mountain in the damp, gloomy fog, was truly ominous. On the one hand, the thought kept recurring to me that surely they would call the assault off since it was impossible to see in this gloom, and then on the other hand, why didn't they get started instead of keeping us here waiting.

The rumor was that we were going to march to the south and cross a bridge over the creek and we were waiting for troops ahead to get into position. We stood there stamping our feet and muttering nervously under our breaths. We couldn't understand what was taking them so long. Then the sound of gunfire erupted some distance south of us. It was light at first, but then became rather brisk and constant. Shortly after that, artillery behind us to the west opened up and we could see the flashes even through the fog in the distance. We could hear the shells as they whistled and screamed overhead and watched as they erupted with a sudden burst of light on the east side of the creek.

I wondered what good they were doing. I couldn't see more than thirty feet in this fog and I don't see how they could have known what they were shooting at either. I suspected that they had determined the range and the location in the preceding days when they still had good light and hadn't moved their cannons since then. Then the rebel cannons on the other side of the creek opened up and returned their fire, for all the good that did in the damp, dark fog.

The skies seemed to lighten. I could tell that because the fog that had been dark gray and gloomy gradually seemed to become lighter; it whitened, almost shining as it reflected the light. But it was still so foggy that you couldn't see more than thirty feet. Occasionally a breeze would erupt which blew the fog apart, but it immediately closed as the wind passed. It was like being wrapped in a shroud, or so I imagined.

Gradually the columns seemed to become more nervous, people began stamping and shuffling their feet and we gradually started moving forward. We were moving south on the west side of the creek. Our division proceeded in column and we were near the end of the column. I was almost hoping that the fighting would be over before we managed to get across the creek ourselves. It was near midmorning before we reached the bridge that had been erected for our crossing. Our engineers had thrown this together first thing this morning. It seemed a rather flimsy affair to me. It shook and trembled as we moved across it, but had held up so far.

The creek didn't seem to be all that wide, but in the fog it was hard to tell how deep it was and how fast that it was running. I suppose it was moving at a fairly good clip due to all the rains we had recently and the thought flashed through my mind that it was probably a good thing we were attacking in this fog because the Confederates were unlikely to see our flimsy contraption. I imagined one solid shot from cannon on the side of the mountain would have sent the whole affair tumbling into the creek.

There continued to be the sound of musketry off to the south and it was obvious that the other divisions in our army had succeeded in crossing the creek further south. We were ordered to advance to our left along the creek, moving back towards the north. We were moving in line and it was difficult to make out the members in the squad around me in the fog. It was impossible to see any Confederates. There, next to the creek, the fog seemed the thickest and my view was restricted to only a few feet. At times a puff of wind would come sweeping down the valley and the fog would seem to lift and clear to where you could see for thirty or forty feet faintly and indistinctly.

I perked up my ears, turning my head from side-to-side to listen better. I glanced out of the corner of my eye looking for movement that might betray a nearby enemy. I also tried to keep an eye on the troops on each side of me. I was afraid that if we didn't keep in line, our own troops would be marching in front of us and that at the first instance of gunfire from Confederates, we might be shooting each other from all directions.

While we were advancing on the east side of the creek, we were moving through trees and brush. Suddenly we came out in a cleared space and shortly thereafter stumbled across the railroad tracks. Then we started to climb on an uphill grade and passed through a cleared spot on the east side of the creek and into the woods and brush that covered the slope. When we started out, we had been told to follow along the east side of the railroad tracks and then on up the bluff, but in the fog, the railroad tracks were quickly out of sight and, from the slope of the bluff, it was hard to tell just where we were in relation to the river. Now, we were moving up a fairly steep bluff, probably at a forty-five degree angle. We would take a few steps forward, and then slide back a step or two and, for every three steps we moved forward, we slid back a foot. The mud seemed to cling to our boots and our feet seemed to weigh ten pounds each. At times our feet would slide, leaving a furrow several inches deep as our feet slid out from under us and we fell to our knees. We would grab at clumps of grass or small bushes and pull ourselves forward until we regained our feet and were able again to start climbing. Then we would come to the top of the slope only to find an even steeper slope going down on the other side and into a deep gulley in which water ran knee deep.

In the dense fog, there was no sunlight to indicate which direction we were actually traveling. I tried to listen for the sounds of the Tennessee River off to my left, but couldn't make out just in which direction it was. There continued to be the sounds of brisk musket fire off to the south, or what I supposed to be the south, and the cannons fired back and forth across the river in bursts. And then, suddenly it happened. Somewhere directly in front, a wall of flames shot out and the rattling of a hundred muskets vibrated through the fog. I had seen the muskets fire, but couldn't any longer pinpoint their exact position because the fog blended with the powder smoke such that, once I turned my head from side-to-side, it was hard to tell just where the rebels had been that had fired on us.

Our troops fired a scattered irregular volley back to where they thought the Confederates had been. I glanced around to each side, but couldn't tell whether any of the troops near to me had been injured or not. We continued to march, crawl, slip and slide our way up the slopes of the mountain. Then we were stumbling down the sides of another ravine and came up sharp against an abatis in the bottom of the gulley. This was merely a barricade of trees that had been cut down and the limbs sharpened to a point. They had been tossed into the bottom of this gulley to impede movement. I knew that that indicated there would be Confederate rifle pits or fortifications of some sort on the top of the ridge that we were forced to ascend if we ever made it through this entanglement of sharp spear-like points.

I took my bedroll from my shoulder and placed my rifle on it and dropped to my knees. It seemed easier to me to crawl through the limbs beneath the trunks of the trees, rather than to try to climb over them. For one thing, if you slipped and fell, you could impale yourself on a sharpened limb, and for the other thing, it seemed like you were a sitting duck, exposed, trying to work your way through. I crawled and wormed my way from side-to-side and finally made it through the bottom of the gulley and started the ascent up the other side.

I could hear my comrades crashing, cursing and trying to force their way through the sharpened stakes behind me. I threw my bedroll back over my shoulders and, lying flat on my belly, began to worm my way up the slope, digging my toes into the mud for traction. I would crawl forward for a few feet, and then look from side-to-side through the fog and gloom. I was listening carefully, trying to pick up the slightest sound. Suddenly off to my right, I heard the distinct click of a musket being cocked. Peering in that direction, I noticed a slight motion which soon materialized as the shape of a man raising a musket to his shoulder and pointing it in our direction. I couldn't have testified as to whether he was a Union or a Confederate, but since he was higher on the bluff than I and was pointing in the direction of my troops, I brought my rifle up quick, took aim and fired. My musket fired and, what little gun smoke erupted from the barrel sufficed to obliterate any view of the Confederate soldier. Almost immediately there was a volley of flames from in front of me and especially off to my right.

I don't know how they could tell what they were shooting at. I suspected that my gunfire had merely startled them and they had fired back in our direction. I could only hope that my troops were in the deepest part of the gulley, or even then ascending the slopes because it seemed that the fire was directed across the gulley too high. I rolled over on my back and quickly reloaded my musket, and then I rolled back over on my belly and began to inchworm my way up the bluffs.

I was moving ever so slowly in the direction that I thought the rebel had been that I had fired at seconds before. As I moved slowly uphill and slightly to my right, I could hear the distinct sound of metal on metal and I knew that to be the Confederates hurriedly loading their muskets and forcing their ramrods down the barrels. Since I had been crawling up the slope on my belly, I had taken my Remington and placed it in the small of my back, tucked into the belt of my trousers.

I could make out what appeared to be a Confederate rifle pit. There was a small elevation of dirt with some logs crowning the top of it that I could barely make out in the gloom. I didn't think it was more than ten feet away. As I watched I spied the shape of a Confederate soldier as he rose up and pointed his musket down towards the gulley. I imagined that I was close enough to him that, if I had taken my rifle and reached it out with one hand, I could have almost placed it against his chest. I was lying on my belly and was afraid to roll over on my side to actually aim at him, so that's precisely what I attempted to do. I took the rifle and held it up in my right hand, pointed it in his direction and pulled the trigger. The flames leapt out and I could imagine that they must have actually burnt him as he dropped back and disappeared from sight.

My next thought was, Oh, God, I'm in for it now! Surely there must be more in this emplacement. I snatched out my Remington, leapt to my feet and stumbled up, nearly falling over the lip of the Confederate fortifications and firing rapidly at anything I could see. I think I must have surprised them and terrified them at the same time. Possibly they were unsure as to just how many people were there, or possibly they hadn't finished reloading because there was a sudden scramble as men took off in all directions up the hill.

I turned my head and fired from left to right at shapes as they disappeared into the fog. I thought I saw a couple of more fall and one actually rolled back down the slope and into the pit with me. Then I dropped down into the pit just before a volley of rifle fire from the bottom of the ravine shook the air all around me. I screamed out, "God dammit, Johnny, don't shoot me, you dumb German." What better way to identify myself to the boys in my squad than that. There was no reply and, as I waited protected in the

Confederate emplacement, I hastily shifted a cylinder from my pocket into the Remington and placed the empty cylinder in a pocket in my trousers, and then I reloaded my musket.

I had just finished when I heard a soft whisper from the fog just over the head log of the Confederate rifle pit. I instantly recognized Johnny's voice. "Corporal Everett," he whispered. "Are you in there?" "Who in the hell else would it be?" I whispered back. One by one, the men in the squad gathered there about me. We had managed to lose contact with the rest of the line, but had been able to keep in touch with ourselves.

We started back out, back up the slope. I directed the squad to move to my left and get some distance between each man, and then I started feeling towards the right to attempt to link up with the rest of the line. We tried to continue moving up the slope, keeping each other in view through the fog as we moved forward and moved slightly to the right to try to link up with our own troops. I crawled forward. I had given up the idea of trying to stand erect and climb, feeling too exposed and too open, even in the fog. I could make out movement of men who seemed to be proceeding up the hill in the general direction we had originally started. It was impossible to tell if we were moving east along the ridge, or directly south up the ridge, but at least we were moving uphill and I thought that was a good indication.

I turned more to my left so that we seemed once again to be moving in line and managed to communicate to my squad on the left that we were back in the proper order and we began to move forward again. Suddenly, way off to the right and in what I thought was a southerly direction; there was a very brisk and intense volley of musket fire. I had the impression that it was the troops that we had been listening to all morning, but there was no way to be sure of that. If, indeed, it was them, they were considerably closer now than they had been.

I got to thinking it must have been ten, ten-thirty or even eleven when we started moving along the slopes of the mountain. No one in my squad had a watch and it was hard to tell just what time it might be now. The fog seemed to be brighter and it seemed to be especially brighter when I looked straight up, so I thought it might be getting on towards eleven, or possibly even more like noon.

Another fifteen minutes or so later, we seemed to come to a place where the slope of the mountain was less acute and even began to level out. The ground here was scattered with large boulders. Some seemed to be rounded on the top, some seemed to be flat, and some seemed to point skywards in almost a triangular fashion. Some of them were as big as a house, others were the size of a wagon and still others were half the size of a mule. I think they were clustered here more than elsewhere because they probably would have rolled down the side of the mountain if they had been any further downhill. The slopes of the mountain had been fairly thickly covered with trees and brush, but here the ground was mainly cleared.

I don't know why, but it seemed like the fog was considerably thinner here. Looking back down into the valley we had just ascended out of, the fog seemed as thick as ever. Maybe it was because there was a bit more of a breeze here that blew it away to the east, or maybe it was just that it was warmer here on this plateau but the denseness of the fog had definitely dissipated.

Anyway, visibility was now probably up to two hundred yards. As we crept out slowly from the lip of the bluff and into the open, we fanned out to move forward behind the boulders that seemed scattered widely over the field. Looking to my right, I could make out a long line of men in blue as they moved into the clearing. Looking to the left, there was a shorter line of men. When we had started, we had been positioned on the left end of the line, but now somehow in the ascent up the hill we had moved towards the center. There must have been, in the distance, at least a hundred soldiers in blue emerging onto the plateau.

I moved forward to a wagon sized boulder that seemed to come to a point in the center. I approached it bent over double at the waist, dropped to my knee behind it and then to my belly and crawled to my left to peek around the side of it. A hundred yards or so towards the center of the clearing was a line of Confederate entrenchments. I rose carefully to my right knee and placed my left foot forward. I was keeping my head low, looking around the side of the boulder, trying to pick out a target. As I looked into the distance, I noticed as blue clad soldiers came up to my left and moved stealthily forward. As I watched one of the soldiers that I recognized as Frank Martin crept up behind a boulder that was rather squarish in shape and about four feet high. It reminded me of the upright piano that had been in the church back in Osceola.

Frank crept up behind it and slowly began to raise his head to peer over the top. I was about to call out to him to keep his head down, when out of the corner of my eye I noted movement along the Confederate breastworks ahead. I brought my rifle up to my left shoulder, sighted quickly and fired. Even as I did, the Confederate line erupted in a blast of flames and dense grayish black powder smoke. The top of their line was obscured again in the fog of war.

I rolled back behind my boulder, leaning up against it and quickly reloaded my rifle, and then I crawled to the right edge of the boulder and peered around it at the base. It seemed to me that sticking your head up, peeking over the top of a boulder, was a sure giveaway. I didn't think that most people paid much attention to the sides of the boulder, especially if your head was only a foot or two off the ground. I got into position, peering around the boulder, and brought my rifle up to my shoulder to take aim. I had no sooner steadied my rifle, sighting along the top of the Confederate logs, when I saw a gray clad soldier raise his head and shoulders and musket to take aim.

I had managed to reload faster than they had and, before he was ever able to fire a round, I had taken a good clean shot. This time, our line of blue to my right erupted in flames and smoke as the union soldiers who had not managed to get off a volley previously, were set for the Confederates when they rose up to take aim. Then the Confederate lines belched forth smoke and flames in return. I could only imagine this from the sound because I was already safely tucked behind my boulder and had nearly reloaded.

I managed to fire another eight or ten rounds, always seeming to get my rifle reloaded before the Confederates did theirs and always being ready, spotting at their head logs for them to rise up to take aim. Our lines of troops seemed to blast forth lead from north to south nearly in unison. However, I managed to always be safely behind my rock by the time the Confederate fire burst forth.

Our own little battle seemed to last for upwards of an hour with us head-on blasting away, but it soon became apparent that the Union line overlapped the Confederate fortifications on each end and, as troops moved forward along their flank and they were in danger of being caught in the crossfire, they gradually began falling away and moving up the slight slope of the plateau toward the palisades that loomed in the distance.

I had heard this formation of solid rock that towered seventy-five to a hundred feet or more straight up in the air, so called by the officers. It was still what appeared to be nearly a mile in the distance, although it was hard to judge due to the fog. The shape reminded me of the prow of a ship. From where we were positioned, it seemed that I was looking at it nearly head-on. The sides of the mountain seemed to rise up straight from the plateau on which we were presently fighting. And, indeed, on the point that was facing directly north, it seemed that the highest rocks towered up away from it. Yes it definitely resembled the front of a ship; at least those were my thoughts at the moment.

The Confederates had disappeared into thicker brush and trees on the farther side of the plateau where it again began to rise gradually towards the upper slopes of the mountain. I slid from behind my boulder on the right-hand side and, crouching to where my hands nearly drug on the ground, I moved forward, sliding from boulder to boulder towards the Confederates line. As I came up to and ducked down behind the logs of the Confederate works, Tom Sinclair came up on my left. As I looked to the left, I recognized a couple of other men in the squad. I also failed to recognize some of the men that were immediately next to us. They not only were not members of our squad, they weren't even of the same regiment, but we were all wearing blue and that was a good thing.

My gun was reloaded and I was taking a moment to rest as I watched to my right as a whole line of blue clad soldiers came up to the logs. I took a moment to rinse my mouth out with water from the canteen, swilled it around, spat it out to freshen my mouth before drinking. The water that I spit looked black and felt gritty as it escaped my lips. Then I took one good swallow and plugged the cork up in the canteen again. I whispered to the boys in the squad to keep their heads down and a couple of the soldiers that I didn't recognize nodded their heads in vigorous agreement. Then, looking at the logs carefully, I found a place where there was a chink between the first and second logs on the top to which I could peer at the slopes of the hill to the south.

Down to the southwest in the distance, there was what appeared to be a farmhouse and a cluster of buildings. There seemed to be an intense fire fight to the south beyond that. I reasoned that must be General Geary and the paper collared troops of the 12th Division. Other troops of my own division seemed to be extending in line to my left and facing south or southeast. Immediately to our front, were probably three hundred yards of fairly cleared ground without much cover. I thought I could determine the outline of a road running nearly through the center of this, maybe two hundred yards away. On the farther side of this open area, there appeared to be another line of Confederate works extending along the base of the slope there.

I knelt there, peeking through the crack in the logs, thinking of what to do next. It seemed to be exceedingly dangerous to me to attempt to move beyond the line behind which we were crouching across that clearing towards the Confederate works. And, indeed, it must have appeared the same way to the officers commanding the regiments because no one else seemed inclined to move forward either.

I turned to face towards the house that I had seen in the distance off to my right. There was still a tremendous rattling of muskets around it, and the fog that I thought had lifted, seemed to hover around the tops of the buildings, but I knew it was gun smoke and not fog. Even as I watched, the first rounds from artillery began to crash down in the farmyard and on that side of the plateau. I realized maybe for the first time that artillery directly north across the Tennessee River stationed on Moccasin Point were firing over our heads at the Confederate works. I had thought the only artillery firing had been those from west of Lookout Creek behind the position from which we originally started.

I could almost feel sorry for the Confederates who were having shells rained down on them from two directions. I don't know if it was a result of the combined artillery fire, but it wasn't long before Confederate troops could be seen moving away from the farmhouse and fading out to the east and up the slopes of the mountain. The artillery slackened and soon we could spot Union troops moving through the farmyard towards the base of the upper slopes. It seemed that the Confederates across from us began moving to their right, towards the east, even as the troops that had been in the farmyard moved in amongst them.

It was long range, probably close to eight hundred yards I had estimated, but I couldn't resist firing at the Confederates. The wind seemed to be blowing fairly briskly from the west, northwest, in gusts, and at eight hundred yards, I knew my shot would be well east of where I aimed, but I thought there was a slight chance I might do some damage and, besides, when the rest of our lines opened fire, there would be several hundred Minnie balls screaming out towards the Confederates and, if nothing else, it would cause them to keep their heads down while the Union troops to the west pushed them further around the end of the mountain.

The Confederates continued moving back to the east slowly and, as time passed, I realized we were running low on cartridges. I whispered to the boys that they should conserve their ammunition and, as it was becoming extremely foggy again, the line soon fell into silence. I rinsed my mouth again, took a few swallows of water and retrieved some of the hardtack from my pocket. It was much the worse for wear. I had had it in my front trouser pocket and, crawling through the mud and the grass, my uniform was thoroughly soaked, and so was the hardtack. It had a rather muddy taste, but at least it was soft enough that it could be bitten off with relative ease. Not to say that it still wasn't hard, but it wasn't like trying to eat rocks.

As the fog settled in, all fighting ceased and I took the time to crawl up and down the line. I found the rest of the squad leaning up against the Confederate logs to my left. They were leaning with their backs up against the logs two or three feet apart. They seemed tired, worn out and thirsty, but thankfully none the worse for wear, at least none seemed to be seriously injured. Otto Kerner was complaining about an injured ankle, and Johnny was showing him no mercy. "I thought your family came from the Alps," Johnny said. "How could you hurt yourself on this little hill?" Otto cursed him as he said, "We're used to climbing rocks, not mud." Naturally this was said in German and I had to listen as Johnny translated for me.

Johnny helped hold Otto's leg up as I untied his boot and slipped it off. His ankle and foot were already extremely swollen and starting to turn blue. It was with difficulty that I managed to get his sock and boot back on. Then, I had the boys from the squad donate their bedrolls so we could make a pile to elevate Otto's injured foot. It was only then that I realized that one of us was missing. Frank Martin was nowhere to be seen. I wandered left and right down the line after having told Tom Sinclair to keep an eye on things. I went for a couple of hundred yards in each direction before I realized he was nowhere along the line of men leaning on the earthworks.

As I made my way back to the squad where they were still resting against the logs of the fortification, I found Johnny and Christian and they volunteered to come with me to look for Frank. We moved back in the direction that I had thought we had come from, but somehow nothing seemed familiar. I began sweeping east and west along the slope of the plateau, working my way toward the level plateau that was cluttered with boulders. I reached the level and hadn't seen anything familiar. We came upon groups of soldiers who were looking, like we were, for missing comrades. Some were carrying corpses back towards our position along the log fence.

Others had injured comrades slung between them in blankets. I wondered why I hadn't been smart enough to bring blankets or something else to fetch Frank back to our lines. We finally came to the lip of the plateau where it fell steeply down the bluffs and I decided to move to the east along the top of it. We had moved probably a hundred yards along the top of it before I thought I recognized something. Of course, it was hard to tell anything in the fog. I moved back to the south or southeast, sweeping back and forth until finally I spied that piano shaped rock. As we neared the rock, I nearly stumbled over Frank. It was nearly too blurry to make out the soldier, but I knew it was Frank from the shape of the boulder behind which I had last seen him hiding.

I called out his name, but there was no reply. We knelt in the mud on each side and gazed down at Frank. He was lying flat on his back with his head slightly downhill from the rock. His arms were bent at the elbow and his blood soaked hands were raised up along each side of his face with the fingers clenched in a claw-like manner. His head was tilted back and his chin was pointing up and his mouth was opened in a gaping round O. Blood dribbled from both sides of his face and his eyes weren't visible as they were covered by small puddles of blood that had pooled overlying the eyeballs. There was an egg-sized hole in the top of his skull just below the hairline in the middle of his forehead. The whole crown of his skull was gone. Brain matter was visible through the clots of blood pooled in the gaping wound. Surprisingly, the brain itself looked nearly intact. It's almost as if the top of his skull had been taken off from mid forehead to about halfway to the back. I wondered for a moment what could have caused such a devastating wound, but I pictured Frank as he was raising his head up to peer over the boulder just before the Confederates had sent a volley in our direction.

I stood up and looked at the top of the piano shaped boulder and, sure enough, there was a bright silver dollar sized patch of rock shining with a bright sliver of stone exposed pointing to where Frank's head had been. I could picture a 58 or 69 caliber lead ball ricocheting and skipping across the top of the stone as it traveled upwards at a shallow angle and striking Frank's forehead. It had taken off the bone, leaving the brain relatively uninjured. I could imagine Frank lying on his back and feeling the top of his head with both hands and then dying in fright as he realized the ghastly extent of his injury.

Johnny and Christian passed their hands beneath his upper thighs and his mid back, locked wrists and lifted him gently up as I cradled the back of his head in the palms of my hands. We made our way to the south to where the Confederate line had been and where our troops were now resting. I was walking directly towards them, I thought, but managed to strike our line well to the left of where the boys were presently situated. Once we found the log works, we turned to the right and moved along until we came up with the group.

We laid Frank a good ten or fifteen foot away from the squad because I was reluctant to have them see him this way. I took my knife and cut his bedroll loose and covered him with a blanket, then went and sat down next to the boys. I knew that they had seen us as we approached, but no one asked any questions. They didn't need to be told that Frank was no longer amongst the living. Johnny, however, couldn't help but make a comment. The only thing he said was, "Damn, and he never even got to see the hookers." No one felt like laughing.

CHAPTER FIFTEEN

We made a sad and somber little group of men as we sat there, leaning back against the logs of the Confederate barricade. We couldn't help glancing out the short distance to where Frank Martin's body lay covered with the blanket.

The heavens opened up again and it began to rain fairly hard. I had drunk most of my water throughout the day, trying to conserve it by taking only a sip at a time, but still it was nearly empty. It's hard to believe we could be so thirsty and yet so miserably wet all at the same time. I had unfurled my bedroll and put on my greatcoat, I sat on the groundsheet and covered up with one blanket and tried to cover up with my poncho. I folded the edges of the poncho up so the rain that ran off would funnel into my canteen and managed to get it filled to a little over halfway before the rain drizzled off and became just a heavy mist. It didn't seem to be worth trying to funnel anymore water into the canteen, so I corked it up and drew my poncho up around my shoulders.

I had eaten a little more hardtack, saving about half of what I had for the next day. Then, leaning back against the logs, we attempted to get some sleep. No one seemed to feel energetic enough to form the ponchos together to make a tent, so we simply sat there leaning back against the logs and attempting to nap.

Throughout the night there were occasional flurries of gunshots that seemed to come from the south and somewhat from the west and indicated that the Confederates were still there, possibly skirmishing with General

Geary's troops who were along the base of the palisades and probably attempting to move forward through the trees and brush that lined the slopes there.

We had several hundred yards of open ground between us and our barricade and didn't feel inclined to venture out into the open, and I suppose the rebels didn't either because there wasn't any activity in our immediate vicinity. Some time during the night, the rain dissipated the clouds and fog lifted and we had a bright moonlit night. We took turns during the night making sure that one man in the squad was constantly peering out across the open ground to keep an eye on the rebels, but all remained quiet.

It must have been around midnight when Hans shook me awake and said, "You need to take a look at this." I opened my eyes rather groggily and looked around and then saw that he was pointing up. As I watched, the nearly full moon slowly became darker as a big shadow moved across from east to west and blocked the light of the moon. It gradually became pitch-black all around us so that we couldn't see more than a few feet in any direction. Shortly after the shadow seemed to pass and moonlight was visible again from the eastern side of the moon. Gradually the shadow cleared and there was once again bright moonlight. I was amazed. Before I could question Hans about what we had just seen, he said, softly, "I've never seen an eclipse before." I felt relieved that I hadn't been so stupid as to ask him what had happened.

I kept my eyes on the heavens thinking that possibly it would happen again, but wasn't about to ask him about the likelihood of that. After a while, since the moon remained a brightly lighted globe reflecting down from the heavens, I sat down again, covered up with the poncho and began to nap.

It seemed like the rest of the night passed quickly. Gradually it became lighter in the east and, as the sun came up over the top of Missionary Ridge to the east, it seemed to shine directly into our faces. The boys rousted themselves up and rolled their gear back in their ponchos and draped the bedrolls over their shoulders, and gradually troops began to move up and down the line behind the Confederate works.

We watched cautiously and intently towards where the Confederates had last been yesterday before it became too foggy and then too dark to see. We couldn't make out any sign of movement and gradually it dawned on us that the Confederates were no longer there. The troops became more relaxed and moved up and down the line and we saw troops in blue uniforms moving along the base of the ridge in the distance.

The rumor that there was hot food for us available down along Lookout Creek, spread up and down the line, but we weren't inclined to march back down the hill just to get a hot meal. We munched on the hardtack we had left and washed it down with water. A group of soldiers passed down the line distributing more ammunition for us. We were told that we were to begin to march at 10 o'clock in the morning down the road and into Chattanooga Valley. We had been given orders to cross the creek in the middle of the valley and proceed on up in an attack towards Rossville and the southern slopes of Missionary Ridge.

Some time after 10, the order came to move out and we crossed the Confederate barricade and moved to the road that went from the little white house down the eastern slopes of Lookout Mountain. I had thought about trying to bury Frank Martin's body, but as we had nothing to dig with, I took one last look towards the blanket covering him where he lay and moved off.

We formed up in column on the road and began the descent to the valley. As we marched along, the sergeant passed by and spoke to us briefly. I told him what had happened to Frank Martin and told him that we had to leave Otto Kerner behind because he simply couldn't walk on his sprained ankle. The sergeant said, "Well, son, you needn't worry. They'll take good care of him. There are burial details coming up to take care of Frank and the other casualties. I'm sure Otto will be back with the squad in no time." Then he chuckled and said, "That dumb German is one tough character." "That he is, sir, that he is," spoke up Johnny.

As we moved down the road on the eastern slope of Lookout Mountain, we could see General Grant's army in the valley below to our left in front of the Tennessee River. It looked like they were a mile or more outside of the town and were forming up in the valley. Long lines of blue infantry were visible as well as teams of artillery moving into position and cavalry moving back and forth along the lines. It was a splendid sight.

We moved south along the eastern slopes of Lookout Mountain for several miles, and then gradually descended to come out on the valley and move east across the flat ground towards where Lookout Creek ran near the middle of the valley. We came to where the bridge had been crossing the creek, but the Confederates had very thoroughly destroyed it. The column queued up in line along the road, looking east across the bridge.

General Hooker himself came forward on his horse, accompanied by General Osterhaus, who commanded our division, and our own General Woods. They rode forward to the creek and inspected the bridge and soon individual officers went galloping back down the column to fetch up the engineers and equipment and supplies for rebuilding the bridge. It seemed that we were safe from the Confederates as long as we were on this side of the river.

Looking towards the northeast, I could see the bulk of Missionary Ridge a mile or so in the distance, sloping gradually down and then passing directly east of us and continuing towards the south. Straight ahead of us and to the south, it didn't appear anywhere near as high as it did off to the north. It took probably an hour for the engineers to fashion together enough of a bridge so that some troops could be sent across.

The 27th Missouri Regiment crossed first and moved gradually and cautiously away from the bridgehead on the eastern side, spreading out and covering the ground as they moved away from the bridge. Then it was our turn to make our way across the narrow span of the bridge that they had pieced together.

The 27th Missouri moved pretty much straight east, skirmishers in the lead and the line of infantry following a hundred yards or so behind them. We proceeded several hundred yards to the east across the valley. The 27th Missouri was probably a hundred yards in front when suddenly they came under fire from Confederate artillery. Looking into the distance a half mile or so away, we could make out Confederate troops, with cavalry and what appeared to be supply wagons moving behind the artillery.

The order was given for us to move by the right flank parallel to the lower ridge that ran to the south of the gap. Meanwhile, the 27th Missouri had dropped to the ground where they were in an attempt to find shelter. As we marched away to the south, the artillery zeroed in on us and we quickened our pace to get away from their bombardment. I don't supposed they had anything larger than twelve pound smooth bore cannon and we were probably at the limit of their range, but the shells were coming dangerously close and a few impacted and exploded along the line as we moved south.

I saw men go down, but we couldn't hesitate to assist them. The rest of the column was marching hard behind us and the Confederates were getting us in range. I stepped over dead and wounded men never even bothering to look at them. Thankfully, we were soon far enough south of their position to feel safe from any further shelling. Then the order came to face to the left, form line, skirmishers forward and we moved out across the valley towards the gentle slope of the most southern tip of the Confederate positions.

I led my squad forward a hundred yards ahead of the rest of the line and we dropped into our skirmishing posture. Bending over at the waist with my rifle in hand and hands nearly trailing along the ground, we moved forward, sliding from side-to-side, trying to take advantage of any cover possible. Picking our way carefully eastward, we soon came to a shallow drainage ditch that ran in a southeasterly direction and we went into it at a shuffling run. We moved a short distance down it, and then peering to the east over the edge of the ditch, I could make out a slight rise that would keep us hidden until we reached its crest. We dropped to our hands and knees and crawled up the slope so that we could inspect the terrain. We spied another ditch that seemed to run nearly to the east, and then with a burst of speed, we sprang to our feet, and rushed forward into the ditch. We were moving quickly to stay ahead of the line of our troops as they moved east behind us.

As we neared the western edge of the ridge, we could make out Confederate troops moving through the trees and brush on its western slope. We carefully sighted in and, as one, fired a volley. It wasn't much of a volley as there were only seven men in my squad now, but we loaded and fired rapidly. I'm sure we got off four rounds a minute, then the rest of our line was moving up beside us. The Confederates fired a volley and, with that, the whole line lunged into a shambling run towards the ridge.

At fifty yards from the base, we pulled up short and fired an unbroken volley from north to south along the line, and then we charged forward again. It seemed like an unbroken line of blue soldiers as we raced to the east, extending all the way up to the road that passed through the gap in the ridge. As we ran, I threw my rifle over my left shoulder with the barrel extending forward a foot in front of my left ear. Biting off a bullet, I poured the powder down the barrel, spit the mini ball in the palm of my hand and shoved it down the barrel, and then tapped it home with the ramrod as I ran with the butt of the gun nearly trailing on the ground behind me.

The rest of my squad followed my example as we had perfected this technique in previous battles. I slipped the ramrod back in the stock of the rifle, brought it up over my shoulder and placed another cap on the nipple as we entered the brush and woods on the slope and proceeded, still on the trot, up the slope and across the top of it. The Confederates were retreating from in front of us, moving off to the north, apparently heading for the road as it passed on the other side of the gap.

We turned to the north and passed along the eastern side of the slope and soon were coming in view of the road as it cleared the gap on the eastern side. There were still Confederate troops manning the gap, putting up what resistance they could as they tried to limber up their artillery and escape with it. We could see blue clad Union troops approaching the Confederate positions and, as we turned west to rush upon the Confederates from their back, they didn't seem to be aware of our presence. At just under a hundred yards, we pulled up abruptly into line and fired a volley, and then rushed forward again.

The Confederate artillery was bringing up the horse teams, attempting to hitch up their cannon to retrieve it from the field. Some of the troops nearest to us saw us coming and let loose of the reins of the teams which bolted off to the north. They raised their arms in surrender without putting up much of a fight. As we rushed up to surround them, a Confederate officer further, near the cannons themselves, turned around and, seeing what was happening, brought up his revolver and fired a single shot towards us.

We were probably close to fifty yards away, which is a long shot for a revolver, and he hadn't taken the time to aim at all. I doubted whether he had managed to hit anyone, but his actions infuriated me. They were surrounded on three sides, but still he was not willing to give up the fight. I slid to a halt, pulling my revolver from my belt and brought it up to shoulder height while standing sideways facing him. I sighted down it, taking careful aim for the base of his throat and fired a single shot. I watched as he staggered a half step back, rose up on the tips of his toes and bent his head and neck forward as the slug knocked the air from his lungs.

I knew that at that distance the soft lead ball would drop nearly a foot, so I expected I had hit him in the center of his body. The revolver's barrel slowly tilted forward, the revolver spun towards the ground and dropped from his hand as he crumbled into the dust.

I had only stopped for a second, but that allowed the rest of the troops charging forward with me to move forward at least ten yards in advance. I raced forward again. Surprisingly, there were still some of the Confederates who didn't seem to realize their predicament. There were two teams of horses facing us as the Confederates attempted to limber up the cannon to make off with them. There were men holding the reins of the horses and grasping at their halters, trying to keep them from bucking and rearing and stampeding away, while others attempted to lift the trail of the cannon and connect it to the limber.

As I watched, one of the gunners who was holding the halter of a horse team to my left looked over his shoulder and spied us. He had a cannon ramrod in his left hand, and as I watched, he released his grasp on the horse, grabbed the ramrod with both hands near the end and swung it viciously at the nearest Union soldier approaching him. I watched as Johnny brought his musket up with his right hand on the butt and his left hand grasping the stock near the end of the barrel. The blow knocked the rifle loose from his left hand and it went spinning to the ground. I watched horrified as Johnny ducked his head to the right and his left arm was thrown up to protect his head. He was literally lifted off his feet by the next blow and knocked like a rag doll to crumble in the mud on his right side.

I was maybe fifteen to twenty feet away at the time, and with a cry of rage, I snapped the revolver around and shot the rebel cannoneer through the middle. I dropped into a crouch, spinning from left to right, spied another gunner with a ramrod holding to the muzzle of a horse, and as he turned around and noticed us, I shot him also. I charged forward a few more feet, and between the teams of horses that were pitching and rearing, I spied another Confederate just as he turned, I think in an action to run from the Union troops that were even then starting to scramble over the barrels of the cannon to get at the Confederates, and I shot him also.

As I crouched like a cat ready to pounce, spinning from left to right, I was watching for the slightest sign of resistance, but by this time the Confederates had wisely decided to give the fight up. Everywhere I looked, they were dropping whatever they had in hand and raising their arms in the air. As I glanced back over my shoulder, I noticed a Union soldier approaching. When he was no more than a few feet away, I happened to glance up in his face. He was looking at me with a wide-eyed expression of terror or concern, or a mixture of both, and he said, "Are you alright?"

I realized that I was breathing hard, trying to catch my breath. I think that that my gasps for air sounded almost like growls. My eyebrows were narrowed and my lips were curled in a vicious snarl. It dawned on me that Johnny was concerned, not so much for me, as he was about me. I slowly straightened and stood erect and suddenly a tremble passed over me. I could feel myself shaking from head to toe. I merely looked up in his face and said, "I thought you were dead!"

I saw his face lighten and it seemed that he nearly smiled, then I said, "I thought that he knocked your head clean off." And then Johnny did smile and said, "No, I'm too fast for that, but I think he may have broke my arm and maybe a couple of ribs." Now, with that, he took his right hand, placed it in his armpit and began to massage his chest and arm. "He sure packed a wallop," Johnny said. Anything further he was going to say was obscured by the cheers of triumph and the jubilation of the troops around me.

As I looked around, there were several soldiers sitting astride the barrels of the cannons, tossing their hats in the air and bouncing like they were riding on the back of horses. Other troops were absolutely hopping up and down in celebration. A few of the more dedicated, or somber troops, were gathering up the Confederate prisoners, shoving them roughly into a group and starting to march them off to the west. I merely looked around, trying to pick out the rest of the men in my squad and herd them together.

The troops were wild with celebration, mingling amongst and slapping each other on the back and shoulders, grasping one another by the forearms and dancing little circular jigs, the whole time cheering, whistling and cavorting about. Thankfully, I was able to recognize the rest of my squad all still on their feet. I was beginning to think we might come through this without any more casualties in our group.

In the distance to the north, the cannons still rumbled and the sound of musketry reverberated from the sides of the ridge. Somewhere a major assault was still in progress. Now that all appeared safe, senior officers began to gather around us. They were eager to take control of the situation. The cannon were wheeled around to face down the east toward the gap and we were brought back into formations. We formed up in column and were marched to the east through the gap.

We marched between a quarter and a half of a mile straight east down the road, and then were formed up obliquely to the north to ascend the eastern side of Missionary Ridge. As we started in column up the ridge, I could look back to the west and see as other troops were sent directly north up the beginning of the slope of the southern end of Missionary Ridge. We were towards the head of the column. I felt the excitement of the hunt. I realized that very soon the leading elements of the troops on the south end of the ridge would probably be encountering Confederate troopers that we knew were positioned there.

If we moved fast enough, we would be able to arrive on their flanks, or even in their rear. If we maintained the pace that we were, they would probably be able to retreat back up the hill past us. I managed to reload my musket while we were moving and holding this by butt and barrel crossways of my body, I began shoving the men in front forward faster.

Before long, it seemed that the whole column was moving at double-time, in fact even faster than that. We were moving along at a brisk trot. As we started up the slopes of the mountain that was Missionary Ridge, we were able to maintain this pace for only forty or fifty yards until the slope of the mountain took our wind away. The leading elements of the column seemed to put some distance between them as it seemed like further back the column jammed together and slowed down. Then we turned to face directly up the ridge and moved almost in line towards the top. We no sooner had gotten into this formation somewhat accidentally when an intense firefight broke out south of us towards the top of the ridge. It was apparent that our troops moving up the extreme southern slope had found the Confederate fortifications and they were making some show of resistance.

We were in a mood to celebrate still. Troops to each side along the side were cheering and shouting. It was almost like we were trying to flush the game to run before us. Then, sure enough, a few men in gray were seen making their way north along the top of the ridge. They were being driven by the Union troops to the south. I was thinking only that I didn't want any of them to get away. I brought my rifle up to my shoulder and shot the first one that I saw. All up and down our line there were scattered irregular bursts of firing as our boys in blue let loose at anyone in gray on sight.

We continued to move along the eastern slope of the ridge disarming obliging Confederates; it seemed, one after another. Then we were on top of the ridge, and looking down south along the top of the slope, I saw what appeared to be at least a brigade, maybe two or more, of Confederate troops who were obligingly throwing down their arms and putting their hands in the air. They were being pushed and jostled back up the hill towards us by Union troops visible behind them. Looking down to my right, I could see another line of blue coated troops moving forward. We had managed to bag the whole bunch of them.

I thought the celebrations around the cannon were one of the most joyous events I had witnessed, but there was nothing to compare with this. The troops were yelling and cheering, and some were even firing their rifles in the air in celebration. The celebrations were as loud and joyous as they had been in the valley, but nowhere near as long-lived. As I glanced around at the faces of the southern prisoners standing with their arms in the air and an utter look of dejection, defeat, and concern on their faces, my mood for celebration quickly passed. It seemed that most of the Confederates glanced around with looks of apprehension.

I think a lot of them thought that we were going to round them up and shoot them. On sudden impulse, I reached into my pocket and pulled out a piece of hardtack, I managed to bite off a chew and passed the rest to a Confederate standing tensely nearby. He took it rather meekly, I thought, and managed to gradually chew off a bite, and then passed it to the Confederate next to him. I had only a couple more pieces of hardtack in my pocket, but I took them out, bit off a chunk and passed them to the Confederates around me. Soon, Union troops around me were passing out their hardtack also. I think we all knew that we would be getting something to eat later, but who knows when the Confederates would next be given any rations.

Surprisingly by this time, the senior officers were already making their appearance on the scene. I think they managed to sense an easy victory because they were not far behind the rest of the troops doing the actual fighting. They soon had the Confederates marching off under guard down the slope of Missionary Ridge and had us digging in for the night pretty much where we had been at the time the surrenders took place.

There were far too many troops clustered here on the top of the ridge, so our brigade made its way further to the north until we came to a place that had been abandoned, but appeared to have been a camp used by the Confederates on the peak of the ridge. We hastily improved the fortifications with ditches facing north and east and settled down for the night. It was already near pitch-black.

Guards were posted and cook fires were lit and, as the men laid down to spread out their bedrolls, food and ammunition were being brought up for the troops. Ammunition was distributed, and as I loaded up my cartridge box and pockets, I settled back to clean out my rifle and my revolver and reload. By the time I was finished, hot food was ready and we formed up, filled our tins and cups with hot food and hot coffee and returned to settle down on our blankets and eat.

That night was one of the most cold and miserable nights that I had spent thus far on this campaign. I don't think that my uniform had ever managed to dry out from the damp, drizzly rain of the day before. It was most certainly still damp; however, I thought this was more from the sweat of our exertion marching across Chattanooga Valley, up one ridge, down the next, and up another. I was absolutely worn out, bone tired and frozen like a chunk of ice.

I lay on the ground in my greatcoat, covered up with one blanket and my poncho and shivered throughout the night. I don't think I ever slept and was glad to see the sun coming up the next morning. Hopefully it would be a little bit warmer now, I thought. Hot food and coffee was again prepared and soon we were back on the march.

We were on the march again probably before 10 o'clock in the morning. We went down the eastern slope of Missionary Ridge and struck the road that we had been on yesterday, turned east and began marching off in column. It seems that General Hooker had taken the bit in his teeth and was determined to keep the Confederates on the run. We marched hard throughout the day, picking up isolated groups of Confederate prisoners as we went and marching past the debris of an army in flight that lay scattered along the road.

As we marched, the men being curious as always, tried to hesitate as they passed anything discarded to see if there was something of value. We passed teams of artillery horses still hitched to broken down gun carriages. We passed wagons with broken wheels or axles filled with a variety of military junk. There were rifles, muskets, and an assortment of ammunition and artillery shells; but nothing of any use to us. There were clothes, cast off blankets and cooking utensils but nothing to eat or drink. I had snatched up the revolver that the Confederate officer of artillery had used to fire at our troops yesterday and had given it to Johnny. It had been a Colt 44 army revolver. I kept my eye out for any other revolvers, thinking it would be a fine thing if each of the men in my squad possessed one but never found any.

Even though we were ordered to march hard, we never managed to come up with any major groups of Confederate stragglers. Before it had even started to turn to dusk, the column had been called to a halt and instructed to fall out to each side of the road. We dug rifle pits along the eastern front of our line of march as well as down the north and south sides. We threw the dirt up facing the direction from which the Confederates had been fleeing and drug together what we could find in the way of logs, lumber from broken down wagons or any other type of debris that we had found discarded by the Confederates, formed up our little barricade and, feeling secure, settled in for the night.

The day had been cool, but thank God it had been dry. My uniform was very much the worse for wear but at least it had managed to thoroughly dry out by this time. Campfires had been built up and down the road and we were lucky to be treated to another hot meal before settling in for the night. We had spent the day marching at a brisk pace, anticipating an engagement with the Confederates. I was thinking that we had them on the run, and if we kept at them hard, we could push them all the way to Richmond, wherever that was. I was thinking that we should find them, hit them hard again and again, and keep them on the move. I suppose you should be careful what you wish for.

It had been another cold night, but I slept well, possibly because I wasn't wet while trying to sleep, or possibly because I had managed to relax after the fight of the day before. But we were up again well before any sign of sunshine. We snacked on hardtack washed down with water, but did manage to get a cup of coffee before we were marching out.

Once again, our regiment was near the head of the column. Possibly because of the fact that it was still dark, we had skirmishers well out in front as well as some mounted infantry. We had marched for an hour and a half or two, and just as it was starting to become light in the east with a faint glow of pink and yellow showing on the ridge in the distance, we came to a bridge across a creek. There was a Confederate rearguard on the other side of the creek and our skirmishers fired a volley. The cavalry charged, thundering across the wooden planks of the bridge and the Confederates retreated pell-mell towards the town in the distance. They ran like jackrabbits.

We charged forward, trying our best to keep up with the cavalry as they thundered hard on the heels of the Confederates racing towards town. It was almost a hilarious sight, watching the twelve mounted men chasing what must have been a couple of hundred Confederate troops down the road towards the town. We did our best to keep up, but it was impossible. The bridge was narrow and the column was crammed together trying to force its way across. When we finally reached the other side, we spread out a little to each side of the road, and then turned both to the right and left to form line facing the town.

As we moved towards the east, we watched as the last of the Union cavalry disappeared into the town. There was a flurry of shots and in seconds the cavalry was racing back out of town towards the safety of our line of troops. Then the men in gray made their appearance, moving rapidly in line, giving chase to the Union horsemen. They continued to move towards us, apparently oblivious of our presence. They had marched a couple of hundred yards from the safety of the town and we had narrowed the distance on our side by at least an additional two hundred yards.

Our troops separated to the edges of the road as the cavalry thundered past, and then we formed up and delivered a quick volley at the Confederates who were hesitating and some even starting to move back towards the town. We were at a fairly long range, probably three to four hundred yards, but the Confederates had realized their danger at last and were trying to move back to the safety of the town. There were a couple of hundred of them out in the open, and even though it was a long shot, it was much too tempting to resist. We must have had twice their number and we delivered one volley which hastened their movements to the rear. Then we reloaded as we marched in line towards the town in the distance.

We moved across the field with four regiments in line leading the rest of the column. As we came to the houses on the outskirts of the town, our skirmishers were well forward. They went flitting from house to house, peering through doors and windows, and soon the whole line was passing through and around the houses. We did our best to stay in line as we moved through the town from west to east.

There were a few Confederates who lingered in town, sniping at us and making a token show of resistance. Whenever firing broke out, we would drop into a crouch and take cover behind any structure, and then move cautiously forward, peering over walls, around trees, houses, shrubs, wagons, outhouses, or any of the other structures that may have formed the residences of the civilian population. Then as we reached the eastern outskirts of the town, we saw the Confederates break away in small groups and race for safety to the east.

While in town, we paused briefly to reorganize and realign the regiments. It must have been nearing 9 o'clock in the morning. We could look to the east for what appeared to be a thousand yards or so and in the distance there was a sloping ridge that appeared to be nearly as high as Missionary Ridge, at least on the southern and northern extreme. Towards the center directly east of where we were, the ridge seemed to slope down to where it was probably half as high. Looking into the distance and getting a feel for the lay of the land, I realized that the road that we had been following must pass through another gap in the ridge there. Even as I was thinking that, Sergeant Shawnasee moved down the line instructing us that we should be moving forward in skirmish formation.

We were on the southern side of the road, a hundred and fifty yards or so, and we moved to the east and spread out gradually in skirmish formation. My squad was in line to my right, and on the opposite end, Tom Sinclair was moving, encouraging the boys, like I was, to keep their heads down and pick out any cover they could. Once again, we were moving across a fairly open field that didn't seem to offer much in the way of cover, but I knew that wasn't true. There is no such thing as a truly level field. If there were not any low places that served as a natural drainage, then usually the farmers would dig ditches to allow water to run off and the ground usually had a natural tendency to roll and undulate. Unfortunately this was one of the flattest, most featureless fields I had ever seen.

As we moved, we shifted slightly to the south so that when we neared the stand of timber at the foot of the ridge, we must have been a couple of hundred yards south of the road. Skirmishing forward north of us were two other regiments. We got to within a hundred yards of the tree line at the foot of the ridge before Confederates to our front opened fire. We dropped to the ground, searching for whatever cover could be found, firing and reloading, and moving forward flat on our bellies searching for the Confederates. Just how many Confederates were cowering in the brush and trees at the foot of the slope, was hard to determine. So far that morning we had only seen a couple of hundred Confederates in total.

As we made our way to the east towards the ridge on which the Confederates were concealed, it became obvious that there was a small spur of the ridge extending west from the main heights of the ridge. This hadn't been obvious from where we had started the advance.

We continued moving carefully to the east as what appeared to be a brigade of troops marched directly down the road and then spread out into line to pass through the gap in the ridge where the road led. I had gotten into position behind one of those granite boulders that could be found along the bottom of the ridges. It was about half the size of a piano, but I had a rather ominous recollection of Frank Martin. I wasn't about to raise my head to peer over the top of it. I was on my right knee, balancing with my left foot and watching as the Union column spread out to each side of the road, preparatory to marching through the gap in line.

There hadn't been any firing or sign of a Confederate presence north of where we were presently cowering. Suddenly there was a thunderous blast of artillery and a rattling of rifle and musket shots. The brigade that had marched so proudly down the road only seconds before was now fleeing to the rear in panic. Then the Confederates in the tree line along the slope of the ridge in front of me opened up with a tremendous volley at our skirmish line as we crouched in what we thought was concealment. A bullet ricocheted off a granite rock on my right side and another kicked up dust and mud near my right foot. I had failed to notice how the spur from the ridge extended out past the right flank of our skirmish line and it appeared that there were a number of troops there, as well as directly in front of us.

The left end of the line was even now well past where we were on the southern end and these troops were in a mad dash for the rear. The line to the north seemed to be caught up in the panic and began obliquely to move back to the rear also. I decided that we were in no position to stay where we were. It was obvious the rebels were strongly entrenched to our east, and also in position on this spur to our south, certainly they had us in crossfire. I told the boys to, "Move back! Move back!" They never hesitated as they complied.

As we started back across the open field, I noticed Tom Sinclair to my left doing his best to help one of the boys as they stumbled across the field. I ran to help him. Tom had his left arm around the waist of one of the boys in the squad and had the soldier's right arm over his right shoulder, holding his wrist as he helped him stumble to the rear. I came up on the left side expecting to see that the soldier had a leg wound from the way he was limping, but was almost surprised to see that his left wrist was dangling at nearly a right angle from his forearm that was held horizontally forward with the elbow being bent at right angles. His eyes were fixed on his hand as the blood gushed and dripped from his injury. I put my rifle in my left hand and threw his left arm across my shoulder which caused him to scream in pain. The bloody stump of his wrist was directly in front of my face with his hand hanging from it. I grabbed his arm between my thumb and fingers and squeezed tightly. This managed to stop the bleeding from his hand, and between Tom and I, we nearly lifted him off his feet aw we rushed him across the field.

I could hear bullets smacking into the mud and dirt at our feet as we moved to the safety that lay west of us. I had never felt so strong before in my life. I like to think that it was concern for Hans' welfare because that's who we were carrying on our shoulders as we fled, but I suspect that it was more a sense of absolute panic that had gripped me. Whatever the cause, we soon caught up and were leaving the rest of the squad behind us as we raced for safety back across the field and into the small town.

We passed through other troops being brought forward, but never hesitated in our mad dash to the rear. We made it into the small town before we took cover on the western side of one of the houses there. We lowered Hans to the ground to lean back up against the building, and as I did so, I continued to squeeze his forearm between my thumb and four fingers. Tom managed to find a strong piece of leather; I think it must have been the reins of a bridle, wrapped it twice around his wrist just above the injury, and then tied it tight. It only took one look at Hans' injury to know that his hand would not be of any further use. He was destined to see the army surgeons.

I gave Hans my canteen and encouraged him to drink, and then I went into the house where we were sheltering in the protection of its western wall. I searched around and found some clean linen and took this out and wrapped his hand with it after washing off any blood and mud with the canteens of the other boys in the squad. Then I wrapped his arm in the clean linen and tied it there in position with some twine around his forearm just where the bridle reins had been tied.

The whole time, Hans stared at his wrist in shock. I wasn't sure that he even felt any pain. We managed to stop most of the bleeding with the tourniquet and I think that Hans was feeling somewhat stronger. I had sent Tom Sinclair back down the road to look for help and he presently reappeared with a couple of stretcher bearers. We loaded Hans on the stretcher with his right arm lying down to his side and his left arm draped carefully across his chest, covered him with his blanket and poncho and sent him to the rear. I told Tom to follow with him and make sure that he received attention as soon as possible. I knew that somewhere in the rear, probably at the western edge of this town, the army would have set up their tents for the care of the injured. I told Tom to make sure and see that they were the first in line.

I think we probably were because, even though the northern end of the line had started their panicked retreat first, Tom and I had managed to beat them in our race for the shelter of the town and we had lost no time getting Hans treated as best as we could and on his way back to the surgeons.

Suddenly, the sounds of severe fighting broke out again in the east. I peered out the windows of the house in which we were sheltering and watched as more troops of the 1st Division were sent forward, marching, climbing and stumbling over the dead and wounded, they neared the ridge to the south of the gap and received the same welcome from the Confederates. I watched as three regiments moved across the same field that we had just retreated over. They were moving well south of the road that went through the gap. I suppose they thought that they would be safe from the Confederate artillery that was positioned in the gap protecting the road.

We hadn't run into any artillery on the southern end of the line, but as the new troops neared the ridge and the position where I knew the unseen spur of ridge curved west, they were suddenly met with a terrific blast of artillery. The troops that had been facing west from the wooded slopes of the ridge opened fire directly into the troops. If the Confederates had had artillery on this spur when we were there, I don't know why they hadn't used it. Maybe they reasoned that we were too panicked and retreating anyway and had decided to keep it as a surprise in the event that we renewed the attack in the same position as we had just done.

Anyhow, with the Confederate artillery taking the troops in the flank from the southern side and the Confederate infantry in the wooded slope of the hill firing west, it didn't take long for the new attack to come rushing back just as we had. In no time, troops from the 13th Illinois and boys from the 3rd and 12th Missouri were sheltering around our farmhouse on the edge of the town. Soon the little farmhouse was filling with injured soldiers from the 3rd, 12th and 13th that we did our best to care for there before seeing that they were moved to the rear. Well, one good thing about these generals is they eventually learn from their mistakes.

We had sent two attacks on the ridge to the right of the road that had both been met with savage repulses. They must have decided that it was about time to try the left side of the ridge. As we watched from the house on the edge of town, we could see what looked like a brigade of Union troops well north of the road, marching across the open field and heading for the ridge on the northern side of the gap. As we watched, they moved up the slope and into the tree line of the ridge that on that side of the gap was considerably higher. It was hard to determine their progress.

As I watched, I noticed troops moving to the front around the house that we were sheltering in. The officers were attempting to reorganize and reform the three regiments that had been sent in a panic to the rear. As all their wounded had been taken back from the farmhouse, I gathered up the men that were huddled within. There were members of our 31st Missouri regiment as well as men from the 3rd and 12th regiments. There may have been a few others.

We formed them up outside of the farmhouse and began to march across the field once more. On the southern side of the road, we were actually closer to the ridge than troops on the northern side, but still we hadn't advanced more than a couple of hundred yards across the open before the sounds of a furious musket and rifle fight broke out near the top of the northern ridge. It lasted unabated for what seemed like several minutes, and as we marched east we noted the first of the Union troops coming out of the wooded slopes at the bottom of the ridge and moving west. We quickened our pace across the field hoping to reach cover before we came under fire.

We were halfway across as the majority of the brigade began to emerge at the foot of the ridge and flee back across the field. I was almost surprised to see men in gray pursuing them. The Union troops were moving rapidly to our rear, but it seemed that the Confederates were moving just as rapidly in pursuit. Our line turned and faced north. We were just coming into position finally when the Union troops cleared the front. The Confederates seemed oblivious to our threat on their flank.

We fired volley after volley as they came to a crashing halt, turned and began stumbling back up the slopes of the mountain in their rear. As the Confederates made their way back up the western slope of the northern spur of the ridge, I watched as what appeared to be several brigades of Union troops moved east along our front. It had been one hectic, confusing morning. I suppose it was somewhere between 9 and 10 in the morning and we were already about to make what I thought was the fourth attack on this ridge.

Once again, Union troops started up the slopes of the ridge to the north of the gap and the sounds of vicious firing began again. I expected to see the Union troops come back down the ridge in a route as had happened on the last attack. The volume of rifle and musket fire rose to an astonishing volume. It seemed that it never faltered entirely, but like ripples on the water, rose in sharp crackling bursts of intensity and then faded to a slow rhythm of isolated cracks before suddenly rising feverishly to a maximum pitch again. I still expected to see blue coated Union troops coming down the sides of the ridge, but never did.

This battle went on in this rhythmic fashion over the next hour and, as I watched and listened, Union artillery came rattling up the road and passed by to the east. The artillery moved to the east until they were within five hundred yards or so of the road in the gap. I expected the Confederate artillery that I thought to still be there to open up on them, but surprisingly it never happened.

Our troops on the ridge north of the gap continued their battle with the Confederates and volley after volley of fire echoed from the ridge and across the gap, but the rhythm to the battle seemed to gradually slow down. The Union artillery, as it came up, moved to the south of the road, and continued facing towards the slope where the men in my own regiment had been repulsed. They were probably five hundred yards distant as they set up. As I watched, the Union artillery let loose barrage after barrage towards the gap and towards the wooded slopes of the ridge south of the gap. What they were shooting at, I couldn't really tell. I suspect they thought there were still Confederates cowering there in the trees, and as I watched, I could see that they were concentrating their fire on the spur of the ridge that extended to the south. It was here that the Confederate artillery had last fired on our line as we had moved forward.

As we stood watching these developments, another column came moving eastward along the road and it seemed that another whole division of troops was moving forward to the attack. It must have been early afternoon when sounds of fighting gradually slowed and then ceased, except for an occasional crack of a rifle that seemed to echo in the distance from the other side of the ridge.

As I watched, men from the new division marched down the road, passed through the gap and moved off north and south along the ridge. We had won this battle at a terrible cost, and as I watched, I could tell that the men of General Davis' division were fortifying their positions facing the Confederates. Gradually tired and wounded troops began making their way back down from the northern ridge to the road and back to the rear. These were the tired troops that had made their way successfully along the top of the ridge and driven the Confederates off. They were followed by the walking wounded and then stretcher after stretcher of wounded being carried to the rear.

I moved with my patched-together collection of men back into town and we separated, individual men moving off to look for other members of their squad, their company, their regiment, their brigade or their divisions. I had a rather ominous feeling. It was almost a sense of dread.

We had come all the way through the Vicksburg campaign without any serious injury in my squad. There had been me and eight other men just a short time ago. Now, Frank was dad. Hans was crippled and would surely lose his hand and would be unlikely to return, even if he didn't die as a result of it. Otto was somewhere with a severely sprained, if not broken, ankle and I wasn't sure about how to go about finding him.

I looked from man to man in our squad. Johnny still had a grin on his face, but somehow it was lacking in humor. Christian Nichols was limping slightly. I'm not sure what his injury was. When I asked him, his only reply was, "Ya, it is nothing." Robert Cantrell and Michael Francis just looked extremely weary and had nothing much to say. Tom Sinclair, when I looked at him, made the intelligent suggestion that we should head back into town and find some place to stay. He said that he had heard that orders had been given for us to remain here and cease in our pursuit of the Confederates. He wisely said, "It would be good if we could find a house to stay in because, with all of these troops, there is going to be a shortage of places to stay." Then he said, "Let's move back to that farmhouse and spread out our bedrolls, fill up on water before we have to go looking for it and then see if we can't find out what happened to Hans." Tom always did seem to have a downright sensible way of looking at things.

We moved back to the farmhouse on the very edge of Ringgold, as I had learned the town was called, and deposited our gear on the floor of the home. Leaving the rest of the squad there, I took Michael with me as we carried the canteens back looking for water and sustenance. We ran into Sergeant Shawnasee who explained in his jubilant Irish accent, "It's good to see you again, son. I was most worried for you."

We chatted as we made our way to the west and passed by where the cooks were setting up camp to make their fires and cook a hot meal for the troops. Sergeant Shawnasee had managed to make friends with some of the cooks which wasn't hard for the tall Irishman with his naturally bubbly disposition. He managed to acquire a large roll of sausage and some coffee and I sent this back with Michael, who was carrying the canteens of water for the troops. Then the sergeant and I made our way back to the medical tents to find Hans.

It took a good deal of searching and pleading with medical personnel, and I'm not sure anyone would have paid any attention to a mere corporal, but Sergeant Shawnasee was big and strong enough to be intimidating and pleasant enough to be charming. It wasn't long before we managed to find Hans in a large tent lying on the ground on blankets next to row after row of wounded soldiers.

We had to pick our way deliberately and carefully as we stepped over one soldier after another until we could find Hans. He was lying on his back with his blood soaked stump of an arm draped across his chest. He seemed to be asleep and seemed to be breathing peacefully, but he opened his eyes at the mere whisper of his name. I said, "I thought you were sleeping." Hans replied, "No, it's hard to sleep. I just like to close my eyes so I can ignore the pain and pretend that I don't have to listen to the cries and moans of the men around me."

"Are you having much pain?" I asked. Surprisingly, he said "No. Not as long as I don't think about it and not as long as I don't move my arm." Then Sergeant Shawnasee said, "Have you had anything to eat, boy?" Hans said, "No, I haven't had anything since hardtack this morning before the fight." To which the sergeant replied, "Well, here you go son. I brought you a little something."

I hadn't noticed as the sergeant had slipped a small piece of sausage and a piece of cheese into his pocket. He handed these over to Hans and we stood looking down on him from each side. There wasn't enough room in the tent to kneel down, and certainly no room to sit, but taking Hans' right hand and helping him to sit up, he ate his cheese and sausage and finished up some hardtack and I helped him sip water from my canteen. After he had finished this brief meal, the sergeant handed him a small flask and said that he should keep this with him at all times. He said it had some good old Irish whiskey which was sure to help him heal in a heartbeat. "And make sure none of those rascally sergeants find it, or it'll be gone before you know it," he said.

Then we made our way out of the tent after helping Hans to lie back and adjust his position to be as comfortable as possible. As we left the tent, the sergeant spoke to me briefly. He said, "Son, I must be checking on the rest of the men from the regiment. You should make your way back to the squad and see that they're taken care of."

By the time I got back to the farmhouse in which we had been sheltering, the boys had made a fire in the fireplace and boiled up some coffee in a large pot that they found there. They had been unable to find an actual coffeepot and had been forced to be creative. They had strained the grounds through a muslin sheet and were doing their best to protect the last tin cup of coffee for me. They had saved me a chunk of the sausage and had protected my bedroll in the farmhouse which was now packed to overflowing capacity.

I gathered up their tin plates and went back through the camp until I found the cooks who had just finished preparing a meal of beef, beans and cornbread for us. I made several trips carrying two plates of food until all the men in the squad had had a hot meal. No one wanted to go for their own food for fear that when they got back they would have lost their place in the cabin. I have to give it to Tom. He could certainly think ahead.

That night it turned out to be unbelievably cold, probably well below freezing. I was actually concerned for Hans being in a tent, lying on the ground, but there were enough other wounded soldiers in that tent that I think the body heat alone would have kept them warm. We had made sure that Hans had a couple of heavy wool blankets over him when we left as well as rolled up blankets for a pillow.

We stayed where we were for the next several days, huddled in our farmhouse, taking meals from the camp in the center of town and checking on Hans a couple of times each day. We made sure that he received as much nourishing food as we could, refilled his flask of Irish whiskey and even filled canteens with hot coffee for him.

One day when we went to check on Hans, we found that he was no longer there. He had been doing quite well and had been moved back to Chattanooga. It seems that most of the wounded men were being taken into town in Chattanooga where they could be better cared for in wooden barracks type hospitals. Johnny Applebaum laughingly said, "You suppose Hans will be making his way to see the hookers?" Otto Kener who had just earlier managed to find his way back to join us, limping on his crutch, spoke up and said, "Yea, yea. If it were Frank, he would be there even with one arm."

I smiled briefly as I thought to myself, he's probably right. Even if Frank were laid up in a hospital a couple of miles from the ladies, I'm sure he would figure out a way to slip away for a visit. It was rather sad to think about. The only thing that Frank had talked about for the last month was visiting Hooker's Ladies in Chattanooga. There seemed to be only two things that Frank cared about in life, whiskey and women, not necessarily in that order. Whatever had induced him to voluntarily join up with the Union army, he never said and I suppose I had never really questioned. The fact that he had volunteered spoke enough for his character that words weren't necessary to try to define it further. I had actually found the man to be somewhat annoying, but I realized now that I would miss him.

That night, we were ordered to pack our gear together, and by the light of a waxing moon, we were up and moving back through Rossville gap to take up camp in the Chattanooga Valley. I found that it was December 1st as we dug and scratched together a camp, set up tents and pieced together lean-tos and other structures for shelter. The Confederates were gone, God only knew where, and we tried to make ourselves as comfortable as possible. It seemed like General Grant had decided to fortify his position all around the town of Chattanooga and it looked like we would be there for a while.

CHAPTER SIXTEEN

We had moved back into the Chattanooga Valley between Missionary Ridge and Lookout Mountain on the first day of December as I was to learn later. We had started setting up what we thought would be a permanent winter camp.

The following day, I asked permission from the sergeant to go into Chattanooga. I told him that I wanted to see Hans Verner and make sure he was doing okay. I made my five mile trek into the town and inquired of the first troops I met on the outskirts of Chattanooga where the hospitals could be found. I headed off in the direction they indicated, but soon became confused. Chattanooga was a large sprawling military camp and the tents all looked the same to me. I had to make inquiry of several other soldiers before I finally reached my destination. Even then, it was hard to find one person amongst all of the many sick and wounded.

I finally managed to track down Hans. As I entered the tent, I glanced quickly up and down the rows and had no trouble spotting him as he sat on the edge of his cot. He looked to be doing surprisingly well. He had a book across his lap and was attempting to write a letter. He never noticed as I made my way towards him and the first he was aware of me was when I said, "It looks like you should be back in the line, soldier. Quit malingering here."

He glanced up with surprise that quickly turned to jubilation. The first thing he said was, "It's good to see you, Corporal Everett. How are the rest of the boys?" I could tell from the look on his face that he truly meant it.

I'm sure he had wondered about the outcome of the rest of the days fighting and any that may have occurred since he had been wounded. He seemed to be relieved when I told him that he had been the only casualty for us. Then I said, "Never mind that. How are you doing?"

He smiled and said, "Well, I expect to be back soon. I can always use this," holding up the stump of his left arm, "To steady my rifle. I'll be able to shoot as good as ever." "Well, that I don't doubt," I said, "But, the devil is going to be in trying to reload." His smile seemed to fade as he said, "Yea, you've got that right."

Then I asked him if I could take a look at his arm. He said, "Well, it is fine by me, corporal, but I doubt that the orderlies will want to wrap it up again." I said, "Well, that's alright, let me just take a look." I took his injured arm in both hands and bent and took a sniff or two. It smelled clean. There wasn't any odor of decay. Then I gently felt of his stump through the bandages and he didn't seem to react with any unusual pain. I felt greatly relieved. I knew that it must be healing well since there was no smell and no unusual tenderness.

Then I sat down on the cot next to him and for a while we talked about old times and the other members in the squad. I found that he expected to be sent within the next week or two back home, as did most of the other men in this tent. I wasn't sure if it was by accident or design, but Hans speculated that the more severely wounded were kept separate from the rest.

It seems we soon ran out of things to say. I thought about asking him about his home in St. Louis and what he planned to do once he returned, and then realized that probably wasn't such a tactful conversation to begin. I'm sure he really had no idea of what he could do with one good hand. So, I sat there and steadied the book on his knee while he finished writing his letter and then helped him fold it and place it in the envelope. We gave it to an orderly who was passing and asked him if he would mail it, and then I made my farewells and left the tent.

It was still early and for a moment I thought about Frank Martin and the Chattanooga hookers, but I had no real desire to seek them out. Before, when we had been in Vicksburg, we had gone as a squad looking for the ladies, but I think that was mainly because Frank Martin had been so insistent and had managed to inflame the passions of the other men.

I know that he certainly aroused my curiosity, but I had no idea where they could be found and really didn't feel like stopping soldiers to make inquiry.

So, I made my way back to our camp and linked up with the rest of the men. I got back just at dusk, in time for supper. It was probably a good thing that I hadn't wasted any further time in town because I was informed that we had been given orders from General Grant to move out at first light and march to Bridgeport, Alabama. My first thought was, what, with all the trouble we had taken to get here, all the marching, fighting, death and destruction, we were headed back to Bridgeport. Well, what did I know? I was only a corporal.

We were up before light, had breakfast and packed up all of our gear in our haversacks and our knapsacks, which had been returned from the regimental supply wagon, and marched out at the crack of dawn. We marched north, and then west and crossed the bridge over the Chattanooga Creek. This had been completely rebuilt and was now a remarkably strong and sturdy structure. We marched leisurely and proceeded up the winding road of Lookout Mountain, around its northern tip, down to the west and across Lookout Creek.

As we had made our way around the northern tip of Lookout Mountain, I kept my eyes peeled for the piano sized rock where Frank Martin had met his end. Surprisingly, I wasn't able to recognize it as we marched past. Then, I watched as we marched past row after row of new graves. Most of them didn't have any markings to indicate who was buried there. I don't know whether I expected to see Frank's ghost as we marched by waving to me or just what I was thinking, but I knew that he must be lying there peacefully under one of those mounds of fresh dirt.

We made our way winding up the side of Raccoon Mountain and camped for the night in the shallow valley on its top, just outside the small town with the stone bridge over the creek. The next day we spent descending the western slopes of Raccoon Mountain and crossed the Tennessee River and entered into Bridgeport just at dusk.

The following day, we were given orders to begin work extending the fortifications and preparing winter quarters. We moved outside the town to the south and west and went to work. There had been a line of fortifications erected just beyond the periphery of the town and we were marched off a couple of hundred yards in all directions from this line of fortifications and set to work with pickaxes and shovels.

Day after day we worked, digging out a trench and piling the dirt along the inner side to make a wall on the inside of the ditch ten feet high and ten feet thick. The ditch itself was probably five or six feet deep and ten feet wide. At locations chosen by the officers, we built redoubt and lunettes in the line that would be used for artillery emplacements.

We lined the wall of the entrenchments with dugouts reinforced with plank walls and plank roofs covered over with several feet of dirt. We dug pit latrines and drainage ditches towards the river. We set up row after row of tents, some quite large and others with enough room for eight people.

Day after day, more and more troops of the 15th Corps arrived and soon the whole corps was there. A few days later, the first of our wounded were brought over from Chattanooga. They were placed in some wooden plank barracks that we had constructed that had potbellied stoves for heat.

One evening, Sergeant Shawnasee passed through and reported that Hans had made it in that day from Chattanooga. After supper, the whole squad and I went off searching for Hans. We located him in a large tent that had been set up around the wooden barracks. It had been decided that the wooden barracks were for the more seriously injured. He was glad to see us and we laughed and joked for a few minutes until the orderlies came by, shooing us off. It seems they couldn't have too many visitors at one time, but Hans was continuing to do well and apparently these wounded were being moved in stages and shortly he expected to be headed back to St. Louis.

We spent the next four or five days doing our best to stay warm. For the last few days, it had turned extremely cold and we had flurries of light snow and the usual drizzling freezing rain. I had been mistaken in my belief that, once we had finished this new camp and settled in, we would be here for the winter because surprisingly the next day we were told that we would be packing up and moving out south along the west bank of the Tennessee again.

That evening, as we huddled in our tent trying to stay warm, Sergeant Shawnasee passed by and stopped in for a quick chat. I had previously complained to him about having to leave the Chattanooga Valley. His reply then had been that it was easier to keep the troops supplied if they were separated, and also in case of an epidemic breaking out, it was better for the general health of the army to have the corps in different camps. He also went on to relate that moving to Bridgeport had enabled us to hold more territory, scout and defend it and keep track of the movement of any of the Confederate troops.

I thought the sergeant knew everything, but surprised that he really had no good idea and certainly no explanation for why we were moving out from here. His only reply had been a jesting, "Well, that's the way of the army, son. You can't expect to know what they're thinking. If we knew what they were thinking, it wouldn't be long before the rebels knew what was up." Well, there might be some truth in that, I thought, but I couldn't help wishing I knew where we were going and why.

We were up before the sun again the next day, had breakfast and loaded up and marched out. The roads were a terrible mess, nothing but mud over the top of your boots and running rivulets coming down the side of the hill across the road and into the Tennessee River. At places, the roads were washed out such that wagons couldn't pass. We filled these little gullies with two foot logs placed perpendicular to the road. I supposed that was done so that water could run between them. Then we covered these with longer logs, maybe a foot thick, running in the direction of the road and covered the top of these with smaller logs, and then limbs and brush, and piled dirt on top of it all. In this manner, we made our way south and spent the first night in Stevenson. We had been through this small hamlet on our way north and found it to be the most depressing dingy sort of little village consisting mainly of log huts and very little else. It hadn't improved any since the last time we were here.

We spent the next couple of days marching through the mud in the flurries of snow and cold rain, sleeping alongside the road and repairing it in places as we went. One night as we lay shivering in our blankets, huddling together to keep warm in our two-man tent, while we lay on our backs looking up at the stars since the day had finally cleared and quit raining. Johnny Applebaum suddenly remarked, "What a way to spend Christmas."

I thought about it and did some quick calculating and realized he was right. Today had been Christmas. I studied the stars through the near cloudless night and said, "Which one do you suppose is the Christmas star?" Johnnie just laughed and said, "That star only appeared to signify the birth of the Savior. It doesn't come every year." Then he said, "You know, I wonder if there is anything to save." I didn't say anything, but I thought I knew what he meant.

Some time during the night it started to rain again and it was still raining when we got up and rolled our muddy blankets and tents together and started off down the road. We soon left the road and started following the railroad tracks. The road was muddy, difficult to march on and extremely disagreeable, but I think the railroad tracks were worse. The railroad ties were too close together for a normal step, but too far apart for one either. With our muddy, water-sogged boots, stepping on the edge of the wooden ties was treacherous.

We marched, or rather stumbled and tripped along throughout the day and just at dusk came into a small hamlet along a railroad station. I couldn't have cared less, but as we spent the next few days here, I came to learn that we were in Woodville, Alabama. We spent the next few days here, cold, wet and muddy, and extremely miserable. With perfect timing, one morning we were formed up and a proclamation was read calling for reenlistment of the troops. It seemed that most of the men in the division and maybe the entire 15th Corp, as far as I knew, had signed up three years ago. Their enlistments were up.

The men in my squad had enlisted only a year ago and I had enlisted two years ago, so we were stuck. It may have been due to the weather, the rain, the mud, and the cold, but there wasn't any rush forward by any of the troops to immediately sign up. I think the officers reading the proclamation were somewhat disheartened by the lack of enthusiasm. Maybe that's why they announced shortly later that we would be establishing winter camp here. My first thought was, 'Why in the Hell would we want to stay here?'

We went to work rather unenthusiastically, digging trenches in the mud and erecting fortifications and setting up tents in the rain. Digging pit latrines that filled with water as rapidly as you threw the mud out, was an exercise in futility. Then our enthusiasm for the job soon picked up as a day or so later it became extremely cold, the rain turned to snow and the wind seemed to whip and swirl around us. We needed better shelters in a hurry!

Groups of men were sent out on various chores. Some returned with rocks and stones to construct foundations and chimneys. Others returned with logs and planks to build cabins. Other continued digging fortifications and forming dugouts. Surprisingly the harder they worked at erecting shelters; the happier they seemed to become.

I had never been so cold in my life. I thought that in the south things were supposed to be warm, but this cold beat anything I had ever seen in my long fourteen years of existence. I wondered if the men worked so enthusiastically because they knew that whenever they got a shelter finished, they had a chance of warming up and possibly not freezing to death.

As we worked to erect shelters, some squads were sent out on a daily basis, looking for food and supplies, but they picked a miserable place to make a winter camp as there weren't many people in the vicinity and, as I had noticed last year when we marched through this area, the soil was poor, the farming difficult and the livestock rare, if not nonexistent. Thankfully the railroad seemed to be working, and just about the time I thought we were in for a period of starvation, a trainload of supplies arrived.

After nearly two weeks of the coldest weather I could imagine, it began to warm up somewhat. The ground that had frozen hard beneath our feet, started to turn back to mud. I wasn't sure what I preferred, unbearably cold with frozen ground or moderately cold with sticky mud, but by now we had adequate shelters made.

We had erected a dugout in the wall of our frozen fortifications. We had made a fireplace that was dug into the barricade itself and had a chimney extending four or five feet above the rampart. Above ground, we had done the best we could to fill in the cracks between the rocks with mud. It was a poor excuse for a chimney, but it sufficed to draw smoke out of the dugout.

We had cut armload after armload of thin pine limbs and piled these up around on the floor all over the inside of the dugout for insulation from the ground and mud. We had placed our ponchos over these, then our groundsheets on the poncho, and our blankets on top. We were actually comfortable indoors. Having established our meager shelters, we then had some days of near leisure.

We used the first few days to bathe and wash our clothes and polish our gear and equipment. This almost made us feel human again. One evening, as we were sitting around before it was time to turn in, Sergeant Shawnasee stopped in for a quick chat. He sat cross-legged on a pile of pine limbs, leaning back against the wall of the dugout, and passed a small flask of liquor around. Each man took a small sip. I had never really seen the sergeant drunk except maybe once after Shiloh when we had been celebrating in the sutler's tent on the bluffs of Vicksburg Landing. Where he managed to find the liquor to refill his flask, I had no idea, but whenever he stopped off for a chat with the boys, he usually passed the flask around. Of course, we only had these little meetings maybe once a month, so maybe it wasn't such a strain on his resources.

After we had all taken a sip and returned the flask to the Sarge, he said, "I just stopped in to see how you boys might be doing." By which we knew that he was open for any questions or conversations we might want to bring up. My first thought was about the reenlistment proclamation.

"Is it true, sergeant," I said, "that they're giving out four hundred dollars for people to reenlist?" "That they are son, that they are." Then I joked and said, "Well, can I reenlist?" He merely laughed and said, "No, son, you're already in, at least for another year. But don't worry. If the war lasts long enough, you might get five or six hundred dollars to reenlist. Now, isn't that something to think about?"

"What about furloughs?" Christian said. "I hear that people that reenlist are getting a one month furlough. What about us? Do we get any furloughs?" The sergeant thought for a moment and said, "Well, son, you know it does seem that that would be reasonable, but I haven't heard anything about it yet."

Then Tom Sinclair spoke up and said, "How are the reenlistments going, sergeant?" "Well, son," said the sergeant, "It seems to depend on which troops you're talking about. Some regiments signed up quickly and others seemed to be less enthusiastic. Besides the bounty for signing up, they are offering special tags and stripes for the uniform to designate the troops as veteran regiments. In addition to that, I understand they will get a slight increase in monthly pay. That applies to any regiment that gets more than seventy-five percent of their troops to reenlist. It's not necessary to get everyone in the whole regiment to reenlist to qualify. Personally, I think that most of the regiments would end up signing on again, but there are some that I think are unlikely for any reason."

Then he said surprisingly that he thought that the 13th Illinois would not be signing up again and were likely to all go home when their term was up. This was rather surprising to me as the 13th Illinois had been in the first division with us and, on most occasions, we had been side-to-side in the fighting and while marching. But it was still early and we had only had a couple of weeks to think this over. What, with the extreme cold, the snow, the mud and the gusty winds that seemed to buffet this place, it wasn't a good time to even think about asking troops to reenlist. I believed that when spring came and the weather began to mellow, that they would probably change their minds.

Then, almost as an afterthought, the sergeant said, "Here, son. I have got something for you." I realized he was talking to me and, as he leaned forward and stretched his arm out, I lifted my hand to take what he had. In the flickering light of the campfire, I looked down at the palm of my hand and recognized the sergeant stripes that he offered. Surprised, I looked up into his smiling face and the only thing I could think to say was, "For me?" "Yes, for you," he said, smiling. I sat there staring at the stripes in the palm of my right hand as the men of the squad leaned forward, congratulating me and slapping me on the shoulders.

I looked up at the sergeant and was at a loss for words to speak. I almost sputtered out 'What do I do now?" but realized that would sound stupid. However, I think the sergeant read my mind because he said, "Well, for the first thing, you need to get those stripes sewn on your uniform and then you need to make a choice as to who you would like to see named corporal of the squad."

I know my face must have shown consternation and probably a little hesitancy, and again the sergeant seemed to read my mind. "Of course," he said, "We will be making the final decision, but it never hurts to get your input." And, with that, he stood up as straight as he could in the dugout, spoke a work of encouragement to each of the troops and then ducked his head as he pushed the blanket aside that we had tacked up as a door.

I felt like jumping to my feet and following the sergeant outside, but knew I couldn't do that. I sat there on the mound of pine limbs that I had erected for my bed. The boys in the squad continued to congratulate me and I knew they were all sincere. Tom Sinclair said, "Well, aren't you going to sew those on?" I said, "I'll have to do it in the morning. It's too dark in here to thread to needle." With that, everyone laughed.

Then, we began to talk about other things. We talked about the reenlistment proclamation. It seemed that the men in the squad were all unanimous in their assertions that if they were given the opportunity, they would all reenlist. The suggestion was made that we should visit the 13th Illinois and encourage them to reenlist. We decided that we would individually, more or less on our own, arrange to make incidental contact with the troops and discuss the situation with them. I said, "I think it would be better that way than to approach them in a group. That might bring on some hostility." Then, gradually as it was getting late, we ran out of things to say and turned in for the night.

CHAPTER SEVENTEEN

Over the next few weeks, the weather took a turn for the best. It gradually warmed up until it really felt good to be out and about. The officers celebrated the change in the weather by forming us up to march in parade and drill around through the camps. We had been eating pretty well after the supply train had come through and hadn't been doing much else. I think we had all put on a little bit of weight. We marched and drilled as a regiment, and then in brigade strength, and then in battalion strength. We had inspections frequently and were encouraged to keep our uniforms neat and clean, and our weapons polished.

One night, it snowed about two inches, but the next day it was gone. It warmed up enough that we could be out marching without our greatcoats. As we were passing by on the parade ground, I noticed Sergeant Shawnasee standing with a group of other officers, and as we passed nearby, I took note that his uniform which he always kept neat and brushed seemed even more spiffy than usual. Then I noticed that he was beaming at me broadly and, when he turned to say something to an officer standing next to him, I noticed on his shoulder a lieutenant's badge. I thought, that sly old fox, I wondered when he received that.

That evening after supper, Sergeant Shawnasee made his way to our dugout. Once again, he wasn't wearing his greatcoat. He stepped in and inquired in a thick Irish accent, "How be you boys doing?" I just laughed and said, "We'd being doing fine, lieutenant. When were you going to tell us? When did this happen?"

The lieutenant dropped down on a pile of pine branches and smiled as he announced, "Oh, a couple of days before I passed out your stripes." "And you never said anything?" I said. "Well, no," he said as he passed around his flask. "I didn't want to dampen your good news. Besides, I knew you would find out shortly." Then I said, "Well, congratulations, sir. You deserve it." He, rather somberly said, "We lost a lot of good men over the last year. I would gladly have remained a sergeant if we could have kept them all."

I got to thinking of the men that I had known that were no longer with us. Sergeant Ernest Francis Smith had died during the Vicksburg campaign. He had come down with some abdominal pains and gone off to the hospital and never returned. Then, Jacob Koontz had lost a foot at the battle at Rossville gap. As we had marched down the east side of the Chattanooga River, hurriedly ducking the artillery fire to get into position for the assault on the southern ridge, he had been one of the soldiers I had stepped over in my hurry. I'd never even noticed my old comrade from the 21st Mo.

We had lost a Lieutenant Robinson in battle at Vicksburg and a Sergeant Snyder who I hadn't really known. We had lost a Captain Judd and a Captain Dougherty at Chattanooga. I understood what the lieutenant meant when he said he would just as soon have remained a sergeant, if it meant that those men were still alive. It cast a pall over the whole idea of the promotion.

Then the sergeant said that he was here to inform me that tomorrow we would be leaving to go out on a scouting expedition and to relieve the guard stationed at a small outpost overlooking the Tennessee River. We turned in early, but I had difficulty sleeping. Tomorrow seemed like an auspicious day to me.

I was up early and met up with the Sarge and we proceeded to the tent where we would be briefed. Major Fredrick Jaensch was conducting the meeting. There were a few other sergeants and lieutenants with us and we were detailed a line of march and a specific outpost to report to.

I gathered up the boys in the squad and met Lieutenant Shawnasee on the parade ground. We linked up with another squad and their corporal. Then we marched out of camp and down south to the banks of the Tennessee River and followed it west along the bluffs until coming to an outpost about ten miles distant. This was simply a small fortification that had a shallow trench around it with four foot high dirt embankments and horizontal logs notched together on the top extending the height another three feet or so. There was a head log which left a space between the fifth and sixth logs on the top of the barricade through which we could fire.

From a distance, we announced our presence and intentions and then marched up to the outpost, up the dirt embankment, stepping over two logs that formed like a doorstep and into the compound. Inside the compound there was just barely enough room for one eight-man tent and two smaller tents that would have held about four men each. The outpost was situated on a bluff that was overlooking a ford in the Tennessee River and was within easy view of the railroad tracks that ran further north of the fort. The fort was intended to block access from the ford, thereby safeguarding the rails.

The men here who had spent the last two weeks patrolling and scouting around the area were quite happy to see us arrive. So happy, in fact, that they couldn't wait to be gone. Lieutenant Shawnasee and the lieutenant commanding them discussed the situation briefly and the lieutenant made some suggestions to the Sarge as to how best to go about their responsibilities and finally informed him that over the last couple of weeks they had occasionally seen Confederate cavalry on the other side of the river. However all had basically been quiet. Then, as the last of his troops were even then passing over the step and out of the outpost, he quickly ducked inside one of the smaller tents, grabbed his gear and followed them. We were now on our own.

It seems the lieutenant was in command and I was second in rank. Well now, this was something different. I wasn't quite sure what to do next, but Lieutenant Shawnasee wasted no time. He directed the members of the other squad and their corporal to take the large eight-man tent as there were seven of them. Then he directed us to reposition the two smaller four-man tents so that their entrances faced each other. He then had us fastened together several of the rubberized ponchos, that were used to form two-men tents, and instructed us to drape these over a rope strung between the apex of the two tents. Lastly we tied them down to the ground of the embankment. This formed a sort of a lean-to, which served to partially connect to the two four-man tents. They were close enough together that when the flaps were opened, it seemed almost to make one large tent.

That way, in the evening, we could sit around like usual and enjoy the companionship of the entire squad.

We had positioned the tents to where the entrances were on each side of the fire pit and this would provide a slight degree of warmth at night, plus sitting around the campfire was also somewhat reassuring and relaxing. It seems the lieutenant had only been here for a few minutes, but he had already come upon this simple improvement to the arrangements inside our little fort.

The flaps of the larger eight-man tent could be opened, and in the evening we would all be easily visible as we congregated around the campfire. It provided an ideal means for us to get to know the members of the other squad with whom it appeared we would be spending the next couple of weeks.

We had marched nearly ten miles that day and didn't feel inclined to exert ourselves any further. Besides, with us marching west and the other squad marching east, we felt secure from any Confederate threat as apparently no one had seen anything in their patrols before we had arrived at the outpost. Therefore, we decided to put together something for supper.

Cooking equipment consisted of a three-legged, five gallon cast iron pot, into which we poured water, some salt pork from a barrel and some dried beans from a sack that was kept on top of the pork barrel. There was another sack on top of a barrel of hardtack to the other side of the entrance of the eight-man tent and in it we found several onions. We chopped up a few onions and threw them in the pot also. Then we had placed a large pot of coffee on the coals to boil. While we were doing this, we placed one man in the southwest corner of the fort and another in the northwest corner of the fort to keep an eye out for any sign of Confederate cavalry or raiders.

We settled in around the cook fire, relaxing and making conversation with the soldiers of the other squad, while we waited for supper to cook. After supper we stationed another guard at the northeast corner of the compound, dropped a couple more logs through the slots on each side of the step through the doorway in order to barricade it and arranged for the troops to rotate guards throughout the night. Feeling satisfied with these precautions we turned in.

The following day, the lieutenant woke me earlier than the rest and asked me a simple question. He said, "Well, Sergeant, have you decided who is to replace you as corporal of your squad?" Of course, I had given this some thought, but had been somewhat reluctant to make my recommendation. I liked all of the boys in the squad and didn't wish to offend any, but rather reluctantly, I admitted to the lieutenant that, "In my opinion, Tom Sinclair would be the best choice."

"I heartily agree," said Lieutenant Shawnasee. "And, in fact, we have already designated him such." I said, "Why ever, in that case, did you even ask me to make a choice?" The lieutenant just laughed and said, "Well, Sergeant, in the future you're going to have a lot of choices and I just wanted to see how good your first decision would be."

Then he instructed me to go roust the squad up and give Corporal Sinclair his new stripes. I lost no time in doing that, congratulating Tom on his promotion and feeling relieved as I hinted to him that the decision had been made by Lieutenant Shawnasee. Then I returned to talk with the lieutenant and kicked together the embers of the fire, added some new wood and set the coffee to boil.

After breakfast of hardtack and coffee, Lieutenant Shawnasee asked me my thoughts as to our duties for today. I thought about what the lieutenant had told us yesterday as he had been leaving, and spoke aloud, "I wonder, Sir, about the Confederate cavalry he mentioned spotting on the other side of the river a day or two ago. I don't think it would hurt to take a scout out in that direction and see what we can find."

The lieutenant looked at me and queried, "How many men do you think you should take?" he asked. I thought about it briefly and said, "I think four, Sir." "And who would you plan to take?" "I think I'll take Johnny Applebaum, Otto Kerner, Robert Cantrell and Michael Francis," I said. "Why not Tom Sinclair?" the lieutenant asked. And I replied, "I think he should get his corporal stripes sewn on first thing this morning, and besides, if anything should happen, I think it would be best if he were here to take over. Besides, after Tom, I think Otto would have been my next choice for corporal and I think the five of us should suffice."

"Very well," said Lieutenant Shawnasee, "See to it."

I went to the entrance to our tents and called out for Johnny, Otto,

Bob and Michael to get their gear together, because we were going out on a scout. In a few minutes, they were ready. In the meantime, I ducked back into the tent that I was using and rummaged through my knapsack. Now that I was a sergeant, I had taken to wearing one of my revolvers in my belt at all times. I grabbed the other Remington and slipped it into the pocket inside my blouse and took the two small Colts and gave one to Otto and one to Bob. I told them to place them in their belts in case we had any trouble, but not to think about keeping them.

I was thinking that it was senseless for me to have four revolvers for myself, but there was something about these two matching Colts that kept me from wanting to give them away permanently. I couldn't bear to part with either one of the Remington's as they had belonged to my father and older brother who had been killed at Osceola when our cabin had been burnt. But, as I felt somewhat uneasy leading this first scout across the river, I felt it would be best if we all had some extra weapons on-hand.

Johnny had the Colt 44 Army that we had picked up from the Confederate officer of artillery at Rossville Gap, which meant that four out of the five of us would have a revolver. That fact made me feel almost as if I was leading twice as many men on this scout.

We left the outpost and moved away to the north as I attempted to slip down to the Tennessee, taking advantage of every bit of cover I could find. I reasoned that if our fort was under observation by the Confederates, if we took off heading north and then worked our way back to the south and across the river; possibly we could make it at least to the river without being observed. This was probably ridiculous as I knew there was no way that we could ford the river without being seen, but if there were Confederates on the opposite side, maybe we could get to the river's edge unobserved which would prevent them from setting up an ambush while we were in the water.

We came to the river's edge and made our way safely across. Then, for no particular reason, I turned the men to the west and moved down the river just at the edge of the vegetation on its banks. I didn't feel like sloughing through the mud on the banks and also didn't want to leave anymore of a trail than was necessary.

We moved west, keeping an eye on the mud of the banks heading down to the river, as we watched for tracks. We scouted through the vegetation on the top of the banks, watching for any movement, or any sign of enemies there.

We proceeded for about three miles in that direction, moving cautiously, slipping from one clump of brush to another, from one large tree to another, or from one depression in the ground to the next. Then we turned to the south and moved a quarter of a mile inland before we circled back to the east and crossed the road leading up to the ford. We proceeded to the east three or four miles, before heading north to hit the banks of the river and coming back west to the ford. I hadn't noted any sign that there had ever been any Confederate cavalry in the vicinity. I wondered if the lieutenant had been imaging this or maybe his sighting of cavalry had been a few days before what he had said and any trace had been washed out by the rains.

We made our way back across the Tennessee, up the bluffs and into the little outpost, and marched in just in time for salt pork and beans and onions for supper. We washed it all down with hot coffee and I gave my report to the lieutenant. For some reason, I was feeling especially proud of our little adventure of the day, but then I tried to think of it through the squad's point of view and realized it had been nothing other than a long walk. What a difference it all made according to whose eyes you were viewing it through.

Over the next week, we continued with the same schedule that the preceding lieutenant had been following. We would send four men, both east and west along the bluffs of the Tennessee River, marching out four or five miles, then returning, keeping any eye on the river below for any sign of Confederates.

Once again I conducted another scout across the Tennessee as I had before, taking two members of my squad and two members from the other squad with me. It was as uneventful as previous. After another week of scouting along the tops of the bluffs and we were relieved and marched back to our home in the fortifications at Woodville.

The first two weeks of February passed uneventfully. We spent it polishing our equipment, marching, drilling and parading, and having inspections. One fine morning we learned that the order had come that we were to have our gear packed and ready because in the morning we would be moving out. Now that I was a sergeant, I felt that I could inquire of

Lieutenant Shawnasee, and searching him out, I didn't hesitate to ask if he knew where we were headed.

"Well, Sergeant, the only thing I have been told is that we are to be marching back up to Bridgeport. We're to take all of our gear and be ready in case we don't come back here. What our final destination is, I haven't been told myself."

So, that evening, I cleaned and polished all of my equipment. I had come to the conclusion that it made no real sense for me to be carrying four revolvers. I gave one of the .36 Caliber pocket police pistols to Tom Sinclair and the other to Otto Kerner, emphasizing that when this war was over, I would appreciate it if they would return them.

Then, we turned in for the night. Tomorrow, it looked like we would be on our way to Bridgeport, and from there, God only knew.

CHAPTER EIGHTEEN

Once again, we were up well before dawn. We had a warm breakfast, washed down with hot coffee, and then we loaded up our gear and marched off. We headed east, and then as the Tennessee River curved back to the north, we marched along its western banks. The roads were much improved, so much so, in fact, that Major Seay had obtained three wagons and our knapsacks and heavier gear were being hauled for us. That enabled us to march right along and we made good time. Surprisingly, the wagons were able to keep up without much trouble, seldom getting bogged down in the mud.

The weather was cool during the day, but thankfully it wasn't raining or snowing. At nights, we would fallout and bivouac right along the road. The evenings were frosty cold and each morning we woke up with a thin layer of ice on the vegetation and skimming the surface of the hard packed earth.

We made it into Bridgeport on the afternoon of the 2nd day of the march. I was surprised at how much the town had improved. The camp that we had worked to establish now had a considerable number of wood framed buildings and it seemed that the citizens in the town itself were much more prosperous, expanding the limits of the town in all directions.

We marched into the fortifications and were shown some tents that we could occupy at the present time. We were each issued more rations for a continued march in the morning, brushed our clothes and polished up our weapons, and then had a hot meal, the first in two days. After eating, we returned to our tent. I made sure the men were squared away, and then said

I was going to pay a visit to Hans if he was still in the hospital here. The rest of the boys wanted to come along, but I knew that we couldn't all go.

I ducked back out of the tent and found Lieutenant Shawnasee and suggested that we stop in on Hans. He said, "I wish I could, son, but we have a meeting to attend to later." I asked him, "Is it okay if I go?" The lieutenant replied, "Sure, just don't cause any trouble."

I marched through the gated camp, taking advantage of my new rank. I saluted the privates at the gate who returned the salute, never bothering to question me. Then I made my way to where the hospital barracks had been set up on the edge of town next to the river landing. I inquired about Hans Verner and was rather surprised by the deference the orderlies showed to me.

I was shown to an officer in the medical corps who consulted the records and informed me that Hans had been doing well when he had been sent back to St. Louis. The officer then explained to me that it was probable that he would be assigned to the invalid corps after a few more weeks of healing. I didn't wish to look stupid, but nevertheless I couldn't help inquiring as to just what he meant by the invalid corps. The officer went on to explain how there was a lot of work that needed to be done in the army that didn't necessarily involve fighting and marching. There was always considerable paperwork to be dealt with and such things. He indicated that a lot of the orderlies helping with the wounded soldiers here had been serving in the invalid corps because there was always work caring for other wounded soldiers that didn't involve having two good arms or two good legs.

I felt somewhat relieved by that prospect. I could just picture Hans volunteering to continue to serve in some form or fashion. It was good to know that he would have an occupation, at least as long as the war lasted. With that, I returned to the tent to let the rest of the squad know what I had found out.

We turned in early that night knowing that the next day we would be up and on the march again, and indeed we were. We were marching out of the fort earlier than I expected. I don't think it was even seven o'clock by the time we started to move.

We went over the bridge, around Nickajack Point, up over Raccoon

Mountain, stopping to camp just east of the little town on the other side of the stone bridge again. The town looked like it was prospering nicely due to all the military traffic going back and forth along the road. I bet they never planned on becoming so rich.

It had rained all day on us as we marched and it continued throughout the night, but I suppose we were getting used to it. The good thing was that the roads were in much better shape, having been worked on continuously, I think, for the last six months.

The next morning we marched down the eastern side of Raccoon Mountain, made our way across the creek on the bridge leading to Lookout Mountain, then up and over Lookout Mountain and down into the Chattanooga Valley. We marched into the fortifications immediately surrounding Chattanooga and were assigned tents for the regiments.

Major Seay, who commanded the 32nd Missouri Regiment, was in charge and, as we formed up to pass through line that evening for the first hot meal in two days, we were treated to a good sized shot of whiskey in our tin cups. The major himself was at the end of the line, keeping an eye on the cooks as they dispensed the whiskey. Each man in the two regiments thanked him as they passed through the line. It was a nice gesture on his part, one I'm sure nobody expected.

That evening before we went to bed, we drew rations for two days and sure enough we were up again before the sun made its appearance and marched through camp, across the valley and up and over Missionary Ridge. Surprisingly as we marched, the weather became colder instead of warmer. The sun was up and shining, but it didn't seem to have any effect at all. The ground stayed frozen hard which actually made marching easier. As long as we were marching, it didn't seem too bad, but I dreaded the prospect of making camp for the night. We had nothing but the rubberized ponchos that we could fasten together to make two-man tents, but the way the wind was gusting and blowing, they wouldn't provide much protection.

We marched twelve or fifteen miles, made camp for the night, snacked on hardtack and hot coffee, and then shivered through the cold night. We marched to the east, and then the southeast on the following day and moved over another high, steep ridge and into the valley beyond it where we camped again. It had remained unbelievably cold throughout the day and the wind blew such that it was hard to maintain your balance.

We sheltered in the little two-man tents for the night, but during the middle of the night were awakened by what almost sounded like small bullets striking on the rubberized canvas of our tent. There was a continuous drumming on our shelter that increased almost likes volleys of musketry. I thought for a minute that it was hailing, but there was no thunder or lightening. I rolled over on my belly and stuck my head partway out of the tent, and stretching out my right arm, scooped up a handful of the pellets. They were solid balls of ice about half the size of a mini-ball. They continued to drum down so fast that within the next half hour, they were piled three inches deep on the ground. I can honestly say I had never seen anything quite like it.

We were up early the next morning, snacking on hardtack and water, and marched away to the east. We passed through a small town and only went a few miles past it before going into a camp there. Just where we were headed, we still hadn't been told. I had expected that now that I had the rank of sergeant, I might be better informed, but even Lieutenant Shawnasee didn't know. However, we were lucky that we had regular eight-man tents to set up now and we were able to make cook fires and have a hot meal again. It almost seemed like we were on some type of schedule, one hot meal every two days, then hardtack and water

in-betweens.

We stayed camped where we were for the next three days. We had two hot meals a day and managed to get well rested and even began to feel warm, despite the fact that the weather remained bitterly cold. Then, we were ordered to be ready to move out in the morning.

We were up well before any sign of light in the east and marched rapidly all morning. I knew we were destined for a little town called Red Clay. Around noon we were allowed to fallout to each side of the road and take a quick rest and munch some hardtack and water, but told to be ready to march at any time. I had the fear that they had been fattening us up and getting us well rested in anticipation of some hard fighting to come.

We were soon up and marching to the south, keeping up a steady tramping pace. We were bringing up the rear of what appeared to be an entire division. When we went into camp that night, it was well past dark, maybe even approaching midnight. We set up our small two-man tents on each side of the road and dropped down, exhausted. I think we must have marched twenty-five miles or more that day.

As I tried to go to sleep that night, it was difficult because of the anticipation I felt. I was thinking that we would probably be involved in fighting the next day, and it would be the first time that I would have any, what I thought might be, significant command decisions to be made. I knew I would not have any important decisions to make, but might be given an order that I was expected to carry out and the anticipation that I might be the one to determine how to go about following that order, was somewhat daunting.

We were up long before light again, had some hardtack and coffee to nourish and warm us up, then loaded up our gear and awaited orders. They took a long time in coming and, even then, I was rather surprised to find that we would be moving back along the same road that we had just marched down last night. But we didn't have far to march. We had only marched for a half hour or so when we were ordered to form up in line east and west of the road in battle formation. We remained there throughout the rest of the day and that evening were sent forward of the rest of the troops and spread out along the line, having been detailed for picket duty.

We spread out with five yards or so between each man and took what shelter we could facing south towards the enemy and doing our best to stay awake throughout the night. Periodically during the night, there were a few shots as light skirmishing somewhere along our line kept us tense and on edge. Then, in the middle of the night, nearly constant heavy firing broke out far towards the south. Just how far away it was, was hard to say. When Osceola had been attacked and burnt to the ground, there had been some heavy firing at times, but even though our homestead was only twelve miles away, we had heard nothing of it. This sounded to be far in the distance, so I expected it was probably closer than twelve miles, but certainly more than five or six. That plus the fact that there was some firing up and down where our line was, was enough to keep me awake throughout the night, or at least what little night was left.

It seemed like right in the middle of the night; we were formed up and started marching south towards the sound of the battle. As we marched south, the first rays of sunlight showed in the east, the sky became pink, and then turned to yellow as the sun made its appearance over ridges far to the east.

We were formed up in line again, probably sometime around noon. We waited patiently in line for the orders to move forward. There was a brisk artillery duel going on well to our front and the sound of intense musket fire. All we could do was speculate on what was happening in our front. Then, gradually the firing dwindled away and the artillery ceased and I stood there, if anything, with more dread than I had been feeling all day. I wasn't sure what that signified.

Were our troops in the distance moving back towards us, or were the Confederates moving away from us. The skies began to darken as dusk approached. Still, we waited patiently in line, having dropped our knapsacks and sitting on them to rest. Darkness came, and still we stayed in line. Then, well past dark, we formed up again and marched back to the north. The moon came up bright and shinny; a near cloudless night. There was enough light to make out, faintly, details around us as we marched along the road and finally arrived back where we had camped last night where we fell out to each side of the road to get some sleep in what was left of the night.

We were up early the next morning, breakfasted on coffee and hardtack, and drew three day's rations. Then, just as the sun started to pinken the skies in the east, we were marching away, back along the road that we had come down yesterday.

Sometime around noon, we heard skirmishing behind us as we moved north; however, we were not ordered to form the line, but to continue to march north. We passed through Cleveland and then around the northern edge of the ridge there. About dusk, we turned south to southwest and continued marching through the night, and finally in the early morning we were allowed to fallout and set up our camp.

We were up again at midnight. It was too dark to tell anything about the surrounding countryside, but as we started marching back north, Lieutenant Shawnasee passed by and I couldn't help but inquire as to where we were now and where the hell we were going to next. The lieutenant just laughed and said that he heard we were on the other side of Ringgold,

Georgia where we had fought the Confederates last before returning to Chattanooga. We were marching back north towards Cleveland again.

We marched over hilly pine covered hills for several hours, and then were allowed to fallout alongside the road to snatch a few minutes' sleep. Indeed, that's all we were allowed, it seemed to me, a few minutes. It seems like I had no sooner shut my eyes and then we were being rousted out of our bedrolls and back on the march. However, it was early sunlight as we started out, so maybe I had slept longer than I thought

Throughout the day, we continued to hear skirmishing behind us and it seemed like even off to the east of us. Then, in mid afternoon we were back in Cleveland, Tennessee. As we marched through town by platoons, we gave three cheers to Colonel Dickerman, of the 103rd Illinois, who had been commanding the brigade for the last few days as we had marched in an apparently random and incoherent fashion. He was sitting astride his horse inspecting the troops and conversing with a group of officers. I cheered loudly and enthusiastically, if even somewhat sarcastically.

We marched through town and set up camp and had the first hot meal in several days. We were all tired and exhausted, but at least it had been warming up over the last twenty-four hours. It was cloudy and looked like it might rain, but at least it was considerably warmer than it had been. We found eight-man tents set up and dropped out wearily to rest. We immediately spread our bedrolls and lay down to sleep, even though it wasn't yet dark.

Sure enough, during the night it blew up a storm. Lightening flashed and crackled occasionally and booms of thunder shook the tents, but not enough to cause us any great alarm. There was a gentle breeze and the rain, although steady, was almost peaceful. It was a good thing that we had gone to bed early because sometime well before any sign of light, we were bugled awake rather urgently, and grabbing only our rifles and accoutrements, we were formed into line in anticipation of an attack.

It was still too dark to see. The skies were overcast and the gentle rain seemed to mask any sounds. We waited patiently in line, staring into the distance, attempting to pick up any sounds or any suggestion of movement, but all remained quiet, thankfully. Gradually it seemed to get slightly lighter. The skies to the east turned pink, and then purple due to the clouds and rain. Then the sun broke clear of the ridge to the east and the warmth melted away the clouds and soaked up the rain.

Just after the sun was up in all its glory, Lieutenant Shawnasee passed down the line and gave orders for us to march back to our tents, load up all of our gear and be ready to move out. It seems we were headed back towards Chattanooga. We marched away, leaving the tents behind, knowing that after they were allowed to dry out, they would be taken down, loaded upon the wagons and brought along after us.

We marched back towards Chattanooga, camped in the valley east of town at the foot of Missionary Ridge, and then continued on the next day back up over Lookout Mountain, across Lookout Creek, up Raccoon Mountain, finally camping on the summit again. I was beginning to think I should purchase property and build a little house for myself in that hamlet as we had passed through there so many times.

The following morning we tramped down the western slopes of Raccoon Mountain and marched back into Bridgeport. I had anticipated that we would be camping in Bridgeport where we would be allowed some rest and a hot meal, but surprisingly we were loaded immediately onto flat cars and freight cars and rattled out of town south along the Tennessee by train. We snacked on hardtack and water as we rattled down the rails with the engine whistling and tooting around every bend. It was a nice warm day and, as we rattled along, we sat there back-to-back leaning against each other for support and managing to nod off occasionally. We continued rattling, jostling and whistling down the rails and gradually the day passed and the skies began to darken.

It got fairly cool that night, especially riding out in the open on a flat car. It made me tend to wish that we had been lucky enough to get inside a freight car, that plus the fact that in the darkness, bouncing and rattling down the rails as we were, it was somewhat alarming. I feared that if you fell asleep, you might accidentally tumble off the train. I think we all found it hard to sleep and were grateful that early in the morning we rattled into town where we disembarked and were given a good hot meal.

We were shown into a little camp that had been set up there and ushered to our tents where we soon turned in for a more peaceful nights' rest. Early the next morning we were rousted up and loaded back on the trains, heading south again.

The day came and went. It was peaceful riding on the rails, watching out over the Tennessee River to the east and glancing up the sides of the tree covered mountains as we whistled and rattled down the road. There was nothing quite like it, I thought.

We munched on hardtack and washed it down with water. The day passed uneventfully. Dusk approached and soon became pitch black, and well after sundown, the train slowed, squeaked and rattled to a halt and we were back in our camp at Woodville, Alabama.

As we sluggishly and rather stiffly lowered ourselves from the railroad cars, we gave one long cheer, having arrived home in safety. We walked slowly and stiffly back into camp, found our familiar dugout and went in, dropping on our dried out, crackling and crunchy pine limbs without even bothering to roll out the bedrolls. We just spent the last fourteen or fifteen hours moving by train, and although it sure beat walking, it was surprisingly tiresome. I was asleep in no time.

CHAPTER NINETEEN

After breakfast, we returned to our hut. We hadn't received any other orders and I couldn't think of anything else to do. I took off my boots and stuck them on two sticks leaning out over the embers of the cabin fire to let them warm up and dry out some, intending to give them a good rubdown with beeswax to help waterproof them. Then, I set about cleaning my weapons and oiling them down also.

As I was leaning back against the wall of the dugout, Johny came over, sat down cross-legged opposite me and said, "What do you think that was all about, sergeant?" Of course, I knew what he was talking about because I had been wondering pretty much the same question myself. Why on earth had the officers found it necessary to march us a hundred or more miles over the last week? It seemed to me that all we had done was go on one long march. True, there had been a couple of days that we thought we would see action, but the only sign of action was in the distance with the artillery and musket fire well beyond sight.

We had marched through Bridgeport and Chattanooga on the way to getting there and there were tens of thousands of troops in the vicinity. My initial thought was "How the hell should I know?" but I didn't wish to voice this to him. Instead, I paused to think and took on a rather contemplative know-it-all attitude. Then, I said, with what I thought was with an air of confidence, "Well, Johnny, I have it on good authority that the generals were all sitting around conferring about how the whole division seemed to be becoming fat and sassy. They took a vote and decided that we were the fattest, sassiest regiment in the whole corps and decided that we needed some exercise to run the fat off of us and toughen us up some. So, they decided to send us on a long march."

I was rather surprised that Johny leaned forward, and with a look of incredulity on his face, said, "Really, Sarge?", which brought a howl of laughter from Otto Kerner. "Yea, yea, you dumb German," Otto said. "Just because he's a sergeant doesn't mean they tell him anything. He doesn't know any more about it than I do." I was momentarily amused because it seemed that Otto had finally gotten one over on Johnnie, but Johnny wasn't to be outdone. He promptly replied, "Yea, everybody knows more than you do, Otto." To which Otto promptly replied, "Yea, if you knew so much more than I did, how come you had to ask?" Pretty soon, the boys were all ridiculing and teasing each other.

I settled back and continued to finish cleaning up my weapons, accoutrements and gear. I gave my boots a good waxing down and then polished them up. I did this rather hurriedly thinking that at any time we would probably get orders to load up and go for a march or a drill, or do extended duty at one of the guard posts, but we weren't bothered throughout the rest of the day. In fact, over the next week I had the feeling that they had almost forgotten about us.

Throughout the day, we were left pretty much on our own. One day, as it seemed fairly warm compared to the previous week, we marched down to the Tennessee River and stripped down and went for a swim and a good scrub. Then, we washed our clothes out, and hanging them on branches, wrapped up in the blankets to wait for them to dry. Of course, we kept our weapons handy and were never out of sight of the fortifications on the bluff. The Tennessee was several hundred yards wide here and we picked a spot that was relatively shallow and had a sandbank with driftwood covering our front. Of course, even so, we took turns keeping one man detailed with his rifle ready to stand watch.

After bathing we sat around for several hours letting our uniforms dry in the sunshine before we dressed, while they were still moderately damp, and returned to the hut. There, we hung the uniforms around the dugout to let them finish drying and wrapped ourselves in blankets to stay warm.

Then, we took turns using a hot iron that I had borrowed and a three foot long piece of plank to iron our uniforms out. We turned them inside out and took care to give the seams an especially good pressing with the hot iron in order to kill all the lice. After we redressed, we threw all of the pine limbs in the fire and replaced them with new pine limbs for bedding. I was feeling almost as comfortable as at home.

A day or two later, Lieutenant Shawnasee came by to visit. He inquired about our health and our families individually. The lieutenant always wished to make sure that we had written home recently and was quite anxious to hear what we heard in return. I always thought that this was because he had lost his own family to the cholera epidemic that swept through Canton a few years before the war and now had no direct relatives in the United States. He still had family and friends back in Ireland, but I don't think they had ever kept in touch.

He went through the squad and inquired of each and every one of the boys, and especially encouraged Otto, who seemed reluctant for some reason to write home, to send his family a letter. Then, he stopped briefly and asked me about my family. I told him that my uncle and aunt were doing well, that their business at the trading post at the mouth of the Osage River was prospering and that my younger brother was healthy and growing like a weed, and that the oldest of my younger sisters had a boyfriend that lived in Jefferson City and pestered them constantly about making visits to that town for some reason. Jefferson City was twenty-five miles or so away from Osage City, so apparently it was infrequent that they made the trip. I couldn't help but think that that was good because Mary wasn't anywhere near old enough to have a boyfriend. She couldn't be more than thirteen, I thought. No, I thought again and realized she couldn't be more than twelve. Then, I tried to remember exactly when her birthday was and finally gave up.

Just as he was turning to take his leave, the sergeant mentioned that we should take our rifles apart down to the smallest pieces, clean them good and give them a coating of grease. With that, he reached into the pocket of his greatcoat and brought out a couple of jars of what looked like heavy axle grease. He tossed me a jar and tossed a jar to Tom Sinclair and then announced, "In the morning, you will all be receiving bright new shiny rifles as a courtesy of your good Uncle Abe and the U.S. Government." And, with that, he pushed the blanket aside and ducked through the low door to the dugout.

Tom Sinclair spoke out, "Well, what do you think about that?" And I thought to myself, "Yea, big deal!" I had spent the last several months trying to help the boys improve their marksmanship. The army never really allowed for that, therefore, we had had to practice it almost on the sly. I felt that we had just finally gotten adjusted to the weapons and had figured out the trajectory and fine-tuned our sighting, and now we were going to be given new weapons.

I pointed my rifle at the ceiling and pulled the hammer back to full cock. I shook it vigorously back and forth and bumped the butt of the rifle up and down on the ground to try to get as much powder to trickle back out of the nipple as possible. Then, I took the pigtail screw attachment out and placed it on the end of the ramrod, tamped down the muzzle and screwed it into the lead ball that was there and managed to successfully pull it out of the barrel. Then, I took the gun apart, cleaned it down good, oiled it all over and then applied some of the heavy grease that the sergeant had supplied us and put it all back together.

With that done I set about helping the rest of the men in the squad do the same. I had always felt that everyone knew how important it was to keep their arms cleaned and oiled and assumed that they were taking proper care of their weapons. But, as I passed around the dugout, it became apparent to me that several of the men had never taken their gun totally apart and cleaned it, merely confining their care of the weapon to cleaning out the barrel and nipple. A lot of the springs and firing mechanisms were severely rusted and some on the verge of disintegrating from neglect. We cleaned them up and greased them down and put them back together and I scolded each and every man in the squad as I passed through for their neglect in taking care of their weapons, even the ones who had done a fairly good job.

The following morning after breakfast, we were called to line up out in front of the commissary tent. Lieutenant Shawnasee was sitting there behind a makeshift table with a ledger in front of him. On his right-hand side was another sergeant of the regiment next to an empty crate, and as I walked up with my squad, he motioned me forward. He took my rifle, looked it over and wrote down the serial number next to my name in his ledger and handed it to the sergeant who packed it away in the crate. He then instructed me to step to his left where there were several crates of new rifles. I reached in and took one of the top rifles for myself and read the serial number out to the lieutenant and he wrote it down in his ledger.

Then, as the men progressed through the line one by one, they gave their old rifles to Lieutenant Shawnasee and passed through the line to get their new weapon issued by me and the number recorded by the lieutenant. We spent the rest of the morning issuing out the new rifles to the rest of the brigade, and then just before the noon meal, we were relieved and wandered back to our dugouts.

We spent the rest of the day taking the new rifles apart and cleaning off all the packing grease, and then giving them a good oiling down. I was particularly careful to give the new weapons a thorough inspection as I disassembled it, cleaned, oiled and reassembled it. We had also been instructed to turn in all our accoutrements for the old rifle and we had been issued brand new gear for the Springfield rifle. I couldn't wait to try it out.

I put my new belt and gear on, picked up the new Springfield rifle and wandered through the camp to the wood plank barracks where Lieutenant Shawnasee bunked with the other officers. I knocked on the door and entered on command. I glanced around the room and found the lieutenant sitting at a table in conversation with some other officers. He seemed pleased to see me. I hated to interrupt, but the lieutenant spoke up and said, "What can we do for you, sergeant?"

I politely asked him if I could obtain permission to go out and practice with the new rifle. He looked at me, and then looked at the other officers in the room, and said that he thought that was an excellent idea. Then he said, "We're planning on having target practice with the whole regiments over the next few days. I think it would be fine if you were to gather up the other sergeants and corporals and go try out your weapons. Then you would be better off trying to explain their use to the troops."

The lieutenant suggested that I go gather up the noncommissioned officers in the 31st and 32nd Missouri Regiment and return as soon as I had accomplished that. I went through the camp and gathered up the sergeants and corporals of the two regiments, and within a half hour, we were back at the officers' barracks. Lieutenant Shawnasee had been busy seeing that rows of targets were set up and lines at one, three and five hundred yards had been marked off.

The Springfield had a flip-up leaf sight that could be adjusted apparently for those ranges. We took our assigned positions in line and I took a forked stick that I had chosen and stuck it in the ground, wiggling and pounding it in until it was steady, then I knelt down behind it and placed the end of the barrel of the rifle in the fork of the stick. We were each allowed to fire five shots from a hundred yards, and then inspected the targets. Then we went back to three, and finally five hundred yards, firing an additional five shots from each position.

We soon realized that at hundred yards, the rifles all seemed to fire nearly a foot high, but at distance of three to five hundred yards; the sight seemed to be dead-on. Keeping this in mind, we agreed to instruct the troops to aim low, right at the belt buckle, whenever firing at targets less than a hundred and fifty yards. With that, we broke up to return to our barracks just in time for the evening meal. Before going to bed that night, I again cleaned and oiled up the new Springfield rifle. Over the next several days we had repeated target practice, each of the troops being allowed to fire five shots at two hundred yards.

The weather had been getting progressively warmer and I suspected that we would soon be putting the weapons to good use. Then, one day, we had a cold snap. It snowed throughout the day, initially melting nearly as fast as it came down, but continued snowing throughout the night until nearly noon the next day.

We had been out right after breakfast that morning, walking and kicking through the snow which was probably two feet deep, and in some places had drifted even more. We wandered through the camp and came to the top of the bluff. Looking down over the Tennessee River and off into the distance, I couldn't help but remark on the beauty of the snow covering the hills and valleys and weighing the tops of the pines down. Otto Kerner remarked, "Yea, it's just like Germany." I expected Johnnie to make the quick retort, 'How would you know, you dumb German, you have never been to Germany.' But, on glancing around, Johnnie was nowhere to be seen.

We took one long last look around and then turned and made our way back to the dugout. As we made our way up over the embankment and down the eastern side of the dugout, I was surprised to see Johnnie out in front of it, visibly constructing the largest snowman I had ever seen. He had a round mound of snow, the size of an upright piano, rolled and piled and patted together, and another one not much smaller rolled up next to it. As he looked up and saw us approaching, he said, "It's about time you boys got back. I need help getting this up." Now, here was a challenge.

We formed up in a circle around the huge snowball, squatted down and placed our arms under the sides of it. It was all the seven of us could do to lift it up and manipulate it into position. Then, we grabbed handfuls of snow and packed it in around the bottom of the snowball to pack it in tight so the edges wouldn't crumble and it wouldn't slip off.

The top of it was well over head high. As Johnny, Otto and Christian began rolling up a third snowball, Tom, Michael and I went off in search of some planks, empty boxes or other suitable objects to make some sort of scaffolding so we could get the third snowball on top. We managed to find some empty crates, barrels and boards lying around, enough to form a three foot wide, six foot long platform on one side of the snowman and a ramp of planks to roll the snowball up. Then we built a rather rickety scaffold on the north and south side of the snowman so that, after we had rolled the third large snowball up the ramp, we were able to lift it and then step along the scaffolding on each side and slide it into position. I think the top of the snowman's head must have been eight or nine feet in the air.

Finally we packed a small barrel tight with snow and lifted it up and over the head of the snowman to shake the contents out on top. We then filled up other small barrels of snow and lifted them up on the highest part of the scaffolding and began patting the snow together around the base of the circular mound on the top of the snowman, trying to form the brim of what would be a stovepipe hat. We decided to name the giant snowman Uncle Abe.

Several hundred soldiers had gathered around watching what we were doing, and rather unexpectedly, we were suddenly bombarded with a perfectly aimed shelling of snowballs. It wasn't long before the rest of the men in the 31st and 32nd Missouri Regiments had gathered together to defend Uncle Abe from attack. Soon, most of the officers in the regiment had gathered around and Lieutenant Shawnasee made an appearance with a group of settlers, rolling kegs of beer through the snow. They stood them up and tapped them, and then free beer was distributed, courtesy of the officers. Our snowball battle came to an abrupt halt as we hurried back to our respective dugouts to return with our tin cups and rushed to form line to get our share of the beer.

Lieutenant Shawnasee had disappeared, but presently returned, directing more civilians as they rolled a couple of more kegs up. They raised the kegs to a standing position, tapped them and distributed its frothy yellow beverage. Otto took a long sip, held his tin in the air and smacked his lips as he proclaimed, "Yea, dat is good beer." But, with several hundred soldiers, it didn't take long until it was all gone.

Soon we were back engaged in forming up to defend Uncle Abe from attack. We toppled the scaffolding and platform over to make fortifications around good old Abe, defending him from the gallant assault of the 32nd Missouri Regiment. The officers even got involved in making sure that we all played fair. Some of the boys who had been obviously splattered with snow, refused to admit that they were hor's de combat, insisting that the snow on their uniforms were from previous engagements or from where they had fallen while rushing forward. The officers supervised the affair, escorting troops off once they had been rendered a casualty of war.

Pretty soon, it seemed like there were snowball fights going on all throughout the camp and it looked like most of the whole division was involved. Lieutenant Shawnasee had had the idea of bringing up the beer first but other officers had pitched in and it wasn't long until the sutler's' supply had been used up. Evening came all too soon. Our little battle in the snow was broken off as we went to evening meal and then returned to our dugout for the night.

The following morning, when we left the dugout for breakfast, we were greeted with an appalling sight as soon as we pushed the blanket away to exit our dugout. We had failed to provide a guard for poor old Abe and some vicious, bastard had knocked his head off during the night. We hurriedly downed our meal and returned to repair poor old Abe. We had gotten his head back in place about the time that the troops from the 32nd returned from their meal. It wasn't long until we were back at it. Possibly because the officers weren't so generous today and failed to provide us with any more beer, but the battle never seemed to reach the intensity of the fighting of yesterday. That, plus the fact that the day soon became much warmer as the sun rose in the sky, melting the snow and turning the area all around Abe into mud, caused us to lose interest quickly.

Gradually, the men moved off in ones and twos, and then larger groups and we returned to our dugout to clean up our uniforms and polish our boots. Surprisingly the next day when we exited the dugout for breakfast, the snow had pretty much melted except for poor old Abe, but even he was an unrecognizable mound of dirty looking snow.

We wandered off for breakfast, and when we returned, we walked to the bluffs overlooking the Tennessee and scanned the valley in the distance. The days were definitely becoming longer, and looking down over the valley, you could begin to pick out the brilliant purples and reds of the myrtle, rhododendron and redbuds that dotted the countryside. There were even patches of white which I assumed were cherry trees, but could have been patches of snow that had escaped the ravishes of the sun as it lay piled at the foot of the large pine trees.

I stood there looking out over the beauty of the mountains and the valley laid out at our feet. I should have been enjoying and appreciating all of the grandeur of the scenery before me, but I couldn't help but have an uneasy feeling, that as the weather warmed and cleared, it could only mean that we would soon be back at the business of war.

Easter Sunday, March 27th, 1864, is a day I knew I would never forget. It was a warm beautiful morning and we turned out early for church services. There was a large tent set up on the edge of the parade ground and a chaplain preached a fine sermon. He no sooner had finished, and then we were formed up to march in drill around the parade ground. As we passed by in front of the large tent that had been used for the chapel, there on the platform that had been raised for the preacher, were a collection of officers that I hadn't noted until that time.

As we marched past, I had no trouble at all in picking out Uncle Billy Sherman. I had seen him several times previously, but never this close. I also recognized General McPherson and General Logan from the descriptions I had heard others relate. In addition, there were numerous other officers present. I easily picked out General Osterhaus and Colonel Simpson, Colonel Woods, Williamson and Wangelin. These were the brigade colonels for the 1st Division of the 15th Army Corps. I felt a sudden quickening of my pulse. With all this brass present in one place, I thought it could only indicate that we would be on the march soon.

However, we spent the rest of the month practicing our marksmanship, drilling, parading, and even went out for an extended period as a guard in one of the outlying fortifications. Then, one evening, we were given the word that we should clean and polish our gear and have everything packed up, ready to move out in the morning. It seems that at last we were on our way back to war. I actually felt fairly confident that this would be the last year of the rebellion.

CHAPTER TWENTY

We left our winter camp in Woodville, Alabama at sunup on a bright shiny morning. It was May the 1st. We formed up in column and marched out. Each day was the same, up early for breakfast, pack up and then march all day. We had two warm meals a day, one at breakfast and one in the evening after we were through marching. Usually we were permitted to fall out a couple of times during the day to munch hardtack, rest and replenish our water.

After five days of hard marching, we made it up and over Raccoon Mountain, past the little hamlet in the bowl on the top of the mountain and down the eastern side to the railroad junction at Wauhatche. I think we must have averaged fifteen miles each day of marching since we left Woodville on May the 1st. While we were preparing to form up to march out this morning, we were instructed to get rid of our excess baggage. Murmuring apprehensively the boys sorted through their knapsacks selecting whatever clothing and gear they wished to carry. These items they stashed in their haversacks, or rolled in their blankets. As we passed by the wagon that had been allocated for our use the boys in the squad dropped their packs in and then each, it seemed, turned to ask me for information.

"What's happening, Sarge?" queried Johnny.

"Damned if I know!" I replied to each.

Now that I was a sergeant, I had managed to acquire a snap down holster for my Remington revolver. The second one I placed in the pocket

I had made on the inside of my blouse up over the left breast area. I had placed the saddlebags that I had taken off of the Confederate cavalry officer in the bottom of my knapsack and placed an extra pair of long underwear, socks and personal items in the knapsack as well as an extra pair of pants and my greatcoat. I rolled my groundsheet and blanket up in the gum poncho and tied it at one end, then draped it over my shoulder. The knapsack I deposited with the other men's in the wagon.

In my haversack, I placed the two extra cylinders for the Remington's, a leather pouch full of 44 lead balls and a second one of 36 caliber balls for the Colt pocket pistols. I also packed a small brass flask of fine black powder for the revolvers, a tin of percussion caps, as well as the circular waxed pledgets to plug the end of the cylinders. I stowed my tin with my sewing supplies and flint, steel and matches in the haversack. I stuffed in my grooming utensils and finally I used some rolls of old pieces of discarded uniforms to pad the contents and, at last placed on the top of the contents of my haversack, were several dried sausages and my rations of hardtack.

I had my new Springfield rifle and sixty rounds of ammunition, my bayonet, cartridge box, cap pouch and canteen. I had my brass capper hanging from a leather cord around my neck and tucked down inside my shirt in a pocket I had made over my chest. My grandfathers Damascus bladed knife was stuck in my boot. And, of course, my cute little blue kepi was jauntily tilted on my head. I was all decked out and ready.

That day we marched up and over Lookout Mountain, down across Chattanooga Valley and all the way to Rossville. We were in Rossville some time before noon, having marched for five or six hours uninterrupted. Then, later that afternoon, we were on the march again, not stopping to rest until nearly midnight. Some said we were at Gordon's Mill, not far from the Chickamauga battlefield where General Rosecrans had fought unsuccessfully a year ago and where General Thomas had become famous.

We had marched another fifteen miles or so that day, and when we dropped out for the night, we munched on hardtack and washed it down with water before curling up in our blankets for the night.

We were up and marching in the morning before sunup. Gradually as the sun began to brighten the valley, I noticed what a lovely spring day it was. It was warm with just a gentle breeze blowing from the southeast. We were marching through relatively flat rolling ground, the tops of the hills being covered with pine trees and mixed with a scattering of color. There were pinks and whites primarily as there were clumps of rhododendron, myrtle and magnolias still in bloom. It was a wonderful day all in all.

As we marched we could see an occasional abandoned homestead and around them irises, and other assorted colorful bulbs and plants, were starting to bloom. I wondered if, after the war, the inhabitants would come back to take up their lives as they had been living before the war, but suspected in a good many cases that the only thing that would be there to show something of the previous owner's hopes and dreams would be the bulbs that would flower in the springtime.

We marched throughout the day, stopping only occasionally for a quick break for a drink and to munch on hardtack. As we marched to the south and then southeast we passed a rocky, barren outcropping of stone on our south, then turned to march between it and a higher ridge to the east that was covered with a light stand of pine trees.

We continued marching south through this wide valley and camped for the night after having traveled only ten to twelve miles. We seemed to be moving somewhat slower than we had, possibly because the army had skirmishers out in front of the main column looking for the Confederates. We were indeed marching deep into their territory.

The next day, we were marching early and gradually worked our way towards the high ridge to the east. We had traveled several miles before we arrived at the ridge. It appeared to be pretty high, probably four to five hundred feet or more above the floor of the valley, down which we were marching. We started up the slope of the ridge which was gentle at first, and then about halfway up it became quite steep, maybe as much as thirty or thirty-five degrees. The road on which we were traveling seemed to turn practically due south and we passed through a gap along the top of the ridge with heights of a hundred feet or more, looking almost perpendicular, on each side.

Within a quarter of a mile, we gradually began winding our way down the eastern side of the ridge and about an hour after noon, came out on the floor of a narrow valley between steep ridges, both north and east of where we were. We headed straight east at what appeared to be a fairly solid ridge, not quite as high as the one that we had just come down, but as we approached we noticed an extension of the valley that broke the line of the ridge. It ran north and east and we followed the road as it headed in that direction. Here was a very narrow valley that wound its way between steep ridges on all sides, it seemed. There was a small creek that wound its way through with just a mere wagon track that passed back and forth through the waters of the streambed.

We were marching fairly slowly. I'm sure that the skirmishers out ahead of the column were even then working their way through the steep hooded bluffs on each side of the road watching for ambushes. Then, after only a mile or so of this closely confined valley, we passed through the ridge and entered another wider, even lovelier flat piece of ground between another exceedingly steep and high ridge directly to our east.

As we came down the last of the slope, we could see in the distance a small town, maybe two miles away. We emerged out into the wide valley that must have been five miles across and passed just south of an isolated high mountaintop. I had the feeling that we were being watched by rebel pickets on the top of the mountain and anticipated that at any moment we would come under artillery fire, but all was quiet.

As I watched, a few mounted infantry worked their way down the eastern side of the mountain. I'm sure they were doing their best to keep us from any nasty surprises. It was probably well after noon before we made our way along the southern edge of the small town that was situated nearly in the middle of the valley. We stopped and had a quick meal of hardtack and fried bacon, washed down with water, and then refilled our canteens at the stream that ran along the edge of the town, and soon were marching to the east again.

As we neared the range of mountains on the eastern side of the valley, it appeared that they were higher and steeper than those that we had crossed previously. I expect they were seven to eight hundred feet at least. The march up the western slope of the ridge was even stepper than the ridges that we had crossed earlier in the day. As we made our way up the ridge, the road suddenly took a rather steep turn and we passed down a narrow valley between high ridges on both north and south. Then, we were soon marching south and the ridges were east and west of us.

The road on which we were marching soon became nothing other than a couple of wagon tracks that crossed back and forth through a narrow, shallow, rocky mountain streambed. The places at which we crossed were never more than a foot deep, and in most cases only several inches. The gap between the mountains narrowed to probably no more than forty yards at it's widest with thick stands of pine on both sides of the creek, covering the flat bottomland between the ridges that seemed to be several hundred feet high on each side. They seemed to rise nearly perpendicular from the floor of the valley and in places there were stone walls eight to ten feet high that were sheer rock.

The bluffs sloped back at a sixty to seventy-five degree angle and were thickly covered with pines, laurel and rhododendron bushes. It was an uneasy feeling to be marching down this narrow gap. I felt it was possible that a whole Confederate Corps of infantry could be hidden beneath the green canopy of the brush and trees on the sides of the mountains.

As we marched, it started to darken. I knew it was late in the evening, but I wasn't aware of just how late. Possibly because we had a high ridge on both east and west flanks it went from dusk to complete dark, it seemed, with a snap of the fingers. But, we were marching in column behind another whole division that was feeling its way through the mountains. Hopefully, they could see where they were going.

We marched for a couple of hours, and then the bluffs on each side seemed to gradually widen and we came through the gap into another narrow valley that had high ridges on all sides that could be barely made out in the bit of moonlight that was then showing in the heavens. There in the valley on all sides were campfires that had been set up, reflecting off the hills that surrounded us, and belonging to the division of General Dodge which had made its way through the gap ahead of us.

We moved off to the side of the narrow road and dropped in the meadows where the officers instructed us to spread our bedrolls on the ground. It must have been close to ten o'clock at night. Soon, isolated campfires were going and we fried up something to eat and boiled some coffee to wash it down. I suppose before eleven o'clock we were passed out from exhaustion. We were only allowed a few hours of sleep. At four o'clock in the morning, we were aroused out of bed to have a quick bite of bacon, hardtack and coffee again and then we loaded our bedrolls and formed up to resume the march.

Once again, we were towards the back of the column with General Dodge leading off. It seemed that we not sooner had gotten started than we seemed to jam up and mill about in confusion. The rumor soon spread back through the troops that Confederate cavalry had been seen at the mouth of the gap. The troops in the lead quickly formed into line of battle with a force of skirmishers out in front.

It was just now becoming light enough to be able to make out some of the details of the valley in which we had rested for the night. We were facing southeast and the sun was just starting to shine brightly over the tops of a line of willow trees in the distance. On all sides of us, were sharp ridges and steep bluffs, but probably no more than a hundred and fifty to two hundred feet in height. They were thickly covered with pine trees and colorful bushes. We were on flat ground, so it was difficult to see what happened directly in our front. We could only listen to the sounds of the battle.

There were some scattered fire that I supposed must be the skirmishers making contact with the enemy, and then what sounded like a sustained volley of fire from the line of infantry that had disappeared into the willows. Then, there was a sound of bugling and the wild shrill notes of the cavalry charge being sounded, then another volley of musket fire, and then relative silence broken only by the sound of isolated rifle and musket fire. Then, all seemed to be quiet for the next hour, again with the exception of an occasional shot that to me indicated a sniper playing havoc at the head of the column.

The orders were given for us to form up in line and it seemed that our lines covered the whole floor of the valley from ridge to ridge as we marched forward from right to left along the line towards the stand of willows in the distance. Then, it was our turn to move out to the southeast following the line of the blue clad brigade in front of us by only thirty yards or so. We marched to the southeast at first, and then gradually formed facing pretty much straight east and moved forward. It seemed that the whole division was moving forward in line only as fast as the skirmishers of General Dodge's division in front allowed us to move.

We crossed a wide flat valley and late in the afternoon began moving up the shallow slope of wide ridge in front of us. As we neared the top of the ridge, we could see troops extending across the top and down the eastern slope. The whole army had come to a halt there on this ridge where, looking into the distance maybe a mile away stood our objective. There, in the distance, was a line of Confederate fortifications surrounding the western side of the small town of Resaca.

The fortifications looked strong, but did not appear to me to be heavily manned. Of course, I didn't have a spyglass or any means of getting a closer look at the troops that the Confederates actually had in the fortifications, and besides their butternut gray uniforms would have blended quite well with pine logs and that reddish Georgia clay. I had no way of knowing, but it's possible that the Confederates had thousands and thousands of troops there in attendance. But, we had heard that we had been ordered to take Resaca, and here we were. I anticipated that there would be a bustle and rush of artillery to come up behind us and set up their positions. The lines looked to be a mile away, but I knew that we had rifled artillery that could easily reach the works.

I was expecting to be shoved and bustled to one side or another as the artillery came up and was almost eager to receive the orders to advance to the attack. It didn't hurt my enthusiasm at all that there was another whole division in line ahead of us, but nothing seemed to happen. Seconds turned into minutes, and minutes gradually became hours, and still we formed up with even more troops behind us, looking down across the valley at the Confederates. Gradually daylight faded, and just as it started to become dusk, I noticed that the troops behind us began to turn and march away and soon we were given the order to follow suit.

We covered the distance it had taken us all day to advance, probably within an hour, and were soon back at the mouth of Snake Creek Gap. I thought that that was an excellent name for the creek and the gap in the mountains that we had followed along on the previous days' march. The creek certainly wound its way through the woods like the form of a snake. We marched back into the camp in the gap and I think that we even went to bed that night around the same campfire that we had used the night before.

Over the next two days, we remained in the valley and improved our fortifications. We were in a shallow horseshoe shaped valley, surrounded on the north, west and south by steep extensions of the ridge through which we had marched the preceding day. The valley was possibly a mile and a half from northeast to southwest and maybe a little over a mile from southeast to northwest. Across the open end of the valley, which exited to the southeast, it was maybe three-fourths of a mile across. On each side of the exit was a slightly higher extension of the ridges that, to me, resembled the Caulks found at the opened end of a horseshoe.

Artillery was placed here, on the caulks, as well as at a row of lunettes across the opened end of the horseshoe, the willows being cut and used as head logs for the entrenchments. Well, there is nothing like a good entrenchment to fight from, but I wondered if all of this was really necessary. General McPherson was leading General Sherman's Army of the Tennessee. We numbered over twenty thousand men and I had been informed by Lieutenant Shawnasee that General Thomas, with the army of the Cumberland and over sixty thousand men, was moving into position north of us trying to force his way through Rocky Face Ridge. In addition to that General Sheffield and General Hooker, with the Army of the Ohio and nearly fifteen thousand men, were supposed to be working their way around the northern end of Rocky Face Ridge to reach the valley east of Rocky Face and attack Resaca directly from the north.

I was itching to be at the rebels. I was thinking that if we had hit those rebels in Resaca hard yesterday, we could have forced them to weaken their defenses to their north and northwest. Then we could have crushed them in the palm of our hand. I was certain that that was what General Sherman had had in mind. I felt that if he had been here in command of his whiplash, as it was rumored that he called the army of the Tennessee, we would have already crushed and scattered the Confederates. I had heard it said when we were in winter camp that year and Uncle Billy, and Generals Logan and Osterhaus had come to inspect the division that he liked to brag about his western soldiers in the Army of the Tennessee. I had heard that he called us the marchingous, cussingous, fightingous troops in the Union, and that he bragged that if he had a tough nut to crack, he would just hit it with his whiplash.

Now, there they were, the Confederates, in that little town of Resaca and the whiplash was coiled up in the mouth of Snake Creek Gap. Oh, well, we were safe here, but I sure wished we could get to cracking. I said as much to Johnny as we manned our fortifications, and the dumb German's only reply was that he didn't know what cracking was, but he sure wished we could get to Resaca. I looked at him with surprise and mortification on my face, and when I noticed his grin, I could only barely keep from laughing. "Damn you," I said, "Can't you ever take anything serious?" And he laughed and said, "Where's the fun in that?" "You need to learn to relax; trouble will find us soon enough". He was probably right.

CHAPTER TWENTY ONE

We spent the next couple of days in our fortifications, apparently waiting for the Confederates to get up enough nerve to attack us. Then, one evening, we were given orders to be ready to march out again in the morning.

The next morning, we were up well before dawn. The 15th Army Corps moved through camp and deployed into the line of battle just beyond the willow trees at the mouth of the gap. The 1st Division was in front of the corps and sent out a strong skirmish line to lead the way. The 1st and 2nd Brigade made its way forward on each side of the road that had headed towards Resaca. We made our way in line behind the 1st and 2nd Brigades with a battery of artillery moving along to our right.

We moved forward following the other brigades and soon their skirmishers came into contact with the Confederates. Suddenly there was the brisk firing of our skirmishers in front of the division and shortly thereafter volley after volley of musket fire. Ahead of us and slightly to the north was the high hill that now seemed to be devoid of the usual pine trees. The Confederate artillery soon began lobbing shells toward our lines. The ground that we had passed through recently had been fairly heavily wooded in places but it seemed that during the previous couple of days, when we had been fortifying our entrenchments in the mouth of Snake Creek Gap, the rebels had spent their time cutting trees and clearing the ground for their artillery.

There were clumps of trees stacked together that were still smoldering, having been burned over the previous few days. There were still clumps of isolated trees standing and breaking up the ground which was mainly gently rolling, being broken with a few shallow dips in the ground where rainwater drained off. There were wide patches of ground that had been cleared by the southerners for farming, and as we moved further east, we passed through the woods, over the fields and across the ditches.

As we marched, our artillery came up south of us and opened up long range fire directed at the top of the bald hill in the distance. Soon, the 1st and 2nd Brigade of our division had reached the foot of these slopes and intense musket fire broke out as they worked their way through the felled trees and brush that cloaked the lower ends of the slope. We were soon in range so that we could try firing at the Confederates, but the smoke and dust of the engagement to our front kept us from being able to pick out any clear targets. For a while, the fight seemed to stall on the mid slope of the hill, but as more and more artillery came up and the intensity of our bombardment on the crest of the Bald Hill increased, we noted a definite slacking in the Confederate artillery reply to our advancement.

Then, there was a sudden surge in the volume of the musket fire to our front and we seemed to pick up speed as we fairly rushed up the lower edges of the slope and soon our troops were carrying the top of the Bald Hill. We linked up with the 1st and 2nd Brigades and helped them strengthen the Confederate fortifications that they had taken, building up the dirt embankments on the eastern side of the slope and shifting the downed pine trees and head logs from west to east for protection against Confederate fire.

The bulk of the Confederate troops had made their way down and across the creek in the valley that ran from north to south, but they left a goodly number of skirmishers along the eastern slope of the ridge and they concealed themselves in clumps of isolated pine trees that were still standing and in the mounds of downed pine trees that they had piled up at the foot of the bluff.

We took our positions in the trenches with the rest of the division and fell to skirmishing with a relish. I had been dying to put the squad to work with their new Springfield rifles. We flipped the rear leaf sight up and set it for the five hundred yard range. Then, peering between the head logs, we kept a close watch for any sign of movement by the Confederate skirmishers at the foot of the ridge.

I took a few shots at what I thought was enemy movement through the trees and brush at the foot of the slope, but I'm not sure that I hit anything. The fact is, I'm not sure that what I shot at was even a Confederate soldier. It just seemed to be some suspicious movement in the brush.

It soon became dusk and we settled in for the night. We built up the remains of the Confederate fires that still had hot embers and boiled coffee and fried bacon and hardtack for supper. Then, we settled down and turned in for the night.

The following day, I suspected that we would be once again marching to the front to force the rebels there to abandon Resaca. During the night, considerable batteries of artillery had been brought up and down the line on the top of the bald hill, and then sighted in on the Confederate entrenchments on the other side of the creek that ran north and south through the valley. We were probably about a mile from Resaca itself.

We were up well before dawn, anticipating the battle that I knew was to come, and sure enough, it did. Just as the sun was well up above the ridge to the east of us, intense skirmishing broke out in the distance. We speculated that this must be General Thomas or General Schofield advancing from the north and west.

Throughout the morning, sounds of musket fire rose to a crescendo pitch, and then gradually faded away. It was merely the sound of heavy skirmishing. We waited in anticipation for the sounds of an all out battle. To the east, directly in our front, our own troops picked up the intensity of their skirmishing, but it was difficult for me to pick out anything to fire at.

The 1st and 2nd Brigades had moved skirmishers down the slope towards the Confederates, but we remained in our trenches. The Confederates had set large piles of downed trees on fire and the smoke drifted lazily in our direction, somewhat obscuring our view of the Confederate entrenchments across Camp Creek and on the edge of Resaca itself.

It was late morning before the sounds of major fighting arose in the north. The sound of the skirmishers increased in intensity and soon the thunderous explosions of artillery echoed back and forth across the valley between the ridges. Then, volley after volley of musket fire sounded and it was obvious that a major attack was underway. It was hard to make out just what was happening to the north.

The smoke from the huge bonfires the Confederates had kindled, slowly drifted across the valley into our faces, while to the north the smoke from the artillery and the musket fire seemed to cast a pall over the battle raging there. It looked almost like a thunderstorm on the ground. The clouds of gun smoke were thick, being pierced by flashes of artillery that resembled lightening and the booming and thunder of the cannons reverberating, all added to the effect.

The firing lasted for a half hour or so and then gradually faded away. Throughout the day, the storm would return to buffet the hills to the north. There were two or three other major firestorms to the north, but nothing happened to indicate than any real progress was being made as the sounds of the fighting seemed to remain stationary.

Then, late in the afternoon, there was a stir up and down our line. The skirmishers that had been moved forward earlier in the day began a brisk fire directed against their Confederate counterparts positioned out in the valley of Camp Creek itself. Then, our artillery along the ridge opened fire on the Confederate fortifications, and as we watched, we could see shells erupting in the Confederate lines outside Resaca and it seemed a few shells were landing along the western edge of the town itself. Then, the 1st and 2nd Brigade made its way down the slope, and as we watched, moved slightly to the north across the valley of Camp Creek. We were soon making our way down the slope ourselves, gradually moving to the south until our flank was moving along Resaca Road itself.

Our artillery kept up a continuous bombardment on the Confederate works as we made our way across the valley. We moved in line, not being able to take particular advantage of the terrain. We passed through isolated small stands of trees and were forced to split the line to move around the downed trees that pointed towards the west and into our faces. As we closed the distance, we came under fire from the Confederates in their line of fortifications just along the eastern side of Camp Creek.

We were near enough now that our own artillery ceased fire at the Confederate works there and concentrated all their intensity on the

Confederates along the edge of Resaca itself. With a cheer and a volley, we stormed into the face of the Confederates. We went over the banks of the creek that were no more than two to three feet high at that place, splashed through the water that was never more than much over knee high and dropped on the edge of the eastern bank of the creek with our feet still in the water, but our bodies lying in the mud of the embankment.

We loaded and fired as rapidly as possible at the Confederates in their fortifications no more than fifty to seventy-five yards away. Then, up and down the creek, groups of soldiers arose and rushed en masse across the opened space between the creek and the Confederate works.

With a scream and a cheer, we were up rushing across the ground. At twenty yards I stopped and fired my last shot with the Springfield at a Confederate soldier who had made the mistake of standing up behind his breastworks to fire at us. Then, I flipped the snap on my poster and drew the Remington as I charged the last few yards separating us from the Confederate works.

We leapt to their breastworks; it seemed almost as one man. I fired the revolver left and right and realized that the Confederates were abandoning their line of fortifications. We rushed into the trenches and hesitated only a moment as the rest of the boys in the squads reloaded. Then, with a cheer that seemed to turn into a snarl of rage, we were up and out of the trenches following the last of the Confederates as they made their way across a cleared area and sought shelter in another line of trenches fifty yards away.

Other regiments of our brigade were already halfway across the area and coming under fire of the Confederates in the trenches there. This seemed to stagger them for a moment, but then their mad rush continued. They were paused only momentarily but it allowed us to nearly catch up just to the south of them, and as they stormed into the Confederate works, we were not far behind.

Some of the boys had taken the time to fix their bayonets before we left the trenches, and about twenty yards or so from the Confederate works, we pulled up and delivered a volley. Then, we resumed our mad dash for the Confederate works. As we came to the top of the Confederate breastworks, I was able to get a couple of clear shots with a revolver at Confederates who were still resisting our attack before the rest of the brigade came storming into the trenches with their muskets and bayonets. It seemed like in seconds the Confederates were up and moving back to the east across what remained of Camp Creek Valley.

We started to follow them, but all up and down the Confederate works batteries of artillery opened up on us. We were in the second line of fortifications along Camp Creek, but our attack had become disorganized and somewhat haphazard. By unanimous consent, we took shelter in the Confederate works and began to fortify on the eastern side of the entrenchments to protect us from the Confederate artillery and a possible counterattack. Besides, it was getting almost too dark to see.

We dropped back into the trenches and took shelter, hugging the ground in the deepest part of the trenches as tightly as possible. It seemed like the Confederates continued to bomb and shell our positions for almost an hour before the fire gradually slackened and ceased. We scrambled up out of the depths of the trenches and took position, facing towards Resaca. Sure enough, the Confederates launched an infantry attack across the narrow flat ground that separated our entrenchments from their fortifications along the slight ridge on which Resaca was built.

Their attack seemed determined at first, but as they appeared at no more than a hundred yards and began to form up in line, they were easy targets. With a yell and a scream, they charged realizing that they were receiving a murderous fire as they were trying to form up. They never made it more than halfway across the open ground as we delivered volley after volley into their ranks. Then, they turned and fled back to the safety of their entrenchments.

The Confederate artillery opened up once again and we took shelter in the depths of the ditch. The bombardment seemed to go on forever, but I don't suppose it was more than a half hour before they lost interest in us. Well after dark, other Union troops made their way around us and our regiment was ordered to fall back and we were put into reserve on the slopes of the Bald Hill.

The following day heavy skirmishing broke out between our troops in the fortifications east of Camp Creek and the Confederates in their works on the edge of Resaca. We watched from the heights of Bald Hill as several sorties were made against the Confederates there. Our artillery made continuous havoc along the Confederate lines. Some time in the early morning, furious fighting broke out again to the north. It would swell to a crescendo and then fade away. Time and time again, I thought that the Confederates must surely give way and expected to see a stream of gray uniforms come pouring down from the north followed by our troops in close pursuit, but it seemed that the action remained stagnant.

Later in the afternoon, we were distracted by the sound of major troop movements behind us and watched as General Schofield's army made its way out of Snake Creek Gap and moved to our right along the Oostanaula River and soon a furious bombardment at the Confederate works ensued.

Again and again throughout the day, our troops in the fortifications on the east side of Camp Creek launched assaults on the Confederate works, and as dark approached, we all thought that the next assault by the troops would result in their reaching the Confederate fortifications and entering the town itself. However, darkness gradually approached and the fighting on all sides seemed to wither away to nothing. It seemed that that evening the silence of the night was broken only by occasional artillery bombardments on the Confederate town.

The following day broke and the stillness was surprising. We watched as the skirmishers advanced from their fortifications on the eastern side of Camp Creek towards Resaca, expecting at any moment to see flashes of Confederate artillery and musket fire, but were surprised as all remained quiet. The leading skirmishers made it to the Confederate works, and one by one disappeared. Then, as everything remained as silent as death, all across the valley lines of Union troops in blue arose from the trenches and made their way across the rest of the valley and into the Confederate works and were soon seen moving out and through the town itself. All up and down our line on top of Bald Hill, a thunderous cheer shook the morning air. The rebels were gone and Resaca was ours.

CHAPTER TWENTY TWO

Shortly after the first troops had moved into Resaca, it began to rain. It was a light drizzle at first, but increased rapidly. Large cold drops of rain came down in a perfect torrent for several minutes, and then it eased off, but continued to pitter-patter down about our heads and shoulders. Where we were, we were able to see the Union troops come down from the north and start filing through the town. They started to move to the Oostanaula River and in short order they had the bridge repaired and were moving troops across.

We received orders to form up and move to our southwest and cross the river at Lay's Ferry. We had gotten a late start in marching and tried to make up for it as we proceeded to the southwest throughout the day. We covered seven or eight miles through the rain and mud before we pitched in to make camp alongside the road.

We spent a restless night there, trying to stay dry under our gum ponchos. It rained intermittently throughout the night, sometimes a rather brisk downpour, but never stopping. We were up and marching again by eight or nine in the morning. Our regiment had been sent out as skirmishers, ahead of the main column, as we moved down to what I was told was the road to Rome.

I had a sudden flicker of recognition. It seemed I could remember my father talking about Rome, Georgia and the more I reflected on it, as we moved forward in skirmish formation, it seemed that I could recall my grandfather even as he talked about the plantation that he had worked on as an indentured servant being somewhere around Rome, Georgia.

Try as I might, I was unable to remember what the plantation had been called, but as we moved along, I glanced in all directions trying to soak up as much of the feel of the country as I could. It was around here that my grandfather had spent several years of his life when he first arrived in America. It was an interesting thought that possibly, if he had remained here, I might even now be fighting for the Confederates. I was reflecting on these vagaries of life when, within a few miles, we made contact with Confederate troops.

We had been moving to the southwest and were skirmishing to the left of the road. Trying to take advantage of even the tiniest bit of cover, we moved from tree to tree and along the sides of depressions in the ground from one slight elevation to the next. Off to our right, we heard a scattering volley of fire and dropped to our knees behind whatever protection we could find. I was to the left of the members in our squad and Johnny was to my immediate right. There was another squad of soldiers from the 31st Missouri to my immediate left, and I raised my left arm signaling for them to take cover also. Then I motioned for the two squads to advance, taking care to protect each other. Johnny moved out, snaking his way from one tree to the next while I watched for any sign of Confederates ahead and to each side. Then I moved forward while Johnny covered me.

We worked in two man teams, one providing covering fire, if necessary, while the second eased forward from one place of concealment to the next. Soon we spotted Confederate soldiers to our front and off on each side. We commenced that dangerous long range sniping as we moved ever forward. Primarily I looked straight ahead and to my right to watch for Confederates in front of Johnny and myself. But I kept a good watch to the left also for the soldier who came up on my side there, and then it was my turn to move forward.

I hadn't proceeded so far as to come up even with Johnny when I felt a sudden whiff of air past my right ear and then heard the sound of the musket that had fired the shot. I dove to my left and rose up slightly and could spot the cloud of black powder smoke where the soldier had been. I rolled over once and came up behind a small pine tree that offered no real protection from a mini-ball, but did offer a bit of concealment, and as I brought my rifle up to scan ahead of me, I spotted the Confederate soldier as he turned his back to slink away.

As I brought my rifle up, I made the quick estimation that he was a hundred and fifty yards away and there was a slight westerly wind that was causing the light rain to move slightly to my left. I placed my sights below his right shoulder and squeezed off a shot and saw him tumble headfirst to the ground. My shot was followed by a half dozen shots by Johnny and by the rebels in return.

I rushed forward in a quick burst of speed, taking the two squads with me, in order to take advantage of the fact that it would be several seconds before the rebels could get reloaded. Even as I ducked behind the protection of a fairly large pine tree, I was reaching into my cartridge box, preparing to reload my rifle. When I was finished reloading I motioned for Johnny on my right and the squad on the left and we started forward again in quick alternating bursts of blue.

Just as Johnny ducked in behind a tree, there was a volley of fire from the Confederates in front. A man to my left went down. We immediately shot forward and passed our line of skirmishers that had preceded us and rushed forward another fifteen or twenty yards, taking advantage of the lull in the activity as the Confederates reloaded. Immediately to our front, the trees seemed to thin out and I could make out in the distance, probably fifty to sixty yards, another road that came from the east and intersected the road that we were marching on towards the southwest. Thirty yards across the other road, I could make out a line of Confederate infantry through the woods. Surprisingly, they had thrown up a hastily improvised line of earthworks and fortifications. It appeared there were several hundred men here protecting the crossroads.

We waited in position while the rest of the divisions came up behind us. I kept my eyes peeled to the front. I was able to lean out slightly to the right of the tree behind which I was taking shelter and placed the barrel of my rifle over a limb that was right at head height as I knelt on the ground on my right knee.

Steadying my rifle, I watched off to my right for any sign of movement. Trying to look straight ahead and to my left, caused me to expose too much of my own head. I didn't want to be a casualty for some Confederate sharpshooter. A sudden suggestion of movement caught my eye, and just immediately behind the Confederate earthworks, I spied a soldier standing behind a tree, leaning out far enough to take a look at our lines. I aimed for his left breast area, knowing that my ball would move somewhat to the right and also would be a few inches high at that distance. I gently squeezed off a shot and saw him spin to the right and drop before my vision was obscured by the black powder smoke.

I hastily ducked back behind my tree while I reloaded. Then, I shifted around and knelt on my left knee with my rifle held next to my left shoulder and peering out to my left along the Confederate works. As I was watching the Confederate line, I could hear as our own soldiers came up from behind, moving in line towards us. As I watched, a rifle barrel gradually extended in the space beneath the head log in the Confederate works.

I couldn't actually see a soldier there, but I could guess as to where his body must be as he extended the rifle towards our lines. The quick thought went through my head that usually there were about six inches between a head log and the top of the fortification. If the soldier were resting his rifle on the earth of the fortification, then I should estimate what would be about six inches above the rifle, I quickly took aim and steadied my rifle and squeezed off a shot. I couldn't see much to indicate the success of my attempt as my vision was instantly obscured by the black powder smoke, but as it cleared, I could see that the Confederate's rifle was still there extending beyond the slit in the fortifications.

I assume that meant that the soldier who had been aiming it had been unable to retrieve it. Once again, I ducked back behind my pine tree and stood up as I reloaded. I continued to hug my back up tight against the tree and peeked out to my right. The Confederate's rifle was still lying there.

I finished reloading and turned, facing the tree, and peeked out to the west side again. As I did so, the line of Union infantry came up even with me, and then advanced on past. Perhaps they were not aware that the trees around us thinned out, considerably, forward of where we were. It seemed that as soon as they passed, they were met by a volley of fire from the Confederate fortifications. They promptly halted and moved back into the woods. I viewed this as a good opportunity for our skirmish line to move forward while the Confederates reloaded and we raced forward for another twenty yards before ducking behind trees or dropping into a shallow ditch that seemed to run parallel to the road, crossing from east to west.

Once again, I had come to a halt, kneeling behind a pine tree near whose base was a prickly gooseberry bush. The tree itself was hardly big enough to provide good protection for my body, but the foliage on the gooseberry bush was thick enough to provide me some concealment. I was able to extend my rifle through the leaves of the gooseberry, and pressing gently down on its branches, was able to clear a place that I could see. Johnny was no more than ten feet away and had elected to drop down in the ditch. He may well have had adequate protection as long as he was lying flat in the ditch, but would make a perfect target if he stuck his head up to see.

Even as I watched, he started to snake his way forward to try to see over the top of the earth. I screamed at him as loud as I could, "Johnny! You goddamn dumb German. Get back in that ditch and keep your head down." He stopped and slid back down slightly and turned to face me, smiled widely, and even as I watched, I saw dirt kick up near where his head had been and he was showered with small clods of earth.

He flipped forward on his face and rolled to the bottom of the ditch and I thought for sure he was dead. I took a quick glance at the Confederate earthworks and spotted a puff of smoke as it gradually drifted to my east on the wind. I aimed at what I estimated to be a spot a foot from where the smoke was now drifting and aimed about a foot above the gap in the two logs of the Confederate breastworks and squeezed off a shot gently. Then, as I ducked back behind what there was of my tree and crouched lower to the earth to take advantage of the gooseberry bush, I quickly reloaded, casting an occasional glance towards Johnny.

Even as I watched, he lifted his head and looked in my direction and gave me a thumbs up. "Goddamn it!" I shouted. "Play dead, you dumb German!" And he ducked back down. The ditch wasn't near as deep as either he or I had thought. I wasn't in much better shape than Johnny was. I realized that the tree wasn't near as wide as I thought it was when I ducked behind it. In order to take the utmost advantage of it, I flattened myself on the earth and attempted to peek out from underneath the gooseberry bush, both to the left and right of the tree.

I felt a slight tremor near my left leg and it seems that something brushed against the fabric of my trousers. A Confederate shot had kicked up dirt just next to my leg and sprinkled me with pebbles and small clods of debris. I realized that lying with my head up next to the base of the tree, that my legs extended far enough behind it that Confederates left and right of me could make them out if I moved them. I quickly pulled my legs in and scooted up into a sitting position, sitting on my feet with my knees extended to the right of the tree and trying to keep my back straight to take advantage of the widest part of the tree towards its base.

To hell with this, I thought, as I brought the barrel up in front of my face and gave it a light kiss. I held the gun straight up and down and moved the stock a little bit to the west, thereby making my pine tree just a little bit wider. I decided I wouldn't try to shoot anymore Confederates and possibly, hopefully, they wouldn't try to shoot me either.

We were about a hundred and ten to twenty yards from the Confederate works and I couldn't see any way of getting closer since, on each side of the road, the ground was perfectly clear of obstruction for ten yards or more. I was thinking I might have to stay here until dark and I didn't think it was even noon yet. But, just about then, the Union officers showed they were really good for something as artillery opened up on the Confederate works. It seems they had found a cleared place off to the right of the road we had been moving down and several hundred yards from the Confederate works. It appeared that they had a fairly open line of sight, firing back to their east and down south along the road and were even now beginning to shell the Confederate works that were south of the road, but nearly in front of me. I couldn't help but call out, even though I couldn't see them, "Give them hell, boys! Give them hell!" Then, our artillery from well back behind us opened up at long range, firing their rifled projectiles over the trees and on the Confederate positions.

It seemed like our own infantry's fire increased, and as I carefully peeked out around to the right of my rifle, I could see the Confederates as they prepared to abandon their fortifications. As I watched, it seemed that more and more men in gray rose and went slinking away from their works. Then, our artillery fire ceased and the order was given for the troops to advance.

As I huddled even closer to the ground, a long line of men in blue burst out of the woods and passed me on both flanks, heading for the

Confederates' fortifications. With that, I rose up on my right knee and leaned around the tree, looking for one last shot at the Confederates, but the line of blue soldiers had passed and was now nearly a continuous wall in front, blocking any shot at the Confederates. I burst forward and quickly picked up speed as I passed Johnny in his ditch, and he was instantly on his feet moving along at my side.

As we neared the road, a final volley from the Confederate works sent us diving for cover into a ditch on the northern side of the road, but we were on our feet again in an instant and covered the last thirty or forty yards to the Confederate works. As I raced forward, I unsnapped the holster on my right hip and drew the Remington, but as we leaped and stumbled over the Confederate barricade, I could only make out a few rebels hurriedly ducking through the woods on the other side. I didn't see anyone that I thought was close enough to waste a shot at. I never saw anyone closer than thirty or thirty-five yards and, as they seemed to be determined to make their way off to the south, I decided to let them go.

Our two squads dropped down behind the Confederate works and took a moment to rinse our mouths out and then take a quick gulp of water from the canteen. From the time that our skirmish with the Confederates had first started until the time that the artillery had been brought up and the Confederates blasted out of their works, probably hadn't been more than an hour and a half or two.

We took a few minutes to rest in the safety of the Confederate works and munched on some hardtack. I passed up and down amongst the members of my squad and the squad that had been to our immediate left. I inquired about the condition of the troops and learned that the soldier I had seen, in the other squad, go down had suffered a minor wound to his left hip. He was even then standing there with his pants and drawers dropped as his corporal poured whiskey over the furrow on his hip. It looked to me as if he had been struck with a bullwhip. There was a break in the skin about four inches long and it appeared there was a welt arising above and below this.

After they had washed it out with whiskey, they placed a bandage over the wound and pulled his pants back up and snugged his belt up tight directly over the bandage. With his baggy pants hanging halfway off his butt, one of his buddies slipped under his left arm and, supporting him with his right arm around his waist, helped him limp towards the rear.

Later on that afternoon, it finally stopped raining. The sun came out and it turned out to be a lovely warm spring day. We marched and made camp just at dusk. The rumor was that we were on our way to Adairsville and we were supposed to be ten to eleven miles north and west of there. Lieutenant Shawnasee made his rounds amongst the troops. When he came by to visit us, as we sat on our bedrolls along the side of the road, I couldn't help but ask if he knew where we were headed.

The lieutenant said that it was speculated that General Johnson and his army were retreating back down the railroad south and were expected to make a stand around Adairsville. Just why, the lieutenant really had no idea. Then he informed us that General Thomas was pushing hard down the railroad from the north and we were circling as fast as we could around to the west and that General Schofield with the army of the Ohio was marching down other roads to the east, and if we moved fast enough, we might be able to come at him from all sides and crush him in a vise. This bit of information was met with enthusiastic comments.

Johnny Applebaum said, "Sarge, make sure and get us up early so we can get a good march on. I would like to get this war over as soon as possible." And indeed there was a feeling amongst the squad, and in fact all of the rest of the men in the regiment, that this war couldn't go on much longer. There was talk about how General Grant was locked in a life and death struggle with General Lee out in the east. Stories circulated about how General Grant would force Lee to make a stand, batter him to near death, and then when Lee stepped back for a breath of fresh air, Grant would immediately move to the left and forward to come at him again.

It seems that they felt that Grant had had more success in the few months since he had been in command than the Union Army in the east had had in the previous three years of fighting. Our boys seemed to feel that was all it had taken all along. A good no nonsense western man to lead those Union troops. We were filled with an overbearing pride ourselves thinking that Grant's second in command and his most favorite officer among his staff, General Sherman was now leading us.

Thinking back over the last two years of campaigning, I couldn't remember a time when our western armies had been unsuccessful in any campaign that they had begun. And now, if we could just get up early, march hard and surround Joe Johnson, we might have the cat in the bag. It was just possible that this war could be over this summer.

As expected, we were up early and already marching by six o'clock in the morning, just as the sun started to glow brightly in the east. We marched hard throughout the day, which was extremely warm and sunny, pausing only briefly as we marched for a sip of water, and a munch on hardtack about ten o'clock. Then, we were back down the road marching until one o'clock. It seems we were just west of Adairsville, but the Johnnies hadn't stopped there long enough for us to catch up. They seemed to be fleeing as fast as they could, even faster than we could march.

We were allowed to take a good long rest. We had been marching for nearly seven hours and now we broke out to build bonfires along the side of the road and fry up some bacon to go with our hardtack and water. We even boiled up some coffee to keep up our enthusiasm. Then some of the boys laid back with their heads on their bedrolls and napped in the sunshine while we rested along the side of the road. We hadn't managed to catch up with the rebels at Adairsville and I wondered if the general officers were given us such a long rest while they tried to figure out what the next step in their plan should be.

It took them till at least four o'clock to finally make up their minds, and then we were back on the road marching off towards the south and southwest. From what I could understand of the situation, as relayed by Lieutenant Shawnasee, we were moving south like a giant pitchfork. We had columns out to the east and west of the main force, which was General Thomas, as he proceeded directly south. Sooner or later, we were bound to spit those Confederates on the pitchfork and then we would have them for sure.

As we marched briskly along the road, someone at the head of the column began to sing. Then, all up and down the line, the men broke out individually and soon everyone had joined in with the singing. And why not? It was a warm, sunny spring day. Trees, shrubs, bushes and plants were flowering all along the road and in the distance. The Confederate armies were retreating pall-mall before us and we had confidence in our general officers and our veteran lieutenants and sergeants, and were on the verge of ending this rebellion.

Since we were in such a good mood, the officers took advantage of us and marched us with only a few brief stops until after nine o'clock that night when we went into camp around a little crossroads town called Woodland. We were reported to be only five miles from Kingston and just somewhere to the southwest of it.

We built up our bonfires and cooked our rations and tanked up on water for in the morning. We were still optimistic that daylight would find us successful in having encircled Joe Johnson and his entire command. The thought that there might be a huge battle in the morning was both terrifying and exhilarating.

As we bedded down that evening, we were optimistic that we would surely have those rebels trapped in the morning. There had been nearly constant skirmishing over the last few days of the march, although nothing near as severe as we had had at the Rome crossroads a few days before. However, this night it seemed that the skirmishing was more intense than it had been and we considered that a good sign that there were rebels nearby and that we would have at them in the morning.

CHAPTER TWENTY THREE

The following morning broke extremely foggy. Perhaps that was why we didn't leave camp until nearly seven in the morning. We found ourselves in advance of the division, moving down the road towards Kingston, but we failed to make contact with any rebel skirmishers. We got within a couple of miles of the town and still hadn't found any sign of the Confederates. General Osterhaus halted the march and sent pickets and skirmishers forward to explore the town and discover any ambushes that the Confederates might have arranged for us. But they returned to inform us that the town appeared to be deserted except for civilians.

The columns all moved off the road and we were allowed to fall out for a brief rest. I think that the general officers needed time to contemplate their next move in their attempt to trap the elusive Joe Johnson. While we waited in anticipation for further orders, the sound of a fairly intense fight broke out to the north and east of where we were. It seemed to rage for an hour or more and then gradually tapered off. Then, the order came for us to form up in column and march back the way we had come.

Our division made it all the way back to Woodland where we had spent the previous night and set up camp. Our regiment was detailed to stand guard on a bridge just west of Woodland and we marched down along the side of the north bank of the river and split the regiment in half with Lieutenant Shawnasee leading three squads across the bridge to the south bank where he set up a line of pickets a hundred yards away from the bridge, and kept another three squads in position on the bank immediately around the end of the bridge on the south side.

We scooped out shallow rifle pits and drug down trees and limbs to protect us on the southern side of the hole. The remainder of the regiment was kept on the north side with a strong picket out in the distance.

We passed an uneventful night and the next day were relieved and sent back into the main camp where we were issued rations and had our ammunition replenished. We remained in camp for the next two days where we were treated to two hot meals a day. We were able to supplement our noon meal with fresh greens. The boys went out in search of wild onion, fresh pokeweed, dandelions and squaw cabbage which we fried up in the skillet with bacon grease and a good tincture of corn whiskey. It was surprisingly good.

The day seemed to become hotter and hotter and drier and drier. Thank goodness we were camped along the edge of the river. We were getting somewhat anxious to get going again. We seemed to feel that old Joe must be getting a good jump on us wherever he was headed, that and the thought that if we gave him too much time, he would have his next destination thoroughly entrenched and fortified.

Finally, on May 23rd, we were ordered to march out. Our division was the last to cross the Etowah River and the brigades were separated to march, some in front, some on each side, and some behind the supply wagons for the division. It was a hot and hazy day, and as the day progressed it became even hotter and the haze burned off, which indicated that we wouldn't receive any rain this day.

As we marched, it seemed to become drier and drier. The armies marching in front of us kicked up a fine cloud of dust which seemed to settle on us as we moved along. The ground under our feet became more powdery, almost sand-like in texture, and our clothing was soon covered with a layer of a gritty irritating dust. We took our hanker sheets out and wet them with a little water from our canteens and tied them around our face to keep the dust out of our mouths and nose. It definitely seemed to help.

We moved through a gently rolling, hilly countryside that was covered with a thick stand of pine trees in all directions. We stopped only occasionally throughout the day to much on hardtack and sip our water. It seemed that over the last several months we had never been far from a creek or a river to replenish our water and so, rather unwisely, we continued to sip as we marched throughout the day, and by dark we had used up all of our canteens. But there wasn't to be any relief for us just yet.

We continued marching all through the night and it couldn't have been long before sunup before we came up to the rest of the army where they were encamped along a small creek. We immediately refilled our canteens and tanked up on water. Then feeling exhausted, but at least refreshed and rehydrated, we dropped on our rolled up bedrolls along the side of the road. Unfortunately we were no sooner asleep than we were up and marching again.

A couple of hours later, we marched through a little crossroads town called Van Wert and marched a few miles beyond that. We were into camp not much after noon, I don't suppose. There was a small shallow creek that was all the water that we could find. The water was warm and had a muddy, sour taste that I found hard to describe. I suspected it was due to the thick layer of decaying pine needles along the banks of the stream that was likely the cause of this taint to the water. It was nasty enough that I found it hard to drink but it looked like, if you're thirsty enough, men would drink nearly anything since no one else appeared to object.

We prepared our rations for the midday meal, drank some more of the nasty water and were soon asleep. I think we may have marched as much as thirty miles in the last thirty-six hours and hadn't had more than a couple of hours of sleep at most. During the night, it began to drizzle and then absolutely poured for a half hour or more before tapering off, but continuing to drizzle throughout the night.

Some time just before sunup, the rain ceased and we began to dry off. Whereas before we had been covered with a fine layer of sandy, gritty dirt, now it seemed like we were encased in a rather gluey, gummy layer of mud. The next morning we were up early and moving out. We received orders to leave the ammunition and hospital wagons behind as we broke camp. This was a sure sign that we should be anticipating fairly heavy fighting during the day.

General Osterhaus in the 1st Division led off the march. We moved out in front with the rest of the skirmishers and off to the right side of the road. We were still in dense pine forests and gently rolling hills. We moved from one pine to the next, me taking special care about the thickness of the pine trees I chose to move up behind. We moved along shallow gullies and carefully to the top of small hills where we actually dropped to our knees to crawl up and peer over the tops, looking for Confederate pickets or skirmishers.

We were moving slowly, cautiously, feeling our way through the woods in anticipation of coming combat. We all had the feeling that since the wagons had been left behind and we had taken only pocket ammunition and ambulances that the rebels must be there in force. Possibly that's why we didn't make very much progress that day. However, it was probably just as well that we were so cautious because some time just after noon, the sounds of heavy firing began up in the north and east of where we were.

The fight seemed to rage for hours and it was possible to discern near continuous musket fire and the nearly continuous booming of artillery. Someone must be truly catching hell. The fight lasted for an hour or so, and then broke off for a half an hour or more, and then resumed, quickly reaching an intensity to equal that which we had heard previous. The firing fell off until it seemed that it was merely a continuous light skirmish, but then picked up again in intensity throughout the afternoon and well into the evening. I think it was after dark before the last furious repercussions of the cannon slowed and ceased and the musket fire gradually faded away also. It sounded like we had finally caught up with old Joe.

The next day was hot and dry, and would have been dusty if we had been marching. Instead, we probed cautiously forward. The country remained as thickly covered with pine and brush as it was possible to imagine. We gradually felt our way forward, and just after noon, came in sight of a small southern town. We felt our way forward, successfully avoiding any encounters with the rebels.

As we moved, we were instructed to proceed obliquely to the north and pass on the other side of the town while another division moved up to our right. We had made our way carefully forward and covered five or six miles, then we settled in to develop fortifications for the night. I think General Logan and General Osterhaus must have felt that we were in imminent danger because we scooped out a line of entrenchments and felled small pines for our breastwork. Our division seemed to be nearly in the center of the line with troops to our right and even some facing almost due south on the extreme right side of the line.

We had a couple of divisions to our left and at least a division in reserve behind the line. Late in the evening, another severe firefight broke out just before dark. This seemed to be further east of where it had been yesterday, but was just as intense for about an hour. Artillery joined in and, even at this distance, sounded thunderous and we imaged we could feel the ground shaking beneath our feet. Then the firing gradually slackened off, became isolated shots from individual sharpshooters, and then a brief fight as if some skirmishing might lead to a renewal of the hostilities, but as it was becoming actually dark by this time, all fighting soon ceased.

We manned our entrenchments during the early hours of the night, and then were relieved and allowed to fall back to get some rest. We were still sleeping peacefully when suddenly; it seemed in the middle of the night, that heavy outbursts of firing broke out up along the line of entrenchments that we had dug. When I opened my eyes, I could see that the sun was barely starting to come up, and in the dusk and gloom of the early hours, it was possible to see for fifteen or twenty yards, but not much beyond that.

Lieutenant Shawnasee came rushing by, kicking our feet and waking us up, not as if we really needed any urging, and soon the whole regiment was up and on its feet and, joining in with the rest of our brigade, we moved forward to the line. The firing was intense. We noticed as we moved forward that there were men in blue making their way towards the rear. Then, surprisingly, we saw that there were Confederate soldiers in gray uniforms moving not far behind them.

We had been deployed in line just as soon as we had left the place where we were resting and were moving forward rapidly. For me, I didn't need any orders to know what to do. Here were Confederate troopers passed our line of fortifications and I brought my rifle up and shot the first one that I saw. There was a scattered volley of shots that sounded from the men in the squads next to me and we moved forward, reloading as we went.

I called out to the squad to my left and right to pick their targets out carefully because we didn't wish to be shooting any of our own men. As we moved forward, the order came down the line 'Fix Bayonets!" We continued moving forward through the thick pine and brush and soon could pick out our line of fortifications ahead. Most of the men of the 2nd Brigade were still in position along our weak fortifications. It seemed that we had come upon the location where the Confederates had actually gotten past our lines.

The men in blue were still gallantly struggling to defend their portion of the line and, as we came up, we brought our rifles up and delivered a volley to the left of them where the Confederates seemed to be massing. We charged forward with the bayonet, whooping and hollering as we went. The Confederates were soon returning to the other side of the line, but continued to hold what they had gained by coming to a stand with the little earthworks between us.

As we moved into line, more troops came up to our left and closed the gap that had developed between our 15th Army Corps and the men in the 16th Army Corps immediately to our north. The Confederates hadn't gone far beyond the earthworks. They took up position in the pine forest and continued firing at us. Then they came forward with that undulating rebel yell and loosed a volley of musket fire at us. There was a shallow valley, no more than eight feet deep and twenty feet wide here. The Union soldiers had scratched out a trench about two feet deep and three feet wide and placed the dirt on the lip of the gulley and then had pine trees lying parallel to the gulley on top of the earth.

The Confederates came down the embankment on the other side and then, in what seemed like two leaps, were across the gulley and here they came back up the embankment on our side. I had managed to reload my Springfield, even with the bayonet on. I fired once, and then reached for the Remington in the holster on my right hip. Between the smoke from the Confederates' volley and our volley in return, the gulley was fairly well blanketed in smoke.

As the Confederates came up the embankment on our side of the shallow ravine, they appeared almost like ghosts coming out of the fog. The embankment that we were on was inclined at a shallow enough slope that they could get a running leap up the first few feet and reach the logs that formed the breastworks. In several places on each side of me the Confederates in the lead grabbed the logs in both hands and used their weight to dislodge them, sending men and logs rolling back down into the gulley. Other Confederate soldiers used their bayonets to jab up at us as their companions attempted to scramble over the top of the breastworks.

On all sides, men were using the bayonet freely and some had even reversed their grip on the rifles, holding them by the barrel and using the club to smash and knock down at the Confederates as they attempted to come over the breastworks. Those of us who had revolvers were using them freely. The carnage was hard to describe. Men were screaming in pain, some in rage, some in fear and I suspect a few were even screaming with the pure joy of combat. There was the sharp crack of revolver and musket, and then soon the booming reverberations of cannon fire joined in. Over everything, rose that stench of rotten eggs from the black powder fumes. For some reason, the clouds of smoke seemed to linger in the gulley, and as the smoke drifted slowly upwards, it burned and irritated the eyes such that they were soon watery and weepy.

It seems like we fought for hours, but I suspect it was only a few minutes. Then, gradually, the Johnnie rebs fell back and crossed the gulley to take up position in the pine and brush on the other side. I dropped down, sitting in the ditch and changed out the cylinders to the revolvers and reloaded my musket.

The whole time there were scattered shots up and down the line as the Confederates skirmished with us from across the gulley. I turned over on my side and raised my head, thinking that I would see if I could spot an indiscretion on the part of a Confederate soldier that would enable me to pick him off. However I found that the head log, that had been across the breastworks in front of me, had been knocked or pulled down the embankment into the ravine. I wasn't such a fool as to stick my head up over the log that was there. I took the bayonet off my rifle and began trying to dig out a trench underneath the log that I could see through.

It took me a couple of minutes to have the dirt scooped away far enough that I could see and I stuck the barrel of my rifle through there and scanned across the short distance to the brush on the other side of the gulley. Almost immediately a couple of shots from the Confederates kicked up the dirt around my position. I realized that they could definitely see the three feet of my rifle barrel that protruded beyond the dirt.

I quickly pulled it back in and ducked down into the trench. Then I waited a couple of minutes and slowly crept back up the dirt and peeked from one side to the other through my little portal, scanning the Confederate emplacements across the ravine. Looking to my right, I spied a man in butternut gray leaning up tight against a pine tree. He was perfectly safe from anyone directly across from him, but at that oblique angle, I could make him out about fifty yards away. I put only the tip of my barrel on the dirt under the log and slid down into the entrenchment so that I could look between the dirt and the log above and sight along the barrel.

I had been able to see him quite clearly originally, but for some reason I was unable to pick him out now. I laid the rifle down and crept closer and put my face up against the dirt, peeking through the little window, and once again I was sure I could make him out easily. I took a good look at the tree and the brush around him, and then slid back and lifted the butt of my rifle up against my shoulder. Even though I was sure I knew right where he was at, I really couldn't make him out again.

Nevertheless, I carefully adjusted my aim and gradually squeezed the trigger. When the rifle fired, it actually caught me by surprise. The sparks from the percussion cap burst in my face and the black powder smoke rolled from the end of the barrel and my vision was instantly obscured. I crouched down in the ditch and carefully reloaded, and when I crawled up to peek through the slot, I couldn't make out any soldier where I knew he had been. I knew that didn't mean that I hit him. It simply meant that most likely he had been smart enough to move.

Gradually, the firing all up and down the line dwindled away and ceased, except for an occasional sharp crack of a rifle up and down the line. We knew that the Confederates were still there, but the pine and brush were so thick that they were easily concealed. As the time passed, there were less and less sniping from either side, and in the quiet, I swear we could hear the rebels scratching away at the dirt and thumping on the logs as they developed their fortifications, probably no more than fifty yards away on the other side of the gulley.

I used the time to clean out my weapons and reloaded, and then I crawled up and down the trenches and checked on the men around me. The boys in my squad had suffered only a few cuts and bruises but, in the squad to my left, one of the soldiers had been shot in the head and had toppled over the embankment and down into the gulley. There were cries for assistance coming from the gulley, moans and pleas for help. There were men calling for their mothers and calling for God, but no one from either side was willing to go to their assistance. That is, not until someone actually called a truce.

The one Union soldier from the other squad that had toppled into the gulley made no reply when his friends called his name. They felt that that indicated that he was most likely dead. I was afraid that it only indicated that he was smart enough not to make a reply which, more likely than not, would have caused some Confederates to shoot at him. I thought about raising a white flag on the end of my bayonet and asking for a truce to assist the wounded. Then I decided that wasn't my decision to make being as I was a mere sergeant. Besides, I decided, most of the troops in the gulley must be Confederates. If they wanted a truce they should be the ones to call for it.

So we stayed hidden in our entrenchments, washed the powder and smoke from our mouths and lips with a few swallows from the canteen and nibbled on hardtack. Throughout the day there were occasional shots, both from our side of the gulley and the Confederates' side, which caused me to order the boys in my two squads to simply sit in the ditch and keep their heads down. No sense looking for it. Death would come soon enough.

And so it continued throughout the day and finally it was after dusk before all the sniping ceased. After dark, we took the time to reinforce our emplacement and prepare another head log in front of our position. Then I crawled up and down the line and instructed the boys that every third man should stand watch while the other two slept, and I told them to get what rest they could because I felt that we were to be in for it again tomorrow.

CHAPTER TWENTY FOUR

I spent a restless, near sleepless, night and was just beginning to get my senses back when the soldier to my left gave me a hard nudge and said, "I think they're coming." I was instantly awake and gave Johnny a hard nudge to my right. His only reply was, "I hear them." Then we made sure to give a kick and a nudge to the men all up and down the line on all sides. There was definitely something on the move.

I'm sure the Confederates were doing everything they could to be quiet, but it's hard to move through thick brush and pine trees with a layer of dry pine needles underfoot. The brush catches and pulls on your clothes, and the pine needles crunch underfoot. The damn things are slick when you try walking downhill on them and in places on the east side of the ravine it was actually fairly steep.

Listening carefully, I was sure I could tell when individual Confederates slipped on the pine needles and inadvertently had to grab onto brush or trees to keep from falling. Yea, they were coming alright.

All up and down our entrenchments men stuck their rifles out between the head logs taking aim at the lip of the embankment on the other side of the gulley, not more than ten yards away. We could hear them coming closer and closer and I imagined that I could even pick out a few moving through the darkness. Our boys had been instructed not to fire until the order was given and I knew that they were all holding their breaths in anticipation.

I was surprised to hear individual soldiers to my left and right cock their weapons. I was surprised to think that the Confederates must have heard it also because it seemed like suddenly everything became quiet on their side of the ravine. I think that hearing a weapon cocked would have brought me to a halt. Then, suddenly, there was a rushing, crashing disturbance on the eastern side of the ravine and it looked like a black wave was suddenly moving toward the edge of the embankment across from us.

I took aim and yelled "Fire!" And then pulled the trigger myself after steadying the weapon. I had been unable to pick out any individual targets and had simply fired into the wall of men that I knew were just beginning to come sliding down the embankment on their side and across the narrow gulley. Then I yelled, "Fix bayonets!" I knew that we wouldn't have time to reload before they were struggling up the emplacement towards us.

I pulled one of the revolvers and emptied the cylinder towards the bottom of the gulley that seemed to have taken on a writhing, squirming form in the darkness. Then I yelled, "Down! Down!" as I dropped to my knees in the bottom of the trench, dragging Johnny down with me. Only a split second later the flames erupted from the bottom of the ditch, then the thunder of the volley from the Confederate's guns, and the cracking, snapping sound of bullets hitting the logs of our emplacement. I could only hope that the men in the two squads on each side of me had recognized my voice and had had time to react.

I had had a sudden inspiration that the volley was coming. It was only then that I realized that that was what I would have done precisely if I had been in the position of the Confederate troops. I would attempt to get as close as possible in the dark, quietly, then make a sudden charge forward, and at the foot of the embankment within a few feet of the works, deliver a volley all along the top of the head logs before storming up the embankment and attempting to come into our lines.

I pulled out my other revolver and leapt to my feet, knowing that the Confederate muskets would all be empty and that they would be attempting to come to grips with us with their bare hands and bayonets. It was still too dark to see much, but as I stood up, I could see the outlines of men as they scrambled and grabbed upwards at our logs. I pulled back the hammer and fired six shots left to right as quickly as I could. Then, I stuffed the revolver back in my belt and went to work with the rifle and bayonet.

On each side of me, the soldiers in the squad that had revolvers used them; I'm sure with good effect. Then the sound of firing died off and the only sounds of battle that could be heard were the screams and cries of the men engaged in their combat for life. The sound and blows of wood on skulls came from the left and the right. The screams of the wounded made it sound as if the very night was crying. I could make out individual men beneath me, grabbing up at the head logs and trying to drag themselves over the breastworks. I jabbed quickly and sharply at them, stabbing and slicing with the bayonet.

Men screamed and rolled back into the ditch on all sides. Then there was a notable letup in the activity on each side. I was surprised to think that the fight had taken as long as it had, but as I looked up and across; I could actually make out the faint glow of an early morning sun and vaguely pick up an outline of Confederate troops on the lip of the embankment across from us. It seemed there was another whole wave of soldiers who had arrived there and had failed to be noticed.

I dropped my rifle and grabbed at the soldiers to my left and right screaming as loud as I could, "Down, everybody! Down!" and collapsed in the ditch, taking the soldiers with me just as a volley was fired from across the ditch right into our faces. I could even feel the force of the volley as it pulverized the air around us. Then they gave vent to that petrifying rebel yell and came down the ditch and across the gulley and began scrambling up the embankment on our side. They reinforced the Confederates still in the bottom of the ditch and came up, and on and I felt they would probably be across the head logs for sure. I doubted that anyone had had the opportunity to reload and knew it would be hand-to-hand with these rebs.

Our brigade was spread out all up and down the line and it looked, in the gloom of the early morning, that there must have been two or three brigades hitting us at this point. But then the sounds of artillery sounded from up and down our line. The cannoneers were not able to depress the muzzles to fire directly into the gulley, but their shells were sweeping the edge of the embankment directly across from us.

The rebels were starting to grab and pull at the head logs and we were poking, clubbing and shoving them back down. I dropped down on one knee and snatched out my Remington, worked the lever and popped out the cylinder and shoved it in my trouser pocket and reached in my blouse to retrieve a replacement. For some reason, I had trouble working and slipping it into the frame of the Remington as it didn't want to click and lock into position smoothly. I think it was only my intense anxiety as I had done this many times before without problems. I finally got it in position and snapped the lever up to lock it in place just in time as rebel troops began scrambling and dragging themselves over the head logs to crawl into our works.

I shot one soldier in the back as he slid on his face down over the head log and into our ditch. And then shot another as he threw his right leg up and straddled a head log trying to pull himself up. Then I shot a third through the head as he stuck it up over the top of the head log trying to pull himself up with both arms. I rushed forward to the edge of our embankment and fired the remaining three shots towards soldiers I saw working their way up our embankment. I was surprised to think that I could actually see much clearer in the dusk of the early morning than in the bright sunlight of the battle the previous day, but then I suddenly thought there was very little gun smoke. The rebels had fired from the other side of the gulley and our troops had mainly empty muskets when they charged.

I shoved the revolver back in my belt and retrieved my musket, preparing to take the bayonet to the rebs again. Then immediately, surprisingly, everything seemed to become quiet on our front. However, far off on the right, the sounds of a pitched battle erupted. There were volleys after volley of musket fire, and then the thunder of cannon. We could only wonder what was going on in that direction.

The sky to the east began to brighten noticeably. I had dropped to my left knee with my right leg extended; bracing me on the other side of the trench we had dug. The boys in my squad had been sitting on one hip or the other, keeping their head down, but as I looked towards the south towards the sound of the firing, one of the men in the trenches further down the line, five or six positions away from me, stood up looking in that direction. I'm not sure what he was thinking, obviously he wasn't thinking, but just then his head erupted in a splay of blood and bone, and then I heard the sound of the musket fire that had killed him. He was going sideways to his right and landed on the western side of our ditch.

We had thought the rebels had retreated across the ditch and up the other side, but surprisingly they were still in the ditch. I slithered on my belly up to the top of the dirt to try to peek through the gap between the logs and immediately dirt and bark erupted around my face. I was stung by some splinters of pine and I felt a piece in my right cheek that actually penetrated through to the inside of my mouth. I ducked back into the ditch and reached for my face and, as I did so, I bumped the piece of splinter protruding from my cheek and the piece inside my mouth scratched my gum. I actually laughed.

Johnny turned and looked at me in amazement and quipped, "Well, that's a hell of a way to pick your teeth." Then, he reached over and jerked the wood from my face. I spat out a mouthful of blood and said, "Thank you." Johnny laughed and said, "Well, you're welcome. Any time." Then, in a more serious tone, he said, "What now?" What now, indeed, I thought.

The damn rebels must have had two brigades or more in the ditch. They seemed to fill it from side-to-side and, what was worse; I think every one of them must have been reloaded. To stick your head over the log to take aim or even to attempt to look between the logs, was sure death. You would have to be crazy to try to take a look at them. Suddenly, with a flash, I decided that I knew what the Confederates plan had been, to take the ditch and to occupy it with an overwhelming force that was reloaded and would consequently see to it that we kept our heads down. In addition, they were so close that the artillery couldn't be brought to bear. They could worm their way forward, reach up and tear down our barricades while their buddies kept us pinned down.

Well, you didn't actually have to see your target to fire a rifle. I knew the rebels were occupying that ditch so thickly that they were probably almost shoulder to shoulder. I screamed out, "Reload!" as loud as I could and then nudged Johnny and the soldiers next to me and said, "Just stick your rifle through the head logs and aim towards the ground. You don't have to see them to hit them." Then, I turned to the man north of me in line and repeated it. All up and down the line, the word was passed to, "Reload and fire as quickly as possible. Just reload, point the tip of the barrel at the ditch and pull the trigger. As fast as you can now. Go! Go! Go!"

I knelt there on my left knee with my left foot bracing me, loading the rifle, sticking the barrel through the log, raising the butt of the rifle up over my head and pulling the trigger. I knew damn good and well I was getting off at least four shots a minute and I figured I had another thirty shots to go. All up and down our ditch, the smoke rose and the flames lashed out to the east. Suddenly the rebels were firing back as fast as they could. I don't think any of us ever saw the other. We just blasted away until our rifles were empty.

I think I had used up all of my ammunition a few minutes before the rest of the boys did, so I took the time to slip another cylinder into the Remington. Three of the four cylinders were now empty. I never carried any powder and lead to reload them in the field. It was hard to believe that I fired all twenty-four shots for the revolvers. I had also used up my sixty rounds for the rifle.

Suddenly I had the almost panicked realization that we were probably nearly out of ammunition all up and down the line. I yelled out, "Cease fire! Cease Fire!" and went crablike moving up and down the entrenchments to make sure that the men all up and down our line obeyed. It had sounded there for a while like the Confederates were giving us volley for volley, but maybe they had quit wasting their powder and lead and simply taken what refuse they could in the ditch, waiting for us to run out of ammunition.

As I went up and down the line I told the boys to reload but to hold their fire, keep their heads down and wait, and not to fire again unless they saw a rebel climbing over the barricade. Then, as I moved back and forth along the ditch, I sent every fifth man back for ammunition, until I had designated five or six men to run back to the camp to replenish our supplies. Before they had gotten back the Confederates came, trying to scramble over the top of our barricade, but were met with a volley of fire from our lines. Those of the troops that still had ammunition had passed it out, up and down to lines, to where we had had enough for one last uniform volley from the rifles.

Then, staying down, we continued to jab at any rebs who showed their faces over the top of the breastworks. Finally we settled down to a harrowing game of cat and mouse. There were rebels in the gulley and on the top of the bank on the other side of the barricade and we were in the ditch on our side. We were both looking up at the sky, waiting for anyone to be fool enough to stick their head over the top. We were a little higher than they were and sitting more or less horizontal in our ditch. They were forced to cling to the earth, digging their toes or hands into the ground to maintain their position, possibly even sitting on the tops of the shoulders of their comrades. We were only a few feet apart!

When they tried to stick a weapon over the top of the logs to point it down in the ditch on our side, since they were lower than we, the barrels would come through pointing in the air. We merely grabbed the ends of their rifles and began a struggle to try to pull it out of their hands before they could raise the butt of the gun up high enough to fire into our ditch.

One or two people were actually able to jerk the rifle away from the Confederates and drag it into our ditch on the other side of the barricade. Usually what happened was that the Confederate pulled the trigger and fired the musket and then pulled it back out of our hands. Where they were on their side of the barricade, we couldn't reach them with our bayonet without exposing ourselves from gunfire from their buddies in the depth of the gulley, but they couldn't reach us either. I could only hope that the troops would be back soon with the ammunitions because ,once we could reload, we could wreck havoc on them since we didn't actually have to stick the rifles far through the slit between the head logs in order to shoot down into the ditch.

Throughout this time, it seemed that the fighting off to the south, out of sight of our position, had been raging without slackening at all, but then I reckon that they thought the same was true of us where we were fighting. This was going to be one hell of a day, I decided. I was thinking I should go back to camp and try to find my knapsack with the powder and bullets to reload the revolvers, but obviously couldn't leave the troops. I was thinking of telling Johnny to go off and try to find the knapsack for me, but just then the first of the soldiers I had sent back for ammunition returned.

What the hell, I thought, as I saw he had brought back one cartridge box with forty shells and twenty for his pocket. I was quite furious, but he kept insisting that that was all the quartermaster would allow him to have. It seems the stingy bastard was back there somewhere counting out the bullets. We passed the sixty rounds out up and down the line and I crawled down the ditch until I found Tom Sinclair and sent him back, telling him not to come back without a whole box of ammunition or with that quartermaster's scalp, one or the other. I was satisfied that with Tom it would be one or the other.

Then, one by one, the men that I had sent back joined us in the trenches. Once again we distributed the ammunition they had come back with. Well, at least we had two or three rounds apiece, I decided. We made sure that each man was reloaded and I gave orders to the troops not to fire unless the Confederates were storming over the tops of the breastworks again. We settled back into our cat and mouse combat.

We took the brief break in the fighting to rinse our mouths out and take a few swallows of water. Then we were soon munching on hardtack. As I bit off a piece of hardtack and attempted to chew it, I had a sudden thought. "Hey, rebs" I called. "Would you like some hardtack?" And someone yelled in reply, "Well, sure, yank. How would you like a bullet?" I just laughed and threw the hardtack up over the head log and said, "Fine. Now toss me a bullet." And, sure enough, he did. I took one look at it and said, "Hey, Reb. This here bullet won't fit." He said, "Well, that's too bad, yank. That's your problem." And I yelled back, "Alright then. No more hardtack for you."

We were all laughing and chuckling about this when suddenly I was slapped on the back of the shoulder and turned around to see Lieutenant Shawnasee looking at me. He had a wide grin on his face and said, "No more consorting with the enemy, sergeant." Someone from the ditch on the other side of the barricade called back and said, "Aw, come on, now, sergeant. We could use some more hardtack. And maybe you've got some water too." I replied, "No, I haven't got enough to spare, but as soon as the runners get back, I'll throw you a canteen full." I knew that had to hurt. From where they were in that damn ditch, I don't think they could send back for water, and if they drank all of theirs as I had just finished off the last of my canteen, they would soon be suffering from thirst as it was soon fixing to be a very miserably hot day.

The morning came and went, water was brought up to us in our ditch and I drank half of my canteen and called out, "Hey, Johnnie, have a drink." Then I flipped my canteen over the breastworks and down into the ditch. "You drink that and throw me my canteen back, and I'll get you some more." The rebel called back, "Much obliged, yank." In a minute's time, my canteen came back into the ditch by me. Then, I had another sudden inspiration. I called out, "Hey, Reb." He called back, "Hey, yank." I said, "You better get the hell out of there because somebody is bringing up grenades for us. We're fixing to make that damn ditch into your graves."

I'm not sure we even had any grenades in the whole damn army. We had suffered from the Confederates using them on us at Vicksburg, but I wasn't sure that we even had any here. The things were like an artillery round with long fins, like a dart, on one end and a protruding rod on the other. The more I thought about it, the more I wasn't sure that they would even work here. It took a lot of force to ram that rod back and cause the things to explode. Even at Vicksburg where the Confederates were lobbing them from considerable heights on our troops, they often failed to go off. Then I thought that possibly they didn't even know what I was talking about. I had only ever seen them used at Vicksburg. "Thanks for the warning" the Reb called back. We had been well supplied with ammunition and water and were feeling somewhat more confident.

Then towards late afternoon, the sound of intense fighting broke out again to the south and the thunderous boom of the cannon continued for, it seemed like, a half hour without fail. It gradually became quiet in the distance and I felt the urge to converse with the rebs. "Hey, Johnny!" I called out. "What do you think of that?" But there was no reply.

I gradually wormed my way to the top and peeked over the dirt and looked through the slit, but couldn't see much. I put my head behind one of the bracing logs and gradually raised it up high enough that I could see above the dirt through the slit and noted that the trench seemed relatively empty. We filled one of the empty cartridge boxes with dirt and heaved it up on top of the head log and I raised my head up behind it, getting a better look through the slot on each side and finally chanced sticking my head up to look over the head log itself. The rebs had managed to creep away; I suspected one by one, throughout the afternoon and possibly had left with a rush while the sounds of the fighting and artillery had sounded to the south. Anyway they were gone. Except for the dead and dying who covered the floor of the gully by the hundreds.

CHAPTER TWENTY FIVE

It continued to be miserably hot and dry over the next few days. We were alternately moved back along the line for a spell, given hot meals and allowed to rest and rehydrate, and then were moved back into our fortifications which we slowly, but almost constantly, worked to improve.

We placed crossed pieces under the head log to where, instead of one continuous slot running between the logs, we had gaps between logs that would help to block any diagonal fire, but would also seem to obscure our outlines as we watched for the Confederates on the other side.

Throughout the day they never ceased to take pot shots at anyone or anything they thought they could hit. I'm not sure who was better off. We were in stout fortifications, but they would take shots from a hundred yards away, behind trees or brush on the east side and were slightly higher in elevation than we were. They knew right where we were behind the fortifications and had only to keep their eyes peeled for movement along our line. They, however, could be anywhere up and down the hill on their side. But this fire only served to force us to keep our head down; I don't know that they ever hit anyone.

We had no further severe action in our front. However, up and down our line, there were occasional bursts of what sounded like severe fighting, especially up to the east and northeast. I think the rebs had decided not to attempt any further movement against our right flank. The stories that we were hearing from the other day's fights, in our area, were that the rebs had attacked in column down the Villa Rica road, and had managed to storm our works and capture some of our artillery.

The story being circulated was that General Logan, who was in command of the 15th Corps, had led a furious counterattack and leapt his horse over the entrenchments to personally lend a hand in retrieving the lost cannon. This was the same General Logan who back in the Battle of Champions Hill had personally led the assaults against the Confederate lines. The boys all loved Uncle Billy Sherman and were becoming quite fond of General Logan also. It felt good to have a man in command who wasn't afraid to get himself dirty and bloody, 'so long as he didn't get himself killed', I thought.

I met up with Lieutenant Shawnasee in one of the brief respites we had from manning the trenches. We had a few minutes to ourselves and sat on pine logs around the campfire, sipping coffee. I was eager for information about the fighting over the last several days and the Lieutenant always seemed to know the truth from the gossip. Lieutenant Shawnasee described how General Hooker had flung his command at Confederate forces that were dug in around New Hope Church. Obviously this had been one of the major battles we had heard a few days ago. I had known it had to have been severe but was shocked when the Lieutenant reported that "There were over two thousand casualties in the three hours of fighting". The Lieutenant continued and related how, two days later, General Howard had lost another two thousand men at Pickett's Mill when General Sherman had directed him to probe the Confederates right flank. This had been the day before our own fight at the gulley. Thank God, I thought, that it had been the Confederates who were doing the probing in our case.

"Well, Son. Have you been keeping in contact with your uncle? How are your brothers and sisters doing?" He said. And I said, "Well, you know, Lieutenant Sir. I haven't received a letter from them since winter camp." Then, before he could reprimand me, I told him that, "I do write them more often than that, but it's a lot easier to dispatch a letter than to receive one. The last I had heard, they were all doing well, and I am sure they have written to me since, but I guess they just haven't been able to find me."

The lieutenant simply laughed and said he was sure that was it. "You know son," he said. "We have been marching and moving so fast, I'm not sure that anyone but General Sherman knows just where we are." I laughed and suggested, "You know, lieutenant, I'm not sure he even knows where we're at. He has so damned many troops under his command; I don't know how he could keep track of us."

Then, I asked, "Well, lieutenant. Do you have any idea as to what Uncle Billy has planned for us next?" The lieutenant just laughed and winked at me as he said, "I have got it on good authority that the General is planning on cracking his whiplash again. We have been building entrenchments back behind the lines here, and as soon as they're finished, Uncle Billy plans on moving us back into these fortifications there and abandoning these advanced works. Then, we will be marching back around the whole damn army to try our hand at moving east around the northern flank. You know, when it calls for a long march and a hard fight, Uncle Billy prefers to use his Army of the Tennessee."

I knew that it was true. I had read in the newspapers the General's own words to those effects, and I suspected that was one reason that the boys didn't mind marching hard and long. We all took great pride in General Sherman's good opinion of us. Then, the lieutenant said, "You be sure and take care. Keep your head down, your canteen full and your rifle loaded." He excused himself to move around to visit with the rest of the troops. One thing about the lieutenant, he was well loved by every man in the regimen and I believe every man in the brigade as he didn't hesitate to talk to any one, officer or enlisted man, without hesitation. I believe he was even on familiar terms with General Osterhaus.

Sure enough, a day later we were up and moving in the dark to the rear. We moved away quietly in the dark, brigade by brigade, and headed back to the west. We marched for several hours in the dark and continued marching as it turned to dawn, and then bright daylight. Behind us, we could hear an occasional skirmish break out, but continued without hesitation until about 9 o'clock in the morning when we were moving into the new fortifications around Dallas that had been erected for us.

We spread out left and right along the line and munched on hardtack, washed down with water and coffee that we had just prepared. Soon, the whole right flank was bent back nearly at right angles from where we were and the Confederates, ever curious, followed us with scouts and skirmishers. We rested there for the rest of that day, and during the night it started to rain. It rained lightly at first but then the clouds blew up, the sky darkened, what moonlight there had been was soon obliterated, and it began to rain in buckets. The wind blew, lightening flashed and the thunder rolled through the hills. It continued to rain hard throughout the night and we didn't mind when in the early morning we were given orders to form up and begin marching off to the northeast. May as well be marching in the rain as trying to sleep in the mud! Besides, it was a lot more comfortable marching when wet than when dry and parched, so long as you didn't get struck by lightening. Now, that was a pleasant thought.

We had been moving around to the northeast, attempting to flank the Confederates and force them from their position, and sure enough it worked to perfection. A couple of days later, we received word that the Confederates had indeed abandoned their position and we were given the orders to march north to a place called Acworth. We marched out early in the morning and, within three or four hours' time, had made it to Acworth.

We had passed to the east of the town and made camp a little to the north and immediately began digging ditches and putting up fortifications facing towards the southeast. We developed lunettes at two places towards the center of the line and at the ends made larger barricades, extending slightly in front of the line, where we placed other batteries of artillery. And then we turned the lines back at near right angles from these large lunettes that formed a protection at the corners and ran it back for a hundred yards on each side. With the whole division working, it didn't take long at all.

When securely entrenched, we settled into camp and rested while our first hot meal in days was prepared. All indications were that we would be here for a while. Sometime the next day the railroad was repaired and trains moved from the west and south of us into Acworth itself. It seemed the whole Army of the Tennessee was entrenched from the northeast to the south of town.

Later that afternoon, we received our first mail delivery since we had started out from winter camp. I sat back in the ditch that we had dug, leaning back against the embankment, and opened my mail. I had two letters from Uncle Aaron and one from Aunt Susan. There was one letter each from their daughters, Kate, Anna and Susan, and one from their two sons, Robert and Aaron. I also had letters from my younger brother, Jesse, and my two sisters, Mary and Elizabeth.

I opened Uncle Aaron's two letters first. They briefly related that all my cousins and my two sisters and brother were doing well and were quite healthy. He didn't even take the time to mention his wife and his own children before launching into his talk about the business at the trading post at the mouth of the Osage River. I knew that Uncle Aaron loved his wife and children sincerely, but I sometimes wondered if they took second place to his business. It seems they were more prosperous than they had been in years. For a merchant, I suppose, war can almost be a blessing. That is as long as it's waged hundreds, if not thousands of miles, away. It seems that farmers for fifty miles south and west trucked their produce to him which he bought and then promptly saw to it that it was delivered up to Jefferson City to be processed for military use.

He also did a fair business in horse trading and cattle also. Most farmers in that area raised crops and only a few cattle. The excess they would drive to his trading post and sell and he would place them around the post in the flat grounds bordered by the Osage and Missouri River and by the embankments that we speculated had been built by the Indian culture that had flourished there hundreds, if not thousands of years before that. That, plus the nearly inaccessible ridge that was known as Clark's Bluff, kept them pinned in until they had twenty-five or thirty cattle accumulated when he, his two sons and Jesse, would herd them along to market in Jefferson City.

Then, I took turns reading the letters from Aunt Susan and her daughters. They were all the same basically. They inquired about my health and stated that they were praying that I would survive the rebellion. They all related that they were healthy and seemed to be well contented.

Then, I opened the letters from Robert and Aaron. Surprisingly, or maybe not, Robert, the oldest of my two cousins' letter was not much different from his father's. He inquired about my welfare, neglected to mention that he might be praying for me, and then stated that they were all well and immediately began discussing the family business.

Robert was four or five, maybe six years older than I, and obviously took after Uncle Aaron. My cousin, Aaron, who was only a year or so older than I, seemed to wish to hear in more detail about my adventures in the Army. He ended up writing that had brought up the subject of enlisting in hopes that he might be allowed to join me, but he said the mere mention of this had sent his father into a fury. Then he wrote in quotation marks that Uncle Aaron had said, "Aren't three deaths in the family enough?" And, I thought that when I wrote back to him, I would have to be sure and mention the fact that there was no sense volunteering now, in all likelihood the war would be over within a year and there was no sense in taking a chance on getting killed in a struggle that was already won.

I saved Mary's, Elizabeth's and Jesse's letters for last. Mary's was by far the longest letter of all of them that I received. It started off wishing me well and saying that she was praying daily for my safety, and without mentioning the rest of the family, immediately went to describing her boyfriend. Her last letter had mentioned the fact that she was seeing a young man in Jefferson City. Apparently that was still the case. She felt she needed to fill me in on all the details.

He was five years older than she was. Doing my best, I tried to calculate just how old that would make him. I suspected he must be about three years older than I, possibly as much as eighteen years of age. That thought didn't sit well with me. I couldn't feel that anyone that much older had any business having a girlfriend as young as my sister, Mary. Then, she went on to explain how his father had a prosperous general store in Jefferson City and how he was one of the elected politicians in the town. It seemed he had met regularly with the Mayor of Jefferson City in some capacity.

Then, she related that her boyfriend, Henry, was planning on going into politics himself. She seemed to think that he was exceptionally intelligent and had a brilliant future ahead. Then she communicated to me in the letter things that he had said about the conduct of the armies and the leadership of the country. It seems he was of the opinion that Abraham Lincoln was a fool and it was for sure he would never be reelected. He also speculated that Grant was a drunk and Sherman was insane.

As I finished reading the letter, I was almost furious. It was a good thing I didn't carry writing paper and envelops and a pencil with me, or I probably would have fired back a letter in reply. The first thought through my head was, 'If the son of a bitch is so damn smart, why doesn't he join the Army and give us the benefit of the brilliance of his thinking". I ripped the letter into shreds and threw them on the ground in disgust and was startled to hear Lieutenant Shawnasee say, "That's no way to treat your mail, son. I hope it wasn't bad news," he said. Then, I went on to relate to the lieutenant just what had been in the letter. The lieutenant looked at me and said, "Well, that's not really much of a surprise, Son. You know, up north, Lincoln is not thought of highly in the press." I could only stutter, "What do you mean, Lieutenant?" I knew that Lieutenant Shawnasee read a newspaper every chance he could, but I hadn't had much interest in it.

The Lieutenant sat down next to me on the embankment and said, "Well, folks are sick and tired of the war. They thought it would be over within a few months when it first started. A lot of people feel that political blundering was the only thing that kept us from a quick victory. General McClelland, who was at one time commanding the Army of the Potomac, has been severely criticizing Lincoln in the press and the talk is he will be running in opposition to the President in the other party. Since he's taking command, Grant has fought battles almost daily with the Army of Northern Virginia and Robert E. Lee. Lee has been forced back on all occasions, but Grant apparently is having casualties of nearly ten thousand men a week since his campaign began this summer."

I couldn't believe that. I thought the numbers sounded impossibly high, and I said as much to the lieutenant. He merely laughed and said that he expected the actual numbers were probably doubled, but even so, the numbers were staggering. "Besides, don't you know that the news press only wants to look for the bad in things? They never want to talk about the good. Disaster, incompetence, insanity and drunkenness sells newspapers."

I thought it was no wonder that Uncle Billy Sherman had danced in glee when he thought that five newspaper reports had drowned in the Mississippi when they tried to run the bluffs at Vicksburg. Well, I had had enough of this conversation. I decided to change the topic and handed up the other letters that I had read to the Lieutenant. It had become my habit to share my mail with the Lieutenant since I knew that his family had all predeceased him.

He sat back and read through my mail while I opened the letters from Elizabeth and Jesse. Elizabeth's letter, I felt, was the most touching of the bunch. She hardly mentioned herself or the rest of the family, but inquired earnestly about my welfare and couldn't help repeating how much and how often she was praying for me. Then she wrote how she would often plead with my parents and my older brother William, who she knew were all in heaven, to intercede with our Lord on my behalf. She seemed confident that they would have become close personal acquaintances with God. I wasn't so sure about my father, but I knew if anyone deserved familiarity with the Lord above, it was certainly my mother. I thought about the many nights we had spent reading and writing verses from the Bible. A tear came to my eye as I sat there thinking about the family members that I had lost. Then I quietly said a quick prayer for my deceased kin and a special blessing for Elizabeth. She had always been such a kindhearted child and it was refreshing to see that she hadn't changed.

I passed the letter over to the Lieutenant who was still looking through the others and opened the letter from Jesse. His handwriting had greatly improved as well as his spelling and even his thought processes. He was still a small child, but his writing seemed more mature than his years would allow. His letter wasn't much different than the others, relating how they were all well and inquiring about my health, but then they moved to the topic of the war and he specifically wanted to know where I had been and what campaign we had fought in and concluded by asking me if it was possible to bring him a Confederate cavalry saber. The last brought a chuckle to the surface. Jesse was a lot like me, always interested in weapons. I only hoped that when this was over, he would never have needed to use one, at least not against other humans.

We finished the letters and I folded them up and shoved them in my pocket. They would come in handy a little later to help start the campfires. I always disposed of my letters immediately after having read them. Some of the boys liked to keep theirs, especially Tom Sinclair who was determined on keeping every letter he ever received. I think he carried probably five pounds of parchment around in his knapsack. In fact, not long ago, I had teased him as he had discarded his greatcoat, claiming that it was too heavy to lug on these marches. That had been just before our battle outside Dallas. Up till then the weather had been unbearably hot and dry. But as we spent the time moving from Dallas up to here, it had rained heavily day and night and cooled off. I thought to myself that I bet Tom wished he still had his greatcoat.

It had been nice so far this day but, sure enough, it quickly turned cool and began to rain in torrents again. I unrolled my poncho and the Lieutenant and I stood there with it wrapped around the two of us, trying to stay under its small shelter. For once the Lieutenant didn't have much to say. Usually he commented on the things that my family had written but, on this occasion, we simply stood there enjoying the silent companionship and sheltering from the rain. I think the communication from home had caused us both to start thinking about what we would do when the war was over. At least I know that's what I was thinking. I couldn't say for sure what the Lieutenant had on his mind. But, for now, it was just the rain to contend with, the rain and the war.

CHAPTER TWENTY SIX

We had a good rain. It rained all day and it rained all night. I had never seen so much rain. Maybe this was normal for June in Georgia, but I thought it was most unusual. We were on our third day in Acworth. It had rained on us on the march here and it rained ever day since. We worked hard fortifying the town and building entrenchments, while we worked we joked that our time would be better spent building an arc rather than building a mud fortification. We were constantly digging out the entrenchments and scooping buckets full of mud back onto the embankments and watching the rain wash it back into the ditch almost as fast as we could shovel it out.

The engineers managed to get the railroad back in shape and, after about the second day, trains began to arrive and unload large tents and other gear. However, unfortunately, we no sooner got the tents set up when the trains brought back General Blair and the 2nd Division of the 17th Army Corps. Maybe because they didn't want to get their new uniforms wet and muddy but they immediately occupied the tents that we had just finished setting up and we were left to contend with the rain and the mud in our little poncho two-men tent shelters.

We salvaged pine boughs and anything else we could lie on to keep us out of the mud and rain at night. I usually shared the tent with Johnny Applebaum. We would put our groundsheets down, and then our blankets and then our knapsacks and haversacks and tried to keep ourselves up out of the mud that way. I was thankful that I hadn't discarded my greatcoat as most of men had a few weeks ago when it had been so hot and we had been marching for long distances. I may have been constantly wet and muddy, but at least I was warm.

A lot of troops came down with coughs and high fevers. I suspected that was probably because they were wet all day and became chilled at night since they had discarded their greatcoats. We were actually relieved to be back on the march again about two days later. We started out early in the morning, probably between seven and eight, and marched out following the railroad track and marching on each side of it. We moved out in front in skirmish position. I actually preferred moving in this manner. You were allowed to move forward at your own pace, pretty much. You could move and take advantage of any cover and you were free to fire at any target that offered itself.

We moved south until we came in sight of a settlement on both sides of the railroad. It didn't appear to be much of a settlement, but it appeared that there might be rebel activity in the town. The brigade spread out into line and we moved forward slowly, keeping ahead of the line and scouting for trouble as we went. We got up to within a hundred yards of the settlement before rebel troops actually showed themselves. The brigade fired a volley and we rushed into the town. We took about thirty prisoners who didn't offer much of a fight. I think that they were indoors taking shelter from the rain and hadn't kept a careful guard because we had obviously surprised them.

The settlement wasn't much. I learned that it was called Big Shanty. There was one large building that served as a hotel and restaurant and a bunch of smaller buildings that weren't much more than shacks. We searched through all the buildings to make sure there were no Confederates lurking and, having ascertained that there was no immediate threat in the town, our squad took shelter on the porch of one of the small shacks and sat down to relax. The rest of the division came into town and marched on through it and a few hundred yards south and east, before they began digging entrenchments and making preparations for settling in here for the night.

We were just east of the railroad tracks and straight east of us loomed a large hill. It was called Brush Mountain, I heard. I didn't think it was hardly big enough to justify the description as a mountain. The ground that we had been marching along was fairly level with some gently rolling elevations. A lot of it had been cleared and farmed, but here and there were large stands of pine trees. Brush Mountain couldn't have been over two to three hundred feet high and looked like it may have been about a mile in length. Along its southwestern slope it gradually settled somewhat smoothly into the valley through which the railroad ran. Off to the right, to the southeast of our position, was another elevation called Pine Mountain. This didn't look to be but half the size of Brush Mountain.

From where we were we could tell that there were rebels entrenched on both Brush and Pine Mountains and across the floor of the valley in front of us. Their lines of fortifications were, maybe, two miles ahead of where we were. We had moved about five miles so far that day and managed to locate the Confederates. Now that we had them in sight, the obvious thing to do was to begin again to dig in.

We were getting awfully good at digging. It seemed that the officers simply had to walk along the perimeter of the new camp and point, and the men knew exactly what to do next. By mid afternoon, we had a fine ring of fortifications established and the wagons were brought up with supplies and tents for the men. We established a tent city in no time, the officers of course taking over any of the shanties and the hotel, even going so far as to put us off our porch.

We wasted no time gathering together pine boughs and whatever debris we could find and set up our tents to settle in for the night. At least we were undisturbed that night. Possibly because we had led the march to Big Shanty, the troops that had arrived later were marched on through and, after dark, set to work digging another whole line of entrenchments a couple of miles from the fortifications we had just erected.

It continued to rain which I think was actually a good thing because the troops that were digging the fortifications a couple of miles away were able to do so without any interruptions. The constant rain and the clouds which obscured whatever light from the moon that would have been available, allowed the troops to work undetected. That, plus the sound of the rain, served to block and muffle noise. When the sun came up in the morning and the clouds began to burn off, I think, the Confederates must have been surprised to see that we were within a mile of their position on the floor of the valley between the two mountains.

By eight o'clock we marched out of Big Shanty and moved a couple of miles forward, into the fortifications that had been erected during the night, and went to work strengthening our line there and setting up tents. While we worked in camp, strengthening our position, some of the troops were set to work digging diagonals toward the Confederate lines. The artillery trains were brought up and the batteries were rolled into position in the lunettes that had been sited at strategic points in our fortifications. No sooner were they set up then they began opening up a barrage on the Confederate lines. Soon there were the sounds of sharp bursts of musket fire and it was obvious that some of our troops that were out skirmishing had met some resistance.

Early in the evening, I was ordered to take my two squads forward and dig rifle pits. It was dark enough that we would be provided some concealment. We moved out to the south and east and, after what I had estimated was about a half a mile, we spread out and commenced to digging the rifle pits. Usually these were shallow, almost trench-like depressions. There were a lot of boys who joked, as they dug, that they were merely digging their own graves. Usually we dug them about two feet deep and piled the mud up in a horseshoe shaped fashion around the end that was directed towards the Confederates. We would dig the pits big enough for two men and deep enough that we could sit or lie in them with relative safety. Whenever we could find pine trees, we would place them across the front and sides of the rifle pit as head logs and take advantage of the added concealment this afforded.

When morning came, I was almost surprised to see that the men had extended the diagonal to within a few hundred yards of the Confederate's position. The troops were rotated out and fresh troops were brought up to dig a line of entrenchments parallel to the Confederates at the end of the diagonal. About noon we were relieved and allowed to go back into Big Shanty for rest. We were replaced by troops of the 2nd Brigade who moved up and took over our rifle pits. They were certainly welcome to it. During the night it had continued to rain and the pit had filled up with probably six inches of water.

We made our way back into Big Shanty and looked for available space to settle in. We were shown to a tent that we were told we could occupy. It was a tent that was originally designed for eight men, but we had no qualms about fitting the two squads in the tent. At least we would be out of the rain, and that was an improvement; however it seemed that it was impossible to be out of the mud. We were so covered in mud that, even if we had had a tent with a floor, we would soon be covered in mud as it dripped off our uniforms.

We made up our beds and dropped on our packs to get some rest, having been up digging rifle pits or standing guard throughout the whole night. It seemed like throughout the rest of the day and that night there were sudden bursts of artillery fire and outbreaks of sharp volleys of musketry. I knew that using the cover of darkness, we would be building our diagonals and entrenchments ever closer to the Confederate fortifications.

The next morning we woke up to another day of rain. We had a warm breakfast that morning, the first in a couple of days, and were allowed to relax and linger around Big Shanty watching, in the distance, as our troops advanced. This was the fourth day after we had left Acworth. That would make it June the 14th. Throughout the day, the artillery continued to pound away at each other. It seemed obvious to me that we were firing at least three times as many shells as the Confederates. I wasn't sure if they could actually do much damage at the distance that they were firing, but I knew that the artillery tended to force the Confederates to keep their heads down as our infantry dug entrenchments ever closer towards theirs.

We were treated to another hot meal that evening, and then, after dark, were ordered to move forward to the entrenchments and to be ready for an assault on the Confederate works in the morning. When we moved out after dark that night it was, of course, still raining. We moved forward through the entrenchments, zigzagging, but constantly moving ahead. It was impossible to see, due to the darkness and the rain, just where we were making our way to. We finally arrived and were allowed to drop down in the mud and rest up for a few hours before we would be making the assault.

We dropped down, sitting into the mud, holding our knapsacks and haversacks on our laps to try to keep them dry. It was senseless to check the rifles to see if the powder had become wet because there was still a lot of time between now and morning. The only suggestions I could make for the boys was to be careful when they fired their first shot and make sure that it actually fired, if not, they needed to extract their Minnie ball and clean the damp powder out to reload. I emphasized they should be careful not to pile load upon load in if their musket wasn't firing and had no other suggestions to make.

It's surprising how in the constant rain and the mud, especially with the anticipated engagement in the morning, to think the troops would be able to sleep. But as we sat there leaning back against the wall of the entrenchment, surprisingly, we didn't have any trouble nodding off. It also helped to lean up against one another for support to stay out of the mud.

We slept better than I thought possible and it seemed that we were no sooner asleep than we were being jostled and kicked into wakefulness. We scrambled to our feet and adjusted our gear in preparation for the assault. The dark of the night seemed to take on a faint touch of gray just as I think every piece of artillery in our army opened up on the Confederates' position. They fired for only a few minutes, and then paused, and we were given the order to move forward. We went up out of the trenches and began moving towards the Confederates' position.

I found then for the first time that we were actually moving somewhat to the southeast and going up the lower slope of Brush Mountain. Other troops were headed more directly up to the east on Brush Mountain, and still others were moving forward directly south into the Confederate works across the floor of the valley. We moved forward in skirmish formation at first. We took advantage of any cover there was, moving forward and staying behind one tree, and then moving quickly to right or left to line up behind another. We would drop into any depression in the ground and move forward, keeping as low to the ground as possible. Any time a target offered itself, we were free to fire.

It wasn't long before we could make out Confederate skirmishers and pickets ahead. Occasional shots rang out, but just as often I heard men cursing as their muskets misfired and they took concealment to extract the ball and wet powder and then reload. We moved forward quickly, but when the resistance from the Confederates became too severe, we paused to let our line catch up and pass.

Line after line of troops would move forward, fire, and then drop to their knee to reload as the next wave of blue moved forward beyond them to fire a volley. We kept up a constant and never wavering pressure as wave after wave of men in blue moved forward, passing through the kneeling troops and taking the time to aim and fire.

Once again the artillery opened up. Their shells were now being directed towards the top of Brush Mountain above us. We moved forward into the Confederate entrenchments along the lower slopes of Brush Mountain and found them abandoned. We hastily moved in and began adjusting the fortifications by building up the embankments on the uphill side of the slope. We were in scattered pine and it was difficult to see what was happening in the valley and on Pine Mountain across in the distance.

Throughout the day the fighting escalated. It seemed that several times in the next five or six hours there were brisk outbreaks of fighting, especially in the floor of the valley. Then the sounds of battle would drift away and all would be quiet except for occasional explosions across on Pine Mountain. We finished fortifying our position where we were, and then began moving towards the east along the lowest slopes of the mountain.

We moved forward slowly and cautiously through the pine trees, taking advantage of all the concealment they offered. We gradually forced the Confederate skirmishers back and then remained in concealment sniping and skirmishing with the Confederates as our own troops behind us extended the lines of our entrenchments ever further eastward.

Gradually the day began to darken and we commenced digging out rifle pits on the slopes of Brush Mountain. We were in front of the rest of the troops who dug their entrenchments perpendicular to the slope of the ground, facing north, and up to within fifty yards behind us where they then turned and dug the entrenchments down the slope towards the valley. Johnny and I had managed to dig out our little trench about a foot deep, piling most of the dirt up on the downhill slope. We managed to find a downed pine tree to place along the edge of the rifle pit on the upper side which had large roots from the tree extending across in front of us towards the south and a large limb that passed between us. We could lie with our back up against the tree on one side or the limb on the other. We felt quite safe.

We took turns sleeping throughout the night, with the other man staying awake and watching guard. We were out fifty yards in advance, in case the Confederates attempted any action against our lines during the night, and we could provide first warning. Throughout the night, the rain gradually pilfered away and stopped.

The next day was dry and hot. We stayed in our positions on the mountain, gradually stealing forward some later in the afternoon by which time we had become dry for the first time in a week. Surprisingly, we didn't meet any opposition. We crossed the slope of Brush Mountain and in the distance we could see how the railroad curved north and passed around the face of another mountain. This mountain was at least two or three times as big as Brush Mountain. I suspect it must have been seven hundred feet high. It also looked like it was three or four miles in length. From where I was, on the southeast and lower ridge of Brush Mountain, it looked to me like a giant Easter egg lying on its side facing towards the southwest.

Where we were now, we could watch as Confederate troops worked on fortifications along the northern edge of this mountain and on both sides of the railroad track. It looked like they had abandoned Pine Mountain and Brush Mountain and were falling back from their fortifications in the floor of the valley between these. As I watched, more and more of the Confederate troops seemed to move up the pine covered slopes of that large mountain in the distance. I stood there watching it and I almost laughed. What could they be thinking? They could have the top of the damn old mountain, I thought. We would simply move around it, to north and south, and leave them sitting there trying to hatch that egg. At least that's what I thought!

Throughout the day we extended our fortifications and entrenchments further to the south and east along the slopes of Brush Mountain and took over the Confederate fortifications in the valley floor, working to strengthen them facing south and east. Troops were sent to work their way up to the top of Brush Mountain and take up position there. Indeed, the Confederates had truly abandoned this mountain because they met no opposition.

From where we were we could look down and see our Army of The Tennessee lying close to the foot of Brush Mountain and across the valley and the Army of the Cumberland on the slopes of Pine Mountain and in the southwestern corner of the valley. General Schofield had been farthest south and west and I assumed that he was moving forward to extend our lines around Pine Mountain in that direction.

We moved forward and dug rifle pits along the lower slopes of Brush Mountain, consumed our hardtack and water and a bit of dried sausage and towards evening were allowed to fall back towards Big Shanty for rest as our brigade was relieved by another. We got back into camp, had a hot meal and were shown to a tent where we stripped down to clean our uniforms and bathe before hanging them up to dry. When we turned in for sleep that night our uniforms were still hanging outside and drying in the warm Georgia moonshine and the gentle breeze.

Unfortunately during the middle of the night the warm Georgia breeze picked up and began to blow such that it shook the tent and started to blow in under the bottom of the flaps and lifted it entirely off the ground. Then we saw lightening and heard the sounds of thunder in the distance and it started to rain once again.

We rushed out to gather in our uniforms, which were nearly dry by now, before they became soaked again. I had the feeling that I had known it was too good to be true. Throughout the rest of the night and the entire next day it rained continuously in perfect torrents. We got dressed that morning and managed to get a warm breakfast, and then returned to the tent to await further orders.

Johnny and I went walking through the camp looking for Lieutenant Shawnasee. We found him conversing with a number of other men of the 31st Missouri Regiment and a group of men from the 32nd Missouri Regiment and the 12th Missouri Regiment.

As we moved up Lieutenant Shawnasee was just finishing relating that he had it on good authority that it was General Sherman himself who had directed the sighting of the artillery that had fired the rounds that had killed General Polk. I listened to this bit of news rather intently, and then asked, “Lieutenant Shawnasee, Sir. How could you know that General Polk has been killed?” The Lieutenant replied, “Because we could read their flags from their signal station as they requested an ambulance to bring his remains down from the top of the mountain.”

Everyone gave a good chuckle at that. It was rumored that General Sherman cared no more for preachers than he did for newspaper reporters, and we all considered it a lucky blow for the Union to hear that the Confederates had lost one of their senior officers, especially a General as famous as General Polk. Besides, I liked to think that Sherman was capable of sighting in cannon all by himself and firing with such deadly accuracy. It made for a fine story whether it were true or not.

It continued to rain and storm throughout the day, but we had gotten to where we didn't even pay any attention to it anymore. Throughout the day, we listened to intermittent bursts of artillery fire and an occasional sharp, but brief, outbreak of musket fire. Later in the afternoon we were ordered back to the front. We moved forward and, just before dark, went into the fortifications that I think had once belonged to the Confederates and which we had turned to face in the opposite direction. We made ourselves as comfortable as possible, in the continuing rain, and waited for the morning.

CHAPTER TWENTY SEVEN

We continued to advance our lines in the protection of the darkness. The constant rain seemed to aid by muffling our sound and blurring our shadows. During the day we kept up a near constant skirmish of small arm fire, punctuated by intermittent blasts from artillery. As soon as darkness fell we were back at work on the trenches. Gradually our entrenchments moved closer and closer to the Confederate where they had retreated and set up a defensive line on the lower slopes of the big mountain that I learned was called Kennesaw.

We continued to move to the south, southeast, following along the railroad tracks until they curved and went around the northern, steeper side of Kennesaw Mountain. Between the railroad tracks and the foot of the mountain, the rebels had built a strong fortification. We inched our lines gradually closer and closer to the Confederate works there. Finally, when we had moved to within a hundred yards of the Confederate positions, we were instructed that in the morning we would launch an all out assault against their redoubt.

We had a line of entrenchments that faced the Confederate works, looking pretty much directly to the east, and which curved around their fortifications to where a segment of the line was facing straight south. During the night, the trenches were packed, literally, with row after row of Union troops. It was still dark when the order came for us to begin the assault.

The first line of troops came up out of the entrenchments and over the top of the embankment and began moving straight east and straight south towards the Confederate works. We had been told to move quietly without shouted commands or bugles or drums. Our artillery had been instructed not to commence firing. We were attempting to surprise the Confederates. The second, and then the third line of troops pulled quietly up and over the embankment.

We were in the fourth line of troops, and just as we came over the top of the breastworks, somewhere down the line a shot rang out, followed by several scattered shots, and then a weaker volley of musketry. Apparently the Confederates had discovered our advance. It was quiet enough that even I was able to hear as the order was shouted aloud by the officers for us to return fire.

A prolonged uniform blast of rifle fire echoed out. Even in the darkness, I thought I could see the curving line of flames from east to south directed at the Confederate works. I couldn't make the troops out but I knew that directly in front the first line of troops were even then kneeling to reload and the second line was rushing quickly past them and suddenly I heard the command to fire and another volley of flames leapt out towards the Confederate works. It seemed like our line picked up speed as we moved forward. A third curving line of flames leapt out towards the Confederate and just then we jostled our way through the first line of troops, which were just starting to rise from their kneeling position, where they had reloaded their muskets.

We had picked up speed as we passed through the second and then third line of troops, as they continued to reload, and then it was our turn to deliver a volley of massed rifle fire against the Confederate fortifications. Through the dark, I could actually make out the outline of the Confederate works raising no more than thirty or, at the most, forty yards in front. I brought my rifle up and aimed at what I judged was a foot above the top of the darker outline that I believed would be the top of the breastworks facing me.

Just as I judged my aim to be correct I heard the command to fire from off to my right and yelling 'Fire!' also, we delivered a blast of flames and lead towards the Confederate works and then promptly dropped to our knees to reload. Balanced on my right knee, attempting to reload my rifle, I was jostled from left to right as the first line of Union troops forced their way past us between the members of our squad. Someone stepped on my ankle as I knelt on my knee and nearly toppled me as they rushed by.

The first line pulled up shortly, no more than five yards ahead of where we were, and delivered a blast of smoking lead and flame towards the Confederate fortifications. I struggled to finish reloading my weapon and was bringing it up in my arms to place the percussion cap when it seemed that the second and third rows of troops came rushing past in unison. In the darkness and the confusion, and the blasts of rifle fire, the lines of troops were becoming excited and intermingled. The Confederate troops had been responding to our volleys of fire with intermittent, irregular bursts of firing. I knew that they were firing as soon as they got their weapons reloaded and that their fire lacked coordination and discipline.

Even as I began moving forward to fight my way through the lines of troops that were kneeling and reloading, the troops in the second and the third line delivered what was by far the loudest and most sustained volley of fire yet. Maybe because the two attacks, moving to the east and moving to the south, had closed the distance as they approached the Confederate works or, possibly because the second and third lines of our attack had advanced together but this last volley seemed to lighten the entire Confederate works in flames such that I imagined I could see the Confederate troops' stunned faces as they looked into our lines of approaching death.

Then we were forcing our way through the densely packed mass of men in blue, and as my two squads made their way clear we were packed tightly, shoulder to shoulder, and no more than ten yards from the Confederates. We started forward in a stumbling, tripping rush of muddy boots and went up and over the sloping embankment of the Confederate works. As we reached the crest of their breastworks we looked down upon the men in gray who were tightly packed below. We gave one blast of musket fire and went over the works, clubbing and bayoneting indiscriminately at the troops beneath us.

It was surprisingly difficult to tell friend from foe in the intermingled mass of humanity in which we had plunged. I felt troops at my back pushing and shoving me forward, and I used the butt of my rifle to club and push and shove my way ahead. Anyone to my front, I felt, was an enemy and certainly anyone who stood and attempted to defend their ground must be, I thought, but I had a moment of almost unreasonable fear thinking that anyone of the Union troops next to me who stopped to hold his position or turn around, would probably be considered an enemy combatant and dispatched accordingly.

I was immensely relieved when the troops in front of me seemed to turn as one man and rush away towards the other side of the fortifications and, in no time, we were approaching the southern and eastern sides of the Confederate redoubt. By unanimous consent we pulled up short at the opposite side of the compound and gave a loud resounding cheer and a few hoots of derision as we celebrated the rebel abandonment of their works. Our celebrations were cut short as the officers passing through immediately instructed us to start building up the earthworks on the opposite side of the compound from which we had just entered.

We went to work digging at the mud and the earth with our bayonets and using any type of contrivance that we could find to pile the mud higher on the walls of the fortifications facing the Confederates on Kennesaw Mountain. As I worked, I looked up into the steep and partially wooded slopes of Kennesaw Mountain. It was tempting, I thought, to consider pursuing the Confederates up the slope in the darkness, but realized, as the officers I'm sure already knew, that this would only result in confusion and pandemonium, probably with our Union troops shooting at each other as we moved through the darkness and the partially wooded gullies and ravines of the mountain.

By the time the skies began to lighten, we had succeeded in raising the height of the Confederate works on the south and east sides of the fort several feet and had brought up batteries of twelve pound rifled Parrot cannon to help defend the fort. The Confederates may have had the height of the mountain to use to their advantage, but most of their artillery consisted of smooth bore Napoleon cannons and these Parrot rifled cannon had a much greater range and in all probability we had the advantage over the Confederate's artillery.

We had been moving into position throughout most of the night, and now that the fort was ours, we were allowed to seek what shelter and what comfort we could for a quick rest. It seemed we no sooner stretched out on the slope of the embankment, sheltering under our ponchos, as we sat leaning back against the slope of the embankment when our rest was disturbed by the Confederates making a concerted effort to retake the fort. With the dusk and gloom and the continued rain, they managed to slip back down the side of Kennesaw Mountain using cover from the trees and gullies to get within fifty yards or so of the fort without being detected.

Suddenly they came rushing and stumbling down the steep slopes, but were met with blasts of artillery and sharp volleys from our sentries and troops that were still on guard duty. We rushed back to the top of our embankment and leveled our rifles and delivered a volley of murderous rifle fire directly into their faces from no more than fifteen yards away. I was amazed at the senseless waste of human lives. We had made our attack in the cover of the darkness and the muffling rain, but launching an attack in the light of day into a strongly fortified position was sheer stupidity. I knew that every man in the two squads that responded to my direct commands were perfectly capable of picking out an individual target and hitting it at that range.

It seemed that the whole front line of the Confederate troops went down as one. Then I pulled the revolver from my holster on the right hip and emptied it at the Confederates who were continuing to charge wildly the last few yards of the slope and then across the few feet of level ground before coming up the walls of our redoubt. I had the feeling that the Confederate troops in front would gladly have turned and fled but, because of the slope of the mountain and the troops pushing from behind, they never had that chance. It must have been sheer horror to be pushed forward, up the walls of our redoubt, to certain death.

For a brief moment the two lines came together and muskets were used to push, shove and club each other back and forth until the impetus of the Confederate charge had been spent and they began working their way back up the slope of the mountain.

Their counterattack had come to nothing and I think they must have realized the futility of repeated attacks. We were once again told that we could relax but we kept a very weary, watchful eye on the slopes of the mountain as we attempted to snatch a bit of sleep.

It seems that it wasn't much more than an hour later that we were disturbed again, but this time by Union troops moving into the fortifications from the west. As fresh troops took their positions we were ordered to move back into the entrenchments we had dug and proceeded towards the west and the rear of the division. As we moved, zigzagging back and forth through the diagonals, we could hear the sound of artillery and volleys of musket fire towards the south where the troops of General Thomas were moving forward in the usual fashion. They proceeded with the daily advancement of entrenchments, punctuated by skirmishing, as they gradually forced the Confederates back to the foot of the mountain and up its slope well to our south.

We spent the rest of the morning moving towards the safely in the rear of the division and arrived just after noon to be treated to a hot meal and an afternoon of leisure. After we had eaten, we drifted around looking for a place to sit and make ourselves comfortable. No one felt much like going to bed in the middle of the afternoon. We had been up pretty much for the last twenty-four hours without sleep, but there was something about trying to go to sleep in the bright light of a sunny afternoon. Even as we sat there and commented about this fact, no one seemed to realize its significance. That is, at least at first, and then the awareness seemed to strike us all at once and the boys and I let out a loud cheer that seemed to startle the other troops as they made their way by. I think they were shocked as they turned to look at us with mixed glances of amusement and consternation, but then Johnny managed to shock them all as he suddenly shouted out, "It's quit raining!"

The cry was soon taken up by everybody and seemed to move throughout the whole division. It had indeed quit raining for the first time in two weeks. It looked like the sun had come out and we all seemed to feel good deep inside. It had quit raining!

CHAPTER TWENTY EIGHT

We had been sent back up, in a few days, and set to work improving and modifying the Confederate entrenchments at the north end of Kennesaw Mountain. Now we were rotated out and sent to the rear for a few days' rest. The new troops that were to be our replacements marched in, in the early morning light while still under the cover of darkness, and we loaded up our packs and marched towards the rear. When we reached the old Confederate line of entrenchments, which had run across the floor of the valley between Brush Mountain and Pine Mountain, we were shown the tents which would be our homes for the next few days.

We immediately went in and dropped our packs and waited for further orders. We didn't have long to wait. We had been assigned to the wagon guard detail. We marched back along the railroad lines to Big Shanty where the trains arrived and off-loaded supplies to the depot that had been established there. We helped load supply wagons with different requisitions and then escorted them to the front.

By this time we had troops stationed on the tops of both Brush Mountain and Pine Mountain guarding signal stations that could relay messages, I believe, to practically any location on the field of combat. The signal stations and observation towers could see for miles in any direction. Their major responsibility was to keep an eye on Confederate cavalry that may be raiding our lines to the rear. Even though there had been no sign of a Confederate threat it was still deemed wise to provide a strong guard detail for the wagons as they inched their way forward from Big Shanty along the road by the side of the rail tracks and up to the entrenchments that we had dug surrounding Kennesaw Mountains western slopes.

The wagons followed the rail tracks to the northern end of Kennesaw. Then, turning south and west, the wagons carried supplies to General Thomas's troops in the center of the line and to General Schofield at the far end of the Union line. By moving down just in front of Pine Mountain, they were effectively out of range of the Confederate artillery posted on Kennesaw Mountain.

The next few days we spent marching back and forth along the wagons as they rumbled their way back and forth, supplying the needs of the army presently holed up in their entrenchments and laying siege to the Confederates on Kennesaw Mountain.

As the next few days passed I wondered what was progressing on the field of battle beyond what we could see or hear. The Army of the Tennessee was presently occupying the entrenchments along the northern extent of the Kennesaw Mountain and Thomas' troops were in the center of the line, while Schofield's was farthest south and actually well beyond the most southwest edge of this mountain range. But I wondered what was happening elsewhere as we seemed to be stalled.

As we continued our daily travels back and forth and unloaded our supplies, we had occasion to visit with the troops who assisted us. It turned out that some of the vicious fighting we had heard a few days before had occurred around Gilgal Church and Noyes Creek. There the Union troops had skirmished with Confederates along the base of Kennesaw Mountain as the Union forces moved their way around the southwestern end and attempted to advance to the east.

They used up a fair amount of ammunition during these skirmishes and the wagons that we brought down were loaded with ammunition and artillery rounds. We spent most of this day helping to unload the wagons and replenish their supplies. It was just after noon when we finished unloading the wagons and we were graciously invited to join General Schofield's troops behind the line for a hot meal before returning back to the supply depot.

We had no sooner sat down to enjoy our meal of bacon, beans and biscuits with some hot coffee, when we heard the sound of heavy skirmishing in the distance. This soon attained the sounds of an all out battle. It sounded as if it had started off to our east a mile or so away, as near as you could tell from the sounds of the fighting, but seemed to be moving in our direction. There was sudden turmoil and bustle in the camp as the troops made their way forward the few hundred yards to fortifications that they had erected. These were nothing stouter than a two foot ditch that had been dug with the earth being piled on the eastern and southeastern side. There were a few pine logs placed across the top of the embankment for added protection, but it really wasn't much of a wall.

We rushed up to the defensive works and found that, even as we approached, the Union troops were filling the trenches in preparation for the oncoming assault. Other Union troops came rushing back from the east and came into the defensive works. These troops were patrols and skirmishers who had been sent out by Schofield to feel out the enemy's position. It seemed that they had felt them out alright! The front line seemed panicked and reported, from snatches they heard from the troops as they rushed by, was that a whole Confederate Corps was in pursuit. The panic, I thought, was almost laughable. It had been reported that Joe Johnson had three Army Corps in his whole command. I thought it was unlikely that we would have taken one whole Corps off Kennesaw Mountain to launch an assault against us here. But the troops that were coming into the entrenchments were veteran troops and not likely to panic. Lieutenant Shawnasee had been leading the guard detail for the wagons and had command of three squads. We had moved to within a few yards of the entrenchments and watched as the Union troops were ordered into line facing towards the presumed Confederate assault, which was surprisingly not long in coming.

The sounds of the firing intensified and as we watched, I believe, that the last of the Union forces came into the entrenchments from the east. As they did so the troops that were manning the defenses dropped to their knees or lay prone on the earth facing over the top of the breastworks. The sound of activity and of the movement of large numbers of men from out on the ground in front of the trenches increased and, although we couldn't see any Confederates from where we stood, it was obvious that a large body of troops were indeed moving upon the position.

Then the order was shouted up and down the line to fire and the troops responded with a rankling volley of rifle fire. The thick cloud of black powder smoke seemed to envelop the top of the breastworks as the troops frantically reloaded in the protection of their entrenchments. There was no return fire from the opposite side of the works, but suddenly that shrill Confederate yell rang out from all up and down the lines outside the works.

As the Union troops finished reloading and took position to fire again, there was a sudden blast of fire from the advancing Confederates. Minnie balls went whistling and screaming past our ears as we stood, unwisely, watching the action twenty yards in our advance. I suppose we were lucky that only one man was wounded. We dropped to our knees to more safely observe the combat going on in our front.

The Union troops fired another volley and began to frantically reload. I could almost sense the Confederates approaching the lines. It seemed like the very ground shook from the stamping of thousands of feet. Maybe it was the vibrations in the air from the throats of the Confederate soldiers as they cheered as they advanced. We had the feeling that the Confederates would be in the works before the Union troops could finish reloading and it seemed that, without orders but with unanimous consensus, the troops that were assembled behind the line in the supply depots and camp rushed forward to help man the defensive works.

Our three squads went forward with the rest of the troops. We were still ten yards from the trenches when the Confederates began attempting to force their way over the breastworks and into the Union lines beyond. They were met with bayonet and clubbed rifle butts. As we approached the struggle we stopped, took aim and added what little firepower we carried to the battle. The Lieutenant had stopped five yards from the breastworks and dropped to one knee and was working the level on his Henry rifle as fast as he could.

I made my way into the trenches, the Remington in my right hand, and as I came to the logs separating the troops I fired left or right down the Confederate lines. Their attack faltered and began moving back all along the line. I had the impression that they had been surprised by the number of Union troops that they had encountered and by the fortifications that we had erected.

As we watched the Confederates moved away to the east and south and disappeared into the pines that covered the slightly rolling hill south of

Kennesaw Mountain. More Union troops moved up and into the trenches and batteries of artillery were soon rolled up and into position along the line. We made our way back towards the camp and located our wounded companion. Two of his friends from his squad were with him and had finished binding up his arm and placing it in a sling. It didn't look like a severe wound to me; at least it didn't appear that his arm was broken. That would have meant an amputation for sure. Of course, any wound could end up in an amputation, but at least I felt he was safe for the moment.

We escorted him back to the hospital tents and then rounded up the wagons and began moving back to Big Shanty for further orders. We had offloaded most of the ammunition and placed it in small outbuildings around the farmhouse that we had learned belonged to a man named Culp.

By three or four that afternoon, we were making our way back to the north. As the sun began to settle in the west, we heard the roar of artillery and the sharp rattle of musket fire behind us. It seemed that the Confederates were determined to make another attempt on the Union lines. I couldn't see that they would have much more success than they had the last time. One thing seemed to be perfectly obvious to me and to the rest of the men in the squads; making headlong attacks on entrenched earthworks simply didn't work. Thank God we had a general in command that was smart enough to know better.

We marched throughout the night and by early morning were back in our lines between Brush and Pine Mountains. We dropped out at the tents even as three other squads took their place to provide guard detail for the wagons on the rest of the journey back to Big Shanty. We slipped into our beds just an hour before sunup to get whatever sleep that we would be allowed.

It was noon before we were rousted up for the day. We had a hot meal which served to immensely refresh us after the previous twenty-four hours of near constant marching and wagon guard detail. Then we were allowed time that afternoon to sit around camp and merely relax. As we relaxed around the camp, with no duties to attend to, our conversation quite naturally turned to the upcoming military confrontation. Uncle Billy had yet to ask our opinion or advice on any of his maneuvers, but that never kept us from offering our opinions to each other.

So far we had moved all the way from Chattanooga to Kennesaw Mountain by flanking Joe Johnston and his Confederates out of their positions. Sherman had only made direct frontal attacks on Resaca to enable us to cross the river and flank him to the south. It had also enabled us to gain the high ground from where our artillery could reach the railroad and the bridges in the rear of Johnston's troops and force him to abandon his position. The fighting at New Hope Church and Pickett's Mill had been directed by General Hooker, the story went, without General Sherman's direct knowledge. In our own battles with the Confederates, at Dallas, they had been the ones attacking into our entrenched positions with disastrous results. And it was General Hood who had attacked Schofield south of Kennesaw Mountain at Culp's farm with.

Once again the rumor that was circulating amongst the troops was that this direct assault into our entrenched positions had been devastating for the Confederates. We all seemed to agree on this point! Johnny Applebaum offered the opinion that Sherman should send General McPherson on another one of his whiplash marches around the northern end of Kennesaw to get into the rear of the Confederate lines. "No, Johnny" I said, "He can't do that. If we were to pull out of our position there, it would leave a direct route for the Confederates to come off Kennesaw Mountain and move directly up the valley towards Big Shanty and our supply lines." Johnny thought for a minute, and then said, "Well, we could have General Blair's troops fall back and man the entrenchments in the valley here while we went around the northern end of Kennesaw." Then he said, "We had done alright without General Blair's division for the last six months and we would be alright now."

I offered the suggestion that General Sherman should have half of General Thomas' army march from the center of our lines and extend Schofield's right to move around to the south and that this would accomplish the same thing, but would be safer. Then Robert Cantrell offered the opinion that we should combine all of our available cavalry into one large mobile force that could sweep around Kennesaw Mountain, either to the north or south, and get to the Confederates' rear.

Tom Sinclair didn't find much use in that suggestion. He reasoned, as he said, that that would leave the Confederate cavalry free to move into our rear and attack our vital supply lines and destroy the railroad. But Robert seemed to feel that if we did it quickly, it would be over and done before anyone realized what we were about. Oh, we had a multitude of brilliant schemes alright. It really was too bad that no one ever listened to us.

After the one days' relaxation we were sent back to escorting the supply wagons running from Big Shanty down to General Schofield's position. Here we found that he had strengthened his fortifications and sure enough confronting him were General Hood's troops who had so gallantly, but senselessly, attacked here just forty-eight hours ago. There was the occasional burst of skirmishing but, in general all along the lines, peace and quiet prevailed.

We returned with the supply train to the fortifications in the valley and after another days' rest, which we used in polishing and shining up our gear and uniforms and planning our upcoming campaign, we were sent back into the fortifications that we had taken from the Confederates along the northern slopes of Kennesaw Mountain. We relieved some troops who had been stationed there and watched them move back into the rear for wagon guard detail and relaxation.

As we settled into the fortifications we learned, from snatches of conversation with other troops there, that there was a rumor circulating that General Sherman was planning on launching an all out assault directly on Kennesaw Mountain itself. The mere suggestion of such a thing seemed as ludicrous as to be beyond belief. General Hooker might order troops to assault entrenched, well fortified, positions but surely Uncle Billy was too smart for that. No one seemed to put much credence in such an absurd suggestion.

Our artillery continued to pound at the Confederate works on a daily basis and there were outbursts of skirmishing here and there, but overall it reminded me of Vicksburg where we had laid siege to the Confederates for weeks, but laying siege here was not an option. At Vicksburg the Confederates had been entirely surrounded and their supplies had been cut off. It was only a question of time until they surrendered. Here we confronted the Confederates on only one side. They continued to bring supplies in from the southeast side of Kennesaw Mountain and, unless we were successful in flanking them, I didn't see any way that we could force them off the mountain. But one thing that was certain was that General Sherman would never waste his army in a direct assault.

But, yet, the rumor persisted that that was exactly what General

Sherman had in mind. When we went to our bedrolls that night we received orders for part of the Army of the Tennessee to move out in the morning progressing to our right, down in front of Kennesaw Mountain to its southwestern slope. Our regiment was to remain where we presently were, occupying the old Confederate fortifications along the northern-western slope. I had the feeling that this only confirmed my original thought, that we would move south en masse to flank the rebels off the mountain in that direction. The answer would be revealed in the morning.

CHAPTER TWENTY NINE

We were awakened just after midnight, having gotten very little sleep during the night because of the anticipated movements in the morning. By three o'clock in the morning, our troops began to move south so that they could be in position for whatever maneuvers Uncle Billy had in mind. It was dark enough that we couldn't make out the troops as they moved off to the south, but the noise of an army on the move was hard to cover up. I'm sure the Confederates on Kennesaw Mountain were likewise aware that there was a significant movement of troops off to the south.

I tried to imagine what they would be thinking and how they might be reacting. I decided they were probably not doing anything since it was impossible to tell exactly where the troops were going or even if they were troops and not just supply wagons. But I felt tenseness in the air that was almost palpable and for some reason I imagined that the Confederates could feel it also. In the darkness before dawn, we listened attentively for any sounds that might indicate Confederate withdrawal from Kennesaw Mountain, but the stillness was deafening. Even the birds and insects were silent

We could only stand around the perimeter of the fortifications and stare into the darkness and listen. Gradually time passed and the eastern horizon began to lighten. At first the sky began to turn pink above the top of the mountain to the east, and then the first rays of direct sunlight filtered down through the pine trees along the top of the mountain. The sun soon made its appearance over the top of Kennesaw Mountain and just as it did, at roughly eight o'clock in the morning, artillery all up and down our line commenced a thunderous bombardment of the confederate fortifications. I think every piece of artillery we had in the army fired at the same instant. It seemed like you could feel the vibrations of the cannon blasts through the very air itself. The ground trembled beneath our feet and, as we watched, the flank of Kennesaw Mountain, burst up and out in a shower of dirt and smoke. At first it seemed that the explosions were occurring nearly simultaneously but then, as the better manned gun crews were able to load and fire faster, it became a continuous drumming of explosions. The whistling of the shells as they flew through the air was punctuated by the blasts of the explosions against the side of the mountain.

We were simply awed by the spectacle. I think Uncle Billy Sherman must have been planning on leveling the Confederate entrenchments and smoothing the earth flat with this volume of cannon fire. We joked that he might even be trying to level the entire mountain by simply blasting it into the air. I thought it was actually doubtful that anyone could survive such an onslaught, and yet it continued. The floor of the valley, where our artillery worked, was soon enveloped in the reeking clouds of blackpowder smoke and became invisible except for the flashes of fire that gave away their positions. We joked that it looked like a thunder storm on the ground.

Most officers, who had watches, were frequently consulting them to keep time of the event. I kept a watch on the sun as it came up over the top of Kennesaw Mountain and tried to think back to just where its position had been when the barrage first began. It lasted so long that we were actually becoming bored of watching it. Then suddenly, abruptly, the bombardment ceased. Officers and men were all in agreement that it had lasted exactly one hour. Not being entirely certain how many rounds a good artillery crew could fire in a minute's time, I arbitrarily guessed at three, nor how many cannon were firing, we guessed two hundred; Johnny and I calculated that probably thirty six thousand shells had been fired.

But we were a couple of miles distance from the heart of the mountain that had sustained the majority of Sherman's wrath, and thus were unable to judge for ourselves the degree of damage that had been inflicted on the Confederates. I watched and listened intently for the first sign of activity to our south. Several minutes passed, possibly a dozen or more, until the first scattered blasts of musket and rifle fire broke out. It was obvious we hadn't killed all of the Confederates with our bombardment.

The skirmishing seemed to continue longer than usual and I was just beginning to think that this was a good thing and might indicate that the Confederates were so stunned and devastated by the bombardment that they were unable to put up much of a resistance, but just at that moment a uniform volley of shots rang out. This was followed a few seconds later by a second, third and fourth fairly evenly timed and distinct volley of small arms fire. This then degenerated into a continuous rattle of musket fire which indicated the troops were loading and firing as rapidly as they could and at any target that offered itself.

I began to feel a sinking sensation in my stomach. I could only hope that we were moving forward and doing most of the firing. If that were so, I reasoned, the sounds of the firing should gradually fade, or at least change location somewhat if our troops were advancing up the side of the mountain. The minutes passed slowly, but the direction from which the sounds of the fight came, never seemed to change. Tens of minutes passed and still the firing never faltered in intensity or volume. Our artillery had long since ceased firing but, after the first few minutes of musket fire, the Confederate artillery had responded and the booming roar of their cannon echoed down the slopes of Kennesaw and across the valley.

I closed my eyes and to my horror imagined line after line of our blue clad troops marching gallantly into the face of the Confederate fire and falling needlessly beneath the hail of their bullets. The fight seemed to last nearly as long as the artillery bombardment, possibly another hour, before it gradually began to falter and decrease in intensity except for an occasional burst of frantic skirmishing.

By midmorning, the sounds of combat had ceased except for an occasional solitary cannon discharge. As with the cannon bombardment preceding this, I tried to calculate the number of bullets that had been fired. It was stupid and needless to do that, especially since I had no real idea how many men the Confederates had had on the mountain to begin with. But, even if they had as few as twenty thousand men involved in the fight and each man fired three shots a minute and the fight had lasted for an hour, well, I gave up trying to figure it out. I supposed there could have been as many as a million balls fired. I hated to think how many men could have been killed.

We stood around in shock and amazement, waiting for some word to filter back down the line to us. I looked around, up and down the bluffs of Kennesaw Mountain and out over the valley surrounding us. It was eerily, unnaturally quiet, and then I realized that probably every bird, mammal, or even insect, had been so shocked and stunned by the noise of the battle that they had abandoned the entire countryside.

Certainly the troops around me were too stunned to speculate on the results of our assault and talk was lacking. I realized that possibly I might have been deafened somewhat by the explosions because I was having trouble hearing the usual noise of people moving and brushing past me. It was as silent as a tomb. Mainly because I couldn't think of anything else to do or anything to say, I simply wandered over and sat on the slopes of the embankment of our fortifications, and one by one the boys in the squad moved over and sat down surrounding me. No one felt like saying anything. For once, Johnny was unable to find any humor in the situation.

A sullen gloom settled over the squad as we sat on the slopes of the fortifications, like nature we were stunned into quietness. Suddenly a brisk, but brief, exchange of gunfire echoed up the valley. In a moment it was quiet again. Troops stood up and wandered aimlessly around the emplacement, stopping to peer up the slopes of Kennesaw Mountain or down into the valley at its base, before sitting down again. We were at a loss. Noon came and went. Some troops munched on hardtack but most didn't feel like eating.

It was early afternoon when word came requesting the services of our regimental surgeon. It was my impression that each regiment had its own physician and trained assistants; but I may have been wrong. The fact that assistance was being sought seemed ominous to me. Dr. A. W. Reese began hurriedly gathering his assistants. They rounded up their boxes, crates, and wagons. "Leave the tents" Dr. Reese called "they'll be too damn hot. Just bring the canopies".

On sudden impulse I called "Doc, can Johnny and I be of any use". The good doctor paused, momentarily speechless, then said "Why not? We might need all the help we can get".

I got to my feet lending a hand to Johnny who seemed reluctant and at a loss for words for a change. I don't think he appreciated the fact that I had volunteered him for this, but he wasn't going to say anything.

Soon we were on our way, moving off to the southwest. Lieutenant Shawnasee waved at us as we passed by. I hadn't thought to ask his permission but I could tell he had no objections. We covered the mile or so to where the casualties were being gathered in no time. Dead and wounded men were littering the area by the hundreds, if not thousands. In a few minutes we had erected the canopies and Dr. Reese was setting up his equipment. It was Spartan in its simplicity. Three trestles and several boards made up his table. His instruments were on another board table.

He passed rapidly along the lines of wounded soldiers directing his attendants to fetch one or another. How he assigned his priorities was confusing to me. He passed by soldiers who were obviously more seriously injured than others before choosing his next patient. The soldiers who formed his medical corps never questioned his decisions. Johnny and I did our best to help.

We carried wounded and placed them in line just outside the canopy while Dr. Reese went to work. He rolled up his sleeves and secured them with gaiters before briefly washing his hands. He called out for "hot water" and began cursing and blaspheming in a most efficient manner. One of his assistants dripped a strong smelling liquid onto a cloth he held over the patients face. Another cut away the soldiers' pants leg, while two others held the soldiers limbs down. Then with quick, deft strokes Dr. Reese sliced through the skin with a long knife, then through the muscles. He clamped and twisted small blood vessels and clamped and tied larger ones. Then he sawed through the bone on the lower thigh. As Johnny and I carried the limb out to pile just outside the canopy Dr. Reese' assistant placed several sutures to close the shin, leaving large gaps between the sutures.

The doctor had already turned his attention to another wounded man on another table as Johnny and I were instructed to hold mounds of loose gauze on the stump of his first patient while an assistant wrapped it tightly. He cussed us most emphatically as we kept getting our thumbs in the way. Johnny positively looked ill. I know I definitely felt ill. And so we worked away throughout the rest of the day.

As we worked I watched the activity around us. I became aware of a younger looking preacher who was moving amongst the wounded. He was praying with them, blessing them, forgiving their sins, and rendering whatever comfort and solace he could. While Dr. Reese cursed most wantonly, he was able to work most efficiently. I think he averaged four or five amputations an hour. However the young preacher, who prayed and blessed most fervently, seemed confused and disorganized.

Darkness came. Lanterns and fires were lit, both for comfort and light,. so we could continue to work. Buckets of hot water were thrown over the boards of the tables periodically when the clotted blood became too thick. It was mid morning before we were finished; or rather, before we were allowed to leave.

Dr. Reese walked with us back to our camp. He left his staff to clean up, sharpen, and pack up his instruments and equipment. It was obvious he was exhausted. As we walked he talked constantly, being too wound up to relax. He had ceased to curse and appeared quite pleasant. I had never known him to talk so much or be so lively. I had thought him to be unusually quiet, almost reticent. Surprisingly he didn't mind me asking questions. Amazingly Johnny still acted as if he had nothing to say.

"Sir" I asked "How do you decide who to operate on. I mean, there were several wounded men who were just ignored. I', but he cut me off.

"Son" he said "there are men whose injuries are so severe they can't be helped. Anyone with an abdominal or chest wound will, in all probability, die. We simply dress their wounds and try to keep them comfortable. A few will live but that's a rarity. Even men who are in need of amputations, who are too far in shock, can't be saved. We do what we can for those who have a chance".

As we walked he continued to talk as if he was training us to be his new permanent assistants, or else to find his own sense of solace. I noticed from the corner of my eye that the preacher was following a short distance behind. He was not attempting to catch up, but he was obviously listening. When we arrived back in camp the good doctor invited us to have a drink with him. "Just to relax" he said.

We took our seats on canvas folding stools outside his tent while he brought out a bottle of bourbon. Catching sight of the preacher he called him over to join us. "A fine job preacher" Dr. Reese said. "Very fine work. I'm sure you saved many a soul today. Many more than I did, I'm sure". I thought for a moment he was being sarcastic, but he wasn't. "When a man's about to meet his maker he needs all the comfort he can get. Come have a drink with us" he called.

Interestingly the preacher joined us but refused to drink. I think he simply needed comforting himself. Dr. Reese continued to talk incessantly, drank about a fourth of the bottle, and then stumbled off to bed. I wandered if that was how the rumors started that army surgeons were usually drunks. I knew the doctor wasn't drunk, merely exhausted, and needed a drink to relax so he could sleep. I had drunk as much as he had and I certainly wasn't drunk; at least I didn't think I was.

The preacher finally seemed to loosen up some and began to talk. "You know before the war I preached constantly about the evils of slavery. I exhorted my congregation to march in protests to free the slaves. I believed slavery was a stain on the good name of our country. I portrayed the suffering and indignities heaped on the poor Negro, and preached how it was our duty to see that they were freed. But now I don't know if it's worth it. Seeing the pain and suffering of all those soldiers, all the death. Maybe there was another way. Killing is no way to do God's work. We should have preached compassion and understanding and worked to persuade the Southerners to see their errors in a reasonable manner". Then he went on to say the war must end. "In the upcoming elections we must vote Lincoln out, and elect someone who will end the war. Then we can persuade the South to free the slaves. Oh it may take a few years, but it will be worth it. No one else needs to die". And he continued with his ramblings.

As he talked I felt myself becoming more and more outraged. Or, maybe, more and more drunk. I had an almost irresistible urge to shoot the bastard. The more I thought about it, the more I felt it would be justified. I looked at Johnny, who appeared to be almost himself again, and he laughed and said "Don't do it". Suddenly I felt like laughing and broke down hysterically. I laughed loudly and Johnny kept repeating "No, don't do it" as he laughed along with me. The preacher watched us both in amazement. I know he had no idea what we were thinking.

At last Johnny and I got to our feet by mutual agreement and physical assistance and I turned to the preacher and said "Well Reverend sometimes you reap what you sow". Then we stumbled off to find our tent and our beds.

CHAPTER THIRTY

Conscious awareness seemed to drift back gradually as the early morning light began to filter through the fabric of the tent. A faint jostling of the soldiers in the squad further served to awaken me. As I became more and more aware of my surroundings, I noticed a rather nauseating smell. Seven or eight men in a small tent creates a situation where smells are quite common, but this odor was unlike anything I had previously been exposed to.

As I gradually became totally awake, I sat up and sniffed to try to locate the source of the odor. I finally realized that it was coming from myself and from Johnny who was still sleeping only inches away. As I sat up and sniffed, I noticed that Otto Kerner had also awakened and became aware of the odor. "Ach, fer der lieber Gott?" "What is that smell?" he asked. Then, I realized where the source of the odor was originating. The odor was coming from the old blood and bodily fluids that had soaked into our clothes and, it seemed like, even into the skin of our hands and arms. How we had ever been able to ignore or overlook the stench of death prior to now was startling. By now, the rest of the squad was up and only too willing to procure water for our baths.

While Johnny and I bathed, Otto and Tom scrubbed and washed out our uniforms. Then they stretched them out, draped over the ropes supporting the tent, to dry. It was the second day after the attack on Kennesaw Mountain and the army remained encamped. There was an occasional outbreak of skirmishing off to the south, but in general the day passed peacefully.

We dressed again in our uniforms a few hours later while they were still damp, and that afternoon were treated to a hot meal. As the sun continued to climb into the heavens and the temperatures reached well up into the 90's, we had received no orders or instructions, so we merely lounged around the fortifications enjoying the sunshine.

Gradually, I began to notice the same smell that had permeated my hands and clothes earlier in the day. It seemed it was becoming progressively stronger as the afternoon passed. I frequently sniffed at my shirt and the sleeves of my uniform. They didn't seem to smell that bad, but there was an odor that seemed to drift through the air around us. The breeze picked up, blowing from the southwest and passing up the valley towards us and as the breeze seemed to stiffen, the odor greatly intensified.

We looked off towards the southwest and were amazed at literally thousands of turkey buzzards that flitted across the sky like a huge black storm cloud in the distance. The odor wasn't coming from our clothes as I had originally thought, but from the site of the battle a mile off to the south.

I had been mistaken yesterday when I thought that most of the men who had been killed or wounded on the field had been removed and brought for treatment. It actually seemed that the majority of the dead and seriously wounded had been left in the ground between the two armies. From listening to the disgruntled talk of the troops that passed back and forth through our fortifications, it was apparent that nothing was being done to remove the dead and the wounded from no-man's-land.

As an occasional quick burst of firing broke out, it only served to reinforce the rumors that had been circulating, that until a truce was called, anyone moving between the lines was libel to be shot at. By evening, when we turned in at taps, the odor wafting up from the south was nearly unbearable. Despite the heat and humidity, the flaps were securely fastened on our tent to provide protection from the stench. It was hard to believe that we were at least a mile away from the scene of the fighting and the smells of blood and decomposition were overpowering here.

Gradually in spite of the stench and the continued grumbling of the squad and their complaints about the lack of humanity of the officers who wouldn't acknowledge a truce to bury the dead and care for the wounded, eventually we managed to fall asleep.

The morning failed to bring any relief from the odor that seemed even stronger than it had the previous day. It was midmorning before it dawned on us that we hadn't heard any gunshots that morning, and before long news passed through the troops that a truce had been called long enough for the field of combat to be cleared and the bodies buried. We were thankful we weren't called to help clear the field. Even where we were, the stench was palpable. How long it would last after the bodies were finally buried was something that we speculated on. I wondered if the stench would ever leave!

It was the fourth or fifth day after the battle that a flurry of excitement and movement of troops erupted. Rumors circulated that General Schofield, who had been moving to the south and to the east around the southern flank of Kennesaw Mountain, had managed to flank the rebel forces. Then the story circulated that General Logan had sent troops up the slopes of Kennesaw Mountain and Pigeon Hill and had discovered that the Confederate forces there had withdrawn sometime during the night. Suddenly, the camp was in frantic activity. Tents were being stripped, gear was being packed and loaded, and we were soon on the march. It seemed like we were in a race to try to catch up with Joe Johnson before the Rebels managed to retreat beyond the Chattahoochee River.

There was an air of excitement, almost jubilation, throughout the army. We were marching off to Atlanta, and the sooner we got there, the sooner the war would be over. The only thing between us and Atlanta was the Chattahoochee and what was left of Joe Johnson's army. We whistled and shouted, joked and reveled and thought that, if we could trap Joe before he got across the river and destroy his army, that there would be no fight for Atlanta, we would simply be marching in unopposed. The more we listened to the talk, the more excited we were and the faster we moved. It looked like it was going to be a race.

Every soldier seemed to have his own view of what was going to happen next. I came to the conclusion that the Chattahoochee River must be as big and as wide as the Mississippi. There didn't seem to be another city between Marietta and the Chattahoochee. Joe Johnson had no place to go if we caught him out in the open before the river. The war was nearly over.

The army was moving rapidly, joyously and victoriously. Otto Kerner shouted as we marched along, "Boys, I think it's the 4th of July again. Remember last year on the 4th of July, Vicksburg surrendered. This year, Joe Johnson will surrender. God bless the 4th of July!" he shouted. Other boys in the squad dismissed this idea. Tom Sinclair said, "No, Otto. Today's July the 2nd." I thought about it, and ventured to speculate that I thought that it was actually July the 3rd. I suppose it didn't much matter. One way or the other, the 4th of July seemed to be a lucky day for the Union army.

We marched rapidly throughout the day and well into the evening before dropping along the road from exhaustion but were up and marching early in the morning. We were heading up the eastern flank of Kennesaw Mountain, headed for Marietta, Georgia. General Thomas and General Schofield were well ahead of us and marching rapidly towards the southeast in an attempt to catch up with Joe Johnson.

It was mid afternoon before fairly intense firing broke out again in the distance. We cheered loudly, speculating that at last General Thomas had pinned down the elusive General Johnson. All was excitement, hustle and confusion.

We marched into Marietta, Georgia from the southwest. It was a lovely little town. There hadn't been any fighting in the immediate vicinity and the homes and houses were undisturbed. The town was unbelievably quiet. It seems that all the southerners were staying indoors, possibly trying to ignore the Union troops that marched, cheering and parading up and down the streets. You could almost come to the conclusion that the town was deserted except for the blue clad troops.

Now that we were here, it seemed that there was some confusion as to what to do next. The troops began to fall out and linger around the edge of the streets through town. The firing far off in the distance to the southeast had ceased and the army gradually came to a halt. There didn't seem to be any Confederates to fight here in Marietta and the silence in the distance seemed to indicate that possibly there were no Confederates this side of the Chattahoochee. I began to wonder if General Johnson had managed to remove his troops from Kennesaw Mountain and retreat so rapidly beyond the Chattahoochee that we hadn't been able to keep up with him. The wily old fox had managed to do that all the way from Resaca; it seemed likely he had managed it again.

We camped out along the side of the road in Marietta and spent the night there. We didn't erect any tents or make any type of a fortification. We wanted to be able to continue the pursuit as quickly as we could. We were up early the next morning. Bands were playing in the distance and the troops were singing as we marched along. Today was indeed the 4th of July. We were marching rapidly to the south and the story was circulating that we were looking for a way across the Chattahoochee. Men were cheering, that General Thomas had Johnson trapped west of the Chattahoochee. If we could move to the south and cross the river while General Thomas held him penned there, we could be between Johnson and Atlanta. The news was stunning, if the rumors were true.

Last night, we thought that Johnson had given us the slip again, but today it appeared that he might be trapped at last. I thought that we had marched fast the last couple of days, but today I think we must have set new records. As we marched, we could see other troops passing in the distance. Whose troops they were, we could only speculate. Most people believed that they were troops belonging to General Thomas.

We marched throughout the day and afternoon, and well on into the evening. As darkness came and the light faded, such that it was inadvisable to continue marching, we made camp along the road. We had failed to find any Confederate troops and had failed to reach the Chattahoochee, although advanced units indicated that it was within a few miles. Surely we could be there and across in the morning.

Surprisingly, in the morning, we were slow in rousing and leaving camp. Some of the excitement and enthusiasm had dissipated for reasons that were not clear. We only moved two to three miles to the south and came up to the Chattahoochee River. Looking from the higher bluffs on the western or northern banks of the river the town of Atlanta could be seen in the distance, at least the spires of the churches and the tallest buildings. Everything seemed to be quiet around us. We didn't notice any troop movements across the river.

It was still early morning and the rest of the troops gradually came up, lining the western bank. Mounted troops had been sent further south looking for a way across the river. The Chattahoochee wasn't nearly as impressive as I had imagined. It was nowhere near the size of the Mississippi or Tennessee Rivers that we had marched across previously. I did not think it was much bigger than the Oostanaula outside Resaca. However, it was muddy and apparently deep and just wide enough that it couldn't be crossed easily, at least not crossed easily if there were major Confederate forces in hiding along the south. We seemed to be stuck.

We went into camp that night on the west bank of the Chattahoochee, not despondent, but certainly not as excited as we had been. Things had been quiet for the last two days. There had been occasional outbreaks of firing in the distance, but certainly no sustained battles.

In the morning, we were up and moving to the northeast with the Chattahoochee off to our right. Before noon, we had come to a river in our front and off to our right. Here, the Chattahoochee forked; or rather the Nickajack Creek joined the Chattahoochee as it traveled down from the northwest. This creek wasn't that wide, but ran between steep muddy banks on the north and south sides, and the creek was deep in most places.

It didn't pose much of an obstacle in crossing, but just across from us on the opposite bank, lay the cause of all the troubles and holdup. Joe Johnson hadn't fled across the river. He was entrenched on the western shore of the Chattahoochee and north of the Nickajack. There may not have been a town for Joe to take refuge in, but the wily old general had managed to construct a set of fortifications that was appalling in its depth of defenses. There were long trenches with high embankments and row after row of forts, lunettes and redoubts. It appeared that every tree between here and Marietta had been cut, sharpened and fashioned, and placed into the fortifications. The sight was appalling. I didn't think we had enough troops in all of Sherman's army to dislodge him from these works.

Just as they did, whenever they didn't know what else to do, the officers brought up shovels and picks and set us to work building our own line of fortifications along the southern back of the Nickajack in the bend at the Chattahoochee. Skirmishers were sent forward and filtered down through the brush and along the edge of the Nickajack to skirmish with the Confederate troops on the other side of the water.

While the troops skirmished, we went to work digging and making our own fortifications. It was extremely hot and dry. It's surprising how you can be on the banks of a river and still be thirsty, but hard work on a hot day seems to sap your energy. We dug trenches, piling the dirt to the north, and made our embankments. It didn't appear there was a log available anywhere near for strengthening the fortification and for making adequate protection, the southerners had beat us to it.

After we had dug the trench out deep enough and made the embankment satisfactorily high, we set to work making little shelters dug into the southern side of the embankments. We covered these with brush and canvas. We didn't anticipate being here long, but needed shade and a bit of protection in case it rained.

That evening, as we lay around in our little brush and canvas shelters dug into the sides of our fortification, we speculated on what the next move would be. Johnny was quite certain that we had Joe right where we wanted him. "He is on the west side of the river," Johnny said. "We have the longer ranged artillery, and it doesn't matter how deep and stout his defenses are, we can surround him and blow him back into the river. We don't need to assault his trenches and fortifications; we can simply devastate it with our artillery." We all agreed that that was the sensible thing to do and felt fairly safe and secure for a change.

Morning came and surprisingly we found that Johnson had once again slipped away during the night. I couldn't believe it at first, but skirmishers were sent forward and crossed the Nickajack and found that the fortifications were truly abandoned. We moved up and looked at the Confederate works. I think it must have taken weeks for him to have constructed these works, and then they had been abandoned without much of a fight at all. Why they had ever bothered about building them was beyond me. It seems he could have crossed the river days ago in safety.

As we wandered along the edge of the fortifications, General Thomas' troops moved down from the northwest and began to occupy them in strength. So far, we had failed to find any suitable point for crossing the Chattahoochee south of our present location. We moved back across the Nickajack and went into camp again. We were convinced that we would be moving out in the morning. Johnson may have made it across the river, but if he could do it, we could do too. And the sooner we were across, the sooner we could catch him and put an end to him.

Monday morning came. Last Monday had been the 4th of July. We were up early, not having slept much at all that night. We were in a hurry to be off and marching, but strange to say, we hadn't moved. There was the sound of artillery and gunfire off into the distance to the north and it seemed even farther south, but in general things were quiet around our camp. That afternoon, it clouded up and rained off and on throughout the day.

The next day, once again, found us stalled in our fortifications south of the Nickajack. One thing about being bogged down, at least we were well fed; however, we were impatient to be up and moving. We had started to relax and actually were preparing to spend another night in our brush arbors in camp, but late that afternoon, not much before sundown, we were ordered to march back towards Marietta, Georgia.

I could have imagined practically anything other than that. I could have imagined moving south to a crossing on the Chattahoochee which we had been scouting for for several days, or some place north, but all that distance back to Marietta seemed pointless. Nevertheless, we packed up and were on the march by 5 pm. We marched for the next five or six hours and went into camp just before midnight. We were still somewhat south of Marietta. We fell out and spent the night along the road, getting as much rest in the brief time allotted. It was still pitch black when we were aroused and ordered to resume our march towards the small southern town. By early morning, we were marching past the outskirts of Marietta, Georgia and continuing on to the northeast.

Rumors passed through the line that we were marching to Roswell, Georgia. Even better news was that General Schofield had found a place to cross the Chattahoochee River at Soap Creek and that Colonel Garrard and his Union cavalry had found a place to cross at Roswell, Georgia. The troops marched with a brisk step and a sense of elation.

As we marched, we speculated that General Thomas was fixing the Confederate army in place across the Chattahoochee and we were hurrying to cross, in force, above them and position ourselves to trap Johnson against the river. However, by noon, the troops had lost some of their sense of jubilation. Marching most of the night and from early morning drained our energy and sapped our enthusiasm.

It was dark by the time we were shown where to camp for the night. We shuffled into position and dropped our gear along the banks of the river. One by one the troops collapsed to the ground, too worn out to worry about eating. After resting for a while, we broke into our hardtack and washed it down with water, then rolled up in our blankets and slept on the open ground.

At first light, we were up again. Troops were detailed to cut trees and secure lumber, by any means possible, to repair the bridge the Confederates had destroyed across the river. Troops returned with freshly sawn logs and salvaged planks that had been found at the site of the mill that Colonel Garrard had burned the previous day or two.

Throughout the day, we worked near fever pitch to get the bridge repaired so that we could advance a stronger force across the river. Troops rotated into work on the bridge and others were given periods of rest in which hot meals were provided. By late afternoon, the bridge was deemed satisfactory to begin crossing troops.

We formed up and marched across the river and passed through the flimsy defensive works that had been erected immediately on the opposite bank by the troops who had first reached the crossing. It was becoming too dark to see well, but we continued moving eastward away from the river and then were ordered to prepare our own defensive works.

The 15th Corps was assigned a section of the fortifications around the landing and we were sent forward and began digging trenches and preparing our emplacement. Several squads from the 31st Missouri were ordered to proceed two hundred yards in advance of the emplacements to dig rifle pits for advanced positions and early warning.

I took the squad forward with me, and after having covered our estimated two hundred yards, we spread out in two men teams to prepare our rifle pits at ten yard intervals. Johnny and I began scratching away at the dirt and piling it in front and on both sides of our position. We worked in silence since we were well in advance of the rest of the Union line and had no knowledge of the Confederate troops that might be in our vicinity.

We had barely gotten our pit more than a foot deep when the wind began to pick up and lightening and thunder boomed out in the distance. The rain began as suddenly as the wind had started blowing. It came down in absolute sheets. The heavens were split by bolts of lightening that flashed from high in the sky and crashed against the earth. A large pine tree nearly fifty yards away was split from top to bottom by a bolt of lightening that shook the ground and seemed to toss brush and rocks in the air. Pieces of bark and wood showered down around us. Johnny laughed as he said, "Who would have known the Confederates could call down the wrath of Zeus?" I didn't find anything funny about it because there was probably an inch of water already accumulated in our pit and it seemed that the electricity from the blast caused my skin to tingle and my hair to stand on-end. "Just keep your damn head down!" I said. "No rebels are apt to be out in this weather anyhow." We hunkered down into the bottom of the muddy pit and covered ourselves with our blankets and groundsheets. Except for the wind, rain and lightening, the night was quiet. The storm lasted most of the night before gradually blowing off to the north.

At sunup we were relieved by fresh troops who were rotated forward while we returned to the camp. We returned to the camp muddy and disheveled, but were treated to a hot meal and then allowed to relax in the fortifications. I had been feeling pretty miserable, muddy and soaked, from our night in the storm, but quickly forgot my own discomfort as we listened to talk about how twenty soldiers had been killed or maimed by the lightning. Maybe Zeus really was taking sides! By early afternoon General McPherson had crossed the rest of the Army of the Tennessee to the eastern back of the Chattahoochee and they continued to expand the camp.

We had seen Atlanta from the bluffs south of the Nickajack and had been within eight to ten miles of the city. Where we were now in position, we speculated, we must be fifteen miles or more north of our objective, but we were across the Chattahoochee. Atlanta was nearly in our grasp. Atlanta, the key to victory, was ready to be taken. The war was nearly over. Surely, once we took Atlanta, the Confederates would see reason and surrender. Maybe not today but surely by tomorrow we would be on our way. On our way to Atlanta!

CPSIA information can be obtained at www.ICGtesting.com
Printed in the USA
LVOW110105160212

268877LV00001B/32/P